DEADER TH

A Murder Mystery

This book is a work of fiction. Any resemblance to living persons is purely coincidental.

All rights reserved by Pacific Series Press and James W. Law

Copyright © March 2024

No part of this book may be reproduced, transmitted in any form, or stored in a retrieval system without the express written permission of the publisher.

Published by Pacific Series Press, Las Cruces, New Mexico

www.pacificseriespress.com

Send comments and corrections to: clarelawman@gmail.com

Deader Than A Doornail

First Edition

ISBN 979-8-9903598-2-6

Library of Congress Cataloging   In progress

Law, James W.

DEADER THAN A DOORNAIL, a novel, James W. Law, First Edition

Editing by James Oliveri, author of "Frost Weeds, Vietnam 1964-1965" and others

Cover support by Robert Reno, weareIT, Las Cruces, NM.

TABLE OF CONTENTS

Chapter

1....RANDALL FOSTER – Seattle, Washington	Page 1
2....ROOSEVELT HIGH SCHOOL – Seattle, Washington	Page 6
3 MARKET SPECULATOR - CBOT Building, Chicago	Page 15
4....THE WEBVAN CAPER – Chicago, Illinois	Page 20
5....THE TAX MAN COMETH – Chicago, Illinois	Page 26
6....TEXAS OR BUST – Livingston, Texas	Page 32
7....FORT WILDERNESS – Disney World, Florida	Page 34
8....THE NEW PARTNERSHIP – Gainesville, Florida	Page 47
9....RABINSKI IN ATLANTA – Atlanta, Georgia	Page 55
10....A NEW YORK PROPERTY – Saratoga Springs, NY	Page 58
11....THE BRUTAL TRUTH – Saratoga Springs, NY	Page 67
12....FIVE YEARS OF GROWTH – Eastern United States	Page 71
13....J&R LLC BUSINESS YEAR SIX – Bumpass, VA	Page 73
14....FBI AGENT JAKE FINSTER – Upchurches Pond, NC	Page 82
15....A SINISTER DISCOVERY – Upchurches Pond, NC	Page 92
16....NEW OFFICES – Gainesville, Florida	Page 101
17....DEN OF SPIES – Gainesville, Florida	Page 107
18 THE MISSING PARTNER – Saratoga Springs, NY	Page 116
19....GAMBLING LESSONS – Saratoga Springs Casino	Page 120
20....THE NASTY ROBBERY – Saratoga Springs	Page 125
21....SECOND MEETING WITH FBI – Fayetteville, NC	Page 135

Chapters...continued

22...ANALYSIS AND DISCOVERY – Gainesville, Florida	Page 143
23....SANDSTONE THE SUITOR – Gainesville, Florida	Page 149
24....DISCOVERIES IN NASSAU – Paradise Island	Page 153
25....MERRIWEATHER, MAN IN THE MIDDLE	Page 157
26....BAD NEWS AND VERY BAD NEWS – Gainesville	Page 164
27....FRIENDS AND ENEMIES – Jacksonville, Florida	Page 176
28....THE DEFENSE – Jacksonville, Florida	Page 185
29....THE INCRIMINATING GUN – Cushing's Offices	Page 191
30....WORKING VACATION – Paradise Island	Page 200
31....PRELIMINARY HEARING – Jacksonville, Florida	Page 211
32....CUSHING'S REBUTTAL – Federal Courthouse	Page 222
33....PRELIMINARY HEARING CONTINUED	Page 227
34....GAINESVILLE DETECTIVE – U.S. District Court	Page 236
35....PROSECUTION'S CASE – U.S. District Courthouse	Page 245
36....THE DEFENSE ATTACKS – Federal Courthouse	Page 249
37....PRELIMINARY COMPLETION – U.S. District Court	Page 256
38...THE DECISION – U.S. District Court, Jacksonville	Page 266
39....BAHAMAS FLIGHT – Bermuda – Nassau	Page 275
EPILOGUE	Page 286
ACKNOWLEDGEMENTS	Page 288
MORE BOOKS BY THIS AUTHOR	Page 289

PROLOGUE

This book is a work of fiction. All of the characters are from the author's imagination. It is Law's first fiction work. He has authored a series of four books published on the Pacific War and is working on a fifth.

James W. Law grew up in Seattle, Washington, and graduated from the University of Washington before commencing active duty in the Navy. He had a twenty-four-year career in the Navy and advanced from Airman Recruit to Commanding Officer of a carrier-based Airborne Early Warning Squadron. Law retired from the service in 1983 as a Commander (O-5) and worked as a defense contractor for the next twenty-three years.

Jim "Lawman" Law got the initial idea for this book from some TV ads. It was fun for him to write, and he hopes you enjoy the tale.

Jim is married to the former Clare A. Stewart (55 years), and they have two accomplished children, Ryan and Amanda, and five wonderful grandchildren, James, Bradley, Amelia, Connor, and Christopher.

TITLE PAGE

DEADER THAN A DOORNAIL

A Murder Mystery

By

James W. Law

Dedicated to the health professionals who have given me a long life. My many thanks to the doctors, nurses, and diagnostic technicians who have helped me through eight decades.

Chapter One

RANDALL FOSTER – Seattle, Washington (1995)

Sixteen-year-old Randall Foster hated his stepfather – a hatred that burned in his brain hotter than a magnesium fire. Rafter Peal was rude, crude, and lewd. Contributing little while debasing the Foster family, Peal drank, gambled, and abused Mrs. Peal. He had a low-paying job in the Anderson Lumber Yard and often skipped work.

Randy's mother had married Peal two years earlier. Tired of the older man calling him a freak and a moron, the youngster fantasized about getting rid of Rafter. Randall's head looked caved in on each side from the overuse of forceps during his delivery. The curvature of his upper spine bent him over, and he limped from one leg shorter than the other. His face was narrow, and his dark eyes close together, earning him the nickname "Weasel" in school. As fall approached, he finally had a plan. He agreed to go fishing with his stepdad on an overcast Seattle morning.

At 6 a.m., they rented a fifteen-foot fishing boat and bought bait in Ballard. October's chill had chased most of the green leaves away. Patches of fog hung over Puget Sound like gauze blankets, and a light cold breeze stiffened the boaters' fingers. Steering north along Golden Gardens, Rafter popped his first beer. The fog mostly hid the tree-covered coastline. Their bright, trolling flashers and tempting herring plugs produced no bites.

After thirty minutes, Peal stood to take a piss while they trolled south of Edmonds through low wavelets. Randy also got on his feet as if to relieve himself. Then, as the older man hit midstream, his stepson gave him a vigorous bump out of the boat. The small craft moved away from Peal.
Randy feigned ignorance, yelling, "Rafter, what do I do? Sorry, I lost my balance!"
Peal floated twenty feet off the stern. "Stop the motor and pull the lines in, you idiot!"

Randy moved back to the outboard motor and pulled the choke out to kill the engine. He reeled in the two lines and started his stopwatch as the light wind pushed him away from his stepdad. Rafter floated on his back with the toes of his knee-high boots bobbing above the gentle waves.

Good, thought Randy, *He refused to wear a life jacket; the chilling had begun.*

His stepdad yelled, "Randy, start the motor and move closer to me."

Randy held his head with both hands and grimaced. "How do I do that?"

Rafter said, "Put the shift gear in Neutral, move the speed handle to Start, and pull the starter knob."

The young man pulled the starter cord but left the choke control extended. The warm motor refused to start as the boat drifted further away..

"It won't start!" Randy cried.

"Get the oars out, row back here, and pick me up!" demanded Peal.

Randall made a clumsy grab at the oars and checked his watch - ten minutes. He used one oar and rowed on each side of the boat's bow until he was ten feet from his outraged companion.

Rafter bellowed, "Don't you know how to row, stupid? Put both oars in the oarlock holes and get next to me."

Foster thought, *I'm going to call him Dad. He always wanted me to do that – what irony.*

"Dad, I'm worried. How will you get into the boat without tipping it over?"

"I'm not sure, you ignoramus, maybe from the bow or the stern stepping on the motor shaft."

"Rafter, I'm just a kid. I won't last long in that cold water. Hey, the motor's choke knob is out. Maybe it will start if I push it in. What do you think?"

"Yes, yes, do that and steer to me in idle."

"OK, here goes, Dad."

Randy started the outboard motor in Forward gear and pretended to lose control as the boat sped away from his victim. Finally, he returned about twenty feet from Rafter and put the shifter into Neutral.

"Hey, I've got it running. How about I go to shore for help?"

"You ninny! That will take too long, and you can't come back and find me in the fog."

"What do you mean too long?" asked the boy.

"You shit for brains. After thirty or forty minutes, the Sound will numb my arms and legs and pull me under."

"Rafter, maybe you can swim to shore?"

"It's too far, you dumbass. After taking my boots off, I'm losing touch with my feet. I need to get into the boat, numb nuts!"

"OK, Dad, I'll toss you a rope and tow you to the beach?"

"You retard ass wipe. I knew you were stupid, but this takes the cake."

"Rafter, I'm afraid you will beat me if you get in the boat. You seem very frustrated."

"Frustrated! Do you think I'm frustrated? Wait 'til I get my hands on you, you little twerp."

"See, that's what I mean. If I pull you to the beach, I can stay in the boat, and we both will be safe."

Besides, there will be more time spent in the cold water. Hmmm, we're at twenty-five minutes. I pull dear old stepdad around in circles for ten minutes, and we should be ready for the final act.

He threw the bow rope to Peal, shifted to Reverse, and backed away. *Let's see how long you can hold that rope, asshole. You didn't even realize I'm controlling the motor when I couldn't figure it out earlier. Good. That means you now have mental confusion along with shivering and slurred speech.*

After a few minutes, Rafter let go of the rope in disgust. "This isn't working, nitwit. You're going in circles and just making me colder. Bring the boat to me."

His stepson complied so he could evaluate his target. Rafter tried to grasp the boat and failed. His hands were stiff as boards, and his arms no better. Instead, he held his head above the waves by wrapping the bow rope around his wrists.

Randy Foster sat on the bow seat as they drifted with the engine off. "Dad, would you like a beer?"

"No, dumb dumb. W-w-why would I w-w-want something c-c-cold when I'm f-f-freezing to death?"

Randy acted distressed. "Rafter, it's not looking good. I can't lift you into the boat, and you can't pull yourself up. What are we going to do?"

"It's all your fault, R-R-Randall. You freak. H-h-how did you lose your b-b-balance?"

"I don't know. I was unzipping my pants, and the boat just lurched."

The hypothermic man thought briefly and said, "You conniving little b-b-bastard. Are you setting me up for a f-f-fall?"

"Gee, Dad, why would I do that? You have been such a great addition to our family. Always home drunk or asleep. Making losing bets on the horses and hurting my mom."

"You w-w-won't get away with it," vowed Peal.

"Really? I don't see anyone who can stop me," teased Randy.

Rafter's face showed sheer panic, realizing these were the last minutes of his miserable life. "Y-y-you idiot, how do you think k-killing me will help y-y-you?"

"Gee Dad, I'm just taking a page from your book. You killed your first wife and collected on her insurance. Now, you plan to do the same to my mom."

Randy saw a flash of reptilian anger grip his prey. "Y-y-you think you can g-g-get the b-b-better of me. N-n-never will that h-h-happen."

"Oh, I think so. It's time to bargain for your life, you drunken loser."

He ripped the bow rope from his stepdad's hands and positioned the boat upwind so it pushed on the struggling man. "Stepdad, admit you killed your first wife, and I'll give you a boat cushion."

"W-w-what does it m-m-matter to you, y-y-you ugly s-s-stupid cretin?"

"Sorry, Rafter, I thought you might like to confess your sins before you die."

"You b-b-bastard, you wouldn't k-k-know how to k-k-kill someone and g-g-get away with it."

Randy smirked. "Really? I think I'm doing pretty well so far. No one can see us from shore because of the fog. If we get near another boat, I'll just push you under. You only have a few minutes left. You've been in forty minutes."

"L-l-look, I might have c-c-considered collecting on your m-m-mom's insurance, but it would only be for the s-s-sake of you k-k-kids, so we h-h-have enough t-t-to get b-b-y."

"If you want the cushion, tell me who killed your wife while you were playing pool."

"Screw you. Ugh." Peal swallowed a mouthful of saltwater.

"I'm waiting," goaded the youngster.

"H-h-how would y-y-you know about any of t-t-that?"

"I went to Portland and looked up your case in the library's newspaper files."

"Give, give m-m-me the cushion. His n-n-name is Jamie J-J-Johns."

Randy asked, "Where does he hang out, and how much did you pay him?"

"A b-b-bar called the "Jingle Jangle" in T-T-Tacoma and five thousand. W-W-Why do you w-w-want to know?"
"I think Mr. Johns could be a good source of income for me in the future."
"S-s-so you're a b-b-blackmailer also?"
"Well, Stepdad, I figure the sky's the limit after you kill someone."
"W-w-what do y-y-you expect to g-g-get from t-t-this?"
"Why, your life insurance, Dad. I saw when Mom and you filled out the forms. Two hundred thousand apiece."
"Ha ha ha, t-t-the j-j-jokes on you nitwit. I n-n-never s-s-sent in m-m-my p-p-paperwork."

Randy thought, *I know, you big prick. That's how I decided you were going to kill Mom. Should I lower the boom now or wait until he's a complete basket case?*
"Rafter, you should atone for your sins now. You don't have much time. Your hands don't work, and your face is turning red. If I take the cushion, you'll go under for the last time."
"H-h-how w-w-will y-you explain this d-d-dumb shit?"
"Not to worry, fellow murderer. I've got it all worked out. I will be in bad shape when I get to shore. I'll row to the beach and leave the motor choke out to explain why I couldn't start it. I will be speechless about the horror of seeing my stepdad drown while I couldn't get him into the boat. An eyewitness account of your death will get Mom the double indemnity money from the insurance company."
"S-s-stupid, I t-t-told you the p-p-policy was not s-s-started."

Now's the time!
"Oh, but Rafter Peal, it was. I found your paperwork, mailed it, and have paid the monthly premiums from my paper route money."
Randy saw true evil on his Stepfather's face and furious lips that spat out, "You s-s-stay away from m-m-my money!"
Foster snatched the boat cushion back. "Do you mean the bank book with ninety thousand deposited? I've already moved cash into my new account. Not bad for an imbecile, moron, ignoramus, shit for brains, retard kid, eh?"

His words had precisely the effect he wanted. Rafter sank with a look of pain and horror. A kid he didn't respect had caused his death. Randall sat for several minutes and plotted his next moves. His body shook from the cold and excitement. Acting mute and shocked on shore would be easy.

Chapter Two

ROOSEVELT HIGH SCHOOL – Seattle, Washington

Randy Foster's high school years weren't academically or socially remarkable. He was not interested in his coursework, resulting in a C+ average. He was interested in girls, but they disliked his strange looks and squeaky voice. However, he did excel in one venue, the stock market. He doubled the $490,000 that Rafter Peal's death provided.

Once he and his mom had the initial capital in a bank, Randall went to the public library on Roosevelt Way and studied investment books. Randy learned that there were several investment types: bank accounts, real estate, stocks, bonds, annuities, and insurance. Since the interest on their bank accounts was low, he put most of their funds into New York and American exchange securities. Most books recommended diversification and purchasing shares of larger, well-established companies. Randy placed half his family's funds in ten larger companies that paid regular dividends. He put the other half in Vanguard's S&P 500 Index Fund, which also yielded a modest dividend.

Foster was happy with his investment choices until he met Mr. Noah Weisman at the library. Weisman noticed that the young man was reading Jack Bogle's book, "New Imperatives for the Mutual Fund Industry." He spoke with Randall and found they had much in common. Weisman showed Randy a weekly publication that covered 1,000 stocks. It provided detailed data on which stocks were gaining or losing and their financial data. Weisman liked the high schooler's investment choices but advised that a conservative portfolio would earn only six to eight percent in the long term.

The seasoned investor recommended that Foster invest one-fourth of his funds in growth stocks and monitor them monthly. For starters, he advised buying equal amounts of McDonald's (MCD), Intel (INTC), Home Depot (HD), and Starbucks (SBUX). Noah showed Randy how to check his holdings' quarterly sales and earnings growth. Randall added Cisco Systems (CSCO), Microsoft (MSFT), Amgen (AMGN), and Oracle (ORCL) the following year.

During the next four years, Randall's portfolio value rapidly increased. He and Mr. Weisman became fast friends. They met nearly every Friday evening to update the stock binder with weekly and monthly reports. Over coffee at Starbucks, they debated adding more companies based on revenue growth rates, price-earnings ratios, and profitability. Weisman warned the high school junior to avoid nonprofitable Internet companies, saying most were full of hot air and phony concepts.

Randy had a growth spurt in high school, his voice matured, and he stood five-foot-nine inches tall. Mr. Weisman challenged him to stand up straight, which helped the youngster lose most of his stooped look. Also, Foster bought custom shoes with one sole thicker to "cure" his limp. As his portfolio grew, so did his self-confidence. He now looked other people in the eye and shook hands with a firm grip as demanded by his financial mentor.

During Foster's senior year, Noah, the Comptroller of King County, invited him to dinner. Randy met the Weisman family. Mrs. W. (Rose) was a smiling, slightly overweight homemaker raising her two daughters to be proper young ladies. At least, that was what Randy thought until they showed him the basement recreation room. Mary Anne (14) and Margaret (16) turned down the lights and recruited him for a game of "spin the bottle" and kissing practice. Randy had never kissed a girl. This new exploration was exciting as Margo (Margaret) taught him different types of kisses.

Over the next several months, he was ecstatic to accept Weisman's dinner reservations, followed by make-out sessions in the basement. Margaret was shapelier than her younger sister and added petting to their repertoire. One evening, the girls showed Foster a book by Masters and Johnson about "Human Sexuality" filched from their parent's bedroom. He couldn't believe some of the photographs or conclusions of the two researchers, nor could he hide his physical excitement. Margo demanded that he undress so she could practice pleasing him with her soft hands. He did, and she did, while Mary Anne watched.

This nefarious activity expanded to Wednesday nights when Randy picked up the girls from their luxury home in his sedan car, ostensibly to take them to an upscale drive-in diner. After a quick meal from McDonald's, they parked on a dark street with no sidewalk, and Randall serially entertained each of them in his back seat. Margo called the shots and ensured they did nothing that could result in a pregnancy. Randy understood that they were practicing on him and he was not a boyfriend. But no matter, his stocks were doing well, graduation from high school was approaching, and the girls helped him forget his mother's illness.

Randall's mom died of breast cancer a year after his high school graduation. He paid for a proper funeral and reception. While at the grave site at Washelli, he offered his sister money from his stock accounts. She declined because she and her real estate broker husband were making big bucks. Randy agreed the family savings could be an emergency fund for her or help with future college tuition when she had kids.

Foster accepted these changes in his life with stoic emotion. He bought a new car and decided to move to New York and work on Wall Street. His meetings with Noah Weisman ended while the older man fought charges of embezzlement from King County.

Randall Foster wanted a clean break from his life in Seattle. He changed his name to Roscoe Fuller and thought, *My wealth came from criminal acts. First, I stole Rafter Peal's bank account. Next, Mom and I collected on his life insurance when he "accidentally" drowned. Crime pays. Noah put two million of embezzled county funds into his stock accounts and doubled it. He's now negotiating a payback with immunity.*

Roscoe packed his car, tore up the monthly condo lease check, and drove east on Highway 90 across the first floating bridge. He exited at Mercer Island and took West Mercer Way up to "Lid Park." After parking, he leaned back on the hood of his car and looked out at the bridge and downtown Seattle.

Roscoe Fuller thought, *This is it; I'm never coming back. From now on, I will be a master criminal who takes from the weak and lazy. My schemes will provide cash while my stocks keep rising. What did Noah say? Oh yeah, "money talks, false bravado walks." He also told me never to talk to the police without a lawyer. Unless you confess to your crimes or provide them with evidence, it's difficult for them to charge and convict you. I'm ready for my first score.*

Roscoe had some of his mother's credit cards. On the Internet, he requested that each card provide $20,000 of credit and a maximum of $500 per day for cash withdrawal. All of these requests were approved. He also withdrew $10K from his stock accounts.

As Fuller started his new life of crime, he withdrew ATM cash daily and wrote bad checks to whoever would take them. He had over $50,000 cash and had passed $10,000 in bum checks upon arriving in Topeka,

Kansas. His plan had a flaw. One of his credit cards and a checking account were with the same bank. Fuller bought gas on credit with the card and used a check from the bank for his motel. Two sheriff's deputies arrested him the following day before he had his complimentary breakfast. He was charged with passing worthless checks over $1,000 in Kansas.

Justice was swift in Topeka. Roscoe was held in the county jail for two weeks and took a plea deal of six months in Leavenworth. There, he met Jonathon Reardon, a gambler, dreamer, and big-deal schemer. Roscoe paid no restitution. He claimed to have spent all the illegal funds, and Kansas authorities didn't discover his stock accounts. Roscoe did pay a fine and the Topeka motel to store his car for six months but told no one about the $50,000 hidden in the trunk.

His cellmate, Johnny Reardon, was a big man in all respects. He was six feet tall and weighed over 200 pounds. His chest and arms were muscular from working out. Reardon had dark hair and a broad face. Johnny was doing time for selling real estate to multiple buyers without a license and residential property he didn't own. Cellmates Roscoe and Johnny hatched a new criminal plan during their months together. Reardon said he knew how to make a killing but needed capital – at least a few million. Roscoe replied that he might know where to get the money but provided no details. The third conspiracy member was Rollo "Three Fingers" Marsoni, who developed the criminal business plan and its action steps. Rollo was doing a life sentence for grand-theft larceny and murder. He demanded a five percent fee of "real profits."

The basic scheme was for the younger men to use money made in the stock market to buy small office buildings in different states. Marsoni showed Roscoe how to falsify tax forms to limit taxable income and property taxes. Rollo instructed Johnny on forming an illicit insurance company in each state and how to defraud the policyholders. Roscoe was good with numbers, so he was tasked to keep an accurate set of books showing how much Rollo should receive. The older man agreed to provide continuing consultation. He made sure that Johnny and Roscoe realized he had the means to murder them if they stiffed him.

After one of the training lessons, Roscoe asked, "Rollo, how did you lose your fingers?"

The older man sighed and said, "I was young and borrowed money from the wrong people. I was scammed out of the money and ignored their threats. Finally, they lost patience and showed me the brutal side of the world."

"How's that?" asked Roscoe Fuller.

"You have the givers and the takers," said the older man. "Some takers have no filters. They'll maim and kill to get their way."

Roscoe shook his head. "What about the cops?"

Marsoni chuckled. "Law enforcement barely makes a dent in crime. They make public examples of some criminals, but many crimes in all categories go uninvestigated and unpunished. Crime pays off, but you have to be good at it. If you and Johnny execute my plan correctly, you will be multimillionaires in ten years. If you get sloppy, you will return to jail, perhaps for life. I recommend you move your profits offshore and leave the country when the time is right."

"What about you?" asked Roscoe.

"My five percent will give me funds to buy what I need here and bribe special permissions."

The next lesson was about depreciation expense on a declining asset. Roscoe learned that the government allowed the yearly deduction of a thirty-eighth of a commercial building's cost but not on the land. Rollo explained that Fuller would need to keep track of this accounting cost and inflate it. Once the younger man understood what he was supposed to report on the tax forms, Rolo discussed the primary set of books. These accounts would undervalue the commercial land and overvalue the building. Roscoe learned that false expenses, inflated depreciation, and under-reporting rents would generate profitable cash flows.

Rollo provided sage tax advice, "Always pay something if it is feasible. Government auditors are lazy and look at companies that pay nothing."

He reviewed Roscoe's stock portfolio and judged it excellent. Rolo advised selling the high-performing companies to obtain capital for purchasing Internet stocks.

Roscoe countered, "My financial mentor warned me to avoid the new Internet companies."

"That's good advice as far as it goes," the old man replied. "However, we are in a frantic period of these companies going public at unbelievable prices. There's a lot of quick money to be made in the IPOs (Initial Public Offerings) and moving on to the next one. I'll tell you what: you reduce your holdings from $1.5 million to one million, and I will stake you and

Johnny a million, giving you funds to raid the IPOs. I want $500K paid back in six months and the rest in twenty-four months with ten percent yearly interest."

Roscoe asked, "Rollo, what if it doesn't work, and we lose your money?"

Rollo drew his right index finger across his throat and replied, "Then you pay the ultimate price."

"How do I do this? I always wanted to go to Wall Street and invest my money."

"No. Not Wall Street, youngster. You go to Chicago and work with a regional investment firm. They're always hungry for cash and ask fewer questions. You get to the 'Windy City' and learn about the CBOT."

"Excuse me, Rollo, what's a CBOT?"

"The Chicago Board of Trade, in some ways, Chicago's version of Wall Street. Find a brokerage in that venue that's large enough to handle small IPOs and bend the rules for you to trade in their offices."

Roscoe was pensive. "You think I can do that?"

"I know you can. We need five to ten million to start this plan while Johnny finishes his sentence. You get that done, and someday you will be sipping margaritas by a Caribbean pool with bikini-clad senoritas attending to your every need."

"No kidding?"

"None at all."

Roscoe Fuller completed his six-month sentence, met with his probation officer, and left the state. His next target was Chicago's financial district. He had read every finance book in the prison library and several from the city's library. He no longer wanted to be a wheeler-dealer on New York's Wall Street and chose the Chicago Loop as his next residence.

He negotiated a decent long-term room rate and free parking from a hotel near Franklin and Madison. Then, fascinated by the CBOT complex, Roscoe scouted for his new stockbroker in the building. He had accounts totaling three million to move and wanted two perks – access to a Bloomberg data terminal and receipt of his mail at the brokerage. After three days of research, Fuller had two regional brokers in his sights. One afternoon, he waited outside the largest company and followed a young man into the elevator.

"When they exited, Roscoe said, "Excuse me. Could I ask you a question?"

"Of course. I'm Graham Rabinski; you are?"

"Roscoe Fuller. I'm looking for a new full-service broker. Can I buy you a drink?"

"Sounds great. Heap, Roberts, and Crandall chain us to our desks from eight-thirty to five. I call it digital servitude."

"What about your lunch?"

"Oh, we eat lunch at our screens. We can order it delivered or pull something off a lunch cart. We respond to calls, telephone existing customers, or prospect for new accounts all day."

Roscoe whistled. "I see what you mean. Bloomberg lists your firm as one of their customers. How do you like the terminal?"

"It's the best thing about the job. I can research any stock, bond, or commodity in a flash. I can place market or limit orders on all the major exchanges and get fast feedback."

"That's what I'm looking for, Graham. I'll bring you my account, but I need four hours daily on a terminal."

"Roscoe, that's very unusual – not sure my bosses will go for that."

They ordered drinks.

Fuller said, "Let me talk to them. I can be very convincing."

"It depends on your account; what's the current value?"

"Last, I looked just under three million."

Rabinski smiled. "Boy, that would be a feather in my cap. I'm just starting; it would be my largest account. But I must warn you, I'm not very experienced."

"No problem, Graham. I do my own research and want to place my trades."

Graham frowned, "I doubt that's legal. Tell my bosses you'll research, and I'll input your trades. What are your holdings?"

Fuller replied, "Several high-performing growth stocks, the S&P 500, and fifty percent cash."

"Smart thinking, Roscoe. Is that how you want to proceed?"

"No, absolutely not. While I've been out of action, the dot.com revolution has started. Your firm has brought some of them into the market."

"Yes, we have, and our customers have done quite well with our recommendations."

Fuller frowned. "That won't last forever. Most of these Internet companies are doomed to failure. They're putting services and production schemes onto the net that won't generate profits."

"So, what's your plan?" queried Graham Rabinski.

"I'm going to invest half my account in Internet startups. Then, once my purchase has doubled, I move on to the next Initial Public Offering. Then, as the dot.com IPO frenzy peaks, I pull out."

"Roscoe, are you sure about this strategy?"

"As sure as I'm sitting here with you sipping a good whiskey."

"Hmmm. How about I buy you dinner? The firm will pay since you're a prospective customer."

"Sounds good to me, Graham."

During dinner, Roscoe learned that Graham Rabinski came from a wealthy Philadelphia family and had graduated from Yale. Graham's father was an insurance executive, and the family owned a summer place on Martha's Vineyard. Roscoe's new buddy was self-assured, well-dressed, nearly six foot tall, and had neatly trimmed blond hair and blue eyes.

Roscoe offered few details about his life other than he was from the northwest and his parents were dead. The following morning, Roscoe met with H. R. & C.'s partner, Charles Crandall.

Crandall shook his hand and waved to a sofa and comfortable chairs.

"Graham tells me you want to work with a regional broker. Is that right?"

"Yes, sir. I've dreamed of working in the CBOT Building and increasing my account through active trading."

"Son, I hope you aren't a day trader. Our experience is that most of them make bad bets and lose all their money."

"No sir. I'm a trend follower. Like the old saying, 'the trend is your friend,' I sniff them out and ride them up."

"So, are you a short seller?"

"No sir, I've found that I cannot predict when a stock will drop. But I do need a margin account."

"I see. How much would the value of your account be?"

"Sir, I have twenty K of cash to put in this morning and will move nearly three million dollars to you this month."

"May I ask how a young man like yourself acquired so much?"

"Yes, Mr. Crandall. My parents died with substantial life insurance policies. I have doubled and re-doubled those amounts during the last four years."

"And you want access to our research connections?"

"Yes, sir, I make my own decisions. Graham can input my trades, but I require some discount on the commissions."

"How much?" asked the partner.

"Fifty percent. I'm a large account and plan to be an active trader. I'm not going to lose my profits to high commissions."

"If all that you say is true, we will give you a forty percent discount – no more."

"Done, and I want my mail to come here. I currently live in a hotel and don't know where I'll settle."

"Hmmm. It's all unorthodox, but we will give you a three-month trial period."

"Thank you, sir. You won't regret it."

Chicago Board of Trade (CBOT)

Source: Wikimedia – Antoine Taveneaux

Chapter Three

MARKET SPECULATOR - CBOT Building, Chicago

Roscoe spent the rest of the day exploring the CBOT Building. It was like a small city and offered most of the services its members and tenants needed. He became a retail member of the CBOT, which provided access to their research, announcements, and public events. After receiving a shoeshine, a haircut, and a custom suit and vest fitting, Fuller took the LaSalle/Van Buren subway west and north to the Washington/Wells station. He then bought several food items and Maker's Mark bourbon at the Walgreens on Madison and Wells.

Back in his room, Roscoe took a shower, changed into an old robe, and sipped bourbon while he reviewed his day. *Damn!* he thought, *I'm off and running – got myself into a brokerage house, have thirty grand still in the car, and start moving my accounts to Graham tomorrow. He can advise me on buying more suitable clothes and where the brokers hang out.*

He didn't open the curtains because his view was the wall of another building. Nor did he turn on the TV since it could add little satisfaction to his mellow reverie.

Graham Rabinski met Roscoe in the CBOT Building lobby the following day and escorted him to the twentieth floor. Fuller used his new company phone to sell and transfer his stock accounts – first to a bank account with his old name and then to Graham.

The Bloomberg computer terminal was available while Graham prospected for new customers. Meanwhile, Roscoe learned that a new dot.com company was going public in two weeks. Etoys.com received substantial hype compared to other dot coms coming to market. Roscoe researched the offering and its business model day and night for one week. His only break was when Graham took him to "Block 37" to buy clothes and shoes at Macy's.

Fuller opened an account with the swank store and followed Graham's advice on shoes, socks, shirts, ties, gloves, and hats. He also purchased khaki trousers to complement a Navy blue sports coat and dark trousers for a tan one.

The eToy publicity reached a peak when it became public at $20. Roscoe purchased 10,000 shares and watched them soar to $79 by COB (Close of Business). It was sheer madness; the company had revenue but no profit or profit prospects. He had gladly broken his rule of selling out at $40. During the next three days, he fed his holdings back into the market at an average gain of $50 a share. After fourteen days of concentrated effort and risking $200K, he had a profit of $500,000.

Rabinski and other brokers wanted in on Roscoe's next trade. A month later, DrKoop.com went public at $9. Roscoe, his newfound friends, and thousands of other speculators pushed the price to $45. Fuller sold his 20,000 shares for an average gain of $30 per share. He didn't care if Koop and his AOL partner made a success of the medical advice website. His trading stock account was worth just shy of two million. And his reputation as a securities rainmaker was spreading.

Graham Rabinski insisted they celebrate on their Saturday day off by returning to Block 37 for lunch, shopping at Macy's, and going to a movie. Roscoe bought sunglasses and various clip-on bow ties - Graham was tired of re-doing his neckties each morning. After the flick, they went to The Dearborn restaurant for drinks and dinner.

Graham paid for the drinks and got giddy after clearing $50,000 for his and his dad's account in only two days.
He said, "Roscoe, let's invite those two girls at the bar over for dinner."
Roscoe Fuller was appalled. "Why on earth would they do that?"
"Because, my friend, they're probably here looking to meet some guys and get picked up. I'll be right back."

Fueled with good whiskey and youthful enthusiasm, Graham went to the bar, talked to the young ladies, and led them back to the table. He introduced Roscoe as a stock market maven who was making millions. Fuller now had long hair covering his head's concave sides, braces on his teeth, and upscale clothing. He wore soft tan loafers, jeans, a leather flight jacket over a narrow-striped shirt, and a bright red bow tie. The foursome enjoyed their pricy dinners. Graham suggested they retire to his digs and promised a spectacular view of Lake Michigan.

They took the subway south a couple of stations and walked two blocks east to Michigan Avenue. Graham's two-bedroom suite was on the top floor of an older building. The corner view was north and east from his living room and south along the Chicago shoreline from the balcony. The two couples took their beer outside, and their host lit off propane heaters that made them comfortable. He sat in a lawn chair with his legs up. Before long, Annette joined him, and they started making out.
Susan asked, "Roscoe, do you have your own place?"

"Yes, I do, but it's not as impressive as these rooms."
She smiled. "Good enough. If you have something to drink, we should be quite cozy."
"I have some good bourbon, and we can take the subway."
"Sold," she replied.

    Riding around the loop, he learned that Susan and Annette were waitresses in a Joliet steak house. She held his hand, and he felt worldly while escorting her to his room. She took off her coat, used the bathroom, and thanked him for the tumbler of bourbon and water.
"Roscoe, what are you doing in the stock market?"
"Well, I'm a speculator. We are in a unusual period with a buying frenzy for internet stocks. Companies with questionable earnings and no profit are seducing the public into believing they'll succeed someday. But, unfortunately, many have only a concept of what they'll do."
"But what do you do?" she persisted.
"Oh yeah, I research these losers and buy them when they go public. Then, I sell as soon as I double my money or thirty days elapse – often, I'm out during the first day or two."
She asked, "Is it that simple?"
"Yes and no. It's like a game of musical chairs. The party will end, and you could be left holding a bag full of worthless stocks."
"How do you avoid that?"
"You must sell everything before the big blowoff, which is hard to judge," he answered.
"Why is that?"
"Everyone is making big bucks. You're climbing a mountain of greed, and the market is grossly overbought."
She sipped her drink and smiled. "Mr. Roscoe Fuller, are you really a multi-millionaire?"
"Yes, I suppose so, except it's all on paper, and I could lose it tomorrow."
"No matter. I've never screwed a millionaire. So, get your clothes off, and I'll meet you in bed after I use the John."

    The next day, Roscoe met Graham Rabinski for breakfast at the Halsted Street Deli, half a block south of the CBOT. They stood at a table eating egg sandwiches while Graham gushed about his weekend with Annette. Then he pressed his friend for details about Susan.
Roscoe said, "We went to my place, drank some bourbon, and fell asleep. The next day, she guided me around downtown while I drove my car. We

went to the Field Museum, Oak Street Beach, and had lunch at Gibsons Bar and Steakhouse. After lunch, we went shopping in the Water Tower Place, and I bought her a scarf."

"Yes, I get all that, but did she ever put out? Did you do the nasty?"

"Well, Graham, you are trying to make a gentleman out of me, so I can neither confirm nor deny that question. However, when Annette didn't show up at their apartment the next day, Susan made me dinner, and I stayed overnight."

Rabinski laughed. "All right, back to business, Romeo. Have you picked our next target?"

"It's possible. There's a grocery delivery service that's losing money hand over foot. They have over $400 million in private financing. Rumors are on the street; WebVan will go public in two months."

"Roscoe, what do we need to do?"

"We should look them over and talk to the workers and senior managers. If my gut is right on this one, I'm risking two big ones."

"Where are they?"

"Foster City, California. It's a nice location on the bay near Silicon Valley. They have put warehouses and fleets of delivery trucks in west coast cities and have plans to expand to Dallas, Atlanta, and even Chicago."

"Roscoe, it sounds promising to me. What are the red flags?"

"First, none of their top executives have experience in the grocery business. Second, they're burning through their capital at an alarming rate. Third, they'll take anyone as a customer and then promise a thirty-minute delivery window."

"Wow, why not an hour or two? Thirty minutes is crazy," said Graham.

"Yes, it is, and so is free delivery for low-profit margin products like groceries. It's like the old saw about the druggist selling medications below cost and saying he will make it up on volume."

Graham laughed. "So, what's your plan?"

"We fly next Thursday. Meet with management and inspect their HQ on Friday. We talk to employees on Saturday and return on Sunday."

"Who is going to tell my bosses, you or me?"

"I will. We need a partner to call ahead and explain that we plan to put several million into their IPO."

Rabinski and Fuller flew United Airlines to San Francisco. Then, they drove their rental car to a hotel in Redwood City. The next day, they met with WebVan managers and had lunch with senior executive George

Shaheen. Next, a guide showed them WebVan's computer center with Sun Microsystems servers, Compaq desktop computers, and Cisco Internet routers. They then visited WebVan's automated Oakland Distribution Center (DC). Both facilities were impressive top-drawer operations.

At dinner, Graham said, "Roscoe, what do you think of WebVan now?"

Fuller took a sip of his Maker's Mark 46 bourbon and water. "Graham, I'm blown away. They've spared no expense in assembling the supply chain, web order software, warehouse fulfillment, and retail delivery components. The optics are excellent: snazzy logos, an easy-to-use website, trendy trucks, expensive modern furniture, glitzy HQ, and a two hundred million budget for advertising. It's a first-class effort, and therein lies the rub."

"How so?"

"These guys are spending other people's money like it's water. There's no indication of budget constraints or incentives to make their break-even number as low as possible. That PowerPoint brief they gave us claims it's inevitable that they'll snag at least two percent of a $700 billion retail market. But it had significant flaws and questionable conclusions."

"Roscoe, I thought it was great," complained Graham.

"That was their intent. They made one wrong assumption after another and convinced you that the market was there for the taking. Also, they argued that millions of buyers were ready to buy their groceries online. They're relying on high tech and automation to deliver the goods at a reasonable price. Bullshit, no matter how artfully delivered, is still BS."

"So, what are we going to do?" asked Graham.

"Tomorrow, we return to WebVan's Oakland, DC, and talk to the workers. We find out about the glitches, bitches, and customer attitudes."

On Sunday, the two researchers flew back to Chicago. Graham worked on a brief for his bosses while Roscoe slept. Annette and Susan met them at the airport, and the foursome piled into Graham's vintage Cadillac. They dined at the il Vacinato Ristorante in the Heart of Italy, polished off a jug of Chanti, and enjoyed the Italian feast. Graham dropped Roscoe and Susan at his hotel and agreed to meet him at the deli the following day to finish their brief. Susan stayed over with Roscoe and helped him develop some new sex skills.

Chapter Four

THE WEBVAN CAPER – Chicago, Illinois

Roscoe and Graham presented their WebVan brief to Heap, Roberts, and Crandall at three in the afternoon. The firm's Compliance Officer and the Vice President of Operations were also present. Roscoe wore his custom suit, a light blue dress shirt, and a burgundy bow tie.

Graham started the brief. "Good afternoon, gentlemen. As you may know, Mr. Roscoe Fuller and I just returned from a review of the Internet startup WebVan. We visited their Foster City headquarters, received briefings, and had lunch with the CEO. In addition, WebVan provided guided tours of their computer and warehouse centers. Mr. Fuller will cover why we made the trip. Roscoe."

"Thank you, Graham, and good afternoon to all of you. WebVan is a fast-track dot.com funded at over $500 million. There's a strong rumor that their IPO is a few months away. So Graham and I wanted a first-hand look to determine our approach to the IPO."

Steven Roberts held up his hand. "Excuse me, are you an employee here at H.R. and C?"

"No sir. I'm one of your active trading customers, and I place my trades through Mr. Rabinski. In the past months, I have increased my account to nearly four million by investing in dot.com IPOs and selling out after the initial over-exuberant rise. I'm prepared to put two million into WebVan's stock, but I wanted to see their business model up close to confirm its value. So, I paid my way to San Francisco and back."

Roberts responded, "OK, I guess. However, this briefing seems rather irregular."

Charles Crandall spoke, "Steven, I approve of this arrangement. It's been lucrative for both parties."

Graham Rabinski displayed his first view graph.

SLIDE ONE - WEBVAN BACKGROUND

CEO – Louis Borders (Co-founder of Borders Book Store chain)
Initial funding – Goldman Sachs and Yahoo
Headquarters and software development located in Foster City (adjacent to Silicon Valley)
Business – Credit and Delivery model of Internet placed orders
Products – Full range of grocery items and others
Distribution Centers (DCs) – Oakland, Orange County (L.A.), Seattle, Dallas, Atlanta
Planned DCs – Chicago, San Diego, and others for 26 total

SLIDE TWO – COMPONENTS OF WEBVAN COMPANY

Distribution Centers – 350,000 square feet, built by Bechtel ($30 million cost each)
    WebVan has signed a $2B contract with Bechtel
Website Ordering – thousands of products, including fresh produce
Software Development – hundreds of software engineers work on websites and automated DCs
Delivery Vans & Drivers – guided by GPS software and directed by Palm Pilots
Leadership – several top-flight executives, BUT none of them from grocery or e-commerce

SLIDE THREE – FINANCIAL SITUATION

Fifty Million cost to open business in a new population center (26 large cities)
Currently about 1,000 employees – majority are high-wage earners
Average customer order is $80 – break even estimated at $100+
Already burned through $500 million of private placement capital
Losses are doubling each year
Cost to acquire new customer is $210 (Two hundred million marketing budget)
500,000 customer base – many inactive
Gross Profit has steady increase, BUT Net Losses also have steady increase

SLIDE FOUR – WEBVAN PROMISE TO CUSTOMERS
Easily Order 1,000s of items using a computer and the Internet
Delivery within a customer specified 30 minute-window
Free Delivery
Competitive Prices for ordered products
Mass Market Strategy – anyone can sign up
Max Flexibility for Customer – no order too small and same-day delivery possible

SLIDE FIVE - CHALLENGES FOR WEBVAN
Developing and maintaining high-volume websites with thousands of grocery products
Product complexity expanded by Drugstore, Electronics, Books/CDs, and SEVEN MORE categories
Purchasing and Inventory Management must be a nightmare
Capital-intensive business with enormous inventory costs
Computer Intensive DCs have thousands of moving parts and 5 miles of conveyor belts
Automated Product Placement, Availability Checking, and Order Fulfillment (plucking totes) - workers report that glitches occur at a 1% to 2% rate of thousands of daily orders
Reliance on Automation for Cost Saving UNPROVEN for this Market
Recent $1.5B stock swap to merge with HOME GROCER – another unprofitable company

SLIDE SIX – WEBVAN'S FAULTY LOGIC – THEY BELIEVE…
Top-of-the-line computers and Distribution Hardware will Lower costs
Large numbers of retail customers are Internet savvy and have computers
Most customers want strangers to select their products and produce
Delivery drivers are happy campers (not true)
    Extreme pressure to fulfill the 30-minute window
    Routing software doesn't allow for rush-hour traffic or construction delays
DCs will operate at full capacity – No, currently at 25 – 33% capacity
    4,000 orders per center per day – No, more like 2,500
Delivery cost of $5 to $6 per order – No, $20 is closer

SLIDE SEVEN – THE BOTTOM LINE
WebVan will declare bankruptcy next year after burning through $800M to $1B in capital
They can't make up for daily losses with more transaction volume
The thirty-minute window will be expanded
Minimum order values for "free" delivery will be necessary
WebVan should cut back on the number of products sold but probably won't
WebVan may face a van driver's strike – they aren't happy with stress and pay
    Customers prefer evening and weekend delivery when drivers want to be with their families
Mass Market Targeting is Not Working
Advertising and pricing should target upscale, high-income, computer-savvy market

SLIDE EIGHT – DISCUSSION OF WEBVAN IPO STRATEGY

TBD

    Graham and Roscoe fielded several technical and financial questions from the partners. Finally, Mr. Heap dismissed the Compliance Officer and the Ops Vice President.
He looked at Roscoe. "Mr. Fuller, what are your plans for the WebVan IPO?"
"Sir, I plan to buy as much as $2 million and sell if it doubles. Rumor has it that the underwriter will be Goldman Sachs for a price of $11 to $13. If it doesn't double in seventy-two hours, I'll take whatever I can get before the long slide to zero."
Heap pointed at Rabinski. "And you, Graham, what are your plans?"
"Sir, I plan to follow Roscoe's lead with some of my money and my dad's account. We will not hold for the long term."
Heap stroked his chin. "Hmmm. Compliance has left the room, but I don't think we can recommend WebVan to any of our customers. This meeting is over."
    While Roscoe and Graham waited for the WebVan IPO, they traded two others. On the first IPO day, askjeeves.com soared from $14 to $64. Roscoe had an average purchase price of twenty dollars for 10,000 shares and later cashed out at $100 per share for an $800K gain.

They also bought the priceline.com shares that skyrocketed from $16 to $88 on day one. Roscoe sold the next day for a profit of $550K. Graham's profits were far less but still substantial for his and his father's accounts. H. R. and C. notified customers that, based on a first-hand assessment, it did not recommend investment in the WebVan IPO.

During a quiet weekend in October, Graham Rabinski taught Roscoe, Susan, and Annette how to play bridge. Roscoe loved the card game and learned bidding for tricks using a Goren point count cheat sheet. However, his contract play was a bit ragged. Once he learned to finesse and concentrate on pulling trump, he was hard to beat.

The SEC delayed the WebVan IPO one month due to the excessive public hoopla created by Goldman Sachs. Roscoe and Graham played bridge for money in Chicago's downtown venues. First, they played for a penny per point, then a nickel and a dime. Graham showed his friend the mechanics of duplicate bridge without oral bids or discussion during play. Players held up printed cards to signal their bids, and "bridge boards" holding the four hands were passed from table to table so each table played the same set of cards.

At one of their bourbon and steak dinners, Roscoe stated, "Graham, if we play for a dollar a point, we need to be more creative."

"What do you mean?"

"Well, for example, when I make an opening bid, I will hold the bid card higher the stronger my hand. So, you will know when we should go for a game and when we should stop at a lower number of tricks."

"Roscoe, that's cheating. If we get caught, our reputations will be trashed, and we'll be blackballed from playing."

"Cheating, schmeating, look at these IPOs. Big money is bringing in the lambs for fleecing. You are either a wolf or a sheep, a lion or zebra, a winner or sucker, a taker or loser. I will do anything to be a winner."

Graham got them an invitation to a weekly dollar-a-point game. They used Roscoe's "system" and still lost over $500. Fuller added a scheme that signaled what suit to lead and another that led to a three no-trump game bid. They cleared $400 in the next competition. Then, their bridge playing was put on hold because WebVan's IPO was two days away.

Rabinski and Fuller were tense, keyed up, and frantic about the IPO. WebVan was opening the following day on the New York NASDAQ Exchange at nine-thirty. They needed to be ready to buy at eight thirty

Central Standard Time. WebVan was using the symbol WBVN and was debuting at $14 a share.

Roscoe had two million in cash ready to trade and planned to buy 10,000 shares on each trade. Graham entered his friend's first buy order for 10,000 shares at $15 as the Bloomberg terminal showed eight-thirty their time. A second later, the first purchase of WBVN flashed on their screen. The price was $24! They were shocked.
Fuller yelled, "Get me 20,000 shares at 25 even!"

His purchase was filled, and he bought another 20,000 at $26 and $27. Then, something in the price-to-volume action warned Roscoe to stop purchasing. WBVN went up through $30 and started to Peter out. Roscoe sold out his $1.56 million gamble for a $300,000 profit and called it a day. The big numbers they expected from WBVN were never in the cards. It topped at $34 a share and slid into single digits and bankruptcy within a few months.

Commiserating over a few drinks the night of the IPO, they decided that the investment community knew WebVan was a valiant effort but doomed to failure - they weren't the only clever people in the room.

WebVan Headquarters (after bankruptcy)
Source: Wikimedia

Chapter Five

THE TAX MAN COMETH – Chicago, Illinois

Roscoe kept half his $4.5 million investment account in large companies that paid dividends. He used the other half to experiment with CBOT E-mini future options. Roscoe could bet on the ups or downs of stock indexes using these highly leveraged securities. He concentrated on the NASDAQ 100 and expected to reap good profits until the index crashed. He knew it would collapse, but not when.

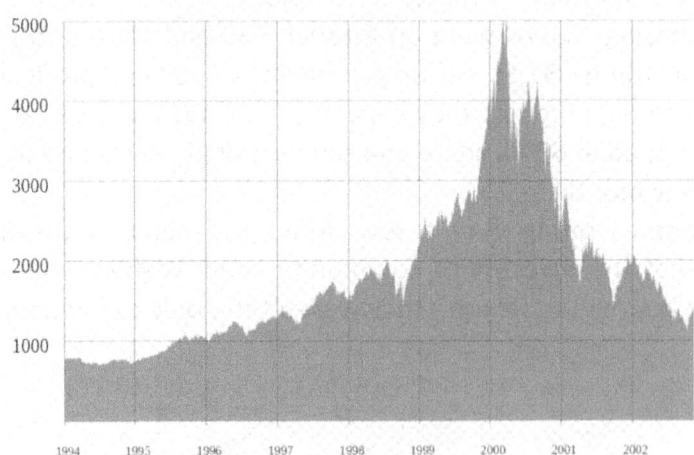

NASDAQ Composite Index showing 2000-2001 dot.com debacle
Source: Wikipedia

Fuller was patient. As the NASDAQ 100 index increased, he profited at 10% per month, 120% yearly.

Roscoe discovered he had a tax problem. A chance meeting with H. R. & C.'s CPA reminded Fuller that the state of Illinois and the federal government would take a large chunk of his short-term profits. He hesitated using Washington state (no income tax) as his legal residence because of his past sins. He had left without paying the rent, car loan, or federal taxes on his stock account as Randall Foster.

Roscoe Fuller had other problems. Steven Roberts, the senior partner at H. R. & C. wanted him removed from their premises. Instead of thanking Roscoe for the heads-up on WebVan, Roberts decided Fuller was influencing the firm's traders without a proper educational background. Roscoe threatened to move his account to another regional broker and Steven Roberts stopped complaining about the high school grad.

Fuller's tax problem was partially solved when Graham's dad visited from Philadelphia. The elder Rabinski wanted to look at the new motorhomes at a Chicago RV show. While browsing dozens of sales booths, one caught Fuller's attention.

"Join the ESCAPEES," proclaimed the banner.

"We take care of your mail, absentee voting, and home address.

20,000 MEMBERS CAN'T BE WRONG

Your BONUS: Texas has no income tax!"

Roscoe talked to the two older ladies at the Escapee desk and learned that he could call Livingston, Texas, his legal home if he joined and had an RV. A salesman told him that used cheaper models were for sale by owners in a back lot.

Graham and his father left for lunch while Roscoe looked over dozens of old motorhomes. Finally, he found a 1975 Toyota Chinook with a motivated seller. It needed new tires, a radiator, and a clutch. The seller wanted $5,000, but Fuller bargained him down to $2,500. After joining the Escapees and towing the Chinook to an RV storage yard, Roscoe felt very smug. He had solved a $200,000 state income tax problem for less than $5,000. He never planned to use the RV or return to the storage lot.

As the new year approached, Roscoe received a letter from Johnny Reardon. Johnny was coming to Chicago once he was released and completed his first probation meeting. Afterward, they'd go to the East Coast and buy their first office building.

Roscoe saw that the Internet bubble of 1999 - 2000 was topping out. He had nearly six million in his Heap, Roberts & Crandall accounts and stopped buying IPOs or CBOT Mini future contracts. What was his next move? He wasn't sure until the first freezing day in October, which energized his brain. He remembered the brutally low temperatures from last winter and thought, *I need to get out of here and head for a warmer climate. How do I do that? I know; I'm a proud RV owner. I'll fix it up and head south as soon as possible.*

Roscoe went to "Big Rick's RV Barn" in Joliet and met with the owner. Rick Parsons wore farmer's overalls and smoked a corncob pipe. He was a Winnebago dealer and asked Fuller what he had to trade. Roscoe told him about his Toyota Chinook and some of its problems.

"How much did you pay for it?" asked Parsons.

"Rick, the owner wanted $5,000, but I paid him $2,500 because it's not running."

"Mr. Fuller, instead of fixing a rig in that condition, you could be driving a larger new RV with a full warranty.

"Big Rick, how much will you give me if we have to tow it here?"

"No promises, but if the outside body and the interior are in decent condition, I could go five grand."

"And what would you sell me?"

"First, I would get you out of that Toyota. It's a good package for the size, but not much larger than a jail cell."

Fuller turned pale. "You may be right. I need something bigger than that." Roscoe, my friend, you need a twenty-seven-foot or twenty-nine-foot model. There's plenty of power in the Ford V-10 engine, and you can even tow your car."

"Wait. Really? I can take my car with me?"

"Absolutetomente. It will cost you a few bucks to add tow gear."

"Money isn't a problem. What else can I get?"

"You have two TVs, a gas heater, and a three-way fridge. I can sell you a bigger, better, more versatile unit today. Add some hoses, bedding, pots, and pans; you're ready to drive away."

"Big Rick, how much is that going to cost me?"

"The retail on a Winnebago Twenty-seven-foot Minnie is $75,000. I can give you $5,000 on your Toyota and $5,000 off as a new customer. This 27P unit has a feature that will knock your socks off."

"Which is what?" asked Roscoe.

"Behind the driver's seat is a slide-out or pop-out that moves the couch and dinette out twenty inches, and there's another for the queen bed in the back. It makes your living areas a home, not a jail cell."

"I can't see myself spending that much money for a RV that I only plan to use for a few months."

Rick said, "What do you have to trade?"

"Huh? What do you mean?"

"I've made deals with farmers for food and others for services like car repair. So, what do you have to offer?"

"Well, nothing that I can think of offhand."

"Roscoe, what do you do for a living?"

"I guess I speculate in the stock market for a living. I've done quite well." Rick swatted him on the back. "There you go! I've got a lot in the market, and I'm not sure what path to take."

"Big Rick, the party is over. There's only one action necessary to save your investments – sell everything now."

"That's not what my brokers say."

"Of course not; they need your account and the commissions. I work beside an honest broker daily, and he can't bring himself to tell his customers to sell it all."

"So, you're telling me to call my three brokers and sell all my stocks?"

"Yes, I sold everything two weeks ago. How much do you have in the market as of today?"

"About three million."

Roscoe whistled. "Good. Sell it all and pay me a five percent advisor fee for every dollar I save you in the next year. So, if you keep one million, you owe me $50,000 off this RV. If it's two million, the RV is free.

"Whoa, Roscoe! You're talking real money here. I have another idea."

"What's that?"

"I have a two-year-old model I took on trade. It's a beauty, just like new. I'll sell it to you for $65,000 and give you ten grand for your RV. Then I will give you two percent of the money I save in one year – that's $20K on a million and $40K on two."

"Rick, make the sales price $60,000, and my fee is three percent, and one other thing. Then we may have a deal."

"What other thing?" asked Big Rick.

"I'm assuming the used RV is out of warranty. I want your warranty for six months of parts and repairs at any Winnebago dealer."

Big Rick offered his hand, and they shook. He said, "I'll call my brokers, show you the RV, and then we'll step out for lunch."

After his bourbon and steak lunch with Big Rick, Roscoe called Susan and picked her up to see his almost-new motorhome. The previous owners had wanted new kitchen items and bedding, so Fuller received all their older furnishings. Susan took the bedding and towels to a laundromat and cleaned them.

Roscoe Fuller and Susan took the Winnebago to a nearby campground the following weekend and found the queen bed entirely satisfactory. Graham and Annette arrived Sunday afternoon with spare ribs, potatoes, and a salad. Roscoe and Graham drove to an ACE Hardware store to buy a portable Bar B Que.

En route, Graham said, "Roscoe, do you mind telling me why you wanted my name on the RV title?"

"Sure, Buddy. My license has expired, and I plan to get a new one in Texas. Besides, when I left the northwest, I owed some rent and other bills that may have people looking for me."

"I see. Also, why did we transfer the title in Indiana versus Illinois?"

"Easy. I will title it in Texas and pay the sales tax there. The dealer has to sell it in another state to do that."

Graham inquired, "When do you leave?"

"In two weeks."

"Does Susan know?"

"No. And don't tell her. I need to break it to her gently."

"Are you keeping your account with me?"

"Yes and no. I'm moving half to Vanguard next week."

"I'm sorry to hear that. My earnings are down since the market peaked."

"Business is business, Graham. I'm not keeping all my eggs in one basket. Say, why don't you come with me? I'm taking my time driving to Texas — probably via Nashville, Memphis, and Dallas. After getting my license in Livingston, I'm heading for a week in New Orleans and another at Disney World."

"Roscoe, it's tempting; I'd like to see some new places. Where to after Disney World?"

"I'm thinking of going down the East Coast to Miami and some fishing in Key West. After that, I'm going to winter somewhere in Florida. Graham, please come with me and help me find a small office building to buy."

"Why are you going to do that?"

"Here's the deal: my strategy is to wait for this bear market to end. In the meantime, a friend of mine and I are investing in real estate and insurance. Like Texas, Florida has no state income tax. The building's expenses and depreciation will provide a good living pretty much tax-free. I deliver the down payment funds, and he provides the business plan."

"Where is he now?"

"He's finishing a consulting contract in Kansas and will join me by spring."

"Roscoe, you want me to quit my job, ditch Annette, and leave town just like that?"

"Exactly, you're not a tree. You don't have to stay here and freeze your gonads off. There's a world out there to see, and we must do it while we're single and well off."

"You think I'm well off? You're the multimillionaire."

"Hey Rabinski, don't snow me – I've seen your trading account. You did quite well on a bunch of my trades. You come from a blue-blood family and must break it off with Annette at some point anyway."

"Why do you say that?"

Roscoe winked. "Come on, are your parents going to accept a waitress into the family? I think not. Look, I'll pay for gas and the RV parks. Your job will be to find us good places to eat and pay for some of the meals."

Graham replied, "I'll think about it. It's tempting. I'm not staying at H. R. & C. forever."

Roscoe had his car modified for towing and gave the hotel notice of his departure. He moved half of his stock accounts to Vanguard and the other half to Fidelity. Fuller also sent $500K and ten percent interest to Rolo Three Fingers.

Graham Rabinski was coming with him. They mollified the waitresses by promising them airline tickets to New Orleans in a month.

Chapter Six

TEXAS OR BUST – Livingston, Texas

On the way to Livingston, Roscoe paid cash for the gas and RV parks. The two carefree travelers stopped for three days in Indianapolis, two in Louisville, five in Nashville, and three in Memphis, where they toured Graceland. They shared the driving from Memphis to Texarkana and then spent four days in Dallas/Fort Worth.

The duo camped in Lake Livingston State Park while Roscoe conducted his business with the Escapees. A week later, he had a mailing address (with forwarding), a Texas driver's license, plus Texas plates on his car and the RV. Graham signed over the Winnebago title to his buddy, who registered to vote in Polk County. Roscoe used the social security number of a deceased hobo in Alexandria, Texas, to open a checking account at the First National Bank of Livingston. He had paid an "Identity Broker" in Dallas $1,000 for the number. The new identity was part of his plan not to file federal taxes on his capital gains. He also prepaid for Johnny Reardon to obtain a different SSN.

Livingston hadn't much going on, so the youngsters planned to leave in two days. Roscoe wore his Escapee hat and T-shirt while Graham had them trolling for dates at the Beacon Bay Marina. After an hour of watching boats, mainly fishing boats, being launched or hauled out, Graham nudged his buddy and said, "Look over there."

Two young ladies had trouble backing a speed boat trailer down the ramp. Graham trotted over and offered to help. He put the boat into the lake while one girl was in it, and the other rode on top of the trailer's tongue. She released the boat and climbed in before her companion lowered the out-drive and reversed off the trailer. Rabinski pulled the trailer out and parked the rig at the top of the ramp. He locked the truck and took the keys to the floating dock where the girls were organizing their MasterCraft for water skiing.

They invited Graham to accompany them and serve as their "flagman." He sent Roscoe for a twelve-pack of beer at the Shell Station, and they cruised out into the lake with two attractive southern girls. The girls liked to ski on the downwind side of Pine Island. Graham skied, and Roscoe begged off.

Instead, he sipped his beer and thought, *I've established a new identity and a home base in a no-income-tax state. Johnny should be getting out in a few months. Good thing he told me to pay off my car loan. Otherwise, the dealer could claim I stole it. The RV is working fine, and Rabinski is a good co-pilot. These college gals are lovely. Maybe we'll get laid tonight. Life is good.*

Roscoe and Graham stayed two additional days in Livingston to enjoy Libby and Violet's company. They then traveled east to the French Quarter RV Park in New Orleans. Promises made to Susan and Annette turned to dust as the young men found plenty of girls to chase on Bourbon Street. They careened from one bar to the next - enjoying the music and exuberant crowds. One music bonus: they saw Pete Fountain at his "French Quarter Inn" club and heard Al Hirt's music played in the "Jelly Roll Club." Finally, after a week of fine music, good booze, great food, and young women sharing the Winnebago, the "Two Musketeers" were ready to move on.

In Tallahassee, they camped at the North Florida Fairgrounds. Roscoe started his search for a suitable small office building, and Graham used their new pick-up routine on the Florida A&M and FSU coeds. He introduced himself and asked if they wanted to meet a millionaire for dinner and drinks. It worked more often than not.

Meanwhile, Roscoe found that determining the size, condition, costs, and value of two or three-story commercial buildings was an art form. He expected to put down ten to twenty-five percent of the sales price but found the prices varied greatly by location. So, he worked with an agent who recommended establishing a Limited Liability Company to make the purchase.

Graham created a spreadsheet for Roscoe to compare various properties. After a week in the college town, no property appealed to Roscoe, and it was time for their Disney World reservation.

Chapter Seven
FORT WILDERNESS – Disney World, Florida

Graham navigated to Vista Boulevard and the Reception Outpost for Disney's Fort Wilderness Resort & Campground. After checking in and making some turns, the "Dynamic Duo" found their camping spot on Timber Trail. They had full hookups, electricity, water, sewer, and cable TV.

Roscoe unhooked the car and then had to move the rig back and forth to get a satellite TV lock-on through the trees. Next, he leveled the rig, put the slides out, and completed connecting fresh water and the sewer hose while Graham looked for a dinner venue. Finally, they put their lawn chairs out and toasted each other with a cold beer. Most of the pads on their loop had motorhomes, trailers, or larger fifth-wheel rigs. Nearly all of them were families with yowling, screaming, crying, and rambunctious kids riding various toys on the road or playing hide and seek in the forest.

Rabinski wanted to have dinner at the Cheesecake Factory. While there, they asked a bartender about the best places to meet young ladies in the Disney complex. He recommended Downtown Disney and the Grand Floridian Resort. After dinner, the lads strolled through the bars and shops in Downtown Disney.

The following day, they slept in and decided to have brunch at the Grand Floridian Café. They wore some of their best casual attire to fit in at the swank resort. After a delicious and expensive brunch, they strolled through the Courtyard Pool area and the Beaches Pool Bar and Grill. Graham ordered a Heineken beer and a single malt whiskey while they surveyed the feminine talent at the Beach Pool.

Disney's Grand Floridian Resort
Source and Permissions: https://commons.wikimedia.org

After reviewing the hotel's amenities, Graham added a new twist to his girl search. He watched for young ladies who ordered bar drinks, picked out the prettiest, and sent them complimentary refills. If they showed no interest, he selected another pair. If they came to the bar or waved him over, he asked them if they'd like to go on a boat ride with a multi-millionaire.

Overhead view of Floridian Resort
Source: Google Maps

The third set of drinks brought him a friendly wave from the pool lounge area. He trotted over and chatted with two coeds from the University of Georgia. After learning they were amenable to a boat ride, Graham called the Captain's Shipyard and booked a pontoon boat for two hours. The girls went to change, and Roscoe scored some beer and ice from the Sandy Cove store. Graham got checked out on the boat, and they pulled it into a berth near the Gasparilla Island Grill.

The foursome motored south along the Floridian Resort and Disney's Polynesian Village Resort. Several people in the Bora Bora-like cabins waved at them. Roscoe steered the boat north toward Disney's Magic Kingdom Park while Graham entertained their guests with stories about Ivy League colleges. Holding his second beer, Roscoe steered down the canal south of the Contemporary Resort and into Bay Lake. The youngsters stopped at Contemporary's marina and used the Sand Bar facilities. The Georgia girls wanted tequila shooters, so each of them sucked on a lemon slice, tossed back an ounce of Patron Silver, and finished with a squeeze of lime.

The party boat continued to the east side of Discovery Island and tied up against a small dock. Graham was pretty bombed by this time and informed his shipmates that he was taking a nap. Melonie joined him, which left Tammy staring at Roscoe.
He said, "What?"
"Are you taking a nap?"
"No, but I'm not drinking anymore. I'm pleasantly relaxed."
"Good; tell me about yourself," she requested.
"Not much to tell, really. I grew up in Seattle and moved to Chicago after my mom died from cancer."
"I'm sorry to hear that. How did you learn about the stock market?"
"I studied it in high school, had a mentor I met in the library, and read more books on the way to Chicago's Loop."
"What college did you go to?"
He said, "None. My business training has come from the School of Hard Knocks. I've learned you must be bold and risk large amounts of money to make it big in the market."
She smiled. "You and my dad would hit it off. He is a self-made man who has done well through hard work and taking business risks."
"What does he do?"
"He was a mason apprentice during high school summers and after graduation. After a few years of brick and concrete block construction work, he decided to learn the brick-making trade. Then, he started his own company. It became one of the southeast's largest brick and concrete materials suppliers."
"No kidding, Bricks? You can make money from them?"
"Yes, dummy. Lots of money if you know how to make them and maintain your quality. There's a lot to bricks that we don't appreciate. There are different types, strengths, materials, and uses. My dad came here from Georgia and promised Walt Disney he would provide various bricks, colors, veneers, blocks, and manufactured cobblestones at fair prices and excellent quality. The rest is history."
Roscoe laughed. "So, Tammy, a pretty girl like you has made bricks?"
"You bet. I've made them, stacked 'em, loaded trucks with forklifts, and even driven the products to market."

Graham woke, took the helm, and steered the boat southwest to Disney's Wilderness Lodge's marina. After using the facilities, the two couples had another shot of tequila at the Geyser Point Bar & Grill. They then cruised along the cabins north of the Lodge, the Magic Kingdom Park shoreline, and back to the Floridian. The girls invited Roscoe and Graham to return for dinner at eight in Citrico's. They also warned them to wear sports coats and bring an appetite for a seven-course meal.

The boys returned to their RV, popped two beers, and sat outside watching the parade of children riding, skating, and running by their campsite.

Roscoe was distressed. "Graham, I've never had such a fancy dinner. How do I know which utensil to use and not look like a hick?"

Rabinski chuckled. "First, don't stress out, my friend. Take it slow and watch the others. The silverware above your plate is probably for dessert. The server may bring more items if necessary. A larger sharp knife is for cutting your meat - pay attention to what our host does. You're right-handed; hold your fork in your left hand, cut your meat, put down the knife, shift the fork to your right hand, and eat the piece you just cut."

"I'm going to screw this up," moaned Roscoe.

"No, you're not. Ask Tammy's dad questions. He'll think you're interesting if you show interest in him and don't talk with your mouth full."

"What kind of questions?"

"Don't worry; it will come to you. But remember this: don't question how much anything might cost."

They showered and shaved, starting at seven o'clock. Roscoe wore his blue sports coat, and Graham's was tan. They met Tammy's parents and the two girls at eight o'clock in Citrico's lounge. Jocko Fleming ordered Golden Haze Margaritas all around. He was a tall, muscular man with a bushy mustache and blue eyes. His battered, strong hand crushed Fuller's during their handshake.

Once they all had their cocktails, Fleming proposed a toast. "Here's to Walt Disney and his amazing vision for Disney World. He's our best customer."

Tammy's dad stood fast as waiters took other patrons to their tables. She asked, "Dad, shouldn't we go in and get our table?"

"No, dear daughter, they'll come for us."

At eight-thirty sharp, the head waiter led them past the tables and into a private room. Roscoe gave Graham an inquiring look, and Rabinski shrugged his shoulders. The table was set for six dinners and had gorgeous linen, goldware, sparkling crystal, and bountiful flowers.

Fleming said, "Welcome to the Chef's Domain. You can order any drink or item from the menu, mix and match anything, or have Chef Andre prepare a surprise."

Jocko had Roscoe sit to his right and his daughter to his left. Mrs. Fleming faced him from the other end of the table. She had Graham sit to her right and Melonie to her left. Mr. Fleming ordered a white wine, and the first course arrived – one prawn, a large scallop, and a shelled crab claw in a chilled white sauce. Fuller sipped his wine and watched his host spear the prawn with a small fork – he did likewise.

Roscoe remarked, "Mr. Fleming, thank you for inviting us to this special dinner. Tammy tells me you're in the brick-and-block business. When did you start?"

Jocko took a bite out of his prawn. "I was a bricklayer right out of high school and decided it might be more comfortable making the product. I was half right, as most of my production was inside. However, firing bricks in the kiln was hellish work in the summer. I learned everything I could about making bricks and cement building materials.

After two years, the owner had me pounding the pavement, selling his products in Georgia and Florida. Unfortunately, he was a drunk and lost control of our finances. I used my savings and a loan from my parents to buy Macon Brick and Block from the bankruptcy court."

"Wow, quite a story. This seafood is delicious, and so's the wine."

"How about you, Mr. Fuller? What's your occupation?"

"Sir, please call me Roscoe. I guess I'm best described as a stock market speculator. But I have pulled out and plan to switch into real estate and the specialty insurance business."

Fleming arched his eyebrows. "Really? Why is that, the pulling out, I mean?"

"Well, in my opinion, the market run-up is over. My buddy Graham and I had a good ride on the dot.com IPOs. He's my broker, and I talked him into this vacation while I look for an office building to buy in Florida."

"Why Florida?"

"No income tax," replied Fuller.

"I hear you, young man. I've considered moving our business here, but many of our product inputs, like clay and rock, are more available in Georgia. Did you only invest in IPOs?"

"No, sir. We were working out of the CBOT Building in the Chicago Loop. I got some training and started trading CBOT Mini future calls on the NASDAQ 100."

"What do you like in the market now?"

"Nothing. The Bear has taken over. Take any index, and the Bears are still in charge"

Tammy interrupted the men. "Dad, you'll like Roscoe's style; he's a self-made man like you. So here comes our next course. You, gentlemen, will now pay attention to this lovely companion who doesn't care about the stock market."

"Yes, dear daughter, sorry," replied Jocko.

Chef Andre came from the kitchen with three servers who placed small plates of sliced roast duck topped with a colorful orange sauce. Roscoe watched his host select a new knife and fork while the waiters removed the first ones used on the seafood plate.

The chef said, "Bon appetite, my friends. I'm here to take your salad and main course orders. I have a petite Caesar salad made with or without grilled chicken, steak, shrimp, or crab and with or without anchovies. You can select a garden salad with any dressing, or we will make you a fruit salad with a flaming rum finish. You can order anything off the menu for the main course, including any vegetable and starch. Otherwise, you can have a cheeseburger, breakfast items, pizza of your choice, or just ask for a surprise."

Roscoe ordered the Caesar salad with crab, grilled medium-rare filet mignon, green beans with sliced almonds in a butter sauce, and truffle macaroni and cheese.

Jocko and his wife said, "Surprise me."

Tammy's dad asked, "Daughter, how was your day?"

"Pops, it was wonderful. Mel and I went swimming, met Roscoe and Graham at the pool, and they rented a pontoon boat. We had drinks and toured past several resorts and the Magic Kingdom. It was very relaxing, and I didn't even think about school or my thesis."

Roscoe asked her, "What's your major?"

"Psychology. I'm working on my master's degree."

Fuller was entranced, she had beauty and brains. "Tammy, what do you plan to be?"

"I'm not sure, but I'm leaning toward teaching on a college campus."

The salad course arrived, along with freshly baked garlic rolls. Roscoe had a small plate of mixed greens, croutons, Dungeness crab meat, shaved Parmesan cheese, and capers topped off with a tangy dressing. He looked at Tamatha, who was enjoying her fruit salad, and she blew him a kiss. Fleming ordered a French Bordeaux and a second bottle after his companions agreed it was excellent. Fuller was dying to know what the wine cost but kept his silence. Roscoe's oak-grilled filet with Bordelaise sauce was the best steak ever. The next course was a sherbet of your choice to cleanse the pallet.

Two waiters brought bottles of Cognac and Port to the table, and it was time for dessert. Roscoe had Bananas Foster, which he had first tried at Brennan's in New Orleans, considering its name ironic. The buttery rum, sugar, and walnuts flamed and served over rich vanilla ice cream and halved bananas were exquisite.

Roscoe was stuffed and feeling no pain from the alcoholic drinks. The Cognac was strong but enticing – it warmed him inside and out. Dinner was over, and the girls wanted to go dancing. Roscoe and Graham thanked Mr. and Mrs. Fleming and stumbled out of Chirico's. The lads returned to their RV at midnight, went to bed, and slept with most of their clothes on. Graham was up at seven, made coffee, and had breakfast before catching the bus to meet Melonie at the Magic Kingdom Entrance.

Roscoe pulled the covers over his head and slept until 9:15. He had a date with Tammy Fleming for lunch at the Floridian. She wanted to work on her thesis in the morning, and he planned to review listings for Orlando's small office buildings. By ten o'clock that morning, he was working with a Coldwell Banker realtor and was shocked at the prices. Structures in Orlando and nearby were more costly than the ones he had rejected in Tallahassee. The realtor called it the "Disney Effect."

Roscoe met Tammy at the Grand Floridian Café at twelve-thirty. She looked ravishing with her blonde hair in a ponytail, white blouse, pink shorts, and running shoes. They had an enjoyable lunch and talked about their quite different projects. Her thesis was on "The Making of the Criminal Mind," which Roscoe found amusing.

He thought, *I wonder what she would feel if I told her she was having lunch with a bonafide crook?*

After lunch, he went to see her parents' two-bedroom suite on the fourth floor of the Sago Cay building. It had a sitting room between the two bedrooms and a spectacular view of the lake and Magic Kingdom on the other side of the lagoon.

Tammy said, "This is one of Dad's favorite spots in the Floridian. He also likes a couple of suites in the Main Building, but they cost double this one."

"Where are your parents?"

"They had to skedaddle back to Georgia to handle a business emergency."

"That's too bad; I enjoyed talking stocks with your dad."

"Boring! What do you want to do this afternoon?"

"I want to go to Epcot Center sooner or later. But I have an appointment with a realtor at three o'clock this afternoon."

"Cancel it, and we'll go to Epcot. We can meet Mel and Graham there for dinner at the Rose and Crown Dining Room – you guys will love the Shepherd's Pie."

"I guess I can push it back. How long are you here?"

"Two more days and nights. You're on vacation, Roscoe Fuller – make the most of it. You can use my dad's yearly pass and VIP parking. We must be back here by eight fifteen for the fireworks at Magic Kingdom. You can't do Epcot in half a day, so we can go tomorrow and have lunch at the Teppan Edo. Ummm…I can't wait. The chefs in the Japanese area put on an entertaining show and cook the food on a grill right in front of you."

Later, the foursome drank French wine in France's pavilion and Guinness beer at the Rose and Crown. The boys sipped single malt whiskey after dinner. Then, they strolled around the larger lagoon and sampled more wines.

Graham drove them back to the Floridian to watch the Magic Kingdom fireworks. Then, he and Melonie departed for the RV and Camp Wilderness.

Roscoe and Tammy held hands on their balcony, and he said, "Tamatha, I'm very interested in your thesis project; tell me more about it."

She replied, "I suppose it's not too unique, but I wanted to use existing research to find a cause for the criminal mindset."

"Just how do you define criminal?"

"I'm working on that. So far, I mean someone who commits multiple felony offenses."

Gee, that's me: check kiting, credit card fraud, skipping probation, tax evasion, and killing my stepdad.

"What are the theories so far?"

"There's a wide range. Some researchers blame genetics, some child abuse, and others claim it's peer pressure, one criminal teaching another."

How about vengeance against society for my physical deformities and deciding crime pays?

"Interesting, babe. Which way do you lean?"

"Don't call me that! I don't think it's genes, only. My theory is that a bad upbringing, lack of a loving, nurturing family, and disrespect for norms and rules lead the serial criminal into a life of crime."

Maybe, sweetheart. But I know a guy that started right out with murder.

"It seems to me that child abuse is a very broad category," he replied.

"Yes, it is. I define it as physical and emotional abuse, including a lack of parental love and poor socialization. Also, loss of parents or a parent can be a trigger."

Yeah, and a stepdad that beats on you and wants to kill your mom for money - there's a good trigger.

Roscoe asked, "Hmmm. What about felons wanting to make more money at other people's expense or cheating the government?"

She replied, "Yes, there can be an element of arrogance, even narcissism, that the rules only apply to weaker people, and the criminal is convinced they're smarter – they expect to get away with their crimes."

Now you're talking! Make crime pay and get a good lawyer if caught.

"You may be right, Tammy. Unfortunately, the authorities can't catch everyone, especially if you keep moving and changing your legal residence."

"Interesting, Roscoe. Is that what you're doing?"

Careful, Randall Foster or Roscoe Fuller; all this booze loosens your tongue.

"Me, I'm no criminal. I'm in Florida because there's no income tax – it's strictly legit."

"I heard you tell my dad that you're shifting from stocks into real estate and insurance. How will that work?"

I'm not sure, babe. My partner is still in prison and a serial felon.
"I have a partner who has worked out the business plan. We buy small commercial buildings and start a new insurance trend."
"Is it Graham? Is he your partner?"

Naw, Graham is no master criminal like Johnny Reardon.
"No, I met a guy in Indiana selling real estate. He showed me how taking depreciation on a building helps your cash flow."
"Too deep for me."

Me too, even deeper when you file phony numbers on your return. Johnny says we make money on the insurance side and lose it on paper with the real estate. Then, we hide our cash offshore.
"Well, I have the cash to get us started, and he has the smarts to shape the business, so we make a good profit – all on the up and up."
She nodded. "Roscoe, we need to talk about our sleeping arrangements. You can take the guest room, the living room couch, or sleep with me in my parents' king bed."
"Hmmm. Let me think. I know - I like choice number three."
"OK, just remember I don't want to be forced into anything."
"Same here. I think you will find me a very understanding and attentive lover. I had two girlfriends show me the ropes, so to speak."
"Good. I'll call the concierge and order us brandy nightcaps."
"Does that come with the room?"
"Yes, it does. The resort stocks the room with drinks and snacks we like, and we can order anything else. They make our reservations at the parks and the restaurants and take care of our smallest need -it's wonderful."
"Because your dad spends a lot of money here?"
"Yes, that's part of it, and because we are on the top tier of the Disney Vacation Club and stay at Club Level rooms."
"Club Level? What's that?" he questioned.
"We get several perks like no wait check-in, access to a private lounge for drinks and food, reservation assistance, and separate areas in buildings with fewer kids running around – and some of the best views like this one."
"This is the nicest set-up I've ever seen. The fireworks were great."
"Roscoe, have you ever been to Hawaii?"
"Nope, should I go?"

"Of course, someday. Tomorrow night, I'm booking us into the Polynesian Village Luau and Hawaiian show. You'll love it, and we can walk there along the bay."

The two couples did enjoy the food and show at the Polynesian. Tammy and Roscoe had spent the day at Epcot on rides, technology displays, Japanese cuisine, and in the country pavilions. Melonie and Graham rented bikes, rode to the Wilderness Lodge for brunch, and spent the afternoon at the Meadow Swimmin' Pool and motorhome. After the Luau show, the foursome had drinks at Trader Sam's and returned to the Floridian on foot. Graham promised to return at 10 a.m. to drive the girls to Orlando's International Airport for their flights to Atlanta and Athens.

After dropping the young ladies, the "Dynamic Duo" enjoyed lunch and music at Disney's Downtown House of Blues. They used Fleming's passes there and at Epcot that night. In the afternoon, they had a strange experience at their RV pad. A woman pushing a toddler carriage stopped and talked to them while they were having an afternoon beer.
She said, "Hey there, young men, do you want to make some money?"
Graham replied, "Ma'am, we are always ready to replenish funds. What do you have in mind?"
"My best friends have created a 'Prosperity Letter' only for campers. It costs only $20 and will bring you luck, good fortune, and a new source of wealth."
Roscoe looked skeptical. "How does it work?"
"Young man, it's all explained in this letter."

GOOD DAY FELLOW CAMPERS!!

We are Robert and Patricia Merriweather. Our friends, Barbara and Ken Johnson started this Prosperity Letter only for campers helping campers. We are doing it for fun and profit. It is only available in campgrounds for true RVers. Do not send it through the mail, that is illegal!

Here is how it works; someone will give you a list of four names of fellow travelers. You give them a GIFT of $20. They send $15 to the first name, and $5 to the second. You remove the top name and add yours to the bottom.

You provide your list to five (5) other campers and receive a $20 gift (preferably in another campground) and send the money ($15 and $5) to the top two. Your name moves quickly up the list. Soon, you should be receiving $5 and $15.

You get Gifts from all over the country as the game spreads to other RV parks. So, repeat, do not send the list through the mail.

You can feel secure knowing that your $20 will be back in no time, and as the list spreads, much more than that. Many people down on their luck may get enough to pay their living expenses for another month or two. Think about them. You are doing a good thing. May God bless you.

YOUR PROSPERITY GIFT LIST

1. Patricia and Robert Merriweather, 422 North 4th Avenue, Gainesville, Florida, 32609

2. Josh and Liz Riley, 1825 Laurel Green Way, Atlanta, Georgia, 30318

3. Rick and Janice Stratmyer, 1619 Dover Street, Mobile, Alabama, 36618

4. Barbara and Kenneth Johnson, 4219 North West 16th Blvd, P.O. Box 3251, Gainesville, Florida, 32653

INSTRUCTIONS

Please remove the first name(s) at the top (number 1).

You are on your honor to move the list up and put your name at the bottom.

Remember, your actions may help a family desperately in need.

Provide the new list to five (5) campers for a $20 gift from each.

Send $15 to number 1 and $5 to number 2 on each list.

Sure, you could keep the money, but where's the fun in that?

That would make you a cheat and a crook.

You could be hurting other campers who need the payments more than you.

If you follow the gift list directions, you may receive as much as a thousand dollars!

Chapter Eight

THE NEW PARTNERSHIP – Gainesville, Florida

Although he had plenty of cash, Roscoe hesitated to buy a prosperity list. Graham judged it the best chain letter he had ever heard of and bought two. He used his buddy's Escapee address for the payments.

Roscoe said, "Ma'am, how many of these have you sold in the Disney campground?"

"Only ten, young man – all in the northern loops. We are the only ones with them in Camp Wilderness, so you should be able to sell yours in the southern loops."

"Hmmm. In that case, I'll take one. You're sure this is legal?"

"Yes, if you only mail the gifts. The postal authorities may get their backs up if you send the lists.

"I see. Are you Barbara Johnson?" asked Fuller.

"No, we are the Merriweathers and have sold this list generation to the Johnsons. They have already received more than $1,000."

"Wow!" exclaimed Roscoe. "And you folks are from Gainesville?"

"Yes, we've lived there several years."

"What's the real estate market like in Gainesville?"

"It's reasonable, unlike property anywhere near Orlando."

He answered. "Yes, I've found that out. The realtors call it the Disney effect."

She replied, "Well, we're 100 miles north. What are you looking for?"

"Me and my partner want to buy a small office building and start a insurance business."

"You should talk to my husband, Robert. He's been trying to finance a building and is already a licensed insurance agent."

"That sounds great. Would he like to come over for a beer?"

"Sure. I'll send him by at five o'clock."

Roscoe and Graham napped in the RV until there was a rap on the door. Fuller opened the door and found a large man, probably in his early thirties, smiling at him.

"Are you Mr. Fuller?"

"Yes, I am; please come in. Can I buy you a beer?"

"Sure, anytime is good for a cold one," said Robert Merriweather.

"Need a glass?" asked Rabinski.

"No, the bottle is fine. My wife says you're looking for an office building in Florida."

"Yes sir, my partner Johnny and I have some capital and want to own a Florida property and start a insurance company."

Robert whistled. "That's pretty ambitious for a young man. Is your partner older?"

"Yes, Johnny is five years older."

"Does he have training in the insurance industry?" questioned Merriweather.

"No sir, not that I know about."

"Hmmm. To sell insurance, a company must jump through many legal hoops and register with the state."

Roscoe nodded. "Johnny has a different idea. He saw an ad where a company buys policies from the owners and another about reverse home mortgages."

"So, you wouldn't have sales agents, processing personnel, or actuaries?"

Roscoe said, "No on most of that. What's an actuary?"

"Someone that computes the longevity of clients and the risks of insurance policy payouts. You would need lots of seed money to start collecting clients in either one of those categories."

"We have several million that I have taken out of the stock market."

"You got out?"

"I did."

"Patricia and I stayed out. We only put our excess funds in real estate."

"She said you're a insurance agent. How does that work?"

"I started with New York Life three years ago. They provided me with a ton of training in the industry and as a salesman. I'm ARM, AINS, and APA certified. I have sold enough policies to keep our heads above water, but now I'm looking for greener pastures."

"Your wife mentioned you were trying to buy a building."

"Yes, our NYLI offices are in a decent building in Gainesville's College Park District. The owner recently died, and his heirs live overseas. I think they'd take substantially less than the building's intrinsic worth, but I can't raise the twenty percent deposit."

"What are the numbers?" asked Roscoe.

"Yeah, considering the floor space, rent receipts, and total property footprint, I think it is worth three million. Since one daughter is in London and the other somewhere in Spain, I planned to offer each of them one million in cash. That makes the down payment $200K."

"Why would they take it? What's your angle?" questioned Graham.

"They both married well, and the inheritance would be tax-free. I know more about the building and their father's wishes than anyone. We were good friends and had lunch together nearly every week. He wanted his traditions to continue."

Fuller was confused. "Tradition? A building has traditions?"

"This one does. It was designed and built by the owner, Mr. Henry C. Arnholdt, a noted architect."

"Never heard of him," responded Graham.

"Not many people have. Potential customers had to come to him to commission a design. He only worked on one project at a time and was very selective. He designed several small and medium-sized buildings in Canada, the U.S., and Europe. They had energy-saving features, unique appearances, and custom designs matching their customers' interests."

"Robert, what makes this building special?" asked Roscoe.

"I'm glad you asked. First, it has plenty of land and parking on four sides. There's a green grass area to the north and a pavilion for weekend band music during the warmer months. To the south is an arboretum garden with labeled trees and plants. The roof and parking lots funnel all their rainwater to underground tanks that water the botanical garden and grass field. Inside the main lobby is the 'Hall of Presidents.' As each President completes his service, his local political party adds his portrait and life history. Gainesville's Republican Party also uses the hall on election eve nights. Other folks book it for weddings and other events. The roof has solar equipment to heat water and provide electricity. I could go on and on."

Roscoe held up his hand. "Hold it. Why have the lawn area, the grass, and the garden? Doesn't that cost money to maintain?"

"Yes, it does, but it was part of Harry's vision that the building should be part of the community's activities, and they enhance rents and occupancy. The foundation is sounder than building codes require, and the walls are cement blocks with steel rod reinforcement. They're filled with insulation and faced with bricks on both sides. Harry called it a 200-year structure with triple-pane windows that should withstand the toughest hurricane."

"How many floors?" queried Roscoe.

"Three. And get this; half the basement has large boulders that help augment the air conditioning. Young architects come to study all the energy-saving features. School children and now tourists come to admire the Hall of Presidents. Volunteer docents provide nature walks in the garden for grades four through ten. Local soccer teams play in the grassy area. The city and county sponsor Fourth of July, Labor Day, and Octoberfest celebrations in the east parking lot."

Roscoe was intrigued. "So, Robert, you're telling me that we might be able to acquire a three-story, well-built building with plenty of rental space for two-thirds of its retail value. It's a property with additional land, and it has many features to reduce the operational costs?"

"That's correct. If you have two million, we can contact the daughters and offer to continue the community features as their father would have preferred. I think that would mean more to them than the money."

"Shouldn't we get a mortgage?" asked Roscoe.

Robert shook his head. "No, too many sharks will get wind of the deal and bid the price up. We can mortgage it later. Roscoe, do you have a Florida business license?"

"Not yet. The realtors have advised me to start a LLC before purchasing." Robert Merriweather responded, "I think that's smart. It limits your financial liability and protects the rest of your personal funds."

Graham said, "Whoa, slow down, buddy. You'll need an appraisal and physical inspection before committing your hard-earned capital. No offense, but you're taking the word of a chain letter seller who's probably not doing well in the insurance business. What's the unrented space? How do the rents compare to similar properties? Are there rent escalation clauses each year or for inflation? Does it make an economic profit? How much depreciation will the daughters have to pay taxes on?"

"All good questions, Graham," replied Roscoe. "Let's go to Gainesville with Robert tomorrow and look the property over, compute the rent per square foot, and see these unusual features. Robert, are you in?"

"Gentlemen, you bet, 110 percent."

Roscoe smiled. "In that case, I think we deserve another cold one."

  Fuller, Graham, and Merriweather drove to Gainesville the next day. Roscoe was impressed with the Arnholdt Building. It was four stories, counting the basement. The entrance hall and presidential portraits occupied half of the first floor. The three men met with Harry Arnholdt's secretary on the third floor and learned that the building was ninety percent occupied, no rent was overdue, and each lease had a two percent yearly escalator. Miss Wickins did her best to manage the building but needed some assistance. Roscoe was sold. He liked the building, its location, and the discounted price.

Graham took Virginia Wickins to lunch while Merriweather showed Roscoe the arboretum walkways, trees, and plants. They sat on a bench under a weeping willow tree.

Roscoe said, "Robert, I think you're proposing a good deal, so I will reciprocate. My partner and me will put up the money from our LLC, and you can manage the building. With your advice, we will start the insurance business when he arrives in the spring. We will pay you monthly, and you can still sell life insurance. Was Graham correct that you haven't done well in the insurance business?"

"Yes and no. I have trouble closing my sales and only have made it through with Patricia's bookkeeping salary."

"I see. So, this would be an important step for you?"

"Yes. I need to move in a new direction," said the older man.

"J&R LLC can provide that for you, but you need to understand the magnitude of your decision."

"J and R?"

"Jonathon and Roscoe Limited Liability Company. Robert, did you ever see the movie or play called 'Damn Yankees?'"

"Yes, I think so. Isn't it when a baseball player makes a pact with the devil, and his team beats the Yankees in the World Series?"

"Yes. Sort of, but it is an older fan who becomes a young long-ball hitter, wins the National League pennant, and owes his soul to the devil."

"Mr. Fuller, why are you bringing this up?"

"Because Robert, me and my partner can set you up in business. You can be our company's public face, but if you double-cross us, the penalties will be severe. I'm a pussy cat, but my partner is very nasty. You may forget we saved your bacon in a few years and take our business away."

"I would never do that." Merriweather protested.

"I hope not since it would be the last thing you would do. Remember that we found you as a marginal insurance salesman running chain letter scams. But that isn't all."

"What do you mean?"

"Johnny and me plan to bend the law until it breaks. We will cheat on our taxes, and you will sign the forms. Your neighbors will admire and respect you, but underneath, our business will have a foundation of tax fraud here in Florida and other states."

"Florida doesn't have an income tax."

"Yes, we know, but we will manipulate the property tax and other charges. We will funnel profits from other states through here and bypass their income tax. We will misstate our expenses and net revenue to lower federal taxes. Can you handle that?"

"Look, Roscoe, I'm desperate but don't want to go to jail."

"You won't if you do what we say. Will your wife keep two sets of books?"

"No. Patricia is a straight arrow. We would need to keep her out of this, this unlawfulness."

"Fine. She can keep the real numbers, and we will file the taxes."

"Do we have to cheat and lie?" pleaded Robert.

"Yes, Merriweather, it's the only way our business plan works and provides a living for all of us. You can call us criminals, pirates, or rebels. We won't pay half our hard-earned profits to city, county, state, and federal taxes. It slows our growth and makes a small pie to share with you. We've had advice from some of the best criminal minds in the country. Are you in or out?"

"Normally, I would run this by Patricia. We discuss everything."

Fuller warned, "Not this time. A year from now, you can buy a nice house and fund a private school for your kid in a few years. What do you say?"

"I need the money. I'm in."

Roscoe shook Robert's hand. "Good. Figure out how to buy this property for two million. We will provide the funding. My partner and me will form the Florida LLC with you as the President and Patricia as the Treasurer. A lawyer will contact you two with papers to sign while Graham and I head for Key West."

"Roscoe, what if the sisters want a real estate agent involved?"

"That's a negative on the sales side. We can't stop them if they want to pay for a buying agent. Pitch the deal that you have a lawyer who will take care of everything and save them on fees. Emphasize it is a cash buyout, and each of them will receive one million in the bank account of their choice. Convince them we will continue their father's traditions and community involvement. Pick an escrow company to hold the money and handle the closing."

Merriweather asked, "What's our long-range plan?"

Fuller responded, "We plan to have office buildings like this one in several states. Our next target is New York; there's lots of money up there. My partner has friends looking for us in Albany and the surrounding area. Next, you must determine what licenses and approvals we need to buy insurance policies and provide reverse mortgages. I expect a briefing when I return from Key West in two weeks."

Roscoe and Graham continued south from Orlando in the RV. Fuller was getting a bit irritated with Graham Rabinski. He had already been there and done that no matter where they went and what they did. He had visited Disney World, Daytona, Cape Canaveral, and Miami. In Key West, he had already been tarpon fishing, prowled the bars where Hemingway hung out, and snorkeled at the coral reef. Riding an airboat and finding alligators was an old hat in the Everglades swamp. Graham's family had a Boca Raton, Florida, home in the St Andrews Country Club complex to escape the Philadelphia winters. When the young men returned from south Florida to set up camp in Gainesville, Graham was eager to join Melonie in Georgia, and Roscoe wanted some time to himself.

The next morning, Fuller met with Mr. and Mrs. Merriweather at the Arnholdt Building. Robert reported he had a verbal agreement from the two sisters to accept a million each from the building sale. He and his wife had moved into the deceased owner's offices, and Virginia Wickins agreed to act as their secretary. A lawyer in the building had prepared a sales agreement, and it was time for Fuller to move the purchase money plus fees into escrow. Roscoe reviewed the LLC paperwork from Florida's Secretary of State, and everything seemed in order.

"Robert, from now on, all rents are ours. Have our lawyer add a clause that any rent outstanding will pay selling costs."

"Consider it done, boss. What's next?"

"What did you learn about filing to buy back insurance policies and writing reverse mortgages?"

"It's less demanding than selling a variety of insurance packages or issuing various loans. I have our lawyer working on the paperwork."

Roscoe said, "Excellent. I learned my partner will meet me in upper New York soon. Your next task is to figure out the best methods of advertising our products. This week, I will meet with you in the morning and research investments at the main library the rest of the day."

"Why is that?"

Roscoe responded, "I think the market has hit bottom. So, I want to start nibbling at some options and strong stocks to get us more capital."

"You might want to talk to Johnson, Johnson, and Prath on the second floor."

"Why is that?"

"They're an investment firm with about ten brokers who always want more space. Harry had to put in dedicated phone lines for them."

"Hmmm. That does sound promising. Do you know if they have Bloomberg terminals?"

"I haven't a clue. J J & P seem to be doing well, driving flashy cars and ordering food delivered."

"Thanks. I'll check them out once I have my strategy. Nothing is sure in the stock market. It really is the largest gambling casino in the country. But in my gut, I think I'm right."

Roscoe thought about the message from his partner in crime. *I'm to work my way up to Saratoga Springs, New York, by the end of next month and meet with one of Johnny's gambling friends. He will introduce me to a commercial realtor who knows the building market. Do I want to see Tammy on the way? Probably not; I'm not going to marry her. And I may end up back in jail. On the other hand, I want to see Graham, who has signed up with an Atlanta brokerage. Maybe he can help me establish a substantial retirement account by hook or crook.*

Roscoe left Gainesville after confirming the escrow papers were on track and transferring the money from his banks and stock accounts. Merriweather was working on state licensing issues, and his wife had hired a graphics firm to develop logos, advertisement copy, and billboard displays. Roscoe changed his mind about seeing Tammy when he learned that Macon was on the way to Atlanta. He stopped for two nights, and they rekindled their romance in the RV. She took him on a tour of the Fleming Brickworks, and they dined with her parents at the Downtown Grill.

Chapter Nine

RABINSKI IN ATLANTA – Atlanta, Georgia

Roscoe drove on to Atlanta with fond memories of Tammy, yet neither party had made any promise. He parked the RV near Buckhead, Atlanta, cleaned up, and joined Graham Rabinsky at his new firm in the Atlanta Financial Center. Graham had a window office with a dedicated Bloomberg console. Roscoe checked his stocks and discovered he still had a mixture of cash, bonds, and dividend stocks worth over six million. Then, the two friends had a late lunch at Maggiano's.

Roscoe started questioning his buddy. "Graham, how did you get this job so fast?"

"First of all, they were looking for a young broker with sales experience that they could fast-track to a VP position. I must prove myself and build my team. Second, my dad knows the senior partner and pulled some strings."

"Do you really want to be here in Atlanta so far from your family?"

"Yes and no, Roscoe. Winter in Philly, like Chicago, is no picnic. I have a stylish company apartment on the other side of Peachtree and paid membership at a private golf club. This Atlanta Financial Center is like our old CBOT Building. It has about every amenity that you can imagine. This whole area is like the Loop, with plenty of restaurants, shops, and entertainment."

"And how far away is Athens, you horny bastard?" asked Fuller.

"There's another plus. Melonie is only an hour away. Sometimes, she comes here for the weekend, or we meet halfway in Lawrenceville."

"So, it's pretty serious, I take it?"

"Yup, she's a great gal, comes from a good family, and we are like two peas in a pod. She has another year to finish her master's, and there may be wedding bells. Speaking of that, how was your time with Tammy?"

"It was good, but not great. I don't think we see ourselves as a long-term couple."

Their lunch arrived, and Roscoe took several bites and sampled the bottle of red wine. "So, Graham, have you figured out how I can do business with your new brokerage?"

"Yes. I put our lawyers on it, and I have a path for you, but you must completely trust me."

"Let's say I do. How will it work?"

"Roscoe, you create an irrevocable complex grantor trust with me as the trustee."

Fuller frowned. "Please explain."

"First, I manage your money under your direction, with no one the wiser. Second, the taxes are your concern. The Grantor, which is you, pays the taxes."

"Graham, let's say I put in a million to buy CBOT futures and stocks on margin – any problem with that?"

"No, the trust papers will allow any investment, no matter how risky."

"Good. What about real estate? I now own that building in Gainesville."

"Good for you, buddy. Did you get a good deal?"

"I think so, two million plus the sales fees. The Merriweathers are managing it for me."

"Outstanding. To answer your question, you can buy real estate from the trust but not a personal residence. How much do you want to put in?"

"Let's start with two million."

"Works for me. Salute!" responded Graham.

They finished their excellent Italian meal and returned to Graham's office, where Roscoe read over the trust papers.

"Graham, I see what you mean about counting on you. You completely control my money, the type of investments, and you can follow my wishes or not."

"Yes, that's how it must look to my bosses and any outside auditor or tax authority. But you and I will privately coordinate how you want it invested or the payments you want. I recommend phone calls only, nothing in writing."

"I like it. Let's start with three million."

"Salute again!" enthused Graham.

Roscoe stayed in Atlanta for several days to tour the city, sign his trust papers, and use Rabinski's data terminal. He had a month to arrive in Saratoga Springs, New York, and decided to tour the East Coast, which was all new to him. Fuller visited the Aquarium, Botanical Garden, the World of Coca-Cola, the zoo, and Jimmy Carter's Library in Atlanta.

He talked Graham into a three-day trip to Savannah, but it was not as much fun as their previous journeys. Graham was always on his phone working with customers, calling Melanie, and showed no interest in chasing some tail.

Roscoe moved on to Charleston alone and followed up with a Myrtle Beach stop. He liked the ambiance in Charleston but found Myrtle Beach overly developed for summer tourists. After a short stay in Wilmington, he took Highway 40 to Raleigh, then 85 to Richmond. The RV park owner said Williamsburg was a must-see attraction. Fuller camped there for three nights, entranced by the colonial atmosphere and good food. Next, he spent a week in the Washington D.C. area, took many tours, and used the hop–on–hop–off trolleys to visit landmarks and museums.

At Baltimore's Inner Harbor, he met a couple of college girls who were delighted that he would pay for sightseeing and restaurants. They stayed with him in the RV, but nothing romantic ensued. Roscoe then toured Philadelphia for three days and New York City for five. Finally, he arrived at the Saratoga Springs Casino Hotel, parked his rig in the parking lot, and unhooked his car.

Williamsburg, Virginia Courthouse
Source: Wikimedia – Bradley Jones

Chapter Ten

A NEW YORK PROPERTY – Saratoga Springs, NY

Roscoe started the RV generator, raised the satellite antenna, and popped a cold beer. He watched some TV programs and ate a ham sandwich.

After a nap, he thought about his instructions; *I'm supposed to go into the casino at eight o'clock tonight and sit at the end of the bar nearest the crap tables wearing a ball cap. I then order a double gin and tonic and wait to be contacted by Johnny's friend.*

He entered the casino at 7:55, found the bar, and ordered his drink.

A few minutes later, the black bartender approached and said, "How's that G&T, suh?"

Fuller took a sip, "It's fine, thank you."

"I've been expecting you. You'all a friend of Johnny's, right?"

"Yes, I am. I go by Roscoe Fuller, you?"

"Ever' body call me Black Ricky, 'cause there used to be a white Ricky also tending bar."

"I see. Why are we talking?"

"I have a building for you at a good price - inherited it from my daddy. I want to retire, sell it, and move to Florida. These old bones can't keep me on my feet all night, and I wants some warmer weather."

"OK, how big is your building?"

"It's a four-story brick building on Washington Street. There are shops on the ground floor, and most of the space is rented. In the back are living quarters that my daddy added and where I grew up."

"Do you know the square feet of rental space?"

"Yes, suh, it's nearly thirty thousand square feet."

"Ricky, what's your rent per square foot?"

"Mostly about ten dollars or less per foot per year."

"So fully rented, you would get $300K annually?"

"Yas suh."

"Ignoring expenses, three million in ten years?"

"Thas right."

Roscoe frowned. "Ten dollars seems on the low side."

"It probably is. Thas one of my problems. I haven't raised the rents in eight years, and some leases have expired."

"Why is that?"

"Most of the renters are white folk. I'm hesitant to ask 'em for more money."

"What other problems do you have?"

"Mr. Roscoe, please come and see the building. I'm going to make you and Johnny the best deal ever."

"How do you know Johnny?"

"Me and him did some hard time down in Georgia."

"I see. When should we meet?"

"I get off about midnight and sleeps until ten in the morning. Come about eleven, and we can get pizza for lunch."

"OK, Black Ricky, see you then."

Roscoe didn't wait. He drove his tow car north on Broadway and turned left on Highway 29. The building was small yet tidy, with retail businesses on the first floor. He paced the four sides of the structure and came up with 29,000 square feet, not counting the one-story living space in the back. There was an adequate blacktop parking space and more dirt parking to the south. He bought a bottle of Jim Beam from the first-floor liquor store and returned to the RV to contemplate purchasing the building.

The following day, Roscoe met Ricky in the morning and received a tour of all the building's floors. The retail space on the first floor was one hundred percent rented, and the building boasted several professional tenants – a couple of M.D.s, four lawyers, and a chiropractor. Roscoe asked Ricky Brown his selling price and was surprised at the answer.

"Mr. Fuller, suh, I reckon it is worth two million in a good real estate market. 'cause of some of my problems and seein' how you and Johnny are buyin', I gonna knock it down to one million."

Roscoe whistled. "That might be a good price depending on its overall condition. What are these other problems you're talking about?"

"Well suh, my daddy owned the building when he passed eight years ago. I was here with him and acted as the janitor. I told everyone he left it to me, and no one was the wiser. But I never put it in my name 'cause the state of Georgia has a warrant out for my arrest. So's you could say there's a bit of an ownership issue."

"Ricky, did your dad have a will?"

"No, can't say that he did. He would have split it with me, my brother, and sister if'n he did."

"I see. So, there's a serious problem with the property's title, and your siblings or anyone who says you owe them money can come forward and lay claim to the property and rents."

"I suppose so. I just wants to pass it quietly to new owners."

"Hmmm. Have you been paying the property taxes and filing income tax with the state and feds?"

"Yes suh, been doin' that in my father's name. Keeping the rents low meant no profits or taxes to pay on income."

"Ricky, this is a mess. No one is going to buy a million-dollar building without a clear title. We couldn't resale it or get a mortgage on it."

"I knows, I knows, thas why I'll sell it at half price. That's a cash price. You do have cash, right?"

"Yes, we have cash. Is there a mortgage?"

"No, suh. My daddy paid it off over thirty years."

"Again, did your dad have any will, even a handwritten one?" asked Roscoe.

"No, he just told me he wanted me to have the building. I said he couldn't use my name, so he added my brother's name on the title a month before he died."

Fuller, "Does your brother know that?"

"No, I never has told him. I'm willing to split the sales price with my brother and sister. Down in Florida, I'll get a good payment from social security; I'm on Medicare and have some savings set aside."

"Good. I'll pay you $800K if we can clear up this title problem. Are there any real estate lawyers in the building?"

"Yes suh, Ralston and Ralston are on the second floor. You wants the older man and make the price nine hundred thousand, so we can split it three ways."

"Ricky, I'll consider that."

Fuller went to the second floor and found a door that announced Ralston & Son in gold lettering. He opened the door and found an older woman organizing papers on a large table.

She said, "Good afternoon, sir. Can I help you?"

"Yes, Ma'am. I would like to see the elder Ralston if that's possible?"

"Without an appointment?"

"Yes Ma'am, I'm from out of town and need some advice about real estate."
"I'll talk to him, but no promises."
"Thank you."
Roscoe sat down but had to stand back up as a large man wearing suspenders and a bow tie approached. "Good afternoon, stranger. I'm 'Bull' Ralston. How can I help you?"
"Yes sir, I'm Roscoe Fuller. Black Ricky said you might be able to help with a real estate sale."
"Come into my office. Do you need some coffee?"
"No thanks."
"Mr. Fuller, what's the real estate in question?
"It's an office building; the problem is the title."
"Keep going. Say, is Ricky thinking of selling this building? If so, what's the price?"
"That's confidential. We have struck a deal, but the title is still in his father's name. I believe Ricky Brown has no right to sell the building."
"Was there no will? Ricky acted as if he inherited it," said Ralston.
"No, no will, only a verbal statement from his dad that he should inherit it."
"Mr. Fuller, Roscoe, I think you should give me a retainer before we talk more. My standard fee is five hundred dollars."
Roscoe counted out ten Ben Franklins. "Here's a thousand. You're now my lawyer."
"Good enough. Has Ricky been paying the taxes and fees?"
"Yes, but in his father's name."
"Holy shamollee, what a rat's nest. If Brown senior had talked to me, we could have set something up, a will, a trust, a gift, or joint ownership."
"Mr. Brown did put Ricky's brother on the deed."
"Does the brother know that? Did Ricky tell him?" asked the lawyer.
"No. They don't have much to do with each other."
"It's a big mess to clean up. It sounds to me that the brother could sell it to you. Is there a lender now or part of the deal?"
"No, my partner and me are paying cash. Ricky wants to split it three ways with his brother and sister."
"Roscoe, I can't advise you to pay him with the title issue up in the air. We need a written and signed will and a friendly escrow company to hold their noses."

"But Mr. Ralston, I said there's no will, only Ricky's claims."

"We need a valid-looking will that you take to the brother and a sales agreement. You get him to sign and pay him one-third out of escrow. You don't ask for a title search. Leave that bag of worms closed. Ricky must also sign the sales agreement and file the will with escrow."

"Sir, I told you there's no will," repeated Fuller.

"And as I told you, young man, we will find one, wink wink. As your lawyer, I'll find a valid will signed and notarized."

"I take it that you're a Notary."

"I am."

"How much will it cost me to 'find' this will?"

"Five grand."

"Five thousand for an hour's work?"

"Look, Mr. Fuller, I'm your lawyer and solving your problem. Go to Ricky and get his father's date of death and a clear sample of his signature. After that, I'll work on your sales agreement, but I will need the siblings' legal names and the purchase price."

"The latter is $900K, so each gets three hundred thousand."

Ralston whistled. "Now, who's taking advantage? This building is worth twice that."

"Maybe so, but Ricky will only sell it to me and my partner. We need you to start the paperwork on a New York company, J&R LLC."

"The purchasers?"

"Yeah, how long will it take?"

"Not long if I walk it through Albany. It will cost you another grand," said the lawyer.

Roscoe grimaced. "Fine, fine, I'll get you the partner info."

Fuller descended to the first floor and met with Black Ricky. "This must be your lucky day, Ricky."

"Why is that?"

"Ralston has a copy of your dad's will. He needs his death date and a clear signature to provide you with the original."

"Thank the Lord! Did he leave it just to me?"

"No. He left it for you to manage and split the net sales profit with your brother and sister. Mr. Ralston is making up a sales agreement for your brother to sign. We need to take it to Georgia and get his approval because his name is on the lease."

Ricky protested, "Oh no, I ain't ever setting foot in Georgia again. I'll tell you where to go and what he looks like."

Roscoe spent two more days working on the sales agreement with Ricky and filing the "found" will with the County Clerk. Then, he flew to Atlanta, rented a car, and drove north of Marietta, where Ricky's brother had a sand and gravel company. Highway 41 took him past the Cobb County Airport.

He thought, *This might be a good place for our Georgia building. Atlanta is too expensive, and a decent airport would let us fly in for the insurance business. Johnny thinks we should have our own aircraft someday.*

Roscoe found Roger Brown's quarry on Dabbs Bridge Road in Emerson. He parked his car and saw a huge man heading his way from the construction trailer. He was a black man over six feet tall and nearly 300 pounds.

Roger Brown spoke with a deep, strong voice, "Good morning, sir. Can we help you?"

"Yes, I hope you can. Are you Roger Brown, Ricky Brown's brother and Jacob Brown's son?"

"That I am. Are you here for sand and gravel or something else?"

"Definitely something else, but how's your business going?"

"When construction is up, we do quite well. When it is down, we starve. Why do you ask?"

"How is business right now?"

"In between. I got five trucks, and only three took out a load today. Just who are you?"

"I'm Roscoe Fuller, a friend of your brother's. I flew here from New York and brought some paperwork from my lawyer's office. Can we go inside?"

"Sure can. Would you like some coffee? Got a pot on."

"Yes, thanks."

Roscoe sipped the hot coffee while he thought about how to proceed.

He said, "Mr. Brown, when did you last talk to your brother?"

"It's been years. We never were close."

"OK, here's the situation; he's about to retire and move to a warmer climate. He's been managing your father's building for several years and working as a bartender. Ricky can now get social security, Medicare, and use the proceeds from selling the building to fund his retirement. But he feels it is only fair if he shares the money equally with you and your sister."

"How much money are we talkin' about?" asked Brown.

"Three hundred thousand for each of you."

"Whoee, you're talking about some real change there."

"Yes, I am, but some problems with the title could prevent the sale."

"Problems like what?"

"Your father added your name on the title before he died. But in his will, he left it to Ricky to live in and manage as long as he wanted. Your dad bequeathed the net sales amount equally to his three children upon its sale."

"Hmmm. Would there be any tax due on that money?"

"No inheritance tax would be due. Ricky has paid all the expenses and taxes from the rent all the years since your father's death."

"But you said we have problems."

"Yes, you need an all-cash deal. No mortgage company will touch a property that doesn't have a clear title. And you need a buyer who's willing to risk losing the building without title insurance."

"Would that be you, Mr. Fuller?"

"Yes, me and my partner who did time in prison with your brother and saved his life. I've spent five grand with a real estate lawyer to put this deal together. We'll use an escrow company the lawyer recommends to hold the funds and close the sale. We won't do a title search."

Brown looked suspicious. "Why not?"

"Because the whole thing is a mess. Your brother has been acting like he inherited the building and paying the bills like your father is still alive. The will states it belongs to the three of you if sold. I have legal agreements with me that Ricky has signed. If you sign them, my lawyer thinks we can complete the sale."

"When can Marion and I get the money?"

"Within two weeks to a month if all goes well."

"Does my sister have to sign anything?"

"No. But it would help if Marion provided a notarized statement agreeing with the sale. You and Ricky are the principal owners here. Him because he has maintained the property and you because your name is on the title. Like I say, it is a legal quagmire. Most potential buyers would have nothing to do with it."

"Can I see the will?"
"Yes, when we close escrow."
"My name is on the property title?"
"Yes, it is."
"Can't I just sell it and keep the money?"
"You could try, but your brother, your sister, and I will sue you. You will have spent more than $300K by the time you finish. The will is airtight. You will look like a greedy asshole in court and queer this sale and any future sale by exposing the questionable title."
Roger said, "I believe you, and I can use the money. My sister really needs it. How much is the building worth?"
"Probably about fifty percent more if there was a clear title and a buyer could get title insurance."
"So, you're getting a hell of a deal?"
"Yes and no. No one else is going to pay a higher amount. We all come out ahead, but me and my partner take the risk of someone challenging the title."
"Mr. Fuller, what do we have to do?"
"I need your notarized signature on the sales contract and your help in obtaining your sister's statement that she agrees with the division of the money."
"I can do that," said Brown.
"Good. Can you recommend a commercial realtor? I might be in the market to buy a business building here."
"In Emerson?" Brown questioned.
"No, in Marietta. And he or she should have a notary to witness your signature."

Roscoe obtained the signatures, had them notarized, and promised payment to Brown's siblings within thirty days. He then returned to Saratoga Springs and met with Ralston Senior.
"Bull, here are the two agreements. What else do we need for escrow?"
Ralston checked the signatures and notary seals. "Son, normally we would have an appraisal of the property and order title insurance. That's up to you."
"No thanks."
"In that case, we need your deposit, and we can start escrow."
Fuller handed over a check for fifty thousand dollars. "Here you go."

"Excellent. In two or three weeks, your LLC will be the owner of this building. Anything else I can do for you?"

"Yes, I would like a notarized sales agreement with Ricky Brown saying we bought the building for $3.9 million. How much will that cost me?"

"I reckon another thousand will do it."

Roscoe frowned. "C'mon, all you have to do is change a couple of numbers and remove two names."

"Yes, that's easy, but the fee is one thousand if you want it notarized. Also, expect my cousin to charge you an escrow fee that includes what title insurance would have cost."

Roscoe Fuller was pissed. "Shit. You both are crooks."

Bull Ralston winked and smiled. "Takes one to know one, son."

Roscoe met with Black Ricky and explained that the purchase was moving ahead for $900K. Roscoe said the J&R LLC would pay the fees, and Ricky and his siblings could expect $300K each.

Roscoe questioned, "Ricky, how did your Dad buy this building in the first place?"

"Well suh, my daddy was a brakeman and switchman on a New York railroad. He fell between two moving boxcars and lost his left arm. The company fired him and even refused to pay his medical bill. Dad got a lawyer and sued them for defective equipment and discrimination."

"What kind of discrimination?" asked Roscoe.

"It were the depression, and none of the black men on that there line could ever be conductors. Dad got cash and a pension for life. This building was behind on its taxes and a mess. My daddy had the down payment and cleaned it up."

Twenty days later, Saratoga County listed J&R LLC as the new owner of the Brown Building. Bull Ralston warned Roscoe not to seek a mortgage for a year or more – after paying all the bills and taxes as the new owner.

Chapter Eleven

THE BRUTAL TRUTH – Saratoga Springs, NY

One month after escrow closed on the Brown Building, Johnny Rivers, AKA Johnny Reardon, arrived in "The Springs" using his new identity. Roscoe briefed his cellmate on their progress. "Johnny, we have two Limited Liability Companies, one in Florida and one here."
"Why is that?"
"They help hide our profits and limit our liability if we are sued. We own this building and a larger, nicer one in Gainesville, Florida. We can live in this two-bedroom space while we improve this property, redo the leases, and raise the rent. I have a trained insurance salesman and his wife managing the Gainesville building, and they're also working on sales materials for our insurance and reverse mortgage business."
"Roscoe, how much did you pay for the two buildings?" asked Rivers.
"I paid two million for the Florida Arnholdt Building. It's worth three or more. I paid $900K for this one, which is worth double that."
"What capital do we have left?"
"We have three million in a trust account with a broker friend in Atlanta and two million more in stock accounts. I plan to open a broker account in Texas or Florida without state income tax. We will put half those funds in CBOT mini future contracts and have a checkbook to buy insurance policies and fund reverse mortgages."
"Roscoe, it won't be enough. We will need several million more to expand our customer list."
"How many are we shooting for?"
"One hundred in each state."
"Hmmm. If each transaction is about fifty thousand, we need five million in capital for each state."
"Yes, that sounds correct. Do you have another source?"
"The increased rents will help, and we can mortgage these first buildings."
Johnny slapped his hands together. "Damn, Roscoe, you have done well. We are off to a great start. Where did you get all of this cash? Did you rob a bank?"
"Nope. My Atlanta friend and I made a killing in dot.com stocks before the bubble burst. The Atlanta Trust can invest in more buildings. Where do you want to buy real estate next?"

"I'm thinking Pennsylvania, Connecticut, or both in about a year."
"Excellent, that fits my investment plan. Where after them?" asked Roscoe.
"Partner, we march down the eastern seaboard, Virginia, North Carolina, South Carolina, and Georgia."
"What about the smaller states?"
"Unless I'm wrong, we want states with lots of territory to spread our customer base."
"Connecticut isn't so big, right?" questioned Fuller.
"Correct, but there's a lot of New York money there."

After months of prison food, Johnny wanted a good steak dinner, so the two partners went to Morton's Steakhouse in the Saratoga Casino & Hotel. Their meal was excellent, and Rivers again complimented Roscoe on his progress with Rollo's plan. They finished the dinner sipping some single malt whiskey, and Johnny was getting looped when Roscoe questioned the timing of their business plan.

"Johnny, you have this planned out more than me, but Merriweather and some other folks don't see how we can collect much money from the insurance policies or the reverse mortgages for several years or even decades."

Rivers sobered up and said, "Partner, that's something we need to talk about on the way back to your building."

"OK, Johnny, I've got the check. I'm so glad you're here to help run the business."

They donned their coats and gloves and walked into the freezing parking lot.

Johnny stopped halfway to their car and talked in a low voice. "Roscoe, I told you this would be a crime caper that could land us back in jail, right?"

"Yes, you did."

"Good. Now, I will tell you something I will never admit I said. You know we are going to cheat on our taxes?"

"Yes, I do."

"Well, that's just the half of it. Roscoe Fuller, are you prepared to do anything, break any law to make us rich?"

"Yes, I think so," replied Roscoe.

"You can't think so; you must be willing to risk your future, your life, everything. Do you have the guts to do that?"

"Johnny, you tell me what to do, and I will do it. You're smarter than me and have the vision for our business. I'm just putting the pieces in place."
"Partner, the people who you've been talking to are correct. It would take decades to recoup our investment if we just buy policies and fund reverse mortgages."
Roscoe grimaced. "So, Johnny, how does this work? I'm confused."
"First, we establish the office buildings to launder the insurance and property money. Then, we create at least one hundred clients in each state. Right now, that would be New York and Florida."
"What's next?" asked Roscoe.
"We expand and do the same in five or six more states until we have six hundred or even one thousand customers. We use building equity loans to fund the marketing and buy into the right types of clients."
Roscoe again looked confused. "What do you mean?"
"We use interviews and questionnaires to find clients passionate about high-risk activities like hang gliding, scuba diving, rock climbing, bungee jumping, parachuting, water skiing, etc."
"Because they might die sooner?"
"Yes. They're at a higher risk and are easier prey."
"Prey? I don't get it," said Roscoe Fuller.
"Roscoe, once we have several hundred total customers in multiple states, we will cause some of them to die early and start receiving our capital back. If they die from accidents, we may receive much more. After a few years, their property values will usually be higher for the reverse mortgages. We have to be very careful how we do this – not too many in any one state or insured by the same company for the policies. Their deaths must look accidental and from different causes such as suicide."
"Murders? Good God, we are going to kill people?"
"Roscoe, that's a very harsh word. We are just going to help them on their way to heaven. You and I will randomly pick the ones to collect from and use professionals to do the dirty work. We concentrate on improving our buildings during the first five years and pumping up the depreciation. Then, with a large client list, we select random policies and mortgages to close out. In another five years, we each will have five million cash stashed overseas. We then sell the buildings and insurance businesses for five mill or more profit and get out of Dodge."
And Rollo Three Fingers gets his five percent, right?"

"He will monitor our progress and tell us how to modify the plan. Believe me, we don't want him coming after us."

"Johnny, I see how it would work, but if we're caught, we go away for life or worse."

"Yes, we do. We're betting the farm on not screwing up and collecting millions of dollars in the long run. We move our cash offshore, and at a certain net worth, sell the buildings, the businesses, and move to a country without an extradition agreement with the United States."

"Are you sure, Johnny? It seems pretty extreme. I've been doing really well in the stock market. Maybe we should put all our assets there."

"Roscoe, we both know the market goes up and down without warning. There's no promise that we can each stash ten million away in ten years."

"What about the Merriweathers? Do we tell them?"

"No. Only the two of us will know what is happening. The hit teams will have targets and no explanation for the motive. Remember Roscoe, we are the lions, and the rest of the flock are sheep waiting for their slaughter. We are the eagles that soar over our prey, grab them in our talons, and take them back to our nest to eat them alive. We are the hyenas that find a tasty morsel and gobble it up."

"Stop. I get the idea. What happens in the near term?" asked Roscoe.

"We improve the two buildings and start scouting Connecticut and Pennsylvania. We develop customers in Florida and New York. It's cold out here; let's get in the friggin' car."

Before hitting the sack in the Brown Building, Rivers said, "Roscoe, buddy, don't worry. We won't do anything extreme for several years. But remember to cut a low profile, no flashy cars or other actions that would advertise we are pulling in big bucks."

Chapter Twelve

FIVE YEARS OF GROWTH – Eastern United States

During the next five years, Roscoe, Johnny, and Robert Merriweather added office buildings in six eastern states: Connecticut, Pennsylvania, Georgia, Virginia, South Carolina, and North Carolina. Their buildings generated a steady, abundant cash flow. They used the cash for advertising while expanding their insurance and mortgage clients to over one thousand in the eight states. They also negotiated favorable new mortgages on the office buildings to supply more cash.

The trio aggressively avoided taxes and conducted business that didn't bring attention to their holdings. From Leavenworth, Rollo Three Fingers provided the goals and activities for each phase. Johnny Rivers organized three "harvesting teams" at the three-year mark and dropped out of sight. He and Roscoe developed "selection criteria" that would go unnoticed by state authorities and insurance companies.

After much discussion, they agreed on a lottery controlled only by God. They used a random number generator to pick a customer number, then nixed them if their county had more than one customer "harvested" in the past calendar year or the policy was with the same insurance company. If so, a new number was generated. Nothing else mattered, not the customer's age, income, family responsibilities, occupation, or community status.

The average annual revenue for one "collection" from each of the eight states was $120,000, or nearly a million yearly. Rollo called this the Initial Harvesting Phase. Meanwhile, the office buildings increased in value, and Roscoe or Merriweather negotiated lower-interest mortgages whenever possible. Besides New York, each building had a manager unaware of the nefarious insurance and mortgage felonies.

Cash bonuses corrupted Robert and Patricia Merriweather into keeping two sets of books. The tax forms signed by Robert yielded hundreds of thousands of dollars of illicit profit. They always paid a small amount but used every illegal accounting trick to pay the least property, sales, and income tax. Rollo Three Fingers monitored the "real" profit and loss statements and balance sheets as he collected his five percent from Roscoe Fuller.

Johnny (Reardon) River's whereabouts were unknown to all members of the criminal conspiracy. He coordinated with Roscoe by phone and selected the customers for harvesting. Rivers had his profits sent to a Swiss bank account. Roscoe Fuller sent his funds to Hong Kong, and the Merriweathers siphoned money from their building rents and put it into Bahama accounts. Rollo informed Roscoe that the next yearly phase would harvest two customers per state and then three and four. Roscoe dreaded receiving calls from Johnny that directed him to assign one of the hit teams to a specific customer. He had trouble sleeping at night yet still yearned to be independently wealthy.

Graham Rabinski married Melonie and had two young children. He was now a Vice President in his firm, and they lived in an Atlanta suburb. Roscoe Fuller still had two million in his Atlanta accounts and planned to move them to Hong Kong during his exit strategy. The last phase would have Roscoe and Johnny "harvesting" five customers per year in each of the eight states, selling the office buildings, paying no taxes, leaving the country, and implicating the Merriweathers for tax fraud.

Chapter Thirteen

J&R LLC BUSINESS YEAR SIX – Bumpass, Virginia

Amelia Talbot was asleep when her security system sounded the alarm. First, it vibrated her bed, and then an electronic voice warned, "Activity at the main gate; activity at the main gate."

Amelia groaned, thinking it was the local teens again trying to come in and use her pool. She rolled on her back and said, "TESS, display main gate."

On the ceiling, she saw a camera view of a car and two people using their cell phone lights to evaluate the wrought iron gate.

She said, "Show infrared."

TESS displayed the heat signature of the two bodies. The larger body boosted the more petite person to the top of her seven-foot wall a few feet from the gate. The wall was not a significant impediment to an intruder, but it had two wires strung along the top that would give pause to anyone. They could have an electric charge or signal that someone was climbing over the wall. The smaller person dropped down inside the wall and returned to the gate.

Hmmm, thought Amelia, *it could be a man and a woman*. "TESS, display microwave radar." The larger body had a gun in a shoulder holster; the smaller one had a short-bladed knife. Mia knew most trespassers would climb over the gate or near it. Her expensive security system pushed unknowing antagonists in that direction. Also, brambles and sticker bushes a few feet from the driveway herded them downward toward the house.

Amelia put on a bathrobe and went downstairs to her office and computer center.

The time was 1:30 am when TESS warned, "Intruder alert, one person in upper driveway."

She said, "TESS, please give me height and weight."

"TESS roger, height estimated five foot eight inches, weight estimated 130 pounds."

Amelia scanned the six displays mounted three on top of three. The gate camera showed the bigger person entering the car and moving it several yards away from the gate. The driveway cameras and motion detectors revealed the intruder moving from tree to tree while closing on Mia's home. She opened her gun case and broke out a Glock pistol and a short-barreled over-and-under shotgun. There was no need to load them. Her guns were always loaded. She had a ten-year history working for the Department of Defense, the CIA, and the FBI. During that time, she'd made enemies who knew her identity and hated her. Several others wanted to know who and where she was - to kill her.

She watched the dark figure close to her home and decided not to use lights or noise to scare them as she had done with the teens. The security system pushed an intruder into breaching the house on the second floor. The first floor had barred windows or metal doors. Amelia donned dark clothing, strapped on the side arm, and climbed the stairs to her defensive position. She put TESS on mute but could still see displays and alerts on her phone. As expected, the subject climbed a trellis and came through an unlocked window in a guest bedroom.

TESS texted, "Intruder in guest bedroom 2."

Amelia crouched inside a dark doorway at the top of the long wooden staircase. She thought, *You've come here to rob me or harm me. If I use too much defensive force, I'll be the one in trouble.* The next text was, "Intruder in master bedroom, holding knife in right hand."

Hmmm, that does not seem like a robber. She typed on her phone, "TESS, play tape three in the office."

Tape three was a recorded phone call between Amelia and her mother. It should draw the assailant to the stairs. Amelia put her phone in her back pocket. She took shallow breaths as she heard the creaking floor in the dark, wood hallway. By design, no one could walk along the hall in complete silence.

As the attacker reached the top of the stairs, Amelia gripped the intruder's right wrist and shoved her headfirst down the staircase. There was a series of thumping sounds, a final terrible cracking noise, and then silence. She had TESS turn on the lights and saw a crumpled, black-clothed figure at the bottom. Amelia ran to the back staircase, descended to the first floor, and moved through the living room with her pistol drawn.

The woman had plunged down the stairs and collided with the inch-thick oak baseboard at the turn for the last two steps. Blood flowed down the second to last stair from her cracked skull. The woman moaned.

"Who are you? asked Amelia. Why are you here?"

"Please help me. I can't feel my legs. I'm hurt bad."

"You're right about that, missy. You broke your skull and have terminal bleeding. In a few minutes, you'll pass out and die. Answer my questions."

"Please, please, I need a doctor. It was just a job. I don't hate you or anything."

"But you came here to kill me, right?" asserted Amelia.

"I'm sorry. I needed the money."

"How much money?"

The woman whispered, "Five thousand when I took the contract and another five after. And another ten thousand if I could make it look like an accident."

"Who sent you? Who's in the car near my gate?"

There were no answers as the stranger lost consciousness and bled out. Amelia went to her office and reviewed TESS's event list. She deleted a few items to match what she would tell the police. Then Mia put on her leather boots, pants, and jacket and went to the main garage. Before starting her Kawasaki Ninja 400 motorcycle, she called 911.

"Louisa County 911, what is your emergency?"

"Yes, this is Amelia Talbot at 48 Promise Lane in North Bumpass. I just had an intruder enter my home on the second floor. A woman came to kill me – I can't be sure. She fell down my staircase in the dark and busted her head open at the bottom. Send an ambulance and police. The front door and garage door will be open. I'm going after her partner. He's in a car near my front gate."

"Hold it, Ms. Talbot. Is this person breathing?"

"No, there's lots of blood. She passed out and stopped breathing and bleeding."

"Ms. Talbot, wait for police at the scene."

"No, I have to know what's going on. Maybe this driver can tell me. Call Sheriff Roberts and tell him what happened. He can go over the event sequence in my security system."

Amelia roared up her driveway with only her parking lights on. As TESS opened the front gate, she passed through with her headlight on a high beam and flasher lights blinking. The accomplice put his car in gear and laid rubber as he fled down the dark two-lane road.

Mia didn't have a plan, but one soon developed. She got on his tail as he sped away at over fifty miles an hour. Racing the K-400 in low gears made a screaming noise, much like a siren. That and the flashing lights scared the crap out of the conspirator. In half a mile, a ninety-degree hairpin turned to the left. There was no way this idiot was going to make that turn. If he slowed down, she would shoot his tires out. If not, he would fly off the road into the forest. Then, she could pick up the pieces and question him.

The driver spent too much time looking back at the motorcycle chasing him. He missed the warning signs for the turn and departed the road at high speed – rolling down an embankment and smashing into a giant spruce tree.

Amelia doused her bike's lights, put down the kickstand, and went after the car. Drawing her pistol, she slid down the grassy slope. She went to the driver's door. A tree branch poked through the open window and had impaled the man's throat. He was deader than a doornail. She patted him down with her driving gloves and removed his wallet and cell phone. Amelia took pictures of his face similar to those she'd snapped of the dead women in her house. Something caught her attention on the passenger side, so she went around and retrieved two manila folders from the floor. Lights came on in the nearest home as she placed the items in a side saddle pouch and left the "accident" scene.

Amelia rode her bike to a Montpelier all-night dinner. Her hands shook as she sipped the hot black coffee and looked at the folders. *Christ, a quiet night turns into a nightmare with two dead bodies. I left both scenes, and that's probably some sort of crime. I need to see what's in these folders and get the FBI involved to override local charges.*

One folder had the words "A. TALBOT" on the index tab and the other, "G. STRONG." She opened her folder and found pictures of her house, a satellite view of her property, and descriptions of her daily activities, including times and locations. There also were several pictures of her and a synopsis of her employment with the U.S. government. At the bottom of the third page were 5000/10000/20000. The data was hand-printed and probably sent to the hit team by email or a postal box. She opened the other file as the caffeine kicked in, and her hands steadied. *Hmmm, G. Strong, are you another target, or did you send these people after me? Either way, we are going to meet - and soon.* The contents were similar, except Gordon Strong lived in an adjoining state and had 10000/20000/40000 on the last page.

Amelia finished her coffee and a pastry. She then drove to a closed car rental lot in northwest Richmond and rented a nearby motel room.

The weather was nasty between Richmond and Strong's home on Upchurches Pond, North Carolina. She wasn't going to make the 200-plus mile run on the cycle. After 7 a.m., she left it in the rental agency's garage, drove to Fayetteville, NC, and rented another motel room. She had lunch and slept in preparation for accosting G. Strong after sunset.

Siri woke Amelia at 6 p.m. She showered and had dinner at Denny's. Returning to her room, she studied the material on Strong. His waterfront home was on the south side of Upchurches Pond on Lake Upchurch Drive. The pictures showed a tall man with a crew cut, a tanned face, and probably in his thirties. Strong's activities were swimming, water skiing, and jogging. He was a member of World Fitness, the Fayetteville Christian Church, and an Army officer. She noted that the Fort Bragg complex was less than twenty miles away and thought, *He could be a snake eater for all I know. Lots of secret stuff going down at Bragg, although I've never been there.*

She used Google Earth on her iPhone to plan an ingress route from the road to his home. Plenty of trees were on the left side of his driveway for cover. But there was only one tree near the back of the house. So, she would have to cross an open area of about fifty feet. *I hope he doesn't have a security system like mine. Don't worry; only a handful of people have something like TESS.*

She'd designed the sensor hardware and area coverage, and her parents developed the software for a network of computers and displays. None of the detection components used the Internet. She had three customers the previous year at a $500K starting price. It helped that her mom and dad were among the first fifty Microsoft software engineers. They'd sold a small portion of their shares to build Mia's home and provided working capital for TSI (Talbot Security Incorporated).

Amelia arrived at Strong's home at about 9 p.m. She parked her car 100 feet from his driveway, put on her ski mask, and placed the Glock in the small of her back. Mia worked along the chain link fence and was surprised Strong had no gate on his drive. She saw no sensors or cameras and merged into the low grass and trees on the left side of the driveway.

Talbot moved from tree to tree, stopped, and waited for any sign of detection from the house. Light shone from several windows as she reached the garage's side door. It was locked. She took out a credit card to release the simple lock. Before it opened, a man's arm wrapped around her body, and she felt the cold steel of a gun held to her neck.

He said, "Struggle, and I will shoot. You'll be lucky ever to use your arms and legs again."

"All right, all right," she hissed.

He took her gun and asked, "Who are you? What do you want?"

"My name is Amelia Talbot. A two-person assassination team tried to kill me last night. You either sent them or are next on their hit list."

"Miss Talbot, believe me, I've never heard of you. Where are they now?"

"They both had an untimely death in Bumpass, Virginia."

"You must be kidding, Bumpass?"

"No joke, Strong. One, a woman, broke into my home and fell down a flight of stairs. Next, I chased a man in the getaway car down a country road with my motorcycle. He got rattled and missed a ninety-left turn. A tree branch skewered him, and he went to his great reward."

"How do you know my name?"

"The man's car had two folders. One for me and one for you. Each had pictures, addresses, daily routines, and biographical data."

"This is crazy. I don't know anyone in the States that has it in for me – Iraq and Afghanistan are another matter."

"So, you're Army?"

"Yes, Army Ranger, long-range sniper, and several times seconded to Navy SEAL Teams."

"You sent no one to kill me in Virginia?" she asked.

"Hell no. I'm on disability leave and hope never to kill again."

"Amen to that. Can I have my gun back?" she demanded.

"Negative. We'll go into the house, and I'll research your credentials. If you check out, we'll open a bottle of wine and try to figure this out. If not, I can't say what will happen to you."

"Lead on MacDuff."

They took an elevator down two floors below ground level. Gordon put Mia in a chair and zip-tied her wrists to the armrests and ankles to the chair legs. Strong opened a small refrigerator and took out a syringe and a vial with a clear liquid.

"What the hell are you going to do?" she questioned.

"Nothing criminal, Miss Talbot. After a shot of this Kickapoo joy juice, your answers will be much more honest."

She snapped, "Bastard. I should have kicked your ass when I had the chance."
"No need for that. Where are your car keys?"
"On top of the driver's side front tire."
"And your purse?"
"Under the driver's seat."
"And the files?"
"In the glove box along with the deceased man's cell phone, wallet, and car rental agreement."
Strong said, "Good. You just relax there while I retrieve your car. Then we get on the computer and find what's what."
"Screw you, Gordon. You're holding me against my will. That's abduction."
"Maybe so, but you come slinking down my property wearing a ski mask, all black clothes, and carrying a loaded gun. Then you try to break into my garage. After that, you spin an unbelievable story about dead assassins, file folders, and such. Do you see my problem?"
"It's all true. I swear."
"Time will tell. I'll be back in a jiffy."

Amelia thought while her host was absent, *I need to get the FBI involved, or local police may charge me with leaving the scene of two fatal accidents. Surely, the two hit persons came across a state line or two. Maybe Strong can help with that.*

Gordon returned with a sack of materials from her car and her keys.
He sat down at double computer displays and started his interrogation.
"Miss Amelia, what's your full name?"
"Amelia Rose Talbot."
"Born where?"
"Seattle, Washington, July 6, 1984."
"Parents' names?"
"Henry and Doris Talbot."
"Now residing where?"
"Bellevue, Washington."
"Employers?"
"They both have worked for Microsoft for decades.
"You graduated from what high school?"
"Bellvue High School, Belvue, Washington."

"College studies where?"

"I first went into the Marine Corps in 2002. After boot camp, they sent me to intelligence school. My first assignment was at Fort Meade. While there, I earned a degree in computer science at Capital Technology University and a minor in accounting."

"What next?"

"After my second Marine tour, I was offered several jobs and became a CIA analyst."

"Doing what?"

"I can't say exactly, but I was good at researching quasi-legal European companies and their banking accounts. I helped establish the CIA's Office of Financial Investigations. After that, I worked as a defense contractor for a similar outfit in the Defense Intelligence Agency (DIA). They provided targets, mostly terrorists or arms dealers. We went after their finances and took away their funding."

"And what are you doing now, Amelia?"

"I steal funds from criminal and terrorist organizations using computers. I also have a security company, Talbot Security Incorporated, for wealthy clients who want maximum protection."

"What's the website?"

www.tessforu.com, she replied.

"What does TESS stand for?"

"Tactical Electronic Security System. It combines advanced sensors, defensive measures, and AI-networked computers."

"Hmmm. Everything you told me seems to check out. I will cut the zip ties, but I want you to remain in the chair. Deal?"

"Yes. You swear you didn't send those crooks to kill me?"

"I swear. But I can't see the connection between us."

"I know. These folders aren't accidental. It may take some digging."

"Agreed; how do you want to proceed." He asked.

"Gordon, my near-term problem is leaving the scenes of two deaths. I need to get ahead of any local charges by involving the FBI. I've done work for them, and we need to turn over this evidence to them – after we process it ourselves."

"Look, Amelia, it's midnight. I know the Fayetteville Agent in Charge. Let's get some sleep and start again early in the morning. Jake Finster lives on Mariner's Landing Drive across the lake. We'll text him in the morning for a meeting."

"I agree. I'm having trouble keeping my eyes open," Amelia responded.
"OK, you can take one of the guest rooms if you promise not to kill me in my sleep."
"I promise. Will you promise the same?"
He chuckled. "I also promise."

Chapter Fourteen

FBI AGENT JAKE FINSTER – Upchurches Pond, NC

Gordon poured two glasses of chilled red wine, and they slept like babes. Strong woke at 0700 and smelled the aroma of fresh coffee. He used his bathroom, splashed water on his face, and entered the kitchen.
"Good morning, house guest. How should we protect ourselves."
"Good morning, yourself, questionable host. I've made a list. But, first, we need to make copies of everything I have for the FBI."
"And what's that?" he queried.
"I have pictures of the woman at the bottom of my stairs and the man in his car. Their fingerprints should be on the folders. Put on some gloves and check the contents of his wallet. We can use our cell phones to copy the folder material and research the name and credit card on the car rental. They rented it in Silver Spring, Maryland, so there's no doubt they came over state lines after me."
He frowned. "How do we figure out why they want to kill us?"
She said, "In my business, it's always about money. So, I'll reciprocate if you let me look at your financial accounts."
"Done. I'm fixing us breakfast, and we have about an hour before we contact Finster."

After finishing the food, Amelia started with his credit card records. She could see he regularly traveled to New York and Washington, D.C., but none of the transactions and vendors correlated to her activities. Agent Jake Finster called at 7:45 and said eight-thirty worked for him – after his teacher wife, and kids had left for school.

Gordon steered his Duffy electric boat across the lake an hour later to Finster's dock. Finster met them wearing his FBI "uniform" – a white shirt, striped tie, shined shoes, and a dark suit. He had a quick smile, a pleasant tan face, and a military-style haircut.
Once they all had mugs of coffee in the breakfast nook that viewed the lake, the agent said, "What's up, Gordo? Your text was very terse, almost mysterious."
"Hey Jake. I've had better nights. Amelia came to my house last night and warned me that I might be targeted for extinction. She has some evidence and quite a story for you to share with your office in Richmond, Virginia. So, Amelia, take it away."

"Agent Finster, you'll find me in the FBI database as a forensic financial consultant. Here's a folder with my data, address, SSN, full name, and so on. The problem is that I didn't put this data together. Two nights ago, a woman broke into my house in Bumpass, Virginia, bent on killing me. Unfortunately for her, she fell down a flight of oak stairs and fractured her skull. She died after admitting she planned to murder me. She confessed to a ten-thousand-dollar payment for the hit and twenty thousand if she made it look like an accident.

A male accomplice drove the getaway car and waited for her not far from my main gate. I called 911 and told them about the woman. Then I grabbed my travel purse and handgun. I went after the man on my motorcycle. He took off like a bat out of hell and departed the narrow road on a tight turn. I wanted to question him but found him terminally skewered by a tree branch. I noticed two folders, one with my name and the other with Gordon's."

"Ms. Talbot, this is quite a story. Shouldn't you have waited for the police?"

"Maybe, maybe not. Our county has only an understaffed sheriff's department, and their experience with a hit squad is nil. Also, at that time, I suspected G. Strong could have sent them to kill me or be next on someone's list. I figured the pair must have crossed state lines, and I wanted to work with the FBI, not local police."

"I see. What do you have in the way of evidence?"

"I have pictures of both assailants on my phone. I bet their fingerprints are on these folders. Here's their car rental agreement. We need to know who sent them and why. The FBI has the best resources for face recognition and fingerprints."

Finster was dubious. "What's the connection between Gordon and you? Why would they execute you and then drive to another state to off him?"

Mia, "We're working on that. So far, we only know that we both worked for the government. We both live in rural communities and don't have spouses or children. We worked in Iraq and Afghanistan in different locations and never together."

Gordon said, "Hold it, Amelia. You were in-country doing your financial hijacking?"

"Yes, sometimes I put on a burka, went right to the source, and stole their books."

Strong whistled. "Jake, watch out for this lady. She never ceases to amaze."

"I can see that. Please excuse me. I'll call my counterpart in Richmond, Virginia, and have them send an agent to investigate the two dead people and collect DNA. Amelia, I take it that you don't have samples for me?"

"No, I don't. Damn, I didn't think that straight."

Finster, "Not to worry, with fingerprints, DNA, your pictures, and this other evidence, we should have their IDs in two or three days. But, in the meantime, it sure would help if you two could determine a motive."

"We're on it," said Strong.

They left Finster's home. Gordon had Mia steer the Duffy back toward his dock while he thought through their problem. Halfway back, he had her close the throttle, and they drifted in a light wind.

"Amelia, what motives could someone have for killing us?"

"Well, people kill for vengeance, financial gain, differing belief systems, and to punish someone else."

"How does that last one work?"

"Let's say a killer wants to hurt my parents. I'm an only child. Losing me would ruin the rest of their lives."

"OK, I'm also an only child. But my parents are dead."

"Gordon, how about your divorced wife? Would she benefit from your untimely demise?"

"No. She married a flush doctor with three kids. She needs nothing from me. We have a good relationship; she brings her stepkids to use my pool or go out in this boat. Sometimes, she must escape her home's chaos and stays overnight."

Amelia rolled her eyes. "She does, does she? Perhaps she has a vengeful husband?"

"Naw, Butch knows we wouldn't do anything behind his back. He's one of my golf buddies. Besides, none of that creates any connection to you and why we have someone in common who wants us dead."

She agreed. "I know, I know. It has to be money somehow. How much property do you own here on the lake?"

"I own the house and the two lots on each side. My wife and I bought them for a song when the lake was almost dry a few years ago."

"Could somebody be upset about that and want revenge?"

He said, "I guess some sour grapes over the property sale are possible but not probable. But again, where's the connection to you?"

"Agreed. We need to return so I can scrub your checking, bank, and stock accounts. Although it's nice and peaceful out here on the water."
"Yes, I like to come out here, read a book, and leave my cell back at the house. But we need to solve this riddle."
"That's right, Sherlock." She shoved the throttle forward. "Full speed ahead."

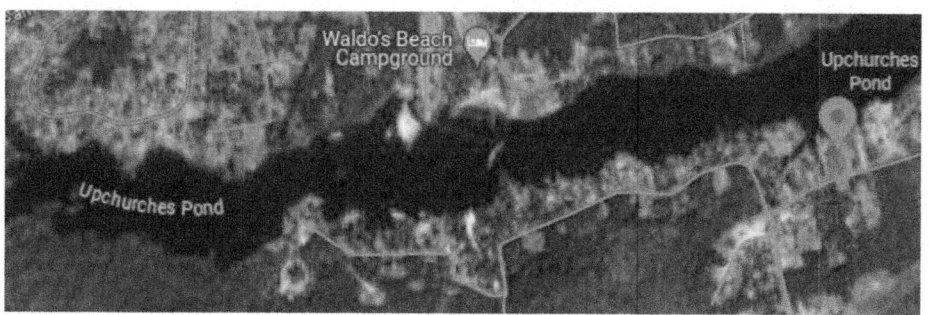

Upchurches Pond – about a mile long

Source: Google Maps

Amelia spent the rest of the morning combing through Strong's financial accounts. When she found something out of the ordinary, she quizzed him about it. One was a $75,000 deposit in his checking account nearly two years earlier.
She said, "Gordon, where did this seventy-five K come from?"
"Oh, that's when I sold my two hundred thousand whole life insurance policy."
"Tell me about that transaction," she directed.
"Well, I had about fifty thousand of cash value and no wife or kids as heirs. So, I saw this ad and called the company. The CFO came here and offered me $75,000. I took the cash, and now they must pay the premiums."
"What's the name of the company?"
"I don't remember, eh, Northeast something. I have a file on it."
"Please let me see the file," she requested.
"Why? Is it important?"
Amelia nodded. "Maybe, or maybe not. I did the same thing and had the president of a small insurance company pay me $45,000 for a policy I didn't need. My folks took it out with New York Life when I was born."
He queried, "Was it the same company?"

"I don't think so. The name was Mutual Assurance of Virginia. Gordon, how did you find out about them? A TV ad or what?"
"No, it was a billboard."
She slapped the table. "Same here!"
He took something from a file cabinet. "Amelia, here's the file."
She looked through the file and agreement with Northeast Assurance Association."
"It seems to be a different company, but we both did it."
"Yes, and they returned a couple of months later and offered me a reverse mortgage on my real estate."
"Is that a smart thing to do?"
"I did it because it helped me buy out my wife. I kept the house, and Northeast paid the mortgage. I pay upkeep, taxes, and insurance costs."
"Insurance payments to the same company?"
"No, to USAA. I've been with them since I got my commission from the ROTC program."
"At which university?" she queried.
"University of Pennsylvania."
"Good school. Tell me about the rest of your career."
Gordon, "As a Second Lieutenant, the Army sent me to BOLC, Basic Officer Leaders' Course at Fort Benning. After ten weeks, I was accepted into Ranger School and went through the three phases in eight weeks. I had already completed Jump School during ROTC summer training."
"What's the Ranger training like? I heard it's really tough."
He smiled. "That's an understatement. It's demanding in all dimensions: physically, mentally, and emotionally. You're sleep-deprived, calorie-restricted, and physically exhausted while solving tactical problems as a leader or follower in small combat teams. In addition, you are constantly being evaluated and graded, which adds anxiety to the mental pressure. Wearing the Ranger tab is important for advancement in the Army, and only fifty percent complete the program."
"What are the three phases you mentioned?" she asked.
"You start with a tactical problem on Fort Benning, Georgia. You also must pass the Ranger Physical Fitness Test (RPFT). If you aren't in top physical shape, you can kiss your ass goodbye. Then you conduct a successful patrol and receive a "GO" by the RIs."
"What's an RI?" she asked.

"A Ranger Instructor. They evaluate your leadership performance, and you can expect peer reviews at some point. You lose twenty to thirty pounds, get only four hours of sleep daily, and deal with all kinds of injuries and painful conditions."

"What's the next phase?"

"The Mountain Phase. It's in rugged territory and usually cold weather. Everyone is tired and hungry by then. You must dig deep within to keep going up and down hills and mountains. Once again, you will be graded by how you lead small teams in combat situations."

"And the last phase?"

He sighed. "Just when you think going on is impossible, they take you to Eglin Air Force Base for the Swamp Phase. It has the same high-intensity demands and concentrates on water transport, swamp survival, and additional small team patrols and raids."

"Do you really eat snakes?"

He replied, "Damn straight, if you can catch them."

"Gordon, what did you do next?"

"I went through various infantry training programs for four months before taking command of a platoon at Fort Lewis, Washington. After a year of training, including some desert training in eastern Washington, the Army sent us to Iraq. I returned to Benning as a First Lieutenant and took command of a company in one of the infantry training schools. I had hunted a lot with my dad, and I was a good shot. My Battalion Commander was impressed with my shooting, and I landed on the base sharpshooter team. Next, the Army sent me to sniper school. Then came my second tour in Iraq. Sniper duty was rigorous and sometimes outright shocking."

"How so?" she questioned.

"You expect to kill some bad guys at long range, but in some situations, you may have women or young kids in your sights."

"I see. That must be difficult."

"Yes, especially when you aren't 100% sure you have the right target. You see two young men burying an IED; what do you do? They have picked a side. You can try to explode the shell or take them out. I have nightmares about my last tour in Afghanistan."

"Gordon, I'm sorry the shit over there has followed you here. Would anyone you fought show up here or pay those goons to kill you?"

He shook his head. "I doubt it."

"Let's get back to your contract with Northeast Assurance. What's the face value of your life insurance policy?"

"Two hundred and fifty thousand."

"And they paid you seventy-five thousand to take it over?"

"Yes."

"What were the parameters of your real estate deal with them?"

"They paid off a $305K mortgage and gave me fifty-thousand cash."

"OK, so they've invested three hundred and eighty thousand in what you own here on the lake."

"Yes. I passed the fifty K to Jean, my X, and I get to live in the house."

"That would be until when?"

"Until I move out or die," he said.

She said, "What's this property worth now?"

"Easily $150K for each of the two lots and five hundred thousand for the house."

"Gordon, I don't like what I'm thinking right now."

"What's that?"

"Forget about the attempt on me. If your numbers are correct, Northeast will gain $125K from your untimely death in life insurance payments. And nearly $500K in property value."

"Amelia, I suppose you're right, but no American company would do what you're thinking."

"Not so fast, Army. In my business, anything is possible. What if they have dozens or hundreds of policies and reverse mortgages? They could create regular income by killing a few customers each year."

He whistled. "I can't believe what you're saying. Some law agency would discover their plot and put them in jail."

"No, not if they were 100% immoral, clever, and spread the kills over unrelated people in different states. Oh shit, oh shit, did your policy have an AD&D clause?"

"Huh. What?" asked Strong.

"Accidental Death and Dismemberment that usually doubles the death benefit."

"I'm not completely sure, but I think so."

"Bingo! I've been trying to figure out the numbers on the bottom of the last page. The hit team got $5,000 upfront and another $5,000 for my murder. But if it was an accident, they got $20,000. You're worth more, so your numbers are higher – $10K up front, $20K for your murder, and $40K for accidental death."

"This is bizarre. I see your logic, but I still don't believe it," he said.

She pointed at the list, "Here's something else; on my activities list, 'AVID SHOOTER' was in caps. On yours, it was JET SKIER AND BOATER. Someone wanted me to die accidentally by mishandling one of my guns. And for you, they were recommending a water accident and drowning," Mia asserted.

He shook his head. "Amelia, the policyholders are different companies in different states."

"Maybe, and maybe not. We need to dig into them. I bet you dollars to donuts each is owned and controlled by the same individuals or corporations. The clincher will be if we find them operating in multiple states under different names and licenses."

"Stop Amelia. You're giving me chills up and down my spine."

"I know. I feel the same. We may be discovering true evil. What will we do if it's true?"

"Turn them over to the police," he replied.

"No, it's never that simple. We'll have to collect evidence that will stand up in court. Or..."

"Or what?" he interrupted.

"If they're coming after us, we treat them with extreme prejudice."

"You mean we kill them?"

"Yes, if it's them or us. My preference is it's them. We're both professional military. Our training has taught us how to kill if it's necessary. Hold your breath; here we go onto the Northeast website. Hmmm. It looks very professional. There's their insurance license in North Carolina. That can help. Let's look under PRODUCTS. They only offer to buy existing whole-life policies and to make reverse mortgages – no other products, it's perfect."

"How so?" he asked.

"They don't need a sales force, actuaries, or underwriters. I bet they have less than five employees. Here at the bottom, I'm clicking on 'OFFICERS.' Write this down. The President is Robert E. Merriweather. The CFO is R. Fuller, and P. Merriweather is the corporate secretary and treasurer. I bet she's Robert's wife. If they have offices, and that's a big if, they may only have a receptionist and secretary. Somewhere, they have a lawyer who files all their forms with each State. And they might have a CPA."

"What about a webmaster and IT person?"

She replied, "I doubt it. It's a good site, but there are dozens of hosting companies and plenty of online designers. It describes their business, has a few customer reviews, and enables an online application – straightforward and effective. They had a graphic designer create their billboard ads, placed a few local radio spots, and bang; they're in business."

"Amelia, what about the site for your insurance company?" asked Strong.

"Cross your fingers; I'm putting in www.mutualassuranceofva.com. Shit. It's the same design, product, and officers!"

"It makes you wonder how many states they're in," he added.

"Yes. It's a simple operation. Set it up in several eastern states. Get a few hundred customers; you only kill a handful yearly for a nice living. The two of us would have brought in about $800K. Think about it; if there are only two officers, they can make a million apiece by harvesting one person in four or five states yearly. Nothing suspicious there; the revenue flows to five different companies."

"It's fiendish, Mia."

"Yes, it is. You're doing a lucrative cash business if you have no morals and enough starting capital to make the initial deals. It's almost as simple as all the new cryptocurrency scams."

"Crypto? Do you know about that investment?"

She grimaced. "Yeah, and there's no investment per se in cryptocurrency unless you're selling it. The whole thing is nothing more than a worldwide Ponzi scheme. You design a virtual coin, set up a website, and advertise that you're God's gift to an international, independent, and stable currency. Then, you put out a false economic narrative that you can't trust governments to maintain their currencies. Still, they say you can trust nameless, unregulated providers or miners worldwide in undisclosed locations."

"Is it that simple?"

"No. There's a bunch of gobbledygook about social justice and financial products of the future. Tens of thousands of people have been scammed for millions of dollars in dozens of countries. Crypto values are having a big runup, and the inevitable collapse and company bankruptcies will follow."

"You seem to know a lot about it."

"I do. One of my financial services for wealthy customers is recovering their crypto losses."

"How do you do that?" he questioned.

"First, we try to do it through lawyers and the courts. If that doesn't work, I may return the stolen funds from the scammers' accounts to my clients."

"Amelia, is that legal?"

"Legal, schmeegal. They're crooks, and there's no regulation. Now, these insurance companies are also stealing money. Even worse, they're murdering their customers. They deserve whatever they get."

He shrugged. "What should we do next?"

"Gordon, let's have lunch and then take the Duffy out on the lake and develop a plan."

**Duffy 18-foot 'Snug Harbor' model
Source: Company advertisement**

Chapter Fifteen

A SINISTER DISCOVERY – Upchurches Pond, NC

Gordon guided the electric boat near Waldo's Beach Campground. He put out an anchor so they could swing with the wind, and he and Amelia fell asleep on the long-padded seats.

After an hour, Mia awoke and started speaking, "Gordon, we are going to stop these creeps from killing any more customers. But, first, we must locate their HQ. Then we go there and surveil their operation and start gumming up their gears."

"Where do you think they're located?"

She replied, "In one of the states where they're licensed. Think about it. They're smarter than the average bear. They need a state with no income tax. That's Florida on the east coast. I bet we find Merriweather listed as CEO of an insurance company in the 'Sunshine State' and several other eastern States."

"Like where?"

She snorted, "Where the money is – New York, Pennsylvania, Virginia, North Carolina, and maybe South Carolina and Georgia. They need to fly north and south periodically, so I think Jacksonville would be perfect. They would have a private plane and a small building."

"I see the plane. Why the building?" he commented.

"They're crafty and don't want to get tripped up on underpaying taxes. So, they have a building worth a few million and rent space. That puts them in the real estate business. It lets them wash depreciation expenses against the death policy/reverse mortgage income and pay fewer taxes. They probably have depreciable assets in every State where they're murdering. They report a low taxable income and run all the money through a Florida corporation. Once we find that company, I can do them some real harm."

"How do you do that?" he asked.

"We take over their financial accounts and move the funds offshore."

"Again, is that legal?"

She laughed. "No, but what are they going to do about it? They already planned to kill us. Turnabout of any kind is fair play. We need to shut them down and stop the murders. Gordon, let's pack up and get out of your house. For all we know, a new hit team could be after us. We can take your car, and I can do more research at a library."

He responded, "OK, let's go down to Fayetteville and meet with Finster. Maybe he can help locate Merriweather and see if he has a record."

"No, not yet. I want to break these crooks financially and then hand them over to authorities."

"Amelia, I'm not sure I agree, but you have more of a plan than I do. About all I could do is beat them up or shoot them. We'll take your Glock, and I have a Walther PDP. I've got a hidden shelf under my dash where we can keep the weapons."

"Good man, I'm only licensed in Virginia."

They drove to the Fayetteville Public Library on Mountain Street. It took Amelia two hours to find CEO Merriweather in four more states: New York, Connecticut, Pennsylvania, and Florida. The Florida company, Southeast Assurance Company, was in Gainesville's College Park area. It owned a three-story building, and Merriweather's home was on the twelfth green at the Ironwood Golf Course.

Amelia suspected the CEO had a private plane at the Gainesville Regional Airport, only a few miles from his home. CFO Roscoe Fuller was more of an enigma. No record searches showed him in Gainesville or any other states serviced by Southeast Assurance subsidiaries. Gordon and Amelia drove to the local FBI office and met Jake Finster. He reported that both would-be assassins were dead and still unidentified. Amelia turned over the dead man's wallet and cell phone to the agent.

She said, "Sorry for the delay. I wanted to find out if Gordon knew the man or contacts on his phone."

Finster questioned, "And the answer was what?"

"Negative," responded Strong. I have no idea why these people were after us."

"Most of your crazy story is checking out," said Finster. "I'm warning you to stay clear of this investigation. Let us professionals handle it and cut a low profile for the next several weeks."

"Yes Jake," they both answered.

The two targets drove south to Savanna and rented adjoining rooms. The next day, Gordon leased a car in Jacksonville with Florida plates. After that, Amelia decided they'd use cash whenever possible. They also shut their phones down and removed the SIM cards. On the way to Gainesville, Florida, they bought two "burner" phones at a Walmart.

Talbot drove Gordon's car to the Alachua County Library while Strong continued west on University. He found Merriweather's building on Northeast Eighth Avenue. Gordon donned a hat and sunglasses and saw no cameras outside the nondescript brick building. Inside the lobby, he took a picture of the tenants' list. Southeast Assurance was on the third floor. He then sat in his car opposite the main entrance and took photos of people entering or departing the building. After that, he met Amelia at McDonald's on Twelfth and University at four o'clock.

Mia took a bite of her "Big Mac" and questioned, "What did you find out?"

He responded, "For starters, no cameras outside the building or inside the lobby," he replied. "Here's a picture of the lobby directory. Southeast is on the top floor."

She took his phone, blew up the picture with two fingers, and laughed. "This is going to be easier than I thought."

"Why is that?"

"There are three vacancies, two on the second floor and one on the third. We will rent space in the building and start surveilling Merriweather and his band of crooks. Sooner or later, we will get sensors inside his offices and monitor their activities in real-time."

"Geez, Amelia, how do you propose we do that?"

"You forget that your partner heads up a security business. We rent some space and then say we are putting up sensors to demonstrate our products. Or better yet, we offer Southeast monitoring of the lobby, elevator, and each floor for free for the first year. I looked at a map of Florida in the library and have developed our cover story."

He dipped a French fry in ketchup. "Which is what?"

"We are a multinational security company going after three large clients, The Daytona International Speedway, The Villages senior living commercial space, and Disney World. We have two years and unlimited funds to land one or more of these whales."

He munched on his double burger. "Do we really have unlimited funds?"

"Affirmative. My parents will fund whatever we need. We'll set up a glitzy security demonstration that we can use to identify Southeast Assurance employees and determine their plans."

"Sounds great. What else did you find out at the library?"

"Our Mr. Merriweather is a high-profile guy. He's a member of the Chamber of Commerce, the downtown Rotary Club, and sponsors a Little

League baseball team. He also sponsors a golf tournament each year at the Ironwood Golf Club. It is a community course, but he's a member and on the steering committee."

Gordon nodded. "So, he's playing his role as CEO to the hilt. Could it be that he doesn't know where his revenues come from?"

"I doubt it. His CFO is just the opposite - hard to find and not listed in any Gainesville database. He's a ghost. I'll bet he handles all the dirty work."

Strong dipped another French fry. "And where are we staying tonight?"

"The downtown Marriott AC Hotel near here. I booked us adjoining rooms for a week."

"Outstanding. What's next on your agenda?"

She responded, "Let's move into the hotel and get some sleep. You drive to the Merriweather house in the morning and observe when they go to work. We need to determine their routine. I'll engage a commercial real estate leasing agent and have them propose buildings for us in the College Park and Innovation District."

Strong was surprised. "Why go to that trouble? Can't we just contact the agent for the Southeast Assurance Building?"

"Nope. We are a class act and must make it look like we are selecting that building from the others. Merriweather is a greedy bastard, so we write an offer he can't refuse. Once we have his verbal agreement, we modify the lease to give us access all over the building."

"Amelia, you're losing me. What would give us access like that?"

"I haven't thought it all the way through, but things like we put up our security sensors so we can demo to prospective customers. We reserve the right to replace the third-floor carpet at our expense to make a better first impression. We require access to the roof for satellite communications and so on."

"Now I see. Those actions let us put sensors next to or above Southeast."

"Exactly."

He questioned, "How do we get into their offices?"

"We must work that out. We could go in with the cleaning crew and maybe even put in sensors with Merriweather's blessing. Say, after the Merriweathers leave for work, please go to the airport and see if you can find his plane. The satellite picture only shows a handful of private jets. Tell the aviation companies you're considering buying one and checking the storage and operating costs."

"You got it. We've been here less than a day, and our plan, I mean your plan, is coming together. Mia, you're amazing."

"Thank you. After I get a leasing agent, I will be in the library. Meet me there, and we'll do lunch at the Hogtown Bar-B-Que."

"OK, what will you do at the library?"

"It's quiet, has free parking, and fast Internet. I'll make up a list of everything we need."

He nodded in agreement, "Sounds good."

They slept that night long and deep. Their adjoining door was open, and each had a pistol under their pillow. Who knew if someone was tracking them and ready to finish what the deceased hit team had started?

Gordon purchased a Starbucks Mocha Frappuccino and arrived on Northeast 16th Terrace near Merriweather's house before seven. Mrs. M. left at seven-thirty with one pre-teen child. At eight o'clock, Mr. M. backed his E-Class Mercedes onto the street and headed south. Gordon called Amelia on her burner so she could photograph their quarry arriving at his building. Then he walked down the road and placed a dark brown infrared sensor on a tree trunk facing the house's front entrance and garage.

Amelia drove from the hotel to the brick building and attached a narrow-beam sensor on the wall in front of the Merriweathers' reserved parking spots. She thought, *We are closing in on you, you bastard. We will know when you're in the building or home, and the same for your wife.*

Gordo drove to the regional airport and found a man servicing a twin jet near the University Air Center. He spoke with the mechanic and asked how many private jets were based at the airport. The man kept pumping fuel into a Gulfstream G400 and replied that there were usually five or six outside and fewer in the hangers. Gordon asked about aircraft types, and the mechanic gushed about the Gulfstream and Cessna business jets. He also pointed to a Learjet on the tarmac and said it was the group's hot rod. Strong asked if any were for sale and explained he worked for a large security company, starting a Gainesville office.

The man answered, "Naw, I don't think so. If you can afford to buy and operate one of these beauties, you don't want to give them up except for bankruptcy or buying a more prestigious aircraft."

Gordon said, "Who owns these planes? What kind of group would we be joining?"

"Most of them are corporations. They use their planes for business or getaway vacations. A few are wealthy individuals who no longer want to deal with busy airports and crowded aircraft. Instead, they travel where they want to go when they want to with family and friends."

"What about that Learjet? It's pretty old, right?"

"She's a classic, a model 24D built in the sixties – flies above 45,000 feet at nearly the speed of sound. I've acted as co-pilot up to New York and back."

"Wow! How long did it take?" Gordo questioned.

"Just over two hours. We climbed to 45,000 feet, had a sandwich, and in no time, we had to start descending."

"Man, what was your groundspeed?"

"Over 500 miles per hour – what a ride!"

"What's the lettering on the side? Some insurance company?"

"Naw, that's Mr. M's Assurance company."

Gordon feigned interest in the plane. "Do you think he would sell it?"

"Not on your life. He loves that baby. It's been re-engined and has the latest Garmin navigation equipment – she practically flies herself."

Learjet 24 series
Source: Online sales advertisement

"So, where did you land in the State of New York?

"Albany International, I think he has a small building there, like here in Gainesville."

"Oh, you've been to his business here?"

"Yeah, he and his wife invited me to the yearly Christmas party. Also, I've gone there to help Mr. Merriweather plan flights out of the country."

"How far can that Learjet go?"

"One thousand five hundred miles if you cruise below 500 knots. Mr. M. and his missus like to toot down to the Bahamas. They have a condo there on Paradise Island. Sometimes, he goes for a round of golf or sport fishing. We turn around the same day and return here without refueling." Gordon nodded. "That's cool. So, you're a pilot? Can you pilot an aircraft for our company?"

"Yeah, but not on a full-time basis. I'm certified on the Gulfstreams you see over there. But, say, I just heard about a Gulfstream G100 in Orlando for $2.5 million. It could be a sweet deal, depending on flight hours, electronics, the engine maintenance program, and number of landings. The G100 flies further than the Lear at a lower cost per mile."

Strong answered, "That sounds good. Who flies co-pilot on the Lear when you don't go?"

"Mrs. Merriweather. She's a damn good pilot. I re-up her twin-engine certificate each year."

"Roger, you've given me a lot to consider. Here's my card. Please get all the info you can on that G100 and pictures. I'll bring my boss back in a few days, and we'll review the numbers."

"You got it, Mr. S."

Gulfstream G100
Source: Online advertisement

Strong met Amelia at the main library, and they took his car to Hogtown. They both ordered and sat at an empty booth near the restroom entrance.

He took a bite of his brisket sandwich and asked, "Did you find anything else about Mr. M?"

"Yes, he's on the local county charities group board. Get this, Robert is also a guest lecturer at the University of Florida's Warrington College of Business."

"What's his subject matter?"

She laughed. "Business ethics, no less. Can you believe it?"

"Amelia, maybe he doesn't know about the dirty tricks. His CFO may be fooling him."

"Yes, it's possible, but not probable. What did you learn this morning, big guy?"

"Mrs. Merriweather leaves at 0730 with their daughter, Amber, in a white Honda Pilot."

She agreed, "Yes, she arrived at work at 0750. She probably dropped the girl at school."

He continued, "CEO Merriweather left the house at eight in his Mercedes. He was nicely dressed - suit and tie. I got a couple of pictures of the car, but none of him. I placed the sensor as you instructed."

"Good. Thirty minutes later, he arrived at the building carrying a small briefcase and Starbucks coffee. Boy, I'd like to know what's in that case. I placed sensors in front of their parking spaces. We now will know when they're in the building or away. The one you placed will warn us when they leave the house. Any luck at the airport?"

He laughed. "You bet. I hit paydirt with one Roger Sandstone. He works on private jets and teaches flying. He may own the flying service and a hanger – that was not clear. Anyway, he instructs Mrs. Merriweather, who has a twin-engine commercial license. Robert Merriweather is a qualified pilot of the company's Learjet. Sandstone sometimes accompanies Mr. M. on flights to New York and the Bahamas. The Merriweathers have a condo on Paradise Island next to Nassau. Roger has flown as co-pilot to Albany, New York, where there's probably another Southeast building."

She said, "Hmmm. They're living the life of the rich and not-so-famous while prematurely ending the lives of others."

"Mia, how did you do with a leasing agent?"

"I talked to three or four and settled on a man meeting us for dinner at our hotel. I told him we needed a prosperous and substantial venue, two or three stories, and established – not modern or in an industrial area. I asked for 600 to 1,000 square feet and an option for more in six months."

"Sounds like a good start. How do we play this dinner?"

"We keep pushing him toward the Assurance Building without looking too eager. It has to be his idea and not ours. We have him go in and photograph two or three offices and measure them."

"OK, boss lady, I have more info from the airport. Sandstone is a friend of the Merriweathers and gets invited to their office Christmas party. I told him we might be in the market for a used private jet. If we take him to dinner and buy him some drinks, he will tell us all he knows about Mr. Merriweather and his family."

"Outstanding, Gordy. When do we do this?"

"In a couple of days. He identified an efficient jet aircraft for two point five million. He can pilot it, and I can be the co-pilot with some work."

"Really? Is this a new skill of yours?"

"No, an old skill. I hold a helicopter pilot's license and a single-engine private license."

"Gee Strong, you never stop surprising me."

"Back at you, Miss Talbot. Do you think we need a private aircraft?"

"No, not completely, but it can't hurt to evaluate one. We may need to follow Merriweather to different cities to find his other buildings. Alternatively, we can look at Southeast's tax forms for last year. They have to list the addresses to take off the depreciation."

"How do we do that?"

"Break into their HQ and find the file, probably in a locked cabinet."

Gordon wagged a finger at her. "Hmmm. One crime after another."

She stated, "Don't forget, they wanted to kill us. We are justified in our actions if we don't get caught."

Chapter Sixteen

NEW OFFICES – Gainesville, Florida

Dinner with the leasing agent didn't go well. He recommended four properties, but none were the Southeastern Assurance Building. Talbot told him they'd evaluate the lease terms and get back to him.

The following morning, Gordon went to the building at seven o'clock. He took the elevator to the third floor and determined that the available office space was on the opposite side of the building from Merriweather's offices. One bonus was that it was in the same hallway as the elevator. So he placed tiny video sensors as high as he could reach at the end of each hallway and opposite the elevator door.

Back at the hotel, he reported to Amelia that he saw no cameras in the building and smelled fresh coffee outside Southeast's doorway. They decided a secretary/receptionist opened the office before the principals arrived.

When activated by movement, their inside sensors sent low-resolution still video frames to the Internet. The Lithium-ion batteries were good for about a week. It was not an elegant surveillance, but it was a start. Two laptops with split screen software showed infrared movement at the house. The others in the building transmitted third-floor hallway activity and a decent view of elevator riders. Amelia called the leasing agent and asked him to add the Merriweather Building to his list. By ten o'clock that morning, several boxes arrived from Amazon containing desktop computers and twelve displays. Gordon and Amelia linked sensor inputs and set up the TESS professional software in their hotel rooms during the rest of the day.

Mrs. Merriweather left the building at four o'clock, and her husband left at five. The secretary left fifteen minutes later. Gordon called Roger Sandstone at the airport and arranged a dinner meeting for the following evening. The next morning, Amelia received a large FedEx box full of sophisticated sensors, wiring, and various batteries. The leasing agent met them for lunch and had the data on the three available offices in the Southeast Building. Amelia told him the third-floor office with 800 square feet and three separate areas would work. She agreed to the asking price per square foot and a one-year lease.

Then, she added additional terms on the back of a paper napkin. "Lessee is an international security firm and requires access to the roof for satellite equipment. With Lessor's approval, Lessee may replace and upgrade the third-floor hallway carpet. In addition, Lessee, with Lessor's approval, may clean and renovate the building elevator. Lessee may offer Lessor one or more years of state-of-the-art building security systems without charge for a demonstration to Lessee's potential customers."

Strong and Talbot entered the Southeast Assurance Building with additional sensors and wiring that night. They wore overalls emblazoned with "Talbot Security Systems," and Gordon carried a short ladder. On the third floor, they raised the foam ceiling panels next to the fluorescent lights outside Merriweather's office and plugged in a new set of listening devices. They embedded them every ten feet into the wall above the removable panels.

The next morning, they monitored the Merriweathers' departure from home, arrival at work, and conversation with their secretary, Virginia. They could hear the secretary taking calls and some of Merriweather's conversations in an open area but nothing from their private offices. Merriweather accepted their lease terms, and the leasing agent showed them the spartan space. Amelia signed the lease and rented office equipment from a nearby furniture store.

That night, Gordon and Amelia met Roger Sandstone for dinner at Mark's Prime Steakhouse on Southeast Second Avenue. Amelia looked ravishing. She wore a short tan skirt, a white blouse, and a blue blazer. It was the first time Gordon had seen her wear makeup. He realized she was quite a looker. Sandstone was smitten by his hostess, who insisted they start with Prime Fusion Martinis. She then encouraged Roger to order the filet mignon and lobster.

He said, "Ms. Talbot, are you sure? They're costly."

"Not to worry, Roger. Our company pays all the expenses. How do you like the champagne?"

They sipped Anderson Valley Roederer Estate Brut while enjoying jumbo lump crab cakes with a lemon beurre blanc sauce.

Amelia ordered a red wine for the main course. After the waiter removed the appetizer plates, she asked Sandstone if he liked the wine.

"Ma'am, it's delicious. Where's it from?"

"Roger, it's Niebaum Coppola Merlot from Napa Valley – one of my favorites."

Mia ordered another bottle. Roger was having a great time in a top-drawer restaurant and looked at her with adoration. She had requested that business talk wait until dessert and made small talk with Sandstone as if Strong was absent. Mia ordered the Chocolate Paradise mousse, a Classic Sidecar Cognac with Cointreau, and fresh lime juice for dessert.

She took one of Sandstone's hands in hers and pounced. "Roger, I don't know much about airplanes. We'll have to rely on your judgment. My company wants us to project a first-class image but not go crazy with expenses. Gordon told me there might be an older plane that fits our needs. Is that correct?"

"Yes ma'am, I mean Amelia. It's a beauty if properly maintained. A new plane like the Gulfstream 100 would cost eight million."

She patted his hand. "I think we should buy it if you fly to Orlando and recommend it to us. Then, you could be our pilot and instruct Gordon on becoming co-pilot."

Sandstone took a bite of his dessert and then sipped the Cognac. "I can do that. It would be my great pleasure."

She retook his hand. "Roger dear, we don't expect you to work for free. We will pay you five thousand to do the evaluation. And for every ten thousand you get off the starting price, we will pay you a one-thousand-dollar finder's fee."

The alcohol was getting to Sandstone. He started to slur his words. "Miss Talbot, you don't need to do that."

"Oh yes, we do. We trust you implicitly, and I can't wait to fly with you. But we must have a mutually beneficial business relationship."

Sandstone thought for a few seconds. "So, you're saying if I get the seller down 100K, I get 10K?"

"Exactly. You'll give us the ability to race around the eastern seaboard. I'm also interested in what Gordon said about your taking customers to the Caribbean islands. Can you do that for us?"

"Sure," he replied with a mouthful of chocolate mousse. "I take Mr. Merriweather and his wife mainly to the Bahamas."

"I'll be damned," she said. "What a small world. We're moving our Florida headquarters into Robert Merriweather's building. I think it's owned by Southeast Insurance or something like that."

Sandstone shook his head. "Naw, it's Southeast Assurance. They're nice folks, the Merriweathers."

"So, you take them to Nassau?"

"Sure, whenever they want."

"How do they get around once they get there?"
"They have an older Chevy Malibu that I drive."
She persisted, "Gordon said they have a condo down there. Is that right?"
"Yes, it's in the Casa Del Sol property. I think they rent it out when they aren't there."
Mia clapped her hands together. "Outstanding, Roger. We've been thinking about putting some of our cash offshore. Do the Merriweathers use any banks there?"
"Yes, they use Bank of the Bahamas and Credit Suisse. I know because I drive them there, and they talk about it in the car."
"That's good advice, Roger. We may also want to open accounts there. I hope you enjoyed dinner. Gordon and I are looking forward to working with you."
He smiled. "Gosh yes, this was about the best meal I've ever had."
"Wonderful," she replied. "I'm so excited to meet you. Can you take Gordon to Orlando to look at the plane?"
"Sure. Gordon, I'll meet you at my hangar at 10 a.m. in two days. We can take my Piper 100 down there."
Gordon replied, "You're on, Roger. I can't wait to fly again."

      Back at the hotel, Amelia went over what they'd learned. She said one of their first flights would be to Nassau to rent the Merriweather condo and place audio sensors. Next, Mia planned to hunt for Merriweather's bank account information to transfer funds to a Talbot account later. She also told Gordon that their first employee, "Ratchet Man" Rhodes, would arrive the next day. Rhodes was a computer hacker from Staten Island, New York.
Gordon questioned, "What will he do for us?"
"He can break into any office, computer, or phone and refine our surveillance of Southeast Assurance. We will monitor every phone call and business discussion. We will have video feeds on locked safes or cabinets so we can open them later. Also, he will help monitor the sensors we've placed and separate the wheat from the chaff."
"How so? Strong queried.
Amelia responded, "We tell him the kind of information we want, and he pulls it from hours of meaningless material. There's a bonus. Rhodes is a persuasive security salesman. He can convince Merriweather to install our systems. Once we've done that, we can enter their offices and access their files. That includes their laptops and desktop computers. We record

their keystrokes and look for passwords. Someone is paying the bills, Mrs. Merriweather or the secretary. We get all their credit card information and how to access their checking accounts."

"Damn! Amelia, do you think we can collect all of that?" Gordon exclaimed.

"I know we can. Eventually, we stop paying their bills, empty all the cash accounts, and force them into bankruptcy."

He shivered. "Geez, remind me never to cross you. What else do we need to do?"

"I'm working on a priority list. First, we need to stop the killing. Second, we must find the elusive CFO, Roscoe Fuller, and surveil him. Third, we want to know who the hit teams are and decide their punishment. Fourth, we will need more help. Fifth, we must discover who knows about the conspiracy to commit murder and who doesn't. Sixth, we collect the type and location of evidence the FBI can find – they can't use what we've illegally collected."

"As always, you're two steps ahead of me, Mia. How can I help?"

"Work on getting the aircraft and a co-pilot designation. I think we will see my parents arrive within twenty-four hours."

"Why is that?" asked Gordon.

"They trust me, but they aren't going to fund a two-million-dollar aircraft without knowing the full story. With them on our team, hacker Rhodes, and a secretary/receptionist, we should be ready to dismantle Southeast Assurance."

"Do we all stay here in this hotel?"

Mia, "No, we need to lease a furnished house in the University District with several bedrooms. It will be a secondary command center."

"So, we'll need more computers, displays, high-speed Internet, and another TESS for protection?"

She said, "Yes, yes, and yes. How do you think we did tonight with Sandstone?"

"Gosh, you had him eating out of your hand. I didn't know you could be so, so captivating."

"Gordon, sorry I ignored you. I wanted Roger to feel I was fascinated by his every word."

He frowned. "You did that – holding his hand and putting your arm around him."

"Hmmm, is someone jealous?"

He responded, "No, not jealous – just surprised at your good looks and feminine finesse."

"I'm tired. It's time for my pajamas and makeup removal. Then you'll see the plain Jane Amelia again."

Gordon brushed his teeth, used the bathroom, and stripped to his skivvies before falling into bed and checking his pistol was under the pillow. He was about to drift off into slumber when he felt her slide into the bed beside him.

"Amelia, what gives?"

"Gordo, I'm lonely. I learned tonight that I could easily get a man but never met the right one. I feel safe next to you; however, no hanky panky."

He chuckled. "I felt alone when you ignored me. OK, deal. Did you bring your piece?"

"Of course."

He questioned, "Is there a round chambered, and it's ready to fire?"

"Of course."

"Do you ever sleepwalk or flail around in your dreams?"

"Not that I can remember." She replied.

"Please do me a favor and eject the round so I can get a good night's sleep."

She chuckled, "Done. Good night. Oh, and I do think you were jealous."

"Maybe. You were a much more vivacious and enjoyable lady – especially with all the booze. You weren't your vengeful all-business self."

"Screw you, Strong."

"Nope, sorry, Amelia - no hanky panky."

Chapter Seventeen

DEN OF SPIES – Gainesville, Florida

Amelia's parents arrived at the hotel driving a six-passenger van they'd rented in Orlando. Gordon and Mia brought them up to speed with a PowerPoint projection on a hanging bed sheet. Mr. Talbot was a tall, lanky man with a friendly face and a short crewcut. He listened to the brief and held his questions for the end. Mrs. Talbot wore a spandex running outfit and flashy two-hundred-dollar tennis shoes. To Gordon, she seemed like an older, equally attractive version of her daughter. Doris interrupted Amelia several times with questions and comments.

After the briefing, Henry Talbot's first question was, "Why can't we turn this mess over to the police?"

Amelia said, "Because they'll take forever and can't legally surveil Southeast as we can. Don't forget other targets may be dying as we speak. And another hit team may be looking for Gordon and me. We do have the FBI involved. Job one is stopping the murders. Job two is to point the FBI at the evidence they can use."

Henry pursed his lips while thinking. "Yes, but your plan has us breaking the law. If caught, we will be the ones going to trial."

His daughter responded, "I've been thinking about that. We need to turn someone working for the Merriweathers against them. Virginia Wickens, the secretary/receptionist, should be an ideal target. If we talk Southeast into a free demonstration security system, and she gives us access to their offices, our illegality gets muddy."

Gordo exclaimed, "How the hell will we do that?"

Mia answered, "I don't know yet. We know when her bosses are out of the building and at home. We'll spend some time with her and get inside information and the access needed. She knows what we don't. Who does the marketing and sales? Who makes the payments on the policies and properties? Where's the CFO? How often does he come to Florida? Where are their tax papers and customer lists? What bank account holds the building rent payments? Who pays the building's mortgage, utilities, property taxes, and insurance? How do they maintain the building and the grounds?"

Henry put up his hand. "Mia, for the sake of argument, let's say you have perfect knowledge of all that and their finances, taxes, and assets. Unfortunately, your plan has a fatal flaw, in my opinion."

She responded, "How so?"

"Daughter, you get all this information and data and then want to punish the wrongdoers. Vengeance seems to be your main motivation instead of working with the FBI."

"Dad, has someone tried to murder you? The woman in my house wanted to drug me and shoot me with one of my guns. She said it wasn't personal; it was just a job – how she earned her living. I want to find out who the boss is and make them pay. I want to hurt them where they live, in their pocketbooks."

Henry looked at Gordon. "What were they going to do to you?"

"Mr. Talbot, from the paperwork we found, it looks like I was going to have a jet ski or boating accident. They were probably going to sedate and drown me. Then, they wound my head and put me in our small lake, probably floating in a life jacket. Someone would find my boat or jet ski on the lake, and the local authorities would start a search for my body. I'm with Amelia. These people have to pay. If necessary, I'll take them out myself."

Doris looked horrified. "Good God, are you talking about killing them? We will have no part in a conspiracy to murder anyone."

Amelia stepped in, "Mom, I don't think it will come to that. Gordy doesn't fully understand how I can punish them financially. Once I have the correct information, I can make their lives a living hell. They wanted to kill your only child for money. Doesn't that make you livid?"

Doris, "Yes, it does, but we won't help you kill people, no matter how evil they are."

"Understood, Mom. We need to define our goals and get rolling. Ratchet is setting up our video and listening gear in our new offices. Let's go there and get organized. When the Merrriweathers leave the building, Mom and Dad can meet the secretary. We have GPS transmitters on their cars to plot their latest location. Our hall sensors are picking up some discussions in Southeast's offices, but nothing definitive yet. We've many questions. Does the Secretary know they're murderers? Does the wife know? Does Robert know? What's his relationship with CFO Fuller? Who directs the hit teams? Who pays them?"

Henry stopped her. "You have 'Ratchet Man' Rhodes here?"

"Yes, Dad."

"He's the best and most elusive hacker in the business. He's caused us no end of trouble at Microsoft."

"I know, Dad. I've hired him before. Ratchet always delivers the audio, visual, and phone data I need."

Henry frowned. "Who's paying him? I don't like the idea of our company paying him."

"Dad, he's working on commission. He gets twenty percent of what we transfer from the bad guys' accounts."

Henry scowled. "Mia, you say transfer. I say steal. Is the FBI going to put up with that?"

"Dad, I don't want to involve you and Mom in that part of the plan. Let's just say it's a special skill that our government had me develop and practice on bad people. None of my past bosses will want the details revealed in a trial."

They drove to the Southeast Assurance Building, and Amelia introduced her parents to Ratchet.

He commented. "Miss Talbot, I didn't know your parents were the Microsoft Talbots. It's a pleasure to meet both of you."

Henry replied, "I'm not sure it's a pleasure, but at least we'll work on the same side. What have you set up so far?"

Rhodes, "We have real-time tracking on the two principals' autos on this screen. I have voice-activated feeds from hallway sensors spooling to a massive hard drive. We will be able to search those files for keywords like 'kill,' 'murder,' 'Fuller,' and 'CFO.'"

"I see," responded Henry. "What do we need to accomplish next?"

Rhodes, "Sir, I've been thinking about that. Next, we need video and audio feeds from the secretary's desk and the two Merriweather offices. Then, we need high-definition devices over their shoulders to pick up passwords as they type them, video feeds from above the file cabinets, and safes to capture combinations. At some point, we need to dump the files from their computers on thumb drives. Also, we want taps on their phones and location data."

Doris spoke sarcastically, "No doubt you know how to do all that. So, Amelia, what do we do today?"

"Mom, we wait for the Merriweathers to leave. You and Dad engage the secretary. Ratchet joins you and starts measuring their offices for a security system. While doing this, he will place new audio and visual sensors. Gordon will be here in our offices monitoring the two cars. He will warn us if they head back."

Doris shrugged. "It's that simple?"

"Yes and no, Mom. Ratchet will have to install a fiber optic feed from the new sensors through the false overhead from their offices to ours. We have battery-fed sensors in the hallway. The ones in Southeast's offices will receive 110 power and transmit by wire – making them nearly impossible to detect."

"Amelia, I wouldn't want you going after me. Your plans are clear yet diabolical," replied her mother.

Gordon shook his head back and forth. "Amen to that, Mrs. T."

The Merriweathers left work at their usual times, four thirty and five o'clock. Gordon could see their cars heading northeast on his map display. Henry and Doris met Virginia Wickins in the Southeast office and introduced themselves as new tenants. They engaged Virginia or "Ginny" in a lively conversation as Ratchet arrived and began measuring the rooms. He placed tiny sensors and took 360-degree camera views of each room.

By the time the threesome left, they'd learned that Ginny was from Atlanta, had worked for Southeast Assurance for six years, and paid the building's expenses from a checking account. She also monitored the rent payments from the company's other facilities and their transfer into the same account. She said Mrs. Merriweather paid all the major expenses like mortgage payments, insurance policy fees, and professional services. Mrs. M. also handled payroll for Virginia, the building managers in various states, and the CFO, Mr. Fuller.

Doris asked her if Roscoe Fuller worked in Gainesville. Wickins said he managed the Albany, New York office and rarely came to headquarters. After Ginny locked her office door and left the building, Ratchet made the power connections he needed in the hallway and ran his network wiring to the Talbot offices. Amelia then took them all for a sumptuous dinner at Mark's Steakhouse.

Gordon and Ratchet arrived at the building shortly after Virginia the following day. Ratchet gave her a Starbucks coffee and some cinnamon rolls. He also brought a ladder and connected sensor wires to his network as she made coffee, opened file cabinets, and checked her company email. On his phone, Gordon watched the movement of Merriweathers' cars and warned Rhodes when Mrs. M. was ten minutes away. Finally, the hacker reluctantly stopped flirting with Ginny and packed his gear. She was a shapely redhead, and he liked her smile and quick laughter.

In the Talbot offices, Ratchet started putting up the feeds from the video sensors on displays. He and Gordon saw Ginny take a set of keys from her desk and unlock file cabinets in her area. Mrs. Merriweather arrived, drew a mug of coffee, and went to her desk. The two men noted the four-digit number, 8962, used to open her Windows laptop. Patricia scoured through a few items in her inbox and opened the B of A checking account. Unfortunately, the ID and password slots filled automatically and weren't readable. Then she went to a steel filing cabinet, spun the dial on a combination lock, and took out a corporate check ledger. Gordon captured the direction, the number of spins, and the combination numbers. Next, she opened accounting software and commenced writing checks.

Robert Merriweather arrived carrying Starbucks coffee and placed his laptop on his desk. Ratchet noted his four-digit opening code. Then he and Gordon watched as their quarry launched an elaborate spreadsheet with several sheets along the bottom. After a few minutes, they realized it was a client list from several states. Rhodes did a screen grab and expanded the document on a twenty-five-inch display. The two men observed that Merriweather could sort his clients by age, location (State), type of policy, the value of death policy, or original and current value of reverse mortgages.

Then Robert opened an MS Word document and started making sales calls to applicants in different states. He had a script prepared for each of the eight states that kept him on track with the correct company name and products for the prospective customer. After ninety minutes of calls, he had ten qualified prospects in five States.

Amelia arrived at her offices while her parents signed papers for a home lease at a nearby real estate company.
Gordon and Ratchet shushed her as they listened to R. Merriweather speak to his wife. "Good morning again, sweetheart. How are our finances on this fine day?"
Patricia looked up from her ledger. "We are making a small profit on rental cash flow, and our property values are shooting upward."
"Good," he answered. "Roscoe's plan is working. We add about fifty highly qualified customers each month and lose about ten annually. Do we need to put more funds offshore?"

Pat answered, "No, I don't think so – maybe next month. The rent payments cover our building expenses, and Fuller's actuary seems right on the money. How long do we have to work with that vile little man?"

"Easy, dear. Remember, Roscoe put up all the initial capital in the millions, and we have followed his business plan."

She said, "I know, I know. But I think he's skimming money and cheating us. I can't prove it; it's just a feeling. He gives me the creeps. Ginny agrees. She's asked me never to leave her alone with him."

Robert agreed, "Yes, he's a very unattractive fellow, but he's done a good job running all of our business in New York, Connecticut, and Pennsylvania."

She nodded. "But Robert, you're the public face of our companies. As CEO, you have built a solid reputation in this community, and with the state officials in our other locations. You're the one who travels, meets new clients, and checks on our buildings – what the managers are doing and what they need."

"Yes dear, except in his three states. Also, Roscoe collects on our policies. That's not an easy job as the insurance companies are very slippery. They try to claim suicide or nonaccidental deaths. Our CFO and his lawyer nail their hides to the wall. They're junkyard dogs, our junkyard dogs. They scour every word in the life insurance contracts to ensure we can collect. Something neither one of us wants to do."

"You're right. I give up. I'll bitch only to you, and you do what you think is right."

He said, "How about lunch in an hour at Hogtown?"

"Sounds good. I'll finish today's payments, and Ginny can mail them."

Amelia had a big smile. Ratchet's equipment was working better than she expected. When the Merriweathers left for their Bar-B-Que lunch, the Hacker and Gordon entered Southeast Assurance's office to chat with Virginia. Gordon talked to her while Ratchet went into her bosses' offices. He opened their laptops, entered the access codes, and dumped their files into a thumb drive. Using a short ladder, he also adjusted a couple of video sensors. Back in the reception area, Ratchet gave Gordon a sign for him to leave.

He smiled at Virginia and said, "I think we have all the measurements to propose an A-1 security system to your bosses. Do you think they'll go for it?"

She smoothed her red hair. "I don't see why not if it is free like you say."

"I don't know all the terms, but it would be free for the first year. My boss wants to bring customers here and show them our systems protecting the building. Say, how about I take you to lunch for being so helpful?"

"I would like that. But I can't leave until the Merriweathers get back."

Rhodes said, "OK, here's my number. Call me, and I'll meet you in the lobby."

She said, "Deal. Would you mind watching the office while I go to the Ladies' Room?"

"No, that would be fine – take your time."

Her laptop was open. Dumping all her files on a thumb drive took only a few minutes. When Ratchet returned to the Talbot offices, he transferred the thumb drive contents to his primary desktop computer and a laptop he kept with him when out of the office.

Gordon asked, "What happens next?"

Rhodes replied, "See the blinking storage access lights on these computers?"

"Yeah, so what?"

"The Merriweathers use Windows computers. Windows sorts all the numbers and words in their files for easy location and retrieval. We will be able to search for phrases or adjoining words. It's also helpful that they use Microsoft Office. We can look at their Word, Excel, and PowerPoint files and track everything they've done."

"How long will it take?" quizzed Gordon.

"There are thousands of document files, but we should be able to look up single words tomorrow."

Amelia joined in, "Great work, Ratchet. We sign for the G100 tomorrow and fly to Albany, New York, the next day."

Rhodes asked, "What's there?"

"The Chief Financial Officer for Merriweather's companies. I think he's the brains and maybe the one who orders the murders. We must find his building and start surveilling him and any employees."

Ratchet shrugged. "Do we have his address?"

Mia responded, "No. And we don't know the names of his companies in the northeast. We only know Robert Merriweather has flown to Albany International to meet with Roscoe Fuller, his CFO. The files you're indexing should give us what we need."

Two days later, Roger Sandstone flew the Talbot crew to New York. Halfway through the flight, Amelia replaced Gordon in the co-pilot's seat.

"Roger, this is amazing. In less than three hours, we will be in upper New York. I need to brief you on something very hush-hush."

"What's that, Ms. Amelia?"

"My parents are considering making an offer for the Merriweathers' business. We have a lot of cash, and they think it may be a good business model. No one can know about this, or it can sour the deal. We'll survey all the buildings they own and develop an estimate of value for Southeast Assurance." She stroked his shoulder. "You must promise to keep it secret."

"I promise," he pledged.

"Good. You can advise my folks on the value of this airplane and how many planes we will need if we expand the assurance organization to other states. We may need you to buy more planes and train more pilots. Does that sound OK?"

"Amelia, that sounds great. I can handle several more aircraft at my hangar and provide maintenance."

"Roger, that's wonderful. I'll enjoy working with you."

She got up, kissed his cheek, and whispered, "Thank you so much."

Mia returned to the cabin and watched Ratchet scan files on his monster laptop. "Hey, hacker. Any luck on the New York address?"

"No, Mia. That office is listed as Albany. I have the insurance company name; it's New York Mutual Assurance. But their phone number and address are unlisted."

She asked, "You're on the Internet?"

"Yup, I'm using the hotspot on my phone. Most of this flight is over urban areas. I think I have another way if I don't have it before we land."

"What's that?"

"We land and call Ginny. Her bosses usually go out for lunch, and she handles the mail to the other companies."

Mia, "Good thinking, Ratchet. What's your cover story? Why do you want to know the Albany address?"

"Yeah, well, I'll tell her my boss is going to New York and wants to see if we can provide security to their building up north."

She smiled. "Not bad. Ask Virginia to keep it secret until we have an estimate."

"Will do," promised the hacker.

"Good. You can learn more about Roscoe Fuller during the rest of the flight. Look for correspondence, invoices, checks, emails, etc."

"I'm not into their emails yet. I'd prefer to do that back at their office when I know they aren't on their computers."

They landed at Albany International Airport, and Enterprise delivered a van for a two-day rental. Rhodes called Ginny and got the address for New York Mutual Assurance – it was on Highway 29 in Saratoga Springs. Sandstone stayed with the aircraft. The rest drove north on the freeway and exited at Union Avenue. After passing the famous racecourse, their GPS gave them several turns that put them on Highway 29 heading west. The four-story Assurance Building had retail businesses on the first floor fronting the highway.

Strong parked the van in the adjacent lot and asked Mia, "What's the plan?"

She replied, "Mom and Dad, go into the building and see if they can find Fuller. Ratchet puts on a hat and sunglasses and gets us lunch at Domino's Pizza across the street. We stay in the van because Fuller has probably seen our pictures and could be the one who ordered us murdered."

Doris questioned, "What do you want us to do?"

"Mom, go into the building and look for the Mutual Assurance Offices. If there's a directory, take a picture of it. See if there's any rental space. Check for cameras and security equipment. And if Roscoe Fuller is on site, meet with him and ask what may become available. Ratchet has a sensor for you to place in his office."

Doris grimaced, "Good grief, how do we do that?"

Amelia responded, "I don't know. At some point, lean on Fuller's desk and press the suction cup up under its edge. How about this? Ask to see the layout of the building. That should get you close to him."

Chapter Eighteen

THE MISSING PARTNER – Saratoga Springs, New York

Gordon Strong pulled his hat down and started napping in the van. Amelia opened Rhode's laptop and had a split-screen view of the Merriweathers in their offices. Mrs. M. was checking their bank balances. Mia noted the time so they could check other video later for passwords. Patricia used <u>pmerriweather99@gmail.com</u> for her ID.

Hmmm, thought Amelia, *we may have to get our hands on her laptop if most of the passwords are autofill. Either that or break into her Google account.*

She selected Full Screen for Mrs. M's overhead video as Pat entered the bank account values into a spreadsheet.

Mia whistled and said, "Holy crap!" The Merriweathers had nearly two million dollars in their Nassau accounts.

Gordon responded, "What's up, Mia?"

"It looks like we'll take a trip to the Bahamas. Robert and Patricia have two million squirreled away down there."

"And you're going to take it away from them, right?" he quizzed.

"Exactly, but it may not be so easy. It looks like Mrs. M. checks the balances every day. It will take one hell of a precise plan to bankrupt them in one day."

"I have faith in you. You can do it."

"Thanks for the vote of confidence, Gordo."

Ratchet returned with two large pizzas, and the threesome in the van commenced demolishing a supreme pie. Finally, the elder Talbots returned and grabbed a slice before starting their report.

Between bites, Henry explained, "You enter the building by a side door, but it's locked. Tenants have keys. There's a doorbell and a camera. You push the button, and someone releases the lock. Inside is a small foyer and a directory. Most tenants are professional services, lawyers, accountants, and such. But, get this, neither Fuller's name nor New York Mutual Assurance is listed."

Amelia wiped some pizza grease off her lips. "What did you do?"

"We started roaming the hallways. The first floor has a back hall behind the retail business. It leads to the portion of the building that protrudes into this parking lot. There's another camera, a doorbell, and a placard on another door, 'R. Fuller.'"

"So, he can see regular foot traffic twice before admitting them?"

"Exactly," her Dad said. " We pushed the bell, and this little bent-over man opened the door and said, 'Whadda ya want?' Not a very friendly type. He was wearing a checkered bathrobe and slippers and had a beer bottle in one hand."

"Was he ugly like Mrs. Merriweather said?"

Doris answered, "He's got a gray complexion like he has cancer or something, and his head is misshapen – sort of pushed in on each side. His manner was rude, and he looked me up and down as if visually undressing me. His fingernails were dirty, and he was unshaven. She and Virginia are correct – he's creepy."

Henry continued. "We weren't invited into his office or home, whichever it is. We said we were looking for office space, and he told us to wait, shut the door, and returned with a key. He directed us to an empty, musty second-floor office with no furniture. There were only two small windows on one wall looking south – neither of us wanted to stay there very long. It did have a bathroom, which was a plus."

Their daughter questioned them as they withdrew another lukewarm slice of pizza, "Where was the office in relation to Fuller's quarters?"

Henry said, "We're not sure, but we think it's partially above him. There's another entrance to the building on the south side and two stairways. We saw no elevator."

"It sounds perfect," said Mia. "We rent above him and drill down through the floor to place our sensors. We put a GPS tracker on his car before we go, and we're surveilling the bastard."

Her mother challenged, "Which car is his? There are several in this lot."

"I don't know, Mom. Although I bet it's that dirty Lexus over near his digs. He probably has a private entrance in the back. And I know how to find out."

"How's that?" Doris asked.

There's a Beauty Shop in front on the first floor. We go there and get all the neighborhood gossip."

"What do the men do?" asked Doris.

"They go to the library and look up all the data they can get on this property, Mr. Fuller, and the insurance company. Then, Dad can take a nap."

Amelia and her mother entered the shop and discovered an older woman with white hair sitting in a chair, smoking and reading the local paper. She put on a professional face and determined what the Talbot ladies wanted. During the next two hours, Amelia and Doris learned that the Lexus was Fuller's car. Mia texted the info to Ratchet. The beautician Martha knew a lot about the building and Rosco Fuller.

She said, "He's a cheap screw - shows up here every two months for a free shampoo and haircut. He put it in the lease many years ago. Asshole, he smells and tries to act like a ladies' man. He lives in the back. If you know what I mean, the only women visiting him are ladies of the night. He keeps the rent low, so most businesses are long-term. The rentable space you looked at had a mortgage processing company – mostly women. Several of them were my customers. They felt they were being watched, especially in the John."

Doris exclaimed, "That's awful!"

"He's a creep. I wouldn't put it past him to put one of those tiny cameras in there."

Amelia thought, *He's also a murderer, I bet. Well, Roscoe Fuller has met his match in my team. I'll have Ratchet scan the space tomorrow, especially the bathroom.*

Mia said, "Martha, we have an office key, but how do we get into the building to scan our space for cameras?"

"Ms. Talbot, I have an extra key for this side. Don't worry about the south side camera; it's a fake."

"How does Roscoe get in and out of his living space?"

The hairdresser replied, "He can go through the building or two entrances in the back. He always parks that Lexus facing away from the building – kinda like he's ready for a quick exit."

Doris saw their van pull into the parking lot. They thanked the beautician, paid her a generous tip, and joined the men.

Amelia asked the first question, "What did you guys find?"

Henry answered, "Neither Roscoe Fuller nor his insurance company own the building. The owner is J&R LLC. Mr. Jonathan Rivers and Roscoe own the LLC. Rivers is also a mystery. He was a rather flamboyant gambler several years ago, but there's no record of him here in Saratoga Springs for the past five or six years."

Mia thought for a moment. "Hmmm. Maybe it's good that we are staying at the track casino and hotel. The gambling staff may remember Rivers. Ratchet, did you take care of the Lexus?"

"Yup, I took pictures of your dad in the parking lot pointing to our second-floor offices. He placed the GPS tracker."

"Good. Tomorrow, we sign the lease and place some sensors above Mr. Cheap Screw Fuller."

Doris asked, "Where did you say we are staying?"

"Mom, it's a very nice casino and hotel at the Saratoga harness racing track. You and Dad have one of their suites. We can also use it as a meeting place. Our pilot and Ratchet will share a room. Gordon and I will have adjoining rooms."

Gordon blushed when Doris looked askance at him. "How long has this been going on, Mia?"

"Mom, it's not what you think. Gordon and I are worried that a new team of professional killers may be on our trail. We are armed and feel safer providing mutual support. But, hey, that's another benefit of having your own aircraft. We can bring our weapons with us."

Henry warned, "Amelia, you don't have carry licenses here, right?"

"No Dad, but that's the least of our worries. Don't forget that there are people that want to kill us. It's not a good feeling. OK, gang, we are off to a good start. Let's go to the Saratoga Casino Hotel and take a load off. We have dinner reservations at Morton's Steakhouse at seven tonight."

Chapter Nineteen

GAMBLING LESSONS – Saratoga Springs Casino

Gordon and Amelia took naps in their rooms with pistols under their pillows and the adjoining doors open. Roger Sandstone jockeyed for position at dinner, so he sat beside Amelia. After dinner, she wanted to gamble. So, Gordon stayed with her, and Roger returned to his motel near the Albany airport.

Amelia put two thousand dollars of chips on her parents' American Express card and instructed her partner, "Gordon, when I sip my drink twice or blow my nose or increase my starting bet, you do the same."

"Yes boss; by the way, do you have your piece?"

"It's in my purse. You?"

He smiled. "Got it in an armpit holster under this sport coat."

"All right, let's have some fun and make some money. Do you know how to play Blackjack?"

"Sure, you try for an ace and a face card to make twenty-one or some combination that beats the dealer."

"Gordon, what do you do if you have a sixteen and the dealer shows a four?"

"Well, I might take a card if I feel lucky."

"No, you sit tight and hope the dealer draws a total over twenty-one and busts.

"I suppose you're right, Mia, but I just go by my instinct."

"No, big guy - bad answer. The only way to have almost even odds is to know the statistics of the game. Just follow my lead and do what I say. They have pretty liberal rules here, and only by playing correctly can we use the odds in our favor."

"Mia, this sounds more like work than having fun playing a game."

"Yes and no, my friend. You still need luck even if you make the right moves.

"What else do I need to know?"

"Always follow my lead and increase your bet if I do."

Amelia called the pit boss over and asked for a private table. They started betting twenty dollars a hand as she taught Gordon more strategies. After half an hour, the duo was up a couple hundred dollars. The pit boss changed dealers, and Amelia increased their bet to forty bucks. They had some luck on pair splits and double-downs and won another five hundred. In the second hour, they had a new dealer and had a losing streak until Mia suddenly bet one hundred dollars. Gordon followed her lead and split a pair of aces. They both played two hands and bet two hundred dollars on each. The dealer busted three times in a row. Gordon's head was spinning. The pair had won nearly $2,000 in less than ten minutes.

The dealer started an early shuffle, and Mia said, "Let's get a drink from the bar and then play some craps."

"Fine with me," said Strong. "Shouldn't we have ordered drinks when they were free?"

"No, Gordon. They don't know us as high rollers, so the booze would be cheap. I'm ordering some Courvoisier brandy. How about you?"

"That's fine, very smooth if memory serves."

She inhaled the pungent aroma of the amber liquor and winked at Gordon across the table.

"You know, Gordo, you're a good companion. We've spent considerable time together, and I would usually be bored with most guys."

"Amelia, I feel the same. You have so many talents and are the most decisive woman I've ever met. Besides, once again, you look smashing. Roger's tongue was hanging out as he looked you over."

"Why didn't he stay here with Ratchet?" she asked.

"I'm not sure. He may have a gambling problem or prefer to be alone. He said he wanted to be near our airplane."

"Roger's a good guy, but he's no Army Ranger. What's his story?" answered Amelia.

"Sort of like mine. Sandstone was too wrapped up in his aviation business and ended up divorced. He has a son who is in an Orlando grade school. While I inspected the G100, Roger went to see his ex and the boy."

She nodded. "What were you looking for?"

"Mainly signs of damage, patches to the skin, corrosion, and anything out of kilter. I reviewed the flight logs and maintenance records for major problems and found none. The plane's mechanic came by and opened the engine nacelles. He also explained his maintenance procedures."

"So, you like the plane?" she questioned.

"Oh my God, Mia, I never thought I would be flying a private jet – it's heaven."

She sipped her brandy and winked. "And you like me, how I look and act?"

"Yes, I do. You said you feel safe with me. I feel the same way about you. If the chips are down, I want you watching my back with your piece handy."

"Gordo, I'm enjoying your company, and you don't look so bad yourself."

"Thank you, Ma'am. What's our next move with the Merriweather gang?"

"I've got some ideas but no clear path yet."

He reached across the table and took her free hand. "Amelia, what just happened at Blackjack? We were losing, and wham, you suddenly raised the bet."

"I was counting nines and tens. There was an uneven amount left in the shoe that would bust the dealer. We hit him hard and quit. Do you know how to play craps?"

He answered, "I'm afraid to say yes. I have played but don't really know the odds."

"Well, we've got nearly four grand to play. Let's see if we can run it up a few more to pay for the trip and fuel for the G100."

Gordon replied, "How do we bet?"

"Gordo, we use a betting strategy that lowers the house's odds of winning. It gets them almost even with us. We bet on the Pass Line and take odds on the five, six, eight, and nine."

"I don't know what that means."

"No problem, just do what I do."

He said, "Maybe you can explain it as we play."

"Yes," she replied. "I'll do that. Don't worry; we'll start with low dollar amounts and work up to bigger numbers. We need a shooter to roll many repeat numbers to beat the house – that's the luck factor."

"Mia, I'm feeling very mellow with this brandy. I'll follow your lead."

They started with twenty-dollar Pass Line bets and took odds on the six and eight after the first roll. After thirty minutes, they were down over $200. Mia bumped the pass line bets to forty dollars and "bought all the numbers" (4,5,6,8,9,10) with at least sixty dollars on each. Gordon started his roll with a 7 winner, followed by a 9 as his point on the second roll. Then he had beginner's luck. He rolled one safe number after another as Mia pressed their bets on the point number boxes. She removed winnings when they had over $120 on each number but let the 6 and 8 ride to nearly $600. Gordon kept rolling the numbers and somehow avoided the deadly 7 and out. She started removing the bets on everything but the six and eight and taking winnings when they won. Gordon was in a zone. He rolled six and eight a couple more times and finally hit his nine. His next come-out roll was crap three and out.

Amelia was not as lucky. She hit a 7 and out on the second roll. Still, they were up over $2,000 after Gordon's turn. The dice passed to other shooters, and nothing exciting happened. Amelia racked over $2,000 winnings in their two chip containers and tossed a $100 chip to the banker for the four men manning the table. Back in their rooms, they had another snifter of good brandy.

Gordon said, "Mia, that was amazing. Do you always win like that?"

"No, it was an auspicious night. We could have just as easily dropped a couple of grand. With blackjack, craps, and roulette, you can get close to even odds with the house."

"What's our plan for tomorrow?" asked Gordo.

"I'm going to sleep on it, but I think we need more help here in 'The Springs' to monitor Roscoe Fuller."

"Like who?" he asked.

"Maybe a private investigator to see who he meets."

Their sleep was uneventful, except Strong wanted company and went to Mia's bed and snuggled next to her.

After sunrise, she was in the shower when the room phone rang. "Good morning, Gordon Strong here."

It was Ratchet, "Good morning, Gordon; I was trying to reach Amelia's room."

"You got it. She's taking a shower."

"Hmmm. Very interesting. Tell her I have the Southeast employee list and locations of all the buildings from Mrs. M's laptop. We are meeting in her parents' suite for breakfast."

"Good work, Ratchet. OK, I'll let her know. See you soon."

Amelia entered the room with a towel wrapped around her hair and another around her lithe body. "Who was that?"

"Ratchet, with good news. He has the Southeast employee list and addresses for their buildings."

She jumped into the bed next to him. "That's good news. Why did you join me last night?"

"I was feeling lonely. I just wanted to be with someone – to share your warmth."

"I see." She teased his lips with her fingers. "Maybe we should celebrate Ratchet's good news."

"Yes, maybe we should. I'll follow your lead."

Their lovemaking was brief and fierce, leaving them both spent and embracing.

"He said, "Mia, I'm going to shower and arrive a respectable amount of time after you."

She punched him in the shoulder and then kissed him long and hard. "I'm very fond of you, Gordo."

"Ditto."

Mia went to her parents' suite and selected several breakfast items. The excitement with gambling and Gordon Strong had made her famished.

She took a call from Roger Sandstone. "Good morning, Roger. Is our magnificent aircraft ready to fly?"

"Yes, ma'am. She's fueled, and I did a maintenance inspection yesterday."

"Excellent. When should we leave to land before dark?"

"Sunset is six thirty in Gainesville. How about we leave before four this afternoon?"

"Roger, that works for me, but it will be tomorrow. The ride up here was great. Thanks so much."

He gushed. "Like I said, it's an excellent plane."

"It is, but we also have an exceptional pilot. I feel safe when you're at the controls."

"Thank you, Amelia. That means a lot to me."

"Roger, we found the Assurance building in Saratoga Springs and have more business to transact. So, we'll meet you for dinner tonight."

"OK, Amelia. Please call me when you know the time and place."

"Will do."

Chapter Twenty

THE NASTY ROBBERY – Saratoga Springs

Ratchet entered the living room, made a heaping plate of food, and pulled a Coke from the fridge. He winked at Mia and wagged one finger at her - probably for having Strong in her room. Her parents joined them from the bedroom, and Amelia handed them $2,000 in hundred-dollar bills. Gordon arrived and loaded his breakfast plate.

"Mom, Dad, everybody, let's move to the dining room table," said Mia.

Once all settled, Henry Talbot inquired, "Amelia, I guess you had some luck at the tables last night?'

"Yes, we did. First, we played Blackjack and then craps. Ratchet, I heard you found Southeast's employees and the building locations. Is that correct?"

Rhodes had a mouthful of scrambled eggs and toast. "Yup, Mrs. M. had a file on the workers, probably all building managers. We have their names, addresses, social security numbers, and salaries. There's one building in each of the eight states. We have the addresses, tax payments, parcel numbers, and tenant lists."

"Good work! Mom and Dad, I thought you might like to visit your New York friends on the way to Florida. That's why we're changing the van for a car today. Also, you can visit the insurance buildings in Connecticut, Pennsylvania, and Virginia."

"And do what?" asked Doris.

"Check for vacancies, meet the manager, and place video sensors in the lobbies so we can see who goes in and out – also an audio sensor in the manager's office if possible. Gordon, I, and Ratchet will drive north from Florida to cover the offices of Georgia, South Carolina, and North Carolina."

Ratchet raised his hand. "I, too, would like to stop over in New York. I'm working on a Park Avenue lease there, and a couple of nights with my girlfriend would be good for my morale."

Amelia replied, "World-class hackers have girlfriends?"

"Of course. She's a dancer on Broadway and pretty good with computers."

"OK, go to New York. We'll figure out where to meet you in two days. What about Southeast's financial accounts? Is there any progress there?"

The hacker said, "No. Mrs. M uses Quicken Books. I don't have her login data yet. But I do have the files. When you and Gordon get back to Gainesville, you can scan her video feed and watch for that."

Mia gave him a thumbs up. "Done. Anything interesting on Mr. Merriweather's laptop?"

"I haven't finished looking at the hundreds of files. Most of his stuff is contacts around town, community activities, and customer data. However, I did find an Excel file where he tracks customers who have died, their policies, and collection amounts."

Mia's dad said, "Amelia, what's your plan for today?"

"Dad, we return to Fuller's building and place more video and audio sensors. Ratchet sets up computers for monitoring and reporting to the Internet. We monitor the creep today, and I have more questions for the beautician. You and Mom sign the lease, and we spend the night at this hotel. Maybe we can learn more about Mr. Rivers, who may own half of the Assurance buildings."

Roger Sandstone called about the dinner details. Amelia told him to take the day off and meet for another Morton's dinner at eight. The others drove to Roscoe Fuller's building. They entered on the south side, guarded by the fake security camera, and let themselves into their second-floor office. After an hour, Ratchet had installed several audio sensors against Roscoe's ceiling. Doris and Henry went downstairs to his entrance and asked to sign the lease. Fuller led them into his office, and the other three listened to their conversation.

Doris asked, "Mr. Fuller, should we not be signing with the building's other owner, Mr. Rivers?"

Fuller looked like a cornered rat. "Why do you say that?"

"Well, sir, we looked up the property in the county records, and you both are listed as owners."

He snapped, "I might as well be the only owner; Johnny's never here. You might think of him as a silent partner."

"I see," Doris said. "We usually like to deal with all the owners, but I guess this will be OK since you live on the premises."

Roscoe, "Good, good. Do you have the security deposit and first month's rent?"

"Yes," responded Henry. "Do you mind if we use cash?"

"No, siree. Cash is king, I always say," Roscoe replied, rubbing his hands together.

They paid the strange ugly man with Amelia's winnings. Back in their new offices, Ratchet played their conversation for the elder Talbots. Every word was clear and now recorded. Rhodes brought more computers online and connected the new sensors inside Roscoe's living quarters. Amelia went to Martha's beauty shop, and her parents monitored the audio and video feeds from Southeast's Gainesville office. Lunch again was pizza from Domino's that was delivered to their offices. Some desks, chairs, tables, and couches arrived from an office furniture company, as Amelia had ordered the day before.

Amelia reported her conversation with Martha: "She said that Rivers disappeared about five years ago. One day, he was in the back, living with Roscoe, and there was no trace of him the next. Fuller said Johnny left to see family in St. Louis, but Martha told me Rivers had no family. From then on, Roscoe acted as if he owned the building. He told her he bought it from Rivers. She was surprised when I informed her that Jonathon was still listed as the legal co-owner."

Ratchet broke in, "Hold it, Amelia. Roscoe is calling someone on his speaker phone."

Roscoe, "Ben, is that you?"

"Yes Roscoe, what's up?"

"We may need your services next week."

Ben, "Oh, I thought we were lower on the rotation."

"We've got a ticklish situation. We lost Team 3 last week," reported Roscoe.

"Really? I thought you only worked with professionals."

"It seems both members had fatal accidents. One fell down some stairs, and the other drove off a country road and smashed into a tree."

"They don't sound like pros to me," said Ben.

"I know. You have our best crew, and we will pay more for you to find the customers that may have killed our team."

"Do you have a dossier on them?"

"Yes, but here's the thing. They seem to be missing. We traced them to Florida, and then the trail went cold," stated Roscoe.

"Maybe you should suspend operations for a few weeks. It's not like you're selling vacuum cleaners."

"I agree, but my boss is pressing me to keep the revenue flowing."

"This is the boss that got rid of Team 2, right?" asked Ben.

"Yeah, we all are expendable if we screw up and expose the boss to authorities and investigation. You have to help me! I'm under extreme pressure."

"Roscoe, I don't have to do anything. Money talks: how much are you paying?"

"Ten grand for finding the missing customers. We think they may have joined forces and are hiding - another forty grand for completing Team 3's mission."

"Do you need accidental coverage or not? It seems much harder and riskier in this situation."

"No Ben, use any method that works for you as long as there's proof of death. Although, I'm sure there will be a bonus from the boss for the higher policy amount."

"OK, Roscoe, fifty grand and expenses. I want twenty grand up front. When do we meet?"

"Tonight, if possible. Can you fly here tonight?"

"Perhaps I can catch the last flight. If I can, I will phone you a time at our usual place."

"Thank you, Ben. I owe you one. This is the first glitch we've had in six years."

"What about Team 2? Why did that happen?"

"Ben, they killed a cop who was in the wrong place at the wrong time."

"Roscoe, come alone with a briefcase. If I smell anything phony, it's off, and your ass is mine."

"Yes Ben, see you tonight or tomorrow – many thanks."

Mia turned to Gordon, "Jesus Christ, is there any doubt that we just heard a second contract on our lives?"

He took her in his arms. "No, no doubt. We stopped using credit cards in northern Florida."

Henry was shaking with fear and anger. "Bastards, we have to go to the police."

"No, Dad, we can't reveal how we found this out. We must learn who Ben is and neutralize him and his partner."

Doris was pale and terrified. "Mia, they really want to kill you. I can't believe it. They talked about murder as if it were a rug cleaning contract."

"Yes, Mom. Now you know how Gordon and I feel. We've done nothing wrong except sign policies with this evil company. Roscoe Fuller is the connection to the killers. He scouts the targets and pays the money. Mr.

Merriweather is probably the big boss who picks the policies to collect. He spreads them out by the state, life insurance corporation, and time. Who will notice if they lose a customer or two in each state each year? The collections flow through seven different companies. Property values have increased, and the various assurance companies can easily sell their acquired reverse mortgage properties without raising red flags. These are really bad people, and I'm going to grind them to dust and make them homeless."

Ratchet said, "Amelia, are you scared?"

"Yes, I am. Professional killers are good at finding their victims and completing their hits. But also, my blood is boiling. So, I'm doubly committed to bankrupting the Merriweathers and shutting their operation down. Before I'm done, they will sleep in that Honda Pilot and beg for food on the streets. Gordon, what do you think about intervening with Ben?"

"I think only you and I can discuss that as an option. Let's go for a walk."

They strolled for several blocks on Highway 29 and came to a pleasant grass park with mature Pin Oak trees. The two targets sat on a bench and listened to the birds singing.

Gordon broke their silence. "Mia, if you're thinking of a sniper shot on this Ben, it's not in the cards. I didn't bring a suitable weapon, and we're not sure of his identity. Also, we give away our original plan. If we use a pistol on Ben or Fuller, we have to get close and risk being recorded on a host of cameras."

She replied, "Damn, I agree. We need to take Fuller's money. He must have a hiding place below our offices. It's too risky for him to withdraw large amounts of cash from a bank."

Gordon clapped his hands. "You may have a plausible option there. If we steal Roscoe's briefcase, we stop the contract – at least in the short term. We need him to believe it's a random common mugging. I doubt he will tell Robert Merriweather about his troubles - the penalty is too severe."

"Gordon, we should have two cars to follow him. The GPS unit will tell us where he is; we have three people he has never seen. We get you looking like a homeless person asking for a handout before taking his case. Mom, Dad, and Ratchet can follow him and get a picture of this Ben person. Maybe they can score his fingerprints if he has a drink."

"Mia, it could at least slow them down."

"Yes, let's review our range of options. We can do nothing. That creates the least suspicion and places the most risk on us. We can kill or badly injure Roscoe Fuller as he leaves the building. It's not what I want to do, but it's a viable option. Or you can take the case when he exits his car for the meeting. Since I talked to Martha, the beautician, there's a new twist."

"What's that?"

"She thinks Roscoe is trafficking young women from Eastern Europe."

"How did she come to that conclusion."

"About two times a year, he brings an attractive twenty-something to her for hair and makeup lessons. He tells Martha he's helping them become models."

"Amelia, what's the connection to our plans?"

"If he's holding one hostage and we kill him, it may kill her if she's at another location."

"I see. We have another option you haven't covered."

"Which is?"

"Call Finster and go to the local FBI office and try to shut down the Merriweather operation with what we know."

She paused. "Yes, that's an option, but our surveillance is illegal. And we haven't found their most damning records yet, let alone punished them with bankruptcy. However, once we can point the FBI at fraudulent tax forms, proof of customer murders, and money laundering, we can work with them."

Gordon, "So, your father was right. Vengeance is one of your main goals."

"Yes, and getting my hands on a few of their millions to fund our activities wouldn't hurt. It's settled. You get clothes and a disguise that makes you look like a mugger. Ratchet can rent another car and drop it in New York. We steal the case, break into Fuller's apartment, and place several video sensors so we can find his stash. My parents can warn us when he's returning to his building."

"Mia, let's say we do that, and he has more cash and copies of our files. He can take both to Ben, and the hits are back on, right?"

"Hmmm...I haven't thought that far ahead. How about this? Ratchet and my parents keep track of Ben. He has to sleep somewhere. And we visit him and scare him off. We tell him his cover is blown, and we, an East Coast mob family, are taking over the Merriweather operation. If we ever see him around Roscoe again, it's curtains for his team and family."

"It might work," responded Gordo.

"It has to work. I'm not going to be a lamb led to slaughter. So, in effect, we are saving his life. Gordon, this park is so nice, but we've work to do. Roscoe Fuller will probably meet with his hitman near the airport."

They returned to their new second-floor offices, and Amelia explained the plan to her parents and Rhodes. They heard Fuller take a phone call where he repeated he would meet Ben at the Olive Garden bar on Wolf Road at 10:15 p.m. Mia and Gordon decided to return to the building parking lot at eight-thirty and follow Fuller to Colonie, New York. Ratchet and Gordon departed to rent a car and find Gordon's homeless outfit.

Mia called Roger Sandstone and said her party was working hard on their marketing pitch. She begged off for dinner and said she planned a midday flight back to Florida. Her group met for dinner in the Talbots' suite and refined the timing of Amelia's plan. Ratchet agreed to sit in the bar by nine thirty with his laptop and listening gear to record Roscoe's conversation.

Amelia took a nap and later waited in the rental car for Gordon at the casino's side entrance. When he got into the passenger seat, she almost fled. The man had long, scraggly hair, an unkempt beard and mustache, dirty and torn clothes, dark glasses, and a construction hat.
He said, "Amelia, it's me. Don't you recognize me?"
"Good God, not at all. What's that awful smell?"
"I rubbed dog shit into my tennis shoe grooves."
"Euuh, but there's more than that."
"Yeah, I pissed on the trousers. Hey, smell my breath." He exhaled toward her face.
"Jesus, you're disgusting. What makes that bad breath?"
"Raw onion and garlic that I've been chewing and spitting out."
"It's dreadful. You're awful."
"That's the idea. We want Roscoe to be so disgusted he might not even chase me."
"How do we get his case?"
"He will have it next to him in the car, in the back seat, or the trunk. You drive a couple of spaces past his parking spot. It's dark. I get out and go after him. I get in his face and ask for a handout when he has the case. You drive around the building to the opposite side. I give him a couple of punches and take the case. Then, I will run around the building and meet

you behind the Red Lobster. I dive into your back seat. You drive out of the parking lot like any patron leaving."

"I'm not sure I want you back in the car," she complained.

"Don't worry; I brought a change of clothes."

"What about the dog poo shoes?"

"And replacement shoes also, we'll dump the outfit as soon as possible."

Fuller came out of his building and entered the Lexus at nine forty-five. He took Highway 87 south from State Road 9P. Amelia could follow at a distance because Gordon had put a strip of electrical tape on Roscoe's left taillight. Thirty minutes later, they approached the Albany Airport and followed Roscoe southwest on Wolf Road.

Gordon said, "Showtime. Have your rear window down and the door unlocked. No way he can keep up with me around the building."

"You got it, big guy," she said.

Fuller pulled into the parking lot and passed some lighted spots by the entrance. Once he parked, Amelia passed behind him, and Gordon jumped out. He watched Roscoe open his trunk and withdraw the briefcase.

When the smaller man turned around, Strong was in his face. "Hey, buddy, can you spare a dollar? I'm starving."

"No, I can't. God, you stink. Get out of my way."

"Just a dollar, sir, before your big meal. I'm cold and hungry out here."

Gordon grabbed Fuller's shoulders and exhaled into his face.

"You asshole," said Roscoe. "What have you been eating?"

"A onion, and you're the asshole, asshole - with your fancy car, fancy shoes, fancy case, and fancy dinner."

"Get out of my face, you disgusting bum. "I'm calling the police."

Gordon looked around, and no one was arriving or leaving. He kicked one of Roscoe's shins in a flash and punched him in the windpipe. Then he took Fuller's phone, wallet, car fob, and briefcase. Roscoe was bent over in pain from his leg. He had trouble breathing, and was shocked as Strong sprinted around the building. He threw the case into the back seat and lunged into it. Mia then drove southeast of the Red Lobster lot at a moderate speed and turned right on Wolf Road. In no time, they were heading north on 87 without any cars chasing them.

Roscoe Fuller leaned against the hood of his car as the enormity of his situation washed over him. He thought, *God, I've been mugged by a disgusting animal. He's got the case and twenty grand – doesn't even* know it. *What am I going to tell Ben? What if the boss finds out? No, that can't happen.* He limped toward the entrance and picked up his car fob where the "Manure Man" had tossed it. Inside, he saw Ben sitting at the bar and watching him in the wall mirror.

Fuller sat down as Ben questioned. "Where's your case?"

"Jesus, Ben. I've just been robbed. This long-haired, filthy, disgusting man asked me for a dollar. I told him to get lost. He got more and more belligerent. Finally, he kicked me and sucker-punched me in the throat. Then he took my wallet, the case, and my phone."

"Roscoe, you better not be shitting me, man."

"I'm not. I swear I'm not. He tossed my car key away, but I found it. I can get more cash and return here in an hour."

"No, that won't work, shit for brains. They close at eleven. I have an extra burner in the car. You stay here, and I'll get it. Tomorrow, at seven, I will call and set up a new meeting place. You understand if I'm arrested, my partner will take care of you as her first order of business."

"Yes Ben, it's a freak accident of nature. I was in the wrong place at the wrong time. No one knew I was coming here. No one knew I was meeting you – I swear."

"Roscoe, order a strong drink and look in the bar mirror. You'd be toasting a dead man if you lied to me."

Neither paid attention to the apparent computer nerd in the room's far corner. He was playing a game on his laptop or gambling – oblivious to the other people in the bar. Ratchet had pointed a sensitive directional microphone at the two men and picked up nearly every word. The taller man left and returned to hand Fuller something that looked like a flip phone. He departed while Roscoe nursed his double scotch on the rocks. Ratchet called the Talbots and told them to follow the man coming out the front entrance.

Mia and Gordon drove to the office building in Saratoga Springs and broke into Fuller's apartment. They then placed several video sensors. He either didn't have an alarm or had not armed it. They went to their second-floor offices and paired their computers with the sensors. Strong had changed his clothes and shoes. He was chewing a handful of breath mints that Amelia forced on him.

Amelia's mother called. "Mia, we just followed a man from the Olive Garden to a nearby Red Roof Inn. Ratchet told us to follow him. What do we do now?"

"Mom, sit tight in your car and stay away from him. Be careful; he's a killer. We need to find out his room number."

"Oh, we can help with that. He parked in the middle of the motel. And we saw him enter one of the first-floor rooms and turn on the lights near his car."

"Good work, Mother. Go pick up Rhodes while I think about this."

Amelia turned to Gordon and said, "Got any ideas, Army?"

"Let's see; we need to get to this guy. How about your parents renting a room adjoining his if that's possible? Or one on the same floor will do. They identify his car, and we jump him in his room or when he gets into his car."

"Hmmm. Not bad," she replied.

Mia called her mom. "Mom, have Dad go in and rent a room on the first floor. Then, he can say his business associate Ben should have arrived and request an adjoining room. We need Ben's room number, car information, make, color, and license plate. We'll meet you in your casino suite in about an hour."

"Yes daughter. This cloak and dagger stuff is almost fun."

"Mom, don't mess around with this guy. He would just as soon shoot you as look at you."

"We'll be cautious."

"Good."

Chapter Twenty-one

SECOND MEETING WITH FBI– Fayetteville, NC

Gordon and Amelia were sipping red wine when Roscoe returned to his apartment. They watched as he paced his living room. Finally, he stopped as if he had decided something. He moved the coffee table away from the couch. Then he swung one end of the sofa away from the wall and raised a two-foot strip of carpet. They couldn't see the combination but understood that Roscoe was opening a floor safe. Once open, he took some packets of $100 bills and counted out $20,000 for his morning meeting. Amelia estimated he had fifty to sixty thousand dollars on the coffee table.

She said, "Boy, would I like to go get that twenty K tonight. Can you imagine his distress?"

Gordon protested. "No Amelia, we can't give ourselves away. We have to focus on this Ben character. How are we going to scare him off?"

"I don't know. Breakfast starts at 6 a.m. at his hotel. Let's go meet my parents and figure out what happens next."

When Amelia's parents and Rachet arrived an hour later, Gordon and Mia sipped their bedtime brandy snifters.

"Hey Mom, how did it go?"

Doris answered, "Well, your father went to the front desk and got us a room next to this Ben fellow. The three of us went to our room and heard him snoring through one of Rachet's audio sensors. We opened our adjoining door, and as you might expect, he locked his door. Our hacker believes you could force the lock with a crowbar, but it will make a lot of noise."

Mia replied, "Wow, you've given us good info to consider. We saw Roscoe Fuller access his floor safe under his living room couch. He took out a lot of cash and counted out $20,000, possibly for his second meeting with Ben tomorrow morning."

Ratchet asked, "Did you get the combination?"

"No, we need an additional camera to do that. What did you hear in the Olive Garden?"

"We were lucky; the bar was mostly empty. Roscoe told the other man that a stinking bum had mugged him in the parking lot. The man, Ben, I guess, threatened him if he was lying – said he would kill him. He also said if he was arrested, a woman would kill Roscoe. Roscoe convinced him it was a one-off event - the wrong place at the wrong time. He said the mugger kicked and punched him and took his phone, wallet, and briefcase. Is that true?"

Gordon nodded. "We have the wallet contents over on the dining room table. We can't open the case without destroying the locks – hoped you could help with that."

The hacker said, "I want to see all of it – the case, the phone, and the wallet contents. I'm taking the case into the bathroom and using a powerful stethoscope. Please stop talking or go in the kitchen and whisper."

Amelia put on surgical gloves and showed her parents Roscoe Fuller's credit cards, driver's license, and other items. There were no pictures of family or friends. Instead, there was a picture of a bulldog with the name "Trigger" on the reverse side. He had a Sam's Club card and gas station membership. Ratchet returned to the dining room and placed the open briefcase on the table.

He declared, "Amelia, I'm taking my cut. Four thousand, correct?"

"Yes, how did you get it open?"

"It's similar to a safe, but there's a different sound when the wheels line up. The two folders provide information on you and Gordon but not your current location."

"I see. Mom and Dad, you take $10,000, and Gordon and I'll take the remaining $6,000. Everyone get a drink, and we will go over our status. Ratchet, were you able to collect any fingerprints at the bar?"

"When Roscoe left, I paid the bartender $100 for the two glasses – told him I was an undercover cop."

"Outstanding. We have started on our first goal: stop the killing. Apparently, there are or were three or more hit teams. Team 3 died in Bumpass trying to kill me. Roscoe's boss eliminated Team 2 for killing a cop. Ben is part of Team 1. Ratchet, we need to find a list in the computer files of more teams if they exist."

"Roger that," he answered.

Amelia continued, "We have found the conspiracy CFO, Roscoe Fuller, and commenced surveillance. He connects to the murder teams and reports to a demanding boss, probably Robert Merriweather. That was our second goal. Third, we want to discover the members of the remaining hit teams and inform law enforcement. Fourth, we need more help. We can't stay here and keep tabs on Roscoe Fuller. I propose to hire a P-I tomorrow morning to use our offices, monitor him, and photograph anyone he meets. Goal five still finds us in the dark. We don't know if the Merriweathers or managers of the buildings know about the murders. Mom and Dad, you scout the buildings and managers in Connecticut, Pennsylvania, and Virginia. Find out who owns the building, meet the managers, and request a lease agreement. Gordon and I will visit the ones in Georgia, South Carolina, and North Carolina. That will allow us to reveal some info to an FBI agent, Jake Finster, out of the Fayetteville office. Also, Gordon and I must pick up our passports before flying to Nassau."

Gordon alerted, "Good catch, Amelia. I need mine also. What else?"

"We need to get the Merriweathers' secretary onboard to have uninterrupted access to the company file cabinets and records. We'll look for tax records, bank statements, credit card bills, and creditor accounts. Once Ratchet opens their Quicken Books accounts and we have the bank account access codes, we can start planning B-day."

Henry raised his hand. "Excuse me, Mia, what's B-day?"

"Dad, it's the day we bankrupt the Merriweathers. I think a Friday after all the rent receipts have been paid and Mrs. M. has checked the account balances would be perfect. Last, we need to categorize data that the FBI can use. I imagine tax fraud will be one of them. No doubt, a company that kills its customers probably understates revenue and overstates expenses and depreciation."

Ratchet was only half listening as he scanned the contacts on Roscoe's phone. He announced, "Amelia, Roscoe, and Ben plan to meet in the morning to complete the contract on you and Gordon. What do we do about that?"

Mia replied, "Thanks for reminding me. Gordon and I will put our heads together and devise a scheme to encourage Ben to leave town. We know his room number, and that's half the battle."

Ratchet Rhodes had one more question. "How much of this should we share with Roger?"

Amelia said, "None. As far as Roger Sandstone is concerned, we are business people providing security services."

Rhodes, "Got it. I'll spend a few days in New York working on these files and meet you and Gordo in one of the southern states."

    Gordon and Amelia went to their rooms, dressed in black, and dumped the rest of their brandy. Strong believed they should go after

Ben while he was in his deepest sleep. But they were stumped on where to find a medium-sized crowbar.

Amelia snapped her fingers and said, "The casino maintenance guys are always on the floor working on something. They have large toolboxes; maybe we can borrow one from them."

"Good idea, Mia. Make sure you have a round chambered, and I'll empty mine. I plan to place my piece against his head and don't want it to go off. If things go south, you'll have to shoot him."

"Thanks for nothing, Army."

Forty minutes later, they were in the room next to Ben's. They could hear heavy breathing but not the snoring described by Henry. They put on gloves. Gordon inspected the second adjoining door's lock and placed the prybar against the jam.

"He whispered, "Mia, there's some give here. I'm going to break through the door and pounce on this guy. His bed will be against this wall or the far wall. Either way, you go to the other side of the bed and keep your light in his eyes. One, two, three."

Gordon pried the lock open and put his shoulder into the door. It popped open with a bang. He took three steps across the room and placed his gun against Ben's head.

"Mr. Ben, move, and you're dead. Where's your gun?"

The startled sleeper said, "What? Huh? Who are you?"

Ben tried to reach under his pillow; Strong crushed his hand with the barrel of his Walther.

"Owwww! What the hell? Who are you?"

"Ben, think of me as number one and my partner as number two. We are here as an unwelcoming committee. Your work with Roscoe Fuller is over, done, finished."

"Why is that?"

Gordon explained, "Roscoe and his handlers are weak players. We are going to roll them up and take over their little business. Then, when we expand to every state, we may have work for you. We know who you are and have your fingerprints off your bar glass tonight. We will kill you and the woman partner if you ever contact Fuller again. Is that clear?"

"YYYes, but who are you?"

"We are part of a New York family if you know what I mean. We have the muscle and cash to expand this assurance business in the U.S. and maybe

into other countries. If you get in our way, you, your partner, and any family are history. Do you understand?"
Ben, "Yes, yes, we've other fish to fry."
"Good, because we'll know if you call Roscoe Fuller for your seven o'clock meeting. I'm taking your piece. My number two will shoot you if you move. Relax, we'll be gone soon."

Gordon spread the contents of Ben's wallet on the room's desk and took a picture. Then, he fished his used flight ticket from the trash can and put it back.
After taking Ben's picture and pocketing his cell phone, Strong said, "We know where you live. When our plans are complete, we will contact you for more assignments. Roscoe Fuller and his bosses are under twenty-four-hour surveillance. Their days are numbered. If you warn them, it will be the last thing you do."

Amelia and Gordon left the building and ran to their idling car. Again, they drove south on Wolf Road and headed north on Highway 87.

The following day, Roger Sandstone flew Amelia and Gordon back to Gainesville. Amelia mapped the three buildings they would visit: one on Forsyth Street in Macon, Georgia, another in Sumpter, South Carolina, and the last outside of Charlotte, North Carolina. Gordon called Jake Finster and booked a meeting at the Fayetteville office in four days.
He got off the phone and said, "Mia, what will we tell Jake?"
She said, "I'm not sure I know. We can talk it over while we do all this driving and make a list. Possibly, we alert the FBI to Roscoe Fuller and the general scheme in New York. It's too early to reveal the Merriweathers and their Florida office."
"Why is that?" he questioned.
"Gordo, I think the first ploy to sic the FBI on Southeast Assurance is through their phony tax returns - the problem is, we haven't seen them yet."

Amelia and Gordon left early the following morning and were in Macon for lunch. They met with the building's managers and researched The Assurance Trust of Georgia's property data at the library and with the Bibb County Clerk. They took Highways 20 and 521 to Sumpter the next day and repeated the process. It was an easy drive to Charlotte, and nothing was out of order, so they continued to Gordon's house on Upchurches Pond. Amelia's stay at his house was much more pleasant than her first visit.

They met with Finster and his assistant the next day.

After introductions and coffee, Mia read from her notes. "Jake, we've found that the scheme to kill us started in upper New York. Two felons, Roscoe Fuller and Jonathon Rivers, bought a three-story office building in Saratoga Springs. Somehow, they started an insurance company, Northeast Assurance Company. Northeast Assurance bought whole-life policies and branched into reverse mortgages. They didn't want to wait for their customers to die off, so they hired one or more hit teams to hasten payments on policies or properties owned."

Finster stopped her. "What's the deal about an office building?"

Mia answered, "We believe but cannot yet prove they cheated on their income taxes. We think they overstate the building purchase price and expenses. Then their J&R LLC washes excessive depreciation deductions against income from death policies and sales of reverse mortgage properties. Being landlords gives them an aura of respectability."

Finster was doubtful. "But you and Gordon don't live in New York. How does that fit in?"

"During the last four to five years, they've expanded their scheme to other states, namely Connecticut, Pennsylvania, Virginia, North Carolina, South Carolina, and Georgia."

"How does that benefit them?" asked the agent.

"Think about it, Jake. If they murder too many customers in one state, it might be noticed."

"OK, I see. Where are these guys now?"

"Roscoe Fuller lives in the Brown Building in Saratoga. We have pictures and the address for you. Johnny Rivers is more of a mystery. He disappeared several years ago. A tenant in the building told me she suspects that Roscoe buried him behind the building."

"What do you want us, the FBI, to do?"

"Jake, that's up to you. I'm having a cadaver dog check the flower beds behind Fuller's building."

"Jeez, you don't mess around, do you?"

"No, and my team has visited each office building in the states I mentioned. We have the locations and tax records for you if you're interested. Each building is a phony tax loss front for a similar insurance company in that state. You might consider surveilling Roscoe Fuller to prevent him from sending out another hit team."

"Hmmm. We'll take it under advisement. Our plate is always full of one thing or another. Why are you telling me all this?"

She said, "Because Gordon trusts you, and if we are murdered, we want you to know where to look."

"Fair enough," the agent replied.

Amelia and Gordon drove to Savannah, checked into the Cotton Sail Hotel, and had a delicious dinner at the River House Seafood restaurant. Within three days, the Talbot team was back in Gainesville.

After comparing notes on the various buildings, Mia announced they'd go after Southeast's tax records that evening. They all took naps, made dinner in the rental home kitchen, and drove in one car to the office parking lot at 7 p.m. Amelia and Gordon placed blankets over the two windows in Mrs. Merriweather's office, and Ratchet opened the first file cabinet. Mia wore surgical gloves as she rifled through the three drawers. None of them held tax information.

Ratchet had opened the second cabinet, and Mia hit paydirt in the top drawer. It held Southeast Assurances' yearly taxes and the Merriweathers' personal tax forms. Amelia took a picture of the file sequence in each drawer. Gordon made two trips carrying them to the Talbot offices, where Doris and Henry photographed each page. The second drawer held the tax forms for each state other than Florida. Rhodes and Strong moved them to their office and started making copies.

Amelia began scanning through the third cabinet. At first, she was not sure what it contained. Then it hit her that these side-by-side files were two sets of books for each state and building. Here was the proof of Robert and Patricia Merriweathers' tax fraud. Mrs. M. was very organized and labeled each file with the suffix "Orig" or "Reptd." Amelia remembered that most illegal entities kept two sets of books. The first or original set provided the actual performance of the enterprise – its revenues, expenses, and profit, if any. Also, a balance sheet of assets and liabilities was necessary to judge yearly results.

The second set of printouts reported false data for minimizing taxes. The lower drawer had files marked "Insur" or "Loans." It took Mia a few minutes sitting on Mrs. M's couch to figure out the illegal accounting system. Mr. Merriweather and his CFO, Roscoe Fuller, knew the financial results of the Assurance companies from the original files. They changed revenues, expenses, and asset values on the reported forms to underpay their taxes. To obtain loans, they inflated revenues and assets; for insurance, they picked arbitrary values that provided the best ratio of coverage and cost. She photographed the contents of the last cabinet and locked it, as well as the first. *Don't get greedy*, she thought. *Eight to ten years of taxes for all the businesses are hundreds of pages to process, if not more. We need to find ways for the FBI to prove tax fraud without revealing our search methods.*

Amelia returned to her offices and found the team hard at work. They copied or photographed each file page and then carefully placed the document back in its folder. Each finished yearly folder was turned upside down in the correct sequence. After five hours, the folders were returned to their respective drawers, and their sequence, front to back, was confirmed against Mia's pictures. She turned the lights out, and Strong and Rhodes removed the window blankets.

The elder Talbots popped two bottles of French Champagne, and the midnight conspirators toasted each other. Ratchet stayed to collate the files for the latest year of taxes by company, and the others returned to their home base for a good night's rest. The next morning, Amelia received a call from the Saratoga private eye telling her that the cadaver dog had alerted on Roscoe Fuller's rose bed.

Over breakfast, she discussed the problem with Gordon. "What do we do? We know that Roscoe killed other people; this is just one more body. If we call the police, he may run. Or they may question why we wanted to look there."

"Mia, I think we stick with the FBI for now. Throw it at Jake and see what he does."

"OK, I'll text him and put him in touch with our PI. What are you doing with the rest of your day?"

"I'm getting more dual instrument training with Roger. Amelia, what will you be doing?"

"I'm going to study the Merriweathers' tax forms. I have some ideas about involving the FBI without incriminating our team."

Chapter Twenty-two

ANALYSIS AND DISCOVERY – Gainesville, FL

Amelia went to the office and started with the Merriweathers' personal income tax returns. They'd reported less than $80K in joint yearly income for five years. Robert and Patricia overstated their mortgage payments, property taxes, and charitable deductions. And somehow, they were pulling two or three hundred thousand out of Southeast Assurance each year without reporting it.

Hmmm. Mia thought. *They may be taking rent in cash and then not declaring it. Let's see, how do you do that? You knock five or ten percent off the rent for cash payment; doing that for eight buildings could add up to a significant amount each month. They mix the rents in their Bank of America accounts and transfer the nonreported excess to their Bahamas' banks.*

During the Merriweathers' lunch hour, Ratchet took burgers in for Virginia and confirmed that most renters paid by check or cash. The secretary said that Mr. M. didn't want credit card companies to receive a cut of his rental income.

Amelia had lunch with her parents and tore into the LLC state income tax forms next. The initial building sales data that she and her parents had collected showed the acquisition values were overstated by 100% or more on the tax forms. Also, Merriweathers used a yearly *residential* depreciation write-off (27.5 years) versus the correct *commercial* period (39 years). They claimed extensive improvements for each property that weren't evident from the Talbot teams' visits. Mia also suspected the rents were understated, expenses overstated, and revenue collections for insurance policies and reverse mortgage property sales were underreported.

Past discussions with the building managers had revealed that they only maintained the facilities, collected the rent, and paid the smaller bills. They were not involved in the Fuller/Merriweather insurance schemes or filing taxes and financial reports. The managers, other than Roscoe, received a base salary and a bonus based on the percentage of the property rented. Mrs. Merriweather paid major bills like salaries, mortgages, utilities, and taxes.

Gordon arrived late in the afternoon and asked, "What have you found?"
"How was your flying?" asked Amelia.

"Excellent. Roger Sandstone is a top-notch instructor. You?"

"First, I have proof that they're overstating the value of the buildings by comparing the county data with the tax forms. This enables them to pump up the depreciation numbers and decrease taxable earned income."

"Mia, I hate to admit this, but I'm not sure what depreciation is."

"No problem, you're in good company. Depreciation is the theoretical loss of value of a physical asset, like a building, over many years. It's entered into the books as an expense."

Gordon was puzzled. "But many properties increase in value, don't they?"

"Yes and no. You must consider inflation and can only depreciate the building, not the land."

"Is that important?"

"Yes, they've aggressively assigned the land a lower value to cheat and pump up depreciation. They use the bookkeeping expense of depreciation to offset taxable income."

"Who is doing this?" he asked.

"I guess that it's Roscoe Fuller and the Merriweathers. Tax cheating is a tiny leap if they're willing to kill their customers for income."

Gordon looked pensive. "I suppose so. What about Virginia Wickens?"

"I don't think she's involved. The other three decide what they want to pay in taxes and make the depreciation, expenses, and income reported fit their decisions."

He nodded. "Ginny is a nice young lady. I hope we can rule her out."

"Me too. Ratchet found nothing suspicious on her laptop. We'll check her file cabinet at some point. I expect we'll find she files the bills and payments for each company."

"What about Mrs. Merriweather?"

"She is up to her neck in this; she's a tax cheat. Her husband signs all the forms, but she prepares them. They're very clever. They make small tax payments; only an extensive audit would show their crimes."

He asked, "What can we tell the FBI?"

"Not much. We need someone like Virginia to testify about the fraud."

He said, "But you don't think she's involved, right?"

"No. However, Ginny might have overheard something that proves the cheating. What if the Merriweathers talked about how much tax they'd pay, or she overheard them plotting with Roscoe Fuller on the phone?

Rhodes has become very chummy with Virginia. She's his local girlfriend."

"Besides the one in New York?" Gordo questioned.

Mia smiled. "Yes, and one in Washington D.C. He's single and playing the field."

Gordon said, "Maybe he can get her to turn on her bosses. We still have the problem of who is a murderer and who isn't. We know Roscoe is in the middle of serious crimes and multiple felonies. What about the bugs? What are they telling us?"

"My parents are combing through all the conversations. Mr. M. spends most of his time on the phone selling new policies. Mrs. M. handles all the banking and finances. Virginia completes the smaller payments, mostly by mail. I think it is time to confront Virginia Wickens with the truth and get her on our side."

"Then what?" asked Gordon.

"For starters, she could tell us when both of the Merriweathers will be away from the office, and myself or Ratchet could get the QuickBooks and other self-filling passwords. It's tricky since we must ensure the financial institution won't call her phone to confirm our identity."

"How will you do that?"

"We have to watch the video while she logs in and see if she has to use her phone. I've confirmed that her QuickBooks account does not."

"Who talks to Virgina to convince her?"

"You and me, big guy. We can tell the truth and play the Fuller conversation with the hitman – that should do it."

"When do we go?"

"When the Merriweathers leave for the day. If she doesn't leave with Mrs. M., it takes Ginny about fifteen minutes to close the office. We can track her boss's cars to ensure they aren't returning."

At five o'clock, Robert was the last Merriweather to drive away from the building. Gordon and Amelia walked around the hallway and entered his offices.

Mia spoke, "Hi, Virginia. I'm Amelia Talbot, and this is Gordon Strong. We also work for Talbot Security. Could we have a few minutes of your time? It's very important."

While turning off the coffee pot, Virginia said, "I suppose so. Is it about our security?"

"Yes, in a way," Amelia responded. "A few weeks ago, two crooks came to my home and tried to kill me."

"Oh, my God, that's awful. Why did they do that?" asked the secretary.

"Gordon and I have found out that an insurance company was paying them to collect on my policy."

"More than awful. Who would do such a thing?"

"Miss Wickens, my home is in Virginia, and the company is Mutual Assurance of Virginia."

"MAV? That's one of our companies," said the secretary.

Amelia nodded. "Yes, it is. While chasing one of the assassins, who ran off the road and killed himself, I found these folders in his car. These are copies; we gave the originals to the police."

Virginia looked through the folders. "I see. One is for you, and the other is for Mr. Strong."

"Exactly, so I drove to North Carolina to meet Gordon and see if he was part of the murder plot or another intended victim."

"Oh no, Miss Talbot. Don't tell me he is also one of our customers."

"Yes, I will tell you that. It took us several hours to discover that Gordon's reverse mortgage and life insurance were under the same corporate umbrella."

Virginia was distressed. "I'm afraid to ask. What was his company?"

"Northeast Assurance Association. Also, one of yours."

"Yes, it is, but we would never do such a thing. The Merriweathers are two of the most considerate and honest people I've ever met."

Mia frowned. "I can prove to you that they're committing wholesale tax fraud. Would that change your opinion?"

"I suppose so, but they would never harm our customers."

"Virginia, how about your CFO, Roscoe Fuller? Do you think he's capable of murder?"

"That creep! Nothing would surprise me; he makes my hair stand on end."

"We have a recording of him hiring a hitman to murder us again. I'll play the tape, and you tell me if you hear Roscoe's voice."

Gordon played a .wav file on his phone.

Virginia said, "Oh, my God, that's him! I need to tell the Merriweathers right away."

"No, not so fast," said Amelia. "We don't know if they're aware of these killings. We need to monitor them to see if they talk about or discuss them with Roscoe Fuller."

"Miss Talbot, what do you want me to do?"

"First, you need to know you're in a perilous situation."
"Why is that?" the secretary asked.
"The FBI is investigating Southeast Assurance Company and your subsidiaries for tax fraud. If they find you're involved in that, or you lie to them about your work here, you could end up in jail."
Wickens sobbed, "That would be terrible."
"Yes, it would. We need your help to prove or disprove your bosses' participation in the murders."
"I don't see what I can do."
"You can tell us when they both are out of the office for lunch so we can scan their laptops. We've seen that they bring them in the morning and take them home at night."
"That's correct," Virginia affirmed.
"We need to look for evidence that will clear them of the killings. You need to keep quiet about us looking at their laptops."
"I don't know if I can do that."
Gordon jumped in, "Virginia, you're possibly in a heap of trouble. If the FBI proves you knew or even should have known about the tax fraud and murders, you could end up in a federal prison for twenty years."
"But I'm innocent," she wailed. "I processed the mail and paid minor bills. I don't have anything to do with the taxes, let alone killing anybody."
Mia said, "Ginny, we believe you. Ratchet says you're a good person. You can prove it and help your bosses by letting us collect evidence."
Wickens, "This is overwhelming. I need to see if Herman agrees."
Amelia and Gordon said, "Herman?"
"Yes, Herman Rhodes. You call him Ratchet."
"Agreed," said Mia, "Let's call and see if he can meet you for dinner."

  Amelia arranged the dinner meeting, and she and Gordon returned to their rental home.
Amelia sipped a glass of red wine while discussing the day with her partner. "Gordo, the only way we will know about the Merriweathers' guilt is to bug their home – please develop a plan."
  Gordon took a pad and pencil to the kitchen table and wrote:
THE MISSION – Surveil the Merriweathers in their home
SENSORS REQUIRED – Audio only, voice-activated
INSTALLATION – Install on Wednesday when cleaners are at the house
MONITORING – Use my laptop
SECURITY – Surveillance known only to Mia and myself

Amelia read his notes and asked, "How do we place the sensors?"

"Well, the alarm will be off because of the two cleaners. We wear lab coats and say we are adding to the existing security system. You pick the sensors, and I'll place them while you engage the maids. We bug the kitchen, dining room, living room, and playroom or TV room. We don't bug their bedroom. I have my limits."

She questioned, "How do I engage the maids?"

"Ask them how long they've cleaned the house, whether they want more work, how much for the house we're renting, etc."

"OK, I get it."

Mia and Gordon placed their listening devices without a hitch the following Wednesday.

Chapter Twenty-three

SANDSTONE THE SUITOR – Gainsville, Florida

Roger Sandstone arranged the two table settings atop his hanger. He had agreed to take Strong, Rhodes, and Amelia to Nassau if she would join him for a business lunch at eleven o'clock. She came to his hanger office, and Gordon headed for their Gulfstream in preparation for the flight.

Mia smiled. "Good morning, Roger. What's this business lunch about?"

"Thanks for coming, Amelia. I have some things I'd like to go over with you. Perhaps we can do more business together."

She nodded. "I could use a nice lunch. I've been working long hours and sometimes think I'm being followed."

"OK, Amelia, we'll have a quiet lunch on top of my hanger, and I'll have security block the staircase."

"Roger, what's on the roof?"

"There's a covered viewing area left over from World War II. Ground controllers radioed taxi instructions to student pilots from it."

"Let's go," she said.

They climbed two flights of stairs, and she found a shaded twelve-by-twelve area with a table set for two. It had white linen, crystal glassware, and sterling silver tableware. One waiter poured them chilled water while another made a pink sauce.

Amelia sighed. "Roger, this is very nice. And the view of the hangers and airport is excellent."

"Yes, I like to come up here at sunset and sip some good scotch. I own all of this, by the way, this hanger, the ones on both sides, several aircraft, and the aircraft maintenance service."

"Good for you. Is that what you want to talk about?"

"Yes and no. I have similar properties in Orlando and Tallahassee."

"You've been a busy boy."

"I have, and I would like to expand to several more cities in Florida. But first, let's have our main course, peeled Dungeness crab legs in salmon sauce. I had the crab flown in from San Francisco, and George here makes a dipping sauce to die for."

She smiled. "Ummm...this is delicious. Do you dine up here often?"

"No. This is the first time and with an exceptional lady."

"Why, thank you, sir. What business do you want to discuss?"

"Ms. Talbot, I think you could provide security for my aircraft facilities, and you might want to invest in the new ones I'm targeting. I have a proven formula for buying old hangers, fixing them up, obtaining commercial loans to establish the services, and buying adjacent facilities. We could make a great team."

The waiters removed the chilled crystal cocktail bowls and placed duck pate finger sandwiches in front of Sandstone and Amelia.

"Oh my God, these are also wonderful," she said.

"Yes, my dear. The duck pate is from a farm in Lakeland, and the sourdough bread is from Boudin Bakery on the San Francisco Embarcadero.

"Ummm. Ummm. I can't get enough."

"You better save some room for the main course and dessert. Would you like some wine or iced tea?"

"Unsweetened iced tea, please."

"Mia, I haven't dated much because I worry that women are after my money. I'm worth over ten million and haven't met anyone I wanted to spend my life with until I met you. You're so beautiful and have your own finances."

"Hold it, mister. This is supposed to be a business lunch."

"Yes, but hear me out and try the Kobe beef steak cooked medium rare."

"Very delicious. I suppose you had it flown from Japan?" she kidded.

He chuckled. "No. From a special farm in Kansas. Amelia, this could be our life. I have so much more to offer you than your Army man."

"Roger, I like you very much, but ours is a business relationship. Gordon and I have been through a lot together, and he makes me feel safe and secure. Are you an expert with guns?"

"No, not really."

"Do you exercise daily and keep your body in tip-top physical shape?"

"No, can't say that I do. But I'm good in the sack if you know what I mean."

She thought, *Life with Gordon is a partnership where he'd be content for me to lead if I wanted to. Life with Sandstone looks like he would be the dominant partner, and I would be a trophy wife. On the other hand, we could fly to New York for a Broadway show or overseas on a whim. Gordo would consider those as financially wasteful. Face it, Mia, Roger wants you, but Gordon needs you.*

She blurted, "Gordon needs me."

"Amelia, you're making my point. Why do you need a broken-down soldier when you can have a brilliant captain of industry? Dump the basket case and give me a try. You won't be disappointed."

She took his hand. "Roger, I'm very flattered, but Gordon and I are already a fighting team."

"How's that?"

"It's a long story and part of an insurance scam. Merriweather and his CFO, Roscoe Fuller, are killing their customers and reaping the insurance money."

"Mia, I find that hard to believe. I've known the Merriweathers for several years. They're respected members of our community and support several charities."

"Like I said, it's a long story. They have office buildings in several states and insurance or reverse mortgage customers. They cheat on all their taxes and pick a few clients to murder yearly for immediate revenue. I have the proof; we've been surveilling them for the past few months."

"Well, there you go. Take that to the authorities and be done with it."

"Dear Roger, you don't understand. How we surveilled Fuller in Saratoga Springs and the Merriweathers is questionable."

"Jeez, Amelia, you could be in a lot of trouble. Dump the weightlifter, and I'll get you the best lawyers money can buy."

"Roger, I can't. I love Gordon. You and I can only be friends. But this strawberry parfait is to die for. Oops, bad choice of words."

The waiters cleared the dessert dishes and began strumming guitars and singing love songs in Spanish. Roger held Amelia's hand and went for his closing argument.

"Amelia Talbot, I've been smitten by you from our first meeting. We are both successful business people, so let's do business."

She hesitated. "What do you mean?"

"I will contribute one hundred thousand dollars to your favorite charity if you agree to date me. I believe you will see me in a better light after you give me a few chances."

"That's ridiculous. You want to pay me to spend time with you?"

"No. I know your time is precious, and I can keep you safe. I want to show you how valuable you are to me. There's more. If you marry me, I'll establish a million-dollar trust for you, free and clear. It's yours whether you stay with me or not."

She pouted. "Again, ridiculous. I've never heard of such a thing!"

"Amelia, yes you have. In olden times, your father might have given me a dowry. I'm a modern thinker and offering you a reverse dowry."

Mia took her hand back. "Roger, I'm sorry. You're very inventive, that's for sure. You are nice-looking, and I might be tempted in another situation. This was a lovely lunch. You have made me feel exceptional. For that, I thank you. However, from now on, we must stick to our business arrangements."

"You're sure?" he questioned.

"Very sure. I'll install a security system for you at no cost for your evaluation. If you like it, you can pay a monthly lease."

Roger called the waiters to the table and handed each one a couple of Ben Franklins. Then, he walked her downstairs to her car and opened the door.

Roger motioned for Amelia to lower her window. "Miss Talbot, I want to share my life with you and no other. Tell me, do you plan to have children someday?"

"Yes, I do."

"Good. Please think about all I can do for those children - nothing but the best schools and medical care. Besides that, I will add a million dollars to your trust for every child we have."

"Roger, you're too much! I thought you said there could be no sex?"

"I did. We could go to a fertility clinic if you find me so repulsive. But the natural way would be way more enjoyable."

"Don't put yourself down. You're an attractive man."

"There you go. I exercise in a gym, play golf and tennis, and swim at my country club. Please think about my offers. I've made them to no other woman."

She replied, "Like I said, I don't see us together, but I'm very flattered. Thank you for lunch."

"Mia, if you change your mind, you know where to find me. I'm going to change into my flying clothes. I see no need to share this with Gordon Strong."

She nodded. "I agree."

Chapter Twenty-four

DISCOVERIES IN NASSAU – Paradise Island

Amelia, Gordon, and Ratchet landed in Nassau onboard the Talbot G100 jet. After clearing customs, they drove to Paradise Island and entered the Meriweather condo. Mia had rented it for the minimum period - a week. Ratchet cracked a closet safe open while the other two searched for another. They found a second hiding place under a kitchen cabinet and a false floor. The two men inventoried the stash while Mia ordered lunch. Roger Sandstone was still at the airport, preparing their aircraft for an afternoon flight back to Gainesville.

There were nearly two hundred thousand dollars on the kitchen table and a .38 caliber revolver. Amelia had Ratchet put a hundred grand back in the hiding places. Then she opened the handgun cylinder and emptied the shells into a plastic bag. After she used her laptop to test access to the Merriweather Nassau bank accounts, they ate lunch.

Amelia said, "Our plan is on track, but we still don't know if the Merriweathers are murderers. Hit teams one, two, and three have been neutralized. But are there teams four, five, and more? We're not sure."

Gordon spoke through a mouthful of fried chicken, "Mia, what do we do with this money and the gun?"

"Gordo, we take them back to home base. Ratchet, are you sure you haven't found any accounts for the killing teams?"

"No, Amelia. I can show you large payments to Roscoe Fuller but no accounting entry to other people."

She replied, "Hmmm. Maybe our proof is buried in a small file or even encrypted."

The hacker responded, "It's possible. I've reviewed all the bank account transactions, Excel files, and Quicken receipts and payments. OK for me to pull $20K out of this one hundred?"

"Yes," Amelia agreed.

Gordon queried, "Mia, what do we do about their taxes?"

"We find a way to leak them to the FBI. Virginia Wickens might be willing to help with that. She's in the middle of a rat's nest that may land her in jail. They use Turbo Tax business software; we now have the login info. The printed copies prove they're tax cheats, so we can make a case for the FBI and IRS to discover."

"What cheating can we prove?" queried Rhodes.

"First, they understate the value of their land and overstate the buildings' value, pumping up their depreciation deductions. Second, they underreport revenue from rents, insurance policies, and reverse mortgage property sales. Third, they overstate all their expenses and payments."

"Is it that simple?" asked the hacker.

"Yes, if you're crooks and thumb your nose at the IRS, the agents are hard-pressed to find all the cheaters. I expect Merriweather's companies to pay a minimal state income tax everywhere but Florida. Then, they run all the profitable transactions through the Florida corporation, Southeast Assurance, and pay a minimum federal income tax. I can't prove it yet, but I bet the skimmed cash in our duffel bag is from their five buildings, and Roscoe Fuller does the same with his three."

Rhodes whistled. "Pretty slick. They have been doing this for years without getting caught."

She said, "Yes, the key is don't get too greedy. Only kill a few customers in different states and look legitimate with the office building real estate. Someone diabolical put all these pieces together."

Gordon commented, "The second building purchased was in upper New York, which makes it Roscoe Fuller, Rivers, or both."

She replied, "I think it's the latter. The hairdresser said Roscoe had the money and Rivers had the brains."

"And you think Rivers is dead?" asked Ratchet.

She responded, "It's possible. Once Roscoe Fuller knew how the scheme worked, he didn't need Johnny. He was already killing customers, so what's the problem with one more body?"

"How do the Merriweathers fit into this story, Mia?" asked Gordon.

Amelia pursed her lips. "I think they were recruited to manage the Gainesville building. Rivers and Fuller probably had criminal records. Robert Merriweather was a small-time grifter and failed salesman but not a felon. The LLC founders used Robert as a frontman for insurance licenses and property purchases. They're murdering people in several states while he plays civic leader in Gainesville."

Rhodes stated, "Then there must be a connection from Robert to Roscoe because Merriweather maintains the Excel list of customers. Someone must use that list to pick the next targets."

Amelia thought momentarily and snapped her fingers, "That's it; Rivers is the Big Boss who selects the customers for the killing teams. He's alive somewhere and in hiding."

They landed at Gainesville's Regional Field, and Mia left the cash and revolver hidden under a seat in their plane. After clearing customs, she, Gordon, and Rhodes drove to their rental house and met with the older Talbots.

Amelia's father hugged her and exclaimed, "How did it go in the Bahamas? No, on second thought, don't tell your parents how it went. We're happy to see you back in one piece."

"It went fine, Dad. Our next move is to ID all the Merriweathers' financial accounts and creditors.

"Mia, your mother and I are uncomfortable with all this breaking and entering."

"Fine, you can stay in our offices. With Virginia's help, we have the passwords for the Quicken Books files that Ratchet had already transferred to our computers. You and Mom can sift through and list all the sources of income and expenditure accounts. Look for two sets of books, the actual numbers and the second for tax purposes."

Amelia spent the night doing a deeper dive into the company tax forms. She evaluated six years of unfiled accurate tax forms and phony, illegally filed counterparts for each state business and the Florida corporation. Mia estimated that the Merriweathers and their conspirators were skimming nearly one million dollars a year from taxes due and unpaid. They cheated in every way imaginable.

The tax forms didn't show how the Assurance companies lied, cheated, killed, and stole from their unsuspecting customers and their heirs. Both of their schemes, reverse mortgages and purchasing life insurance policies, were in their infancy and nearly unregulated. Their customers signed long, difficult-to-read contracts that favored the Merriweather companies and stripped customer heirs of any rights to recover increases in property value or any portion of their parents' insurance payouts.

As Amelia and her team pieced together the scandalous and illegal conduct, it was clear that the Merriweathers were up to their necks in contract and tax fraud, but it was not conclusive that they knew about the murders. Ratchet had voice-to-text software monitoring their office discussions and never found the words: "kill, murder, eliminate, harvest, or rub out."

Dorothy also sifted through Robert and Patricia's personal income taxes. She found they paid themselves a decent salary but reported less. Also, they took outrageous phony deductions for property taxes, sales taxes, offices in their home, car expenses, and their daughter's private school tuition, claiming "special needs." The Merriweathers illegally ran many personal expenses through the company's books. Their entertainment, golf, tennis club, and travel were deducted as marketing costs. They funneled all their auto expenses through their two companies and double-deducted them on the federal returns. There were also other suspicious deductions for furnishings that were probably for the Merriweathers' household. So, the question remained: were tax cheats Patricia and Robert also murderers?

Two weeks later, Gordon Strong had the answer. He played a recording from Merriweather's kitchen for Amelia.
They could hear Patricia questioning her husband. "Robert, what's wrong? You seem preoccupied and not yourself lately."
"Pat, I've been struggling with a terrible reality since we went to the insurance convention in Pittsburgh."
"So, it's not about the row you had with your father?"
"No, it's the conversation I had with Richard Pritchard."
She said, "The actuary dude?"
"Actuary software developer, you should say. I gave him an Excel download of the policies and mortgages we collected for five years."
"Why did you do that?"
"Because it seemed to me that we were collecting at a statistically faster rate than I expected. Some of our customers were seniors, but most were middle-aged or younger. Yet one or two passed away in each state like clockwork. I asked Pritchard to use his software to evaluate our results."
"What did he say?" Pat asked.
"Sweetheart, get your coffee and sit down. Good, what I'll say to you can't be repeated."
"Bobby, why all the mystery?"
"Because actuary predictions are always spot on, barring wars, regional disasters, and pandemics. You can take a particular grouping by age and geographic location and know with certainty how many will die."
She looked worried. "Were our numbers different?"

"Not just different, Pat. Our customers are dying at a rate four times what his software predicts."

"Which means what? I'm confused."

He declared, "The policies and reverse mortgages we closed out are statistically improbable, if not impossible."

She frowned. "Robert, how can that be?"

"I don't know, but I felt in my gut that it was happening. Then Pritchard called me yesterday and lowered the boom. He had plotted the deaths by state and said it was not randomly possible to have the results we were having."

"What does that mean?" she asked.

He said, "It means that someone is pulling the strings and spreading out our customer deaths by state, by county, and the insurance companies involved."

"Robert, you're scaring me. Are you saying Roscoe or the Big Boss are making these deaths happen?"

He shrugged. "Someone is, and it's not God. Our customers are dying so that neither the state authorities nor their insurance companies see red flags and investigate. Also, according to Pritchard, our accidental death rate is ten times what his software predicted."

"Bob, honey, what do we do? The cops will think we're involved because of our creative tax filings. One way or the other, we go to jail. Who will take care of Amber?"

He shook his head. "I know, I know, but it's worse than that."

"Worse than murder? How could that be the case?"

He sighed. "Patricia, when we started with Roscoe Fuller, he warned me that the penalty for our family stepping out of line would be severe. He said the Big Boss had no hesitation in using torture and murder to enforce his authority."

"Oh my God, does that also mean our daughter?"

"Yes, I think it does," he replied.

She was angry, "Then how could you get us into this situation?"

Robert responded, "Sweetheart, remember we were living in a trailer and selling chain letters. We barely had enough cash for food and diapers. Our backs were against the wall, and we planned to sneak out of Fort Wilderness owing money to Disney World."

She agonized, "Yes, that's all true, but what a mess we're in, damned if we do and worse if we don't."

"I know. I agree, and a recent conversation with Roscoe just made it worse."

"How's that?" she asked.

"I called him late at night and confronted him about his so-called actuary. He was drinking heavily and slurring his words. I mentioned that our revenues were down. What he said was chilling."

"Bob, what, what did he say?"

"He said, 'Don't be a Nervous Nelly. We'll have nearly a million coming in soon. Pat, how could he know that?"

Patricia was sobbing, "Robert, you have to fix this. We can't lose our family. We have worked so hard to get where we are: a nice home, a good school for Amber, and a respectable standing in our community. It's all in jeopardy because of Roscoe and the Big Boss."

"You're right. We either have to run away and leave all this behind or go to the police with our suspicions."

She said, "What about Pritchard? Could he blow the whistle?"

Robert said. "He could. I asked him to give us a month to figure this disaster out."

Chapter Twenty-five

MERRIWEATHER, MAN IN THE MIDDLE - Gainesville

The following morning, Robert drove to the Southeast Assurance Building and walked south into the forested arboretum. He sat on a bench, sipping his coffee while reviewing his life and current problems.

He thought, *How did I get in this mess? I wanted status and money, but fudging our taxes was not a good choice. Roscoe pushed us further and further until we couldn't claim to have made some honest mistakes. No, we are outright frauds and owe millions to the Feds and seven state governments. How can we prove we aren't murderers? We collected and pocketed the revenue. Roscoe Fuller is the key to unlocking all of our misdeeds. He knows what's happened and works with the Big Boss. What was the name of Roscoe's partner? Johnny something, we never met him. Jonathon Rivers, that's it – it's on the LLC papers. I wonder if he knows what Fuller is doing. Or is he directing the killings? I know Roscoe is deathly afraid of his partner.*

Robert thought about his childhood and that he had never got along with his father, Fred Merriweather. Fred expected his only son to become a steelworker. Robert was not mechanically inclined and announced at his five-year-old birthday party that he planned to attend college. Although Bob had one job after another from twelve and older, Fred didn't respect him or encourage his high school studies. When his son was seventeen, Fred took him to the steel factory and promised him an apprenticeship in the mold foundry. He wanted Robert to follow in the footsteps of his father and grandfather. Fred had advanced to foreman of the ingot-pouring crew and was an active United Steel Workers union member. What was good enough for him was the correct choice for his son.

Fred was a tough old man who had joined the Navy at seventeen and fought on cruisers during World War II. An uncle sponsored a coveted apprentice position for Mr. Merriweather after the war. He retired with a respectable monthly pension and lifetime medical benefits for himself and his wife. Unfortunately, Mrs. Merriweather died of heart disease after only a few years of retirement.

Bob Merriweather turned down the apprenticeship and received a modest scholarship to the University of Pittsburgh. He lived at home and worked two jobs to pay for his tuition and books. In his sophomore year, he met Patricia Marks, who cleared tables at the Student Union cafeteria. She lived at home and paid her way through college. They had a lot in common as she was also a Catholic. Pat was cute, energetic, smart, and enjoyed their steamy sessions in the back seat of Robert's sedan. During their senior year, Patricia got pregnant, and Bob's mother helped her mother put on a family wedding. Patricia later had a miscarriage and graduated with an accounting degree - Robert's was in Business Administration. His dad predicted it would never get him a decent job, and he was somewhat correct. Merriweather struggled with jobs that bored him or were beyond his technical talents.

The latest "row" with his father happened at the Red Chicken restaurant. While at the insurance conference in Pittsburgh, Robert and Patricia took his retired father to the eatery, where Fred had taken the family once a month for decades. Robert ordered the "Leg and Wing Special" for his father and himself and two thighs for his wife.
His father exploded, saying, "What, is she too good for our family? We always get the wing special. What's her problem?"
"Dad," replied Robert, "She likes the thighs more."
"Yeah, and they cost more!" shot back his Dad.
"Not to worry, Dad. We can afford it."
"Son, it's always been good enough for this blue-collar family. Working at the mill, I put a roof over your head, clothes in your closet, and something for the Sunday offering. I don't understand what you two do or how you make money."

Robert realized that since his mother's death, his Dad was becoming even more set in his ways and hard to get along with.
Patricia responded to his father, "Mr. Merriweather, Robert is in charge of a company that buys insurance policies and funds reverse mortgages. He's had great success. We own office buildings in eight states and have over 1,000 customers."
"Ha!" replied his father. "I got the paperwork for one of those reverse mortgage things. It was a mumble jumble of legal BS that made no sense. I figured out that it was a complete scam. The company could take over my house if I left or died and get all the increase in value instead of Robert and his sisters."
"Dad, what was the name of the company?"
"I don't know, it was a rip-off, and my son is probably a rip-off artist cheating hard-working folks like me."

Robert disagreed, "Dad, with a reverse mortgage, you get to live in your home nearly for free the rest of your life. It can be a good deal for both sides."

"Son, I don't believe you. I saw on TV that Congress wants to regulate your industry because of all the cheating."

Robert nodded. "That may be, but our companies live up to the contracts we sign. I'm proud of what we do."

Now, sitting in the quiet, peaceful small forest listening to the bird calls, Robert thought, *Damn me for involving Pritchard. Pat and I now know something is seriously wrong with our business. We can't deny it. If Roscoe and/or the Big Boss are killing customers, how fair are our contracts? Probably not at all. What are we going to do? If we run, either the police or the bad guys can likely find us, and we end up in jail or dead. Amber, we have to protect Amber as our first priority. We could send her to some relatives on the West Coast. It would break her heart to leave us and her friends at school, but it might keep her alive. We could fight Roscoe and his partner, but that means we'd become murderers. We can't just turn them in without exposing ourselves to many years in jail. Damn, when we started down the slippery slope of tax fraud, it was the wrong thing to do. Stupid, stupid, stupid, just like your Dad thinks you are.*

Robert went to his third-floor office and started his daily prospecting for new customers. He resolved that during the day, he would review Assurance's customer contracts and confront Roscoe Fuller with Pritchard's results.

Patricia tried to talk to him about their predicament during the day, and he whispered, "Wait until we get home."

After reading the contracts, he decided his father was correct. Even Robert could not understand what all the clauses were about. The customer had no rights except arbitration with a legal firm selected by Southeast Assurance.

Roscoe Fuller answered his cell phone at half past one in the afternoon. "Fuller here, to whom am I speaking?"

"Roscoe, it's Robert Merriweather. We need to have a serious conversation. I learned something at the Pittsburg Insurance Conference that has me very worried."

"Robert, you worry too much. I keep telling you that. What's this about?"

Merriweather, "It's your actuary. I think he is completely wrong about our collections."

"Why do you think that?"

"Roscoe, I met a man at the conference selling actuary software. I provided him a spreadsheet with our collected insurance and mortgages. His software computed that our odds were all wrong."

Roscoe, "Hold it, Merriweather. Why in the hell would you do that?"

"Well, I've always been concerned that your actuary doesn't know what he's doing. Who are you using?"

"Robert, it is a local, well-respected law firm. Do you still have that phone I sent you?" inquired Roscoe.

"Yes."

"Activate it, and go outside, not in your car. I will call you in twenty minutes."

Robert followed Roscoe's directions and returned to his bench seat in the arboretum.

The phone rang. "Robert Merriweather."

"Robert, it's Roscoe; tell me exactly where you're located."

"I'm sitting on a bench on one of the paths."

"Is there anyone around that can hear us?"

"No, I don't think so."

"Fine, don't use your speaker phone. Now, who is this genius that got you so upset?"

"His name is Richard Pritchard."

"Where's he from?"

"Philadelphia. You can find his website at online actuary dot com."

"Robert, exactly what did he tell you?"

"He said we are collecting at four times the normal rate, and our AD&D is ten times the normal rate."

"I see. Anything else?"

"Yes, he warned me that when you review all eight of our states, it isn't statistically possible to have the same rate of deaths in each state."

"Robert, you didn't give him our customer lists, did you?"

"No, just the collections data."

Fuller cackled. "So, the guy is an idiot. He would have to know how many customers we have in each state to generate accurate data."

"Roscoe, I can send it to him if it will help."

"No! No, you won't do that! If you do, you're fired. These guys try to stir the pot to sell their products. I will call him and set him straight."

"So, I don't have to worry about it anymore?"

"Not a bit; I will take care of it. You won't have anything to do with Pritchard again. Do you understand?"

Robert answered, "Yes, I understand."

"Good, we've got a excellent thing going here, Robert. In five more years, we'll be multi-millionaires. Focus on that."

"OK, I will."

Roscoe, "If you have any more questions, ask me first. Otherwise, I'll get someone else to do your job."

"Roscoe, I don't want that. I need the money."

"Don't we all. Get back to work."

Chapter Twenty-six

BAD NEWS AND VERY BAD NEWS – Gainesville

Amelia Talbot woke up before sunrise in the queen bed with Gordon Strong. She slid quietly out of bed, donned her slippers and bathrobe, and went downstairs to make her first cup of coffee. Mia was the only one awake in the house. Ratchet Rhodes was in New York. Her parents and Gordon slept while she opened the primary desktop computer in the dining room.

Amelia sipped her hot "Donut Shop" coffee while listening to the previous day's recordings from the Merriweathers' offices. Everything was normal until she heard Robert call Roscoe Fuller and challenge his actuary's advice. She realized Fuller had stopped the conversation and probably commanded Merriweather to use a burner phone outside the building. Hearing Robert cut Patricia off earlier had alerted Mia that something important was in the works.

While Gordon and her parents got breakfast in the kitchen, Amelia started listening to the Merriweathers after they got home from work the day before. She could tell their daughter was outside playing, and the parents were drinking their first glass of wine.

Patricia said, "Robert, how did your day go?"

"Not good," he answered. "I signed up only one new customer all morning. Thinking about what my Dad said about our contracts, my heart wasn't in it. Also, I could be putting new customers at risk for their lives."

She nodded. "How did your conversation with Roscoe turn out?"

"Again, not good. He was very cagy and wouldn't talk on a regular phone. Roscoe also was defensive about the predictions of his so-called actuary, who turned out to be a lawyer in his building."

"Did you tell him about Pritchard?"

"I did, and I think it shook him up. He hadn't considered someone looking at all our companies and giving an opinion."

"Did he admit what we are so worried about?" she asked.

"No. He got defensive and tried to downplay Pritchard's credentials without even knowing him. Oh, and he threatened to fire me if I have any further contact with Pritchard."

"Sweetheart, what do we do now?"

He said, "I wish I knew. I made some notes this morning while I had some quiet time. Now that we have well-founded suspicions, we can't ignore

our situation. Second, we must protect Amber at all costs. We can't have her injured or worse because of my stupidity."
She said, "Yes, I agree, but I don't know what to do."
"We must send her to the West Coast to live with your sister. If something happens to us, Marie and Harry can raise her."
"When do we do that?" she questioned.
"This weekend. Amber has school on Friday, and we send her on Saturday."
"I think she's too young to fly by herself."
"I know; you'll go with her and stay there until it's safe here."
"Robert, what are you going to do?"
"I'm not sure. We must stop the killing if that's what's happening. We need additional proof, and only the police can help us. We can't fight Roscoe and his partner and become murderers ourselves. It's a mess. The crimes, if they're what we suspect, are across state lines. We should probably go to the FBI. Maybe I could confront Roscoe and wear a wire. That would show we are innocent of the worst crimes."
She cried, "But the taxes, don't we go to jail for all the tax fraud?"
"Yes, probably. But maybe we can strike a deal, come clean, and pay restitution. Maybe I can take the blame, and you can stay with Amber in L.A."
"No Robert, I don't want to be apart."
"It may be the only way to keep my girls safe, and that's my highest priority. Please book your flights while I consider our next move."
"If you insist," she answered.
"I do."

Amelia had Gordon and her parents listen to the recording.
Henry exclaimed, "Good!" I like the Merriweathers; it's nice to know they aren't murderers."
Amelia nodded her ascent, "Dad, I agree. I'm not nearly as angry with them as I was before. They're two ordinary people who professional crooks have conned."
Dorothy questioned, "If they go to the police, does that affect us?"
Amelia hesitated. "Yes, it might. We need to get Ratchet back here, be ready to remove all our devices, and consider wiping our hard drives. I'll give him a call."

Mia called Rhodes, got no reply, and left a message for him to return to Gainesville ASAP. The Merriweathers went to work at their regular times and acted like it was just another day at the office.

During lunch, Robert called the FBI while sitting in his car, "FBI office, Gainesville, how can we help you?"

"Yes, my name is Robert Merriweather. I want to meet with an agent to explain several income tax violations and possibly a murder for money scheme I discovered."

"Can you tell us who is involved in the tax violations?"

"Yes, my wife and myself. I told her what to do, so I'm the one to blame."

"Thank you, Mr. Merriweather. And the murders, are you involved?"

"No, Ma'am, but I suspect one of my business partners."

"I understand. Can you come to our offices tomorrow morning at nine o'clock for an interview?"

"Yes, I can, thank you."

Robert called Patricia's cell phone. "Pat, please go somewhere private so we can talk. I'll call you in ten minutes."

Ten minutes later, he said, "Pat, where are you?"

"Bob, I'm alone in the Ladies' Room on the first floor."

"Good. Don't turn on your speakerphone. I just called the FBI and have an appointment tomorrow morning."

"Oh, are you sure about this?"

"Yes, I am. We need their help and protection. I feel very much relieved."

She sighed. "I guess that's a good thing. How are you going to prove you know what?"

"Good question. I don't have any texts or correspondence with the professional actuary. I need him to back me up. I'll call him now and see what documentation he can send me. I should be back at the office within an hour."

"See you then. I trust you, and I love you, Robert."

"Love you too."

An hour later, Merriweather entered his offices and barely acknowledged Virginia. He entered his wife's office and closed the door. He threw the unopened MacDonald lunch bag on her desk and sat next to it.

She was alarmed. "Robert, you look awful. What's happened? Your face is pale, and your hands are shaking."

He looked at the floor and shook his head, "I tried to reach Richard Pritchard."

"And?"

"He didn't answer, so I left a voicemail."

"So?"

"I decided it was an emergency, so I called his business number."

"Did you get him?" asked Patricia.

"No, his daughter answered."

"And?"

Robert said, "She was very distressed and crying."

"Why?"

"Her father was killed last night by a hit-and-run driver."

"Oh my God, Mr. Pritchard was killed?" asked his wife.

Robert, "Yes, it's more like he was murdered in front of a Walmart. A white truck accelerated through the parking lot and hit him at high speed. The police found the truck a mile away and determined it belonged to an employee working in the store. The killer stole it, and that's all the family knows."

"Bob, what did you do? What did you tell her?"

"I told her I was sorry to bother her and hung up."

"He's dead? You're sure?"

He gave her a sad look. "I'm sure, and I'm sure I killed him. I told Roscoe who he was and where he lived."

"Robert, you can't blame yourself. If that's what happened, you couldn't have predicted it."

"Yes, I could have if I thought about it. It gives me one more thing to have the FBI investigate."

She took his hand. "Can I help? What do you need to do?"

"Pat, you get ready for your trip. I'll stay late and gather some files for my meeting tomorrow. Please open all your file cabinets. That would be a help."

"Of course, I'll have dinner in the oven for you when you get home."

He sighed. "Thank you, sweetheart."

  Amelia left Gordon at the rental house and headed for the Talbot offices to work after an early dinner. The parking lot was empty except for Robert Merriweather's car. That was curious as he rarely worked after four or five o'clock. Mia started to enter the building when she realized that Merriweather was sitting in his driver's seat.

She approached his car and called out. "Robert, are you all right? It's almost dark. Are you arriving or going home?"

Talbot was concerned when she reached his open driver's window and saw his head slumped forward. There was a bullet hole above his ear, slowly oozing blood. She was shocked and nearly fainted as she grabbed his car door to steady herself. Mia looked around and saw no one in the parking lot or the streets. Her right hand shook as she checked his pulse. Then, she opened the door and took a picture of the crime scene.

As the evening shadows lengthened, Amelia panicked and thought, *If someone shot Robert, I may be next. I'm getting away from here and then calling 911.* She steered her car down East University Avenue and into the main library parking lot, where she backed it under the shadow of some trees.

Instead of 911, she decided to call Mrs. Merriweather and warn her. She heard, "Merriweather residence, can I help you?"

"Patricia, this is Amelia Talbot, your renter from the third floor."

"Yes, Miss Talbot. Is something wrong?"

"Yes, very wrong. I'm so sorry to be making this call. But I think you and your daughter may be in danger."

"How is that?" asked Patricia.

"Again, I'm sorry to tell you this. I just found your husband, Robert, in the parking lot of the building. Someone shot him in his car, and he's dead."

"Oh no! Oh my God!"

"I know it's terrible, but whoever did this may be after you and Amber."

Mrs. M. was panicked, "Amelia, how do you know that?"

"I don't for sure; call it intuition. If I were you, I'd grab my purse and daughter and leave town. I'm calling the cops next, and you can call me anytime for updates."

"I may do what you say."

Mia questioned, "Do you have a gun for protection?"

"I have a twenty-two in my purse."

"Good. I recommend you call me back with a new phone. Good luck."

Patricia said, "Oh Robert, what have you got us into? He was going to the FBI at nine o'clock tomorrow morning. Goodbye, Miss Talbot."

Amelia sat for a few seconds and called Agent Jake Finster's number.

"Jake Finster, here. Is this Amelia Talbot calling?"

"Yes Jake, I'm in Gainesville and terrified. I just found Robert Merriweather shot to death in his car in his building's parking lot. I looked for a suicide gun but didn't find one. I'm worried that Gordon and I may be on a hit list, so I moved to a safer location."

"Amelia, are you safe now?"

"Yes, I think so. I'm under the shade of some large trees in the Main Library parking lot. I'm going to call 911 next."

He replied, "I'll take care of that and send agents to the Assurance Building. As luck would have it, I'm also in Gainesville. You will have police protection in a few minutes. Please sit tight with your doors locked."

"Thank you, Jake. That makes me feel much better."

Amelia exited her car and searched under the fenders for a tracking device. It was under the front passenger's wheel well. She threw it down on the asphalt, stomped on it, and tossed it into a nearby trashcan. A Gainesville police "black and white" arrived with flashing lights. She asked the officers to accompany her into the library so she could use the ladies' room. Then, they returned to their cars, and the cops followed her to her rental house.

Gordon saw her enter through the front door and kidded, "Well, that was fast work."

"You don't know the half of it," she said. "I started to enter the building and saw Merriweather in his car still in the lot. I went over to check on him, and he was shot in the head and bleeding. I opened his door and looked for a pistol in case it was a suicide. There was no gun. That's when I really got scared. It was dusk. I was alone and unarmed. In other words, a sitting duck. I got the hell out of there and called Finster from the library parking lot. Did you know he's here in Gainesville?"

"No. I didn't. What would Jake be doing here?"

"Gordon, I'm not sure, but while I waited for my police escorts, I found a GPS tracker on my car and trashed it."

"You're saying Robert is dead?" he repeated.

"Yes, shot in the head, murdered. They won't find GSR on his left hand because I saw no gun. His window was down, and it was probably someone he knew."

Gordon replied, "Damn. Things are getting violent and murky."

"Yes, I felt I had to warn Patricia to take Amber and go somewhere safe until she can have police protection."

"Mia, you didn't mention the FBI investigation?"

"No, I didn't want to spook her and have her fly to Bahama or places unknown. But she already knew he was turning himself in and told me so. Damn. Do you think she might have done it? She has a .22 pistol and was very upset with Merriweather."

"Mia, I don't think so unless he had a huge insurance policy."

"Gordon, hold it; Finster is calling me."

"Jake, hello, and thanks for the police escort."

"Ms. Talbot, my pleasure. I need you and Gordon to come to our Gainesville office. Whatever you've been doing has stirred up a real hornet's nest."

"OK, Jake. We'll be there as soon as we can."

She said, "Gordon, he wants to talk to us. Do you think we'll need a lawyer?"

"Naw, Mia. Jake's a good friend and on our side."

"But what if the FBI has been spying on us, spies? They could have us on several infractions."

Strong assured her, "Then he will tell us, and we can straighten things out – not to worry."

They followed the Google Map directions on Mia's phone, and Jake met them on the building's front steps. Finster told Amelia he needed to take her evidence about finding Merriweather in company with a Gainesville Police detective. He had her sign a Miranda agreement and asked if she wanted a lawyer present.

She answered, "No, Jake. I think the situation is simple, except we don't know who's killing people."

"Good. Please state your name for the record."

"Amelia Rose Talbot."

"And your residence, please?"

"48 Promise Lane, Bumpass, Virginia."

Gordon went down the hall to talk to another pair of agents. Finster, "Thank you. Where are you staying here in Gainesville?"

"I'm in a rental home in the University Park area."

"Why were you going to the Southeastern Assurance Company Building this evening?" asked the Agent.

Be careful, Mia. If you lie to the FBI, it's about as bad as any crime you've committed.

"My company has rented offices there, and I had some work I wanted to finish."

"What type of work? What's your company's name?"
>*Keep it simple and honest.*

"I own the Talbot Security Company. We provide modern security systems to high-end customers."
>*All provable, only offer a bare minimum of info.*

"I see. What time did you arrive at the building?"

She said, "A little before six-thirty p.m. I looked at the time because I was surprised to see Robert Merriweather's car still in the parking lot."

"Why were you surprised?" asked Finster.

"Robert and his wife are usually on a strict timetable. She leaves at four thirty to pick up their daughter from school, and he usually is gone by five - I guess to have dinner with his family. We work odd hours and have never seen him in the building past five."
>*Slow down, Amelia, don't add your suppositions and conclusions.*

"Tell us what happened after you parked your car."

"I started into the building and saw Robert in his driver's seat. It was starting to get dark, but it seemed he was not moving, and I thought he might be asleep or passed out. So, I decided to investigate - to see if he needed any help."

"And what did you find?"

"As I approached the car, I said something like, 'Hey Robert, are you all right or just sleeping on the job?'"

"What happened next?" asked the detective.

"There was no answer or movement on his part. I started to feel creepy."

Finster said, "Miss Talbot, how do you mean creepy?"
>*How would you feel, Jake? These are folks involved in murders.*

"I started to get scared that something was not right – that he was hurt or passed out somehow."

He asked, "OK, what did you do next?"

"I went to his driver's window, which was down, and looked into the car."

"And what did you see?"

"Robert was bleeding from a small hole above his left ear."

"What did you think at that exact moment?"
>*Robert is dead, and I'm dumb not to have expected it.*

"I panicked and grabbed hold of his car door to avoid fainting. He was pale, and I thought he was dead from being shot in the head."

"I see. Did you touch the body?"
>*Sure, I always go around touching dead bodies.*

"Eh, no. Hold it, yes; I checked his neck for a pulse."
"In your opinion, was there a pulse?"

What a stupid question.

"No, he was dead."
"What hand did you use to check for a pulse?"

Jeez, Finster, what does it matter?

"Hmmm. Let me think. Probably my right hand."
"Did you get blood on your hand?"
"I'm not sure. I was in shock. Our landlord had been shot, and I feared I could be next."
He asked, "Why did you think you might be shot?"
"Well, you're aware of this attempt on my life a few weeks before, right?"
Finster ignored her comment. "Miss Talbot, when you found Mr. Merriweather, did you call 911?"
"No. I jumped in my car and drove away in case the killer was lurking in the shadows."

You should have been there. What would you have done, Jake?

He added to his notes. "Where did you drive to?"
"The downtown library parking lot where I backed under some trees and felt partially hidden."
"I see. Then, did you call 911 to report the incident?"

Incident. Incident? It was a murder, plain and simple. What's your problem?

"No. I decided to call the FBI and dialed you for advice and protection. You said to sit tight, and you would alert the local authorities."
Finster frowned. "Yes, Miss Talbot, that's correct. This will be the third death scene you've left recently. Don't you think that is unusual?"

Is this some kind of trap?

"Yes, Jake, I sure do. Two people came to kill me in Virginia and had accidental deaths. Today, I found our landlord shot in his car. I'm scared, extremely scared."
"Ms. Talbot, have you told us everything that happened at Mr. Merriweather's car?"
"Well, I think so. I was pretty shaken, like I said."
"Did you do anything more than what you told us?"

What's he driving at? Oh, oh, shit, if the FBI is looking at our camera transmissions, they saw me look for a suicide weapon and take Robert's picture.

"There's one thing. I wondered if Robert had taken his own life, so I opened the car door and looked for a gun. There was none. Also, I took a picture of the body."

"Amelia, why did you do either of those actions?"

Watch it, watch it, this is a trap!

"Jake, even in my shock, I was curious why this happened. I wanted a record of his positioning when I was there in case the EMTs and cops messed up the crime scene."

Finster, "In your opinion, was there any chance Robert Merriweather was still alive when you found him?"

We already covered this.

"No. He was not breathing and was cold to the touch. Like I said, there was no pulse, and he was very pale."

"Were his eyes open or shut?" asked the agent.

"I, I don't know. I didn't think about that. Maybe my picture will reveal that. I'll send it to you."

"No, Ms. Talbot, we will need your phone. Do you have it with you?"

Good thing I left it in the car.

"No, I left it back at our rental house."

Damn! He gets my phone, he has my emails and texts to Gordon, Rhodes, Mom, and Dad, and can trace our travel. This isn't good – not good at all.

"Amelia, Ms. Talbot, is it true that you once said you would grind the Merriweathers to dust?"

Danger! Danger! Danger! When the FBI asks if something is true, they already have the proof. If you say no, they have caught you in a lie. Say yes, and they start building their case. Have they been monitoring us while we monitored the Assurance companies? Shit, we may be in big trouble.

"Jake, if I ever said anything like that, it was just a figure of speech. I've never wanted to hurt any member of the family physically."

"But you're planning to bankrupt them. Is that correct?"

Damn! How does he know that?

She replied, "Gordon Strong and my family believe they're tax cheats and grifters. If and when we prove that, I imagine it would result in jail time and possibly bankruptcy."

Finster persisted. "Ms. Talbot, did you not recently say that when, quote, you are done with the Merriweather family, 'they will be sleeping in their car and begging for food', unquote?"

Jesus, I need a lawyer ASAP.

"Again, if I said something like that, it was just a figure of speech. I don't like your insinuations. You can continue this discussion with my lawyer. This interview is over."

Finster called for a female agent to collect Amelia's clothes and photograph her in her underwear. She stumbled out of the FBI office and into her car. Gordon was already there in the driver's seat.

She said, "How did it go with you?"

He laughed. "It didn't. They wanted me to sign a Miranda agreement, and I refused. After that, it was just name, rank, and serial number until they lost interest."

"Gordon, what kind of questions did they ask you?"

"They seemed to all be about you, Mia. I stormed out when they asked if you could have killed Robert."

"Yes. I'm scared. Finster had another agent and a local police detective in the room. I did sign the agreement. I testified about finding Merriweather, and then things turned ugly."

"How so?"

"Jake started asking questions that showed he had inside knowledge about our security team. Someone told him about our discussions, or the FBI has been listening to us."

"Who the hell would do that?"

Mia, "Not you and me. Not my parents. That only leaves Ratchet the hacker. The Feds may have something on him, and he has squealed on us. I told them I took a picture of Robert in his car, and now they want my phone."

"Damn, why did you do that? I mean, tell them?"

"Gordo, it struck me that they may be looking at our outside camera feeds. If so, they saw every move I made in the parking spot."

"What would be suspicious?"

"Well, taking the pic was sort of ghoulish, and I opened his door, looking for the gun to see if it was a suicide. Christ, I left fingerprints all over his car."

"But there was no gun, right?" he asked.

"Not that I could see. When the G-men get my phone, they'll see I called Patricia, and they already know I didn't call 911."

"Why didn't you call 911?" he questioned.

"I panicked and thought we might be next. It looked like a professional hit. I called Pat Merriweather and told her to take Amber out of town and lay low. She's up to her neck in the tax fraud, and they may be after her."

"They?"

"Gordon, I don't know who. It could be the big boss or a hit team. It could be Roscoe. We need to check on his whereabouts."

He asked, "Where do you think we should sleep tonight?"

"Good question. Let's get out of town, make sure we aren't followed, and find a hotel where we can pay cash. My parents should do the same. I don't want them to be collateral damage."

Gordon asked, "Is it time for us to go to Nassau? Are we going after the Merriweather accounts?"

"I don't know. Now I'm conflicted. With Robert gone, Patricia will need the money, and it could be one more felony the Feds can pin on us. On the other hand, we could go to their condo and clean out the rest of the cash, and it could delay my arrest if that happens."

He was surprised. "Do you think it will come to that?"

"It seemed like Finster and the detective wanted a suspect, and I was their first choice."

"I can call Roger and get us a flight for tomorrow."

"Not tomorrow. Try three or four days. Right now, our priority is to get out of Gainesville. See what he says, and I'll book the condo for a week. Gordo, can you open the safes?"

"Yup, Ratchet gave me the combination," Gordon replied.

Chapter Twenty-seven

FRIENDS AND ENEMIES – Jacksonville, Florida

Amelia and Gordon drove to Jacksonville and checked into a small hotel near the city pier. They bought a bottle of wine and some take-out food at a nearby deli and sat on their balcony watching the pool and beach activity. Mia placed another call to Ratchet but received no answer. She left word that Robert Merriweather was murdered, and they needed to pull all their sensors aimed at Southeast Assurance.

"Damn him!" She exclaimed. "You never know what he's doing or whose side he's on. Gordo, do you think he could have killed Robert?"

"Naw, I can't see any reason why he would, and he seemed like an OK guy to me. We know you didn't do it, nor did I or your parents. I think that puts the finger on Roscoe Fuller or his partner, Johnny Rivers. Merriweather finally realized how they'd used him and was going to the cops. They couldn't let that happen."

Amelia responded, "While you drove here, I texted the P-I up in the Springs. She said Roscoe is there, squiring one of his European proteges around town."

Gordon, "Yes, but he could have ordered the hit on Merriweather."

"I suppose so. I bet Roscoe and Mr. Big use burner phones to hide their conversations and decisions."

"It makes sense."

"Gordon, this is nice. It's a little vacation from Gainesville. Here we are, sipping our wine like a couple of tourists. Play your cards right, and you may get lucky tonight."

"Sounds good to me. Where did your parents go?"

"I don't know. I told them to get out of Dodge and use cash. They should call one of our burner phones tomorrow. Mrs. M. also has our number. We'll keep the phones off until tomorrow morning."

"Mia, what do we do about the sensors if we don't hear from Rhodes?"

"Good question. We can pull the ones from their house on Wednesday and follow the wiring for the others."

Strong looked confused. "How do you mean?"

"I've been thinking about it. We don't have to have Ratchet. We lift the false ceiling panels and trace the wires to find where he put each sensor. There are still some in the hallway that are wireless. We know where they are."

"I wonder how Virginia is doing," he said.
"Me too. If someone murdered my boss, I wouldn't come back to work right away."

Gordon called Sandstone and arranged a trip to the Bahamas in three days.

Mia took the phone. "Roger, do you know that Robert Merriweather was shot and killed yesterday?"

"What? No. Who would want to kill Robert? He's everybody's friend and helper."

"I don't know. All I know is I'm the one who found him, and now the FBI seems to be suspecting me."

"You? Mia, that's ridiculous; you wouldn't hurt a fly. You're the nicest lady I know. Won't the Feds get more suspicious if you leave the country?"

"They may or may not. I don't care. I want time to rest and think. Also, Gordon and I may be in danger. We are fending off the FBI that's trying to pin a murder on me and possibly hit teams from Robert's partners."

Roger said, "Why in the hell would you kill Robert? That makes no sense."

She responded, "I know, but I was first to find him, and I panicked. Then I did suspicious things like not calling 911, looking for the gun, and taking his picture."

"Amelia, what were you thinking?"

"It was getting dark, and I worried the killer or killers would go after me next."

"Sounds illogical - why would anyone want to kill you?" asked Roger.

"Like I said earlier, it's a long story."

"Amelia, come here to the hanger. I can provide around-the-clock security by armed guards."

"Thanks, but no thanks, Roger. Gordon and I are staying out of town for a while."

"OK, be safe, and I'll see you in a few days."

Amelia called Virginia Wickens in the Southeastern Building and heard, "Southeastern Assurance, Miss Wickens speaking."

"Virginia, this is Amelia Talbot. How are you doing?"

"Oh, Miss Talbot, it's terrible. Robert Merriweather was shot, and Mrs. Merriweather is missing."

"Virginia, I know something about that. I told Patricia and Amber to get out of town since Robert's murderer may also be after them."

"So, they may be OK out of town somewhere?"
"Yes, I'm pretty sure of that."
"Thank you, Amelia. That makes me feel much better. Sorry, I have some bad news for you."
"What's that?"
"Mr. Fuller called this morning and said you have broken the lease terms and must vacate your offices without delay."
"Virginia, we are out of town now. Can't you give us a few days?"
"I suppose so. I'm the only one here. What do I tell Mr. Fuller if he calls?"
"Tell him we are traveling and will vacate as soon as possible. Goodbye, and be careful, Ginny."
Gordon, "What was that about?'
"Roscoe Fuller finally smells a rat and has ordered us out of his building. We better go back to Gainesville tomorrow," said Mia.

Amelia and Gordon had dinner at a nearby French restaurant, watched TV, and made love before falling asleep. There was a sharp rap on their hotel door in the middle of the night.
Mia put on a robe and went to the door. "Who is it?"
"FBI, open the door."
She looked through the peephole and saw at least three agents wearing FBI vests and guns drawn. "What's this about?"
"Official business, Ma'am. Open the door, or we'll knock it down."
Amelia opened the door, and the tallest agent asked, "Are you Amelia Talbot?"
"Yes, I am."
"Miss Talbot, hold out your arms; I have a warrant for your arrest."
"You must be kidding. What's the charge?"
He placed handcuffs on her wrists. "You're charged with the murder of Mr. Robert Merriweather."
Gordon started to stir in the bed, "Huh? What the hell is going on?"
A second agent aimed a gun at him. "Hands in the air! Swing your legs toward me and get on the floor. Now, put your arms behind your back. Johnson, cuff him while I check these pillows. Hey boss, just as we suspected, there's a weapon under each pillow."
The tall man said, "Bag them and search the rest of the room."
A woman came forward and read Amelia her Miranda rights. She finished with, "Do you understand these rights?"

Mia replied, "Yes, but I'm not signing anything. Also, I need some clothes. Where are you taking us?"

The woman replied, "To the Jacksonville FBI office. I will help you after I finish with him," she said, pointing at Strong."

The agent then Mirandized Gordon and placed a robe over his shoulders and underwear.

Amelia was angry. "This is ridiculous. Call Agent Jake Finster from the Fayetteville office, and he will set you straight."

"That's good to hear," said the tall man. "He's waiting for you at our facility."

Mia thought, *Finster is after us. He must have a good reason to risk his friendship with Gordon. I'm not going to panic because they have no proof that I killed Robert. I might be a suspect, but there's nothing that ties me to the killing. They may have a weak case of Motive and Opportunity without Means. No bullet from Merriweather's head is going to match my Glock.*

Two hours later, Gordon Strong and Amelia Talbot were waiting in an interview room after being processed by the federal authorities. They'd been fingerprinted, photographed, and given their case numbers. Amelia was charged with murder, and Gordon as an accessory to a murder. They sat quietly in the room, knowing that any conversation would be recorded and used against them. Amelia had called her parents and requested they send the best criminal defense attorney in Jacksonville. Gordon used his call to warn Ratchet about their situation. He expected the hacker to cover up their other felonies.

Finally, Jake Finster and the same police detective from Gainesville entered the room.

Finster said, "When I talked to you two at my home, I asked you to let the FBI investigate the Merriweathers and their companies. Apparently, you ignored my advice and decided to move into their building and hand out the harshest form of punishment."

Amelia responded, "Agent Finster, Jake, we can't answer until our attorney arrives. Neither of us had anything to do with Robert Merriweather's death."

He replied, "Detective Granger, from the Gainesville police, doesn't agree."

Granger leaned forward, "Miss Talbot, you had a motive for revenge. You had proximity to the deceased. That we have on video. Your actions after committing the murder were suspicious, according to your own testimony."

She said, "I did not do it."

Show me the Means, you lunkhead.

"So, you say, during processing, both of you tested positive for GSR."

"I can explain that," snapped Mia.

"Miss, I'm all ears," responded the detective.

"We just got back from Gordon's house at Upchurches Pond, where we used his firing range."

Granger, "We will check on that. This morning, you both had loaded firearms. Do you have Florida permits?"

She said, "Our attorneys will respond to that question. Let me assure you that neither of our weapons was involved in this murder."

The detective smiled. "Miss Talbot, I agree with you."

Why would he roll over on that before testing our pieces?

Granger thumped an evidence bag on the table. "I believe we have the murder weapon right here."

It's not mine; what's the big deal?

The detective removed a .38 caliber revolver from the bag and held it up with a pencil in the barrel. "Does this look familiar to either of you?"

Amelia thought, *Shit, the only .38 we've seen recently was the one from the Bahamas. It can't be that one; it's still hidden on our plane.*

"Miss Talbot, would it surprise you to know we matched your prints on this gun only a few minutes ago?"

I'm being set up. If it is from the plane, my prints are on the gun and the bullets. Damn!

Finster again, "Amelia, we think the bullet that killed Merriweather came from this gun. Ballistics will have a report tomorrow or the next day. This is your chance to get ahead of the evidence and take a plea."

"Jake, where was that gun found?"

The detective pounced, "Even worse for you, missy, our officers found it in a trash can not far from where you parked at the library."

Now I'm scared. They may have motive, opportunity, and means wrapped up in a neat package with a bow on the top.

She flared, "I repeat, neither myself nor Mr. Strong had anything to do with Merriweather's murder. And those are our final words."

Detective Granger looked at Gordon, "Anything to add, Mr. Strong?"

Gordo shook his head. "Nope."

Finster escorted Mia and Gordon to separate holding areas. Each had a desk, a single cot with blankets, and a private toilet. Gordon figured the best use of his time was a good sleep and dozed off despite the overhead lighting. Amelia started using a pad and pen to plan her defense and comments to their lawyer. She was seething from the booking process. Their names and suspected crimes were entered into a permanent computer database. They were fingerprinted, and their DNA collected. An officer of the same sex did a full body search of each of the "criminals," but not a strip search.

The last comment from Finster was, "Thanks for coming to Jacksonville. You will be arraigned in federal court at ten o'clock tomorrow morning. The FBI has been monitoring your cross-state activities. We are taking over this case and may add other charges based on the evidence."

Mia had three pages of notes when she finally pulled a blanket over her head and fell asleep on the cot. At 0700, there was a breakfast of French toast, grapefruit, coffee, and milk. They were both taken to an interview room at 8 a.m. to meet their lawyer. Gerald Cushing looked the part of an experienced, successful criminal attorney. He wore a tailor-made pinstripe suit, a Gucci floral tie, a light blue French cuff shirt, and expensive patent leather shoes.

Cushing's first words were, "Mr. and Mrs. Talbot hired me as your defense lawyer. We will not go into detail here about your guilt or innocence. Remember, you're innocent until proven guilty. Do you have anything of value to give me so I can prove you retained me?"

Amelia answered, "They took our wallets and phones. We both have our watches."

"That will do. I will return them later when you're out on bail."

Gordon said, "How does this work?"

"Mr. Strong, we go before the arraignment judge, and the government reviews the charges. You both plead not guilty. Then we argue about bail and other restrictions."

"What kind of restrictions?" asked Amelia.

"If the government has a strong case, they can ask for remand, where you're in jail until the trial. If you post bail, they can request a house arrest and surrender of your passports."

She asserted, "They don't have a strong case yet."

"You're sure?"

"Yes, they need ballistic testing and lack any witnesses. I was the first to find the deceased, and all of my actions are on video - none of which includes firing a gun."

"I see. Your parents are ready to put up a large amount of bail for both of you. Gordon, where were you when Miss Talbot found the body?"

"I was at our rental house about a mile away."

"Was there any idea in your mind that she might kill the deceased?"

"None. She's not that stupid."

"Please explain."

Gordon explained, "Merriweather was shot in his car with his driver's window down, probably by someone he knew. Mia was aware of a video sensor in front of his car. Why would she commit such a crime in front of a camera?"

"The cops say you both had gun residue on your hands. Is that correct?"

Mia answered, "Yes, we shot several magazines at Gordon's indoor range in North Carolina two days ago."

"Excellent. Why do the cops think they have the murder weapon?"

Amelia said, "They found a .38 revolver in a dumpster near where I made the call to the FBI."

"Gordon broke in, "Here again, why would this brilliant woman ditch a gun where the cops would search?"

"Miss Talbot, do you own such a weapon?"

"No. Never."

"Do you have access to such a gun?" probed the lawyer.

"Yes and no. I'm aware of where one is hidden on our private jet. If the police have that one, it has my prints."

Cushing, "Whoa, you have a private jet?"

"Yes, my company does."

"Does the government know that?"

"I don't know."

"Mr. Strong?"

"Not that I know of. We thought we were working with Agent Finster, but I haven't mentioned it to him. And now it seems he's our adversary."

Cushing, "Hmmm...they will ask for ankle monitors and your passports if it comes up. Next question, do either of you have any outstanding warrants, even for traffic tickets?"

Amelia replied, "Not that I know of."

Gordon said, "Nope. Is that important?"

Cushing responded, "It can be. The authorities can keep you in custody based on existing warrants. It also demonstrates that you might be a flight risk."

They spent another hour discussing the reasons why they were armed, the possible attempts on their lives, and the general situation with the Merriweather companies. Cushing cautioned them to let him do all the talking at the bond hearing except for their plea. Then he excused himself to make a couple of phone calls. At the arraignment, Amelia and Gordon entered their not-guilty pleas. Then Cushing argued that they be released on bail.

**The Jacksonville U.S. District Courthouse, 300 North Hogan Street
Source: Google Maps**

He said, "Your Honor, contrary to how the government has portrayed these defendants as conspirators in committing murder, each is a decorated military veteran. Neither has a criminal record, and both look forward to clearing their reputation at the preliminary hearing."
Federal District Judge William Mudd, "You don't say. What is your recommendation on bail counselor?"
"Sir, I think one hundred thousand for each would be fair."
The Justice Department's attorney jumped to his feet. "Your Honor, we believe they should remain in custody. This is a capital case; we should have clinching evidence in a few days."

Judge Mudd frowned. "Does that mean you don't have it now?"

"Eh, no sir. We have a C-I, a Confidential Informant who has assured us that we'd found the murder weapon and Miss Talbot's fingerprints would be on it. He was right; they're on it."

Mudd, "So you do not have ballistics now. Is that right?"

"Technically, yes, I mean no, Your Honor. But we know the defendants had a grudge against the deceased, and Miss Talbot was the one who found him dead."

Judge Mudd scowled. "Counselor, we are not here to argue the case. Why do you think these two veterans will not attend the next proceeding?"

"Sir, they have the financial means to leave the country or return to their respective states of Virginia and North Carolina, where it could be difficult for us to find them."

"Cushing rose, "Your Honor. My clients' immediate plans are to remain here in Florida to help me prepare their defense. I need full access to them 24/7 to completely understand the actions of the deceased and my clients."

The Judge pointed at Amelia. "Miss Talbot, what military service did you perform?"

Mia stood. "Sir, I had two tours as a proud U.S. Marine. My test scores pushed me into the intelligence branch, and I served at Quantico and with the NSA at Fort Meade. After an honorable discharge as a Staff Sergeant, I worked on highly classified projects for the CIA and DIA. Ironically, I'm currently cleared Top Secret for forensic accounting with the FBI. I give you my word as a former Marine that I will attend all proceedings."

He replied, "Thank you for your service. Bail is set at $250,000. Mr. Strong, it's your turn."

Mia sat down, and Gordon stood. "Your Honor, I'm a major in the U.S. Army on medical leave from injuries received in Afghanistan and PTSD. I have a Ranger badge, a combat ribbon, a purple heart, and several other awards and commendations. I too, pledge on my honor as an Army officer to attend all proceedings."

"Good enough," said Mudd. "Bail is set at $200,000. Thank you for your service." He banged his gavel down, "Preliminary hearing two weeks from today. Dismissed."

Cushing shook hands with his clients. "My, that went well. You should be released this afternoon. Call my office, and someone will pick you up."

Chapter Twenty-eight

THE DEFENSE – Jacksonville, Florida

A car from Cushing's office picked up Amelia and Gordon at 3:30 p.m. in front of the FBI Building on Gate Parkway North. At Cushing's office, Amelia was relieved to reunite with her parents. They had rented rooms at the Downtown Marriot for themselves and the jailbirds. Her mother brought her a change of clothes. Gordon continued wearing the jumpsuit provided by the FBI.

Gerald Cushing's offices were on the fifth floor of the BB&T Building at Forsyth and Hogan, close to the Central Metro Station. He offered his clients sandwiches and coffee in his conference room. Mia's parents returned to their hotel.

Cushing, "Welcome to our law offices. This lovely lady taking notes is my wife, Alice. She is a certified paralegal. Your rights of confidentiality apply equally to both of us."

"Miss Talbot, did you know who killed Robert Merriweather?"

"No, I don't."

"Mr. Strong, did you know who killed Merriweather?"

Gordon, "Nope."

"Good. Now that we've got that out of the way, why does the FBI think you, Amelia, had a motive to kill him?"

"Mr. Cushing," she started.

"Stop, please call me Gerald or Jerry."

"Yes sir, Gerald, at one time, I was upset with the Merriweathers. I thought they were part of a plot to kill Gordon and myself."

He was surprised. "Really? Why did you think that?"

She shook her head. "Oh, my goodness, it's a long story."

Jerry Cushing smiled. "Start at the beginning. We have all night to counter the Fed's claims of motive."

"Yes sir. If we go back six months, a woman came to my house in Virginia and tried to kill me. She fell down my second-floor stairs and cracked her head open at the bottom. Before she died, she admitted that she was paid to kill me and make it look like an accident if possible."

Alice Cushing said, "My God, that's terrible. What did you do?"

"I called the sheriff's office and reported the attempted crime and her death. Then, I chased her accomplice's car on my motorcycle. It was dark. He missed a hairpin turn and hit a tree. I went to the car and found him dead. Two manila folders were in the car, one with my name and the other with Gordon's."

Gerald Cushing, "What was in the folders?"

"About an hour later, I looked at them and found personal data and pictures of each of us. The info included where we lived, our usual schedules, and activities."

Cushing, "What was your state of mind at that point.?"

"I was dumbfounded, scared, angry, and filled with curiosity. I thought, Who would want to kill me? And why? Who was this Gordon Strong? Was he another killer or an intended victim?"

The lawyer asked, "What did you do next?"

"I drove the cycle to Richmond, rented a room, and slept. I rented a car in the morning because the weather was bad and drove to Fayetteville, North Carolina. I tried to sneak into Gordon's house that night, but he caught me. After he read his folder, he swore to me that he was an Army officer and not a murderer."

Cushing pointed at the Army major. "Gordon, are Miss Talbot's words essentially true from your perspective?"

"Yes sir. I had some trouble believing Mia at first. It seemed unlikely that someone wanted us both dead. The next morning, we saw a local FBI agent, Jake Finster."

"Where was that?" asked Gerald.

"Jake lives on the other side of the Upchurches Pond, a lake near Fayetteville, North Carolina. He's a friend, and we golf together."

"What did you tell him?" asked Cushing.

Amelia replied, "I told him about the two assassins at my house, and we showed him the folders. None of us could figure out what was going on. Gordon and I returned to his house and spent several hours trying to see what we had in common that would make us targets. We reviewed our histories, education, military service, and recent travel and jobs – nothing clicked."

The lawyer pursed his lips. "But at some point, you did get a theory, right?"

Amelia, "Yes. I inspected Gordon's financial records and found an insurance payment."

Cushing asked, "What's suspicious about that?"

"He had sold his whole life policy to a company in his state, and it struck me that I had done the same."

"Was it the same company?"

She answered, "No, the names were different. But when we looked them up online, the websites were similar, and the company officers were identical."

"Who were they?" questioned Cushing.

"Robert Merriweather was CEO, his wife Patricia was the Secretary/Treasurer, and a man, Roscoe Fuller, was Chief Financial Officer."

"Could you tell where they were located?" asked the lawyer.

Mia smiled. "That took some sleuthing. We found the Merriweathers in Gainesville, Florida. Locating Fuller near Albany, New York, in Saratoga Springs took a couple more weeks. By then, we believed Merriweathers' companies were killing a few clients each year for the insurance money or reverse mortgage revenue."

Cushing pointed to Gordon. "Mr. Strong, do you agree with this account?"

"Yes, I do. I had doubts at first, but when we found different companies in eight states with the same executives, I decided Mia was right."

"Please name the states," said Cushing.

Gordon took a breath. "OK, Florida, New York, Georgia, South Carolina, North Carolina, Virginia, Pennsylvania, and Connecticut."

Amelia jumped in, "Gerald, um Jerry, it's not that they'd a different named insurance company in each state; they also had small office buildings in each one."

"How is that suspicious?"

Amelia said, "I provide forensic accounting as a paid service. I decided they used the building finances for money laundering. After all, if they're willing to commit murder, tax fraud should be right up their alley."

"Is that all that made you decide they were crooked?" asked Cushing.

"No, there was a notation in each folder. Mine was 5,000/10,000/20,000. Gordon's was 10,000/20,000/40,000."

"I'm not sure what that means," said Cushing.

Mia explained, "Neither were we until it hit me that the first number was an upfront payment for the killing, the second for completing the assignment, and the third for making it look like an accident. We both had AD&D coverage on the policies we sold to the Merriweather companies. Gordon also had a reverse mortgage that would bring them over $500K."

"Are you saying that these companies, controlled by Robert and Patricia Merriweather, were killing their customers?"

"Yes, that's what we thought until last week," she answered.

"What changed your mind last week?" questioned the lawyer.

"We overheard Robert tell his wife that he was concerned that the CFO was having their customers murdered. He had consulted with an actuary and found that the pattern of their collections from the eight states was statistically impossible."

"Miss Talbot, until you heard this discussion, did you bear a grudge against the Merriweathers?"

"I did. I believed they must know about the murders," she responded.

"How did you overhear the Merriweathers?"

Mia looked at Gordon, who shrugged. "I'm not sure I should tell you."

"Wrong, young lady. It would be best if you told me everything. I can only protect you if I know the entire story."

"OK, here goes. Gordon and I placed audio bugs in the Merriweather home."

Cushing frowned. "You understand that was probably illegal?"

"Yes, we do. We needed to know if they were guilty. Robert told his wife he was going to the Gainesville FBI the next morning. He had a nine o'clock appointment the next morning, but someone killed him that night."

"Did you place any other of these bugs?"

"Yes, we had sensors in the Merriweathers' offices, motion-activated video cameras outside their house, and the same in front of their reserved parking places."

Cushing licked his lips, "Remind me never to get on your bad side. Let's stick with motive; when you learned that Robert and Patricia were not part of the murder conspiracy, did your attitude change?"

"Yes, I was relieved that they weren't trying to kill Gordon and myself."

"Before that, did you say you would grind them to dust?"

"Yes, I said that to my team in Saratoga Springs."

Gerald asked, "Did you also say they would sleep in their car and beg for food when you were done with them?"

"Yes, during the same meeting while we were starting our surveillance of the CFO, Roscoe Fuller."

Cushing threw up his hands. "Oh jeez, did you bug him too?"

Mia said, "Yes, we did, and heard him talk to a hitman to re-establish the contract on Gordon and me. You need to know that another key player, Johnny Rivers, was Roscoe's partner when they acquired office buildings and formed the insurance companies."

"Where's he now?" asked Cushing.

"That's the problem," she replied. "We don't know. We know that Roscoe is afraid of him, and Rivers vanished about six years ago. I thought the CFO might have killed him and buried him behind his building. I hired a private investigator to keep track of Roscoe's movements and check outside the property with a cadaver dog. The dog alerted on a rose bed in back, but it turned out to be the carcass of another canine."

Gerald sighed. "So, let's wrap this session up. You had a grudge against Merriweather, but you no longer had it when he was killed."

Amelia said, "That's correct."

"Can we get your service record during the next two weeks?"

"Yes, what will we do with it?"

"I want to show you're an intelligent young lady using your test scores. It's doubtful that you would murder in front of one of your sensors."

"I also earned straight As at Capital Technology University while completing a degree in computer science and a minor in accounting," added Amelia.

He nodded. "All the better, we'll need that transcript. This session has ended. We will discuss opportunity in the morning. When would you like to start?"

Mia responded, "How about 10 a.m. so I can sleep in and spend some time with my parents."

Gerald Cushing agreed, "Good enough. See you tomorrow."

  The following morning, Cushing had coffee, tea, soft drinks, and pastries on the conference table.

He welcomed Gordon and Amelia back to his offices, "Good morning, esteemed clients; how did you sleep?"

Amelia replied, "We went to bed late and slept pretty good."

"Excellent. Today, we want to discuss your access to Robert Merriweather. How well did you know him?"

She said, "Not well at all. I never met him face to face."

"Yet, you went over to his car; why is that?"

"I knew his pattern was to go home by five o'clock. It was much later, and I sensed something was wrong."

"In what way did you feel or think that?" asked Cushing.
"He was sort of slumped down like maybe passed out or something."
"So, you were concerned about him? About whoever was in the car?"
"Yes, and I knew he might be at risk."
"How did you know that?"
"We knew he was going to the FBI the next day and Roscoe Fuller, the CFO, or the big boss, Johnny Rivers, might kill him to stop that meeting."
"Again, how did you find this out? What was the basis of your suspicion?"
"As we told you yesterday, we have listening devices in his offices and home. We heard him tell his wife, Patricia, that he was going to turn himself in for tax fraud to stop the murdering."
"Before you heard that conversation you thought he could be a murderer?"
Gordon, "Yes, that's right."
"Was he?"
She said, "No, as it turns out, he had just suspected something nefarious was happening and wanted to stop it."
"You did have the opportunity to kill Merriweather. You knew his schedule, his home address, and worked in the same building, right?"
Mia nodded. "All that is true. We need to scan our parking lot sensors to see if they recorded the murder."
"Excellent. I have personnel here that can help with that."

Chapter Twenty-nine

THE INCRIMINATING GUN – Cushing's Offices

Cushing admonished, "Mr. Strong and Miss Talbot, you must stop these surveillance activities immediately."

"Yes sir, we're trying to do that. We've asked our technician to remove as many sensors as possible," Said Mia.

"Good. How many folks know about this, this spying?"

"Of course, Gordon and I, my parents, and the technician, Herman Rhodes. Merriweather's secretary thinks we were placing burglar alarms, but she might be suspicious."

"Who do you think killed Robert?" asked the lawyer.

Amelia replied, "One of the two men who own his companies, Roscoe Fuller or Johnny Rivers, or even a hit team hired by them."

"I see. If you wanted to murder Mr. Merriweather, how easy would it have been?"

"Unfortunately, pretty easy as we rented offices on the same floor, we knew where he lived, and we understood his daily pattern," Amelia theorized.

"When you say we, who is we?" said Gerald.

"Gordon, myself, my parents, and Rhodes."

"Could this Rhodes have committed the crime?"

"It's possible but not probable. He did know where the revolver was hidden."

Cushing alerted, "Christ, what revolver? Hidden where?"

Mia answered, "Rhodes, Gordon, and I flew to the Bahamas and rented the Merriweathers' condo. We found a .38 caliber pistol there and brought it back with us hidden in our plane."

Cushing, "Did you touch it?"

Mia sighed. "Yes, I unloaded it and put the bullets in a plastic bag."

The distressed lawyer said, "Why did you take it? Why did you unload it?"

Mia, "I don't know. I guess I didn't want them to have a gun they might use on us, nor a loaded gun on the plane."

"Is it possible that it was the murder weapon?"

"I guess it's possible, I don't see how." She replied.

Gerald Cushing hung his head and stated, "Law enforcement thinks it's the same gun. They seem pretty sure of themselves."

Gordon responded, "We agree. We discussed it last night and think only Ratchet Rhodes could have told them about it."

"Ratchet?" quizzed the lawyer.

Gordon, "It's a nickname. He's a well-known computer hacker. He saw us hide the weapon."

"So, he could be the killer?"

Mia replied, "Maybe, but it doesn't make sense."

"Let's drop that for now. Why were you two armed when arrested?"

"Gosh," she said. "Maybe because two hitmen tried to kill us, and when we surveilled Roscoe Fuller, we heard him try to hire a new team to complete the job."

"Where did you surveil him?"

She said, "In his home and office in Saratoga Springs, New York."

"In another state?"

Amelia, "Yes."

"No wonder the FBI is involved," mused Cushing.

He continued, "Why did you and Mr. Strong have gunshot residue on your hands when arrested?"

"We had just come from Gordon's house in North Carolina, where we fired several magazines in his indoor firing range."

"I see. What type of guns did you shoot?"

"Nine millimeters."

Cushing, "Hmmm. Merriweather was killed by a single thirty-eight bullet."

Mia looked quizzical, "How do you know that?"

"I have connections with the local ME's Office. They called Gainesville. Now, Mr. Strong, Gordon, I have questions just for you."

Gordon, "Shoot."

"Have you provided the police or FBI any information?"

"No sir, other than my name, SSN, and address – nothing."

"Good. Presuming Miss Talbot did kill Merriweather, did you have any knowledge that it would happen?"

"She didn't, and I didn't expect her to do any such thing without discussing it with me."

"Cripes, did you two discuss killing him and his confederates?" asked the flabbergasted lawyer.

Gordon, "Yes, we did. When someone is trying to kill you, it's always an option."

Cushing asked, "What was the nature of that discussion?"
"We thought about fighting back and decided not to do it, especially against Robert and Patricia, because we didn't know if they were aware of the murders."
"I see. Did you provide a .38 caliber revolver to Amelia?"
"No, I did not."
"Did you know where *the* gun in question was hidden?"
"Yes."
"Who else knew?"
"Just Amelia, Ratchet, and myself," said Gordon.
"Where was it hidden?"
"In the last seat behind the pilot. It lifted up and had a hollow space beneath it."
"Did you personally see the revolver in that location?"
"No, Mia told me later that's where she put it before going through customs."
Gerald frowned. "So, you took her word on that, right?"
"Of course."
"She could have brought it off the plane or retrieved it later without your knowledge, correct?"
"I suppose so, but she wouldn't have done that."
"Why not?"
"Because we are a team, we care deeply for each other. We trust and love one another."
"Miss Talbot, is that last part, correct? Are you and Gordon lovers?"
Mia smiled. "That's not exactly what he said, but yes, we are - this could be a long-term relationship."
"Gordon, in any way, did you help Miss Talbot murder Robert Merriweather?"
"No, no way."
Cushing held his head. "Let me think. Let me think. Someone killed him. If not one of you two, who?"
Amelia replied, "The CFO, Roscoe Fuller, his partner, Jonathon Rivers, or paid hitmen."
"Then how did they get that particular gun?"
"That I don't know. There's one other," she theorized.
"Who?"

"Ratchet Rhodes. We don't know his location, and he knew about the gun."

"Why would he frame you?"

She said, "I don't know, but someone, probably him, has told the FBI about some of our private conversations."

"The ones where you said you 'would grind the Merriweather family to dust' and 'bankrupt them so they would be sleeping in their car?'"

"Yes, in a manner of speaking. I don't feel that way now."

"Let's cover that again. Why not?" the lawyer asked.

"The real criminals were using Robert and Patricia. The Merriweathers cooked the books but didn't know about the murders. Robert was the spokesman for all the companies but didn't own them."

"Did Robert find out he was the patsy?"

"Yes," Mia answered.

"How?" asked Gerald.

"They went to an insurance convention, and Robert talked to an actuary. The actuary analyzed the deaths of Merriweather's clients over several years and concluded the numbers and locations were statistically impossible."

Cushing shook his head. "I'm not sure I understand. Please explain."

Amelia answered, "My Dad and I think the CFO and/or his partner were killing one or two in each state, in a different location, and with different insurance companies. Looking at it as a whole, it was not random, and it was too early for most of the deaths."

"Do you have that data?" asked her lawyer.

"We do."

"Can we get in touch with the actuary?" asked Jerry.

"Not without a psychic, he was murdered in Philly," she said.

"Let's get back to *the* gun. How did it end up in a trash can next to you at the Gainesville Library?"

"I didn't know for sure, but I thought someone tracked my car. They knew I was at that location because I found a GPS tracker under one fender."

"When did you find it?"

"After I arrived in the library parking lot. When I found it, I stomped on it and threw it into the trash can."

Cushing grimaced. "Oh Lordy, cameras there might show you throwing something into that can, right?"

"Yes, I guess so," she answered.

"Your innocence might sound very far-fetched to the ears of the judge and jury. Who would set you up like this?"

"I don't know for sure, but it could be Ratchet or the other two."

"Fuller and Rivers?"

She said, "My team was dismantling their evil empire, and it's possible they struck back."

Jerry asked, "Could they be in cahoots with Ratchet?"

"It's possible. He works for whoever pays the most."

"That's it. Mr. Rhodes could have done the deed or provided them with *the* gun."

"It's a theory, probably not a good one," Mia responded.

He clapped his hands, "Doesn't matter; we need some alternative for the jury, so they don't convict you."

Amelia questioned, "What about Gordon?"

"His charge is just the government posturing, trying to put more pressure on you. If he doesn't confess, they have no proof. They will drop it at the preliminary."

Gordon sighed. "That sounds good. I feel the pressure. I don't think we can implicate Ratchet Rhodes without warning him. Jerry, can we spare Amelia a messy trial?"

"Not yet. We have to prove the U.S. Attorney doesn't have a case. Amelia, walk me through what you did that afternoon."

"OK, Gordon and I left the building before lunch and went to our rental house."

"How far away is it? Please show me on this map of Gainesville."

"The building is here, and our house is here, about a five-minute drive."

"I see. Please continue."

"We had lunch and then watched some TV."

"What did you watch?"

"It was a movie on HBO, one of the James Bond movies."

Gordon added, "One of my favorites, 'Diamonds are Forever.'"

"Then what?"

She continued, "My parents came back from shopping, and we took a nap."

"Who took a nap?"

"Gordon and I."

"What did your parents do?"

"I don't know. Probably reading - they were reading books in the living room when we got up."
"Then what?"
"The four of us played some bridge. We're trying to teach Gordo the game."
"What time did that end?"
Amelia, "About five o'clock. We ordered Kentucky Fried Chicken for dinner. It was delivered before five-thirty."
"Tell me exactly when you left the house."
"Six fifteen," she said.
"You're sure?"
"Yes."
"Your parents and Gordon can testify that you were at the house all afternoon and departed at six fifteen?"
"Yes."
"Tell me exactly when you arrived at the Southeast Assurance Building."
"It was six twenty."
What did you see?"
"Nothing at first. I left my car, started entering the building, and noticed Merriweather's car in his parking spot."
"Was that unusual?"
"Yes, very. Patricia left at four thirty every day, and he left at five."
"When did the secretary usually leave?"
"Normally, she walked out with Mrs. Merriweather."
"OK, at four thirty."
"Yes."
Cushing asked, "What time did you see Merriweather's car?"
Amelia, "Hmmm. It would have been about six twenty-two.
"Go on; you're near the entrance and see Robert's car," directed the lawyer.
"Yes, I see Robert in his car..."
Cushing held up his hand. "Let me stop you right there. Could you tell it was he?"
"Ummm...no. It was too dark."
"You saw someone in the car; where?"
"In the driver's seat."
"What did you do?"
"I waited a few seconds and didn't see any movement. It worried me."

"Why?"

"I thought Robert, or whoever it was, might be passed out and need assistance."

"What next?"

"I walked towards the car and saw a man slumped forward."

"Good. And next?"

"When I got to his window, which was down, I could see it was Robert Merriweather. A split second later, I realized he had a wound above his left ear seeping blood."

"What did you think? What did you feel?" asked Cushing.

"It hit me like a ton of bricks that he was probably dead. My knees started to buckle, and I wanted to throw up."

"At that precise moment, what did you do?"

"I grabbed the car door to steady myself."

"So, you left fingerprints on his car. Then what?"

"I just looked at him. There was no movement. I thought, What do I do now?"

Cushing raised his eyebrows. "And then you did what?"

"I decided to check for a pulse. What if Robert was alive and needed an ambulance?"

He nodded. "Exactly what did you do?"

"I reached into the car and checked his neck for a pulse."

"With which hand?" he questioned.

"The cops asked me that. I don't know, probably my left hand to the left side of his neck."

"Was there a pulse?"

"No."

"Was his neck warm to your touch, cool, or cold?"

"I didn't think about it. I would say cool or cold."

"How about his eyes? How did they look?"

"The cops asked that too. When I think about it, his left eye was open and not blinking. It was just a few seconds, and I was in a bit of a panic."

Cushing patted her hand. "At that moment, what were you thinking and feeling?"

She said, "I thought, Robert is dead. Someone shot him, or he killed himself. If he was murdered, I might be next."

"What did you do?"

"I looked around the parking lot and trees and shrubs near the building. It was nearly dark, and I imagined a killer in every shadow."

"What action did you take?" asked the lawyer.

"I decided to open the door and look for the gun. I wondered if Robert was left-handed."

"Which hand did you use to open the car door?"

"I'm not sure, probably my left hand."

"Did you have blood on that hand?"

"Possibly."

"So, you could have left a bloody fingerprint on the door."

She hung her head and sighed. "Yes. This is sounding really bad."

"Don't worry about it. What next?"

"I didn't see a gun inside the car. Now I was scared again."

"You said it was dark. How could you see a weapon?"

"The courtesy lights came on with the door open."

"I see. What was your next action?"

"I started thinking that I was at another death scene and decided to take a picture of Mr. Merriweather."

Gerald pounced. "You took a picture of the deceased?"

"Yes."

"Do the police know that?"

"Yes, and they want my regular cell phone. I need advice about that. Isn't that the same as testifying against myself?"

"No, not in most cases. Did you send them the picture or pictures?"

"Yes, it was just one picture."

Cushing continued, "You took the picture. What did you think and feel?"

"I was afraid for my life and wanted to get out of there."

"Did you think about calling 911?"

"Only momentarily. I ran to my car and drove away."

"Where did you go?" he questioned.

"I drove to the city library. I had been there before and backed up to the trees in the dark."

"Then, did you call 911 for help?"

"No, I felt safer and was worried about Patricia and her daughter – that they could be next. I called her cell phone."

Cushing nodded. "That must have been a tough call."

"It was. I had to tell her about Robert and convince her to get out of town."

"What next?" he demanded.

"I decided to call the FBI. Agent Jake Finster knew about our case, and I wanted him to know about Merriweather."

"Did he advise you to call 911?"

"No, he said he would make the call and send some police to protect me."

"Did that happen?"

"Yes, it was only a few minutes before two Gainesville cops arrived."

"What did you do during those few minutes?"

"At first, I cried out of fear and frustration. Then I got angry and wondered if anyone was tracking me. I searched under my fenders and found a device, threw it on the ground, and stomped on it before tossing it in the trashcan."

Gerald sighed. "Let's take a break. I need to think about all that you've related to us."

"OK. Do you think I'm in trouble?" asked Amelia.

"Young lady, if your prints are on the gun, it is currently a slam dunk for the prosecution."

"Currently?"

Cushing, "I believe you're too smart to murder in front of one of your own video devices. We must prove it was not you and provide an alternative theory if possible."

Chapter Thirty

WORKING VACATION – Paradise Island

During their second full day with Gerald Cushing and his wife, Amelia asked if she and Gordon could take their trip to the Bahamas as previously planned.

Cushing said, "I'm not sure it's wise, although it wouldn't be illegal because Mudd didn't take your passports or restrict your travel."

Mia smiled. "Good. I think we need to get away and decompress. We already have a reservation at a resort and a flight scheduled tomorrow."

"Miss Talbot, I don't think we'll be done with all our preparation for your defense."

She responded, "I've thought about that. Why don't you and Alice come with us? There's room on the airplane and a guest bedroom in the condo. The food is good, and the property has a nice pool and spa. You and Gordo can go fishing while Alice and I get pampered at the spa."

He answered, "My, that's a lovely offer. We're overdue for a vacation. Alice, what do you think?"

"Jerry, we're going. Any expenses are business deductions, and I can use some spa treatments."

Gordon called Roger Sandstone and booked a 10 a.m. departure in the Talbot G100. Their bags were stowed the following day, and Strong was strapping into the co-pilot's seat when his burner phone rang. He walked away from the twin jet as Roger started the engines.

When Gordon returned to his seat, Amelia yelled, "Gordon, who was that?"

He yelled, "Tell you later."

Roger Sandstone said, "Startup and taxi checklists complete. We're cleared to taxi to runway 29. Give me the takeoff checklist on the way."

Gordon said, "Roger that, Roger, ha, ha."

With the checklist complete, Gordon called the tower, "Gainesville Tower, Gulfstream 431, ready for takeoff."

"Tower, roger, 431, taxi into position and hold on runway 29."

As Sandstone and Gordon swung the sleek jet into position at the end of the runway, they saw their traffic. A Piper Cherokee was starting to roll several hundred yards ahead of them.

Roger commented, "Looks like a student flight. We need to keep them in sight until we are well above them and climbing."

Gordon replied, "You fly the aircraft, and I'll watch them."

Tower, "Gulfstream 431 cleared for take-off; traffic ahead is a Cherokee at one mile."

Gordon, "We see them and will maintain a safe separation. Rolling."

The climb out and flight were uneventful except for Amelia coming to the cockpit and speaking into Gordon's ear, "Gordon, I'm scared. It's not there. Who was on the phone?"

He squeezed her hand. "Later."

Sandstone landed perfectly at Lynden Pindling Airport, taxied to the visitor area, and secured the port engine so his passengers and Gordon could disembark with their luggage. Once they entered the terminal, he restarted the engine and taxied for his return flight to Gainesville. The foursome cleared customs, hailed a taxi, and moved into their digs at Paradise Island.

As they unpacked their bags, Amelia accosted Gordon. "Gordo, you're driving me crazy about the secret phone call. Who was it?"

"You won't believe it. It was Rachet."

"Ratchet? No, what did he say?"

He held his finger to his lips. "We need somewhere more private. Let's excuse ourselves and go to the pool for a drink."

Once they had their rum drinks with fruit and miniature umbrellas, they sat at a table at the pool's far end.

"OK, spill it. Why all the mystery?" Amelia commanded.

"We have to decide how much to share with our lawyers," replied Strong.

"Did he kill Robert?" she asked.

"No, I don't think so. He just flew down from New York to yank our sensors."

"Damn. That's good news!" she exulted.

"Yes, he has them all, even from their home. He and your parents have wiped the hard drives of all our computers."

"Also, good news, except we can still get at the data, no?"

"Yes, he said it's safe. I didn't ask him to elaborate on the phone. He wants to testify for you and help us with trial preparations. I think he feels guilty."

"Why?"

"The FBI made him wear a wire when he started working with us."

"That's Finster, the SOB." Amelia asserted.

Gordon, "Maybe, maybe not. They'd caught Rhodes red-handed penetrating the Federal Reserve System. His ass was grass, and he was facing twenty years in prison. He agreed to reveal future clients and got a probation plea deal."

She said, "Hmmm, the government might have been very embarrassed by a public trial. I wonder what Ratchet's scheme was."

"He didn't say. Our problem is how much of this we share with the Cushings."

"I agree," she answered. They don't know how successful our surveillance was. Did Ratchet ever stop reporting to the Feds?"

"Yes, after our trip to Albany, he only gave them dribs and drabs and no recordings. They're threatening him with violation of his probation."

"Maybe Gerald Cushing can help with that situation."

"It's up to you, Mia. The more we tell Jerry and Alice, the more crimes they'll know about."

"I know, I know, but he says he must know about everything. I have an idea. Also, did you talk to Rachet about the gun?"

"I did. He swears he didn't remove it from the plane or tell anyone about it. I believe him. I mentioned that our lawyer might paint him as a possible murderer.'

"What did he say?"

"He replied that he has a rock solid alibi in New York when Robert was killed – no worries. He seemed very distressed that you're being charged. She sighed. "Thank God for that. Let's go back inside."

"Mia, I'll follow your lead."

"Thanks."

Back in the condo, the two couples sat around the kitchen table for a planned two-hour session discussing the case. Mrs. Cushing was ready to capture all the information on her laptop. She and Gerald had shifted into sandals, Bermudas, and Hawaiian shirts.

Mia started the meeting, "Gerald, you might have noticed that Gordon got a call before our flight."

"Yes, I did."

"It was from our hacker friend, Herman 'Ratchet' Rhodes."

"I see. Was he helpful?"

"Yes. Rhodes has pulled all our sensors and wiring from the Southeast Building."

"What about those at the Merriweather house?"

"Gordon answered, "I told him where they were, and he confirmed removal."

Cushing asked, "But the FBI still knows you were conducting illegal surveillance on Robert and Patricia, right?"

Amelia, "Probably. Ratchet told them our actions until our trip to Saratoga Springs and even wore a wire. I think hearing Roscoe Fuller order another hit on us changed his mind about reporting our activities."

"Why was he spying on you?" asked Cushing.

Gordon replied, "He was found guilty on federal financial hacking charges and got probation by agreeing to squeal on his future clients. He's stopped fully exposing our activities, so they threaten jail time."

Jerry smiled, "Sounds like he needs a good lawyer. Where does he live?"

Amelia responded, "New York. He has agreed to testify for me and help us any way he can."

"Excellent. Did he know about the home surveillance?"

"No, not until yesterday. Only Gordon and I knew about that."

"OK, what about the computers you used in Gainesville?"

She said, "Wiped clean by my parents and Rhodes."

"You know that's very difficult to do, right?" Cushing admonished.

"Yes, but if anyone can do it, it's those three."

"What kind of data did you have?" persisted the lawyer.

"Gerald, here's a problem. I'm not sure I should tell you. The government can charge us for what we did in Saratoga Springs, but Gainesville is another matter. If questioned, all of us can take the fifth, and they'd have a problem gathering evidence unless they have been listening to us."

He frowned. "Is that possible?"

Mia said, "Yes, but not probable. We had a world-class hacker equipped with the latest technology for finding bugs."

"Amelia, in answer to your previous question about my full knowledge of your activities, the answer is that we can't have any surprises in court. None. We can't have new charges out of the blue. We can't have the prosecution paint you as a serial felon who also committed murder. Regarding your activities in New York, protecting yourself from a provable murderer would be very compelling for the jury to look the other way on invasion of privacy charges."

Mia looked at Gordon, "What do you think?"

"Mia, I'm not sure how many laws we've broken, but we haven't hurt or killed anyone, so maybe it's open kimono time. We need Jerry and his team ready to defend us on everything."

She nodded, "Gerald, ask me anything."

"Good. I want to return to your time in the rental home before driving to the Southeastern Building and finding Merriweather."

"OK," she agreed.

"We can use sworn affidavits from Gordon and your parents for your alibi, but did you do anything else that would time stamp your presence at the house, like make a phone call or use your computer?"

Mia replied, "Let me think. Gordo and I got up from our nap; we talked to my parents at length about what would happen when Robert met with the FBI the next day. We had dinner. Hold it; I ordered dinner from KFC with my phone and had it delivered."

"Who delivered it? Was it the restaurant or a service?"

"It was 'Uber Eats.'"

Cushing, "Excellent. There should be a record of that on your credit card."

"Yes sir, and there's more."

"What's that?"

"I was so happy that the FBI would be finding out about the murders that I tipped the young delivery man twenty dollars. He may remember that."

"Even better. Did you use your phone and personally tip the Uber Eats guy from your purse?"

"Yes."

"Please check your phone for the time of the call."

"OK, this will take a minute."

Cushing turned to Strong. "Gordon, can you confirm Ms. Talbot made the call and received the delivery?"

Gordon smiled, "That's affirmative."

Mia said, "I've got it; it was five ten when I called and probably five thirty when the KFC Family Bucket arrived. We sat down and ate. I then used the bathroom, washed my hands, and left the house at six-fifteen. Does that help?"

Cushing, "I think so. The prosecution always brushes off the affidavits by themselves. Of course, your parents and boyfriend will try to give you an alibi. If the murder happened before you arrived, as you say, then it was committed by someone else."

Amelia shrugged. "Is it that simple?"

He smiled. "Yes, it can be. What's the size of the picture that you took?"
"It should be five megabytes. That's the setting I usually have."
"Outstanding. Taking the picture may be the best thing you ever did."
She was surprised. "Huh, why is that?"
"It's just a hunch I have. I'm giving you the email address of a forensic blood expert. We'll see if he backs my hunch and will testify."
"OK by me," Mia replied.
Gerald Cushing got up and started pacing around the table. "Let's talk a bit about the Preliminary Hearing. It's like a mini-trial and must be held within twenty-one days of your arraignment. Our first decision is whether we want to ask for a week's continuance to prepare your case. Remember that gives the government another week to strengthen their case."
Gordon asked, "Is there a jury?"
"No. Both sides present their evidence and call witnesses, and a federal judge decides if there's probable cause that the defendant committed the crime. If yes, a trial is scheduled. If not, the judge dismisses the charges. We want to win at the Prelim and get your charges dropped."
He kept pacing. "Gordon, in a theoretical sense, is there any way you would have known that Amelia was going to kill Robert Merriweather?"
"No, she would have told me, and I would have helped her."
"Christ, don't say it like that in court if I put you on the stand. Say, 'We are very close, and I know she would have told me or asked my advice."
"OK, am I going to testify?" asked Gordon.
"Usually not, but it might happen if we get Judge Mudd again. Did you see Amelia leave with a gun on the day in question?"
Gordon, "No, I didn't."
"Did either you or Amelia have a .38 caliber handgun in your possession on that day?"
"No, we did not."
"But you knew where the revolver was hidden on the airplane, right?"
"Yes, the pilot had left, and I saw Mia and Ratchet raise the seat and put the money and pistol under the rear seat."
Cushing frowned. "Money? What money?"
"The money we took from the Merriweather condo - several thousand dollars," replied Strong.

"Hmmm. We will get back to that. Don't offer additional information. I only asked about the gun. You saw it placed under the seat, and then you all left the aircraft. Is that correct?
"Yes sir."
"Supposing she did kill him, is there any way that you knew it would happen?"
"No sir."
"Good. At the Prelim, I will request your charges be either proven or dismissed. They have no proof, and they know it. They don't even know that you knew where the gun was hidden if that was the murder weapon. You need to contact this Ratchet fellow and ask if he told the authorities who knew the gun's location."
"I'll do that," said Gordon.
"Fine. Now, Amelia, do you remember what kind of bullets you took out of that thirty-eight?"
"I'm pretty sure they were regular velocity hollow points."
"Why do you think they were hollow points? asked the lawyer.
"Each one had a hole in the center."
"Hmmm. That could make it very hard for the police to match the lands and grooves from a test firing."
Gordon said, "I don't think that was the murder weapon. It was planted, probably with one empty shell. We need to see the feed from the Southeastern parking lot sensor. It should show that Amelia didn't fire a gun. And it may show who did."
Cushing agreed. "I see. How did it work?"
Mia, "I set it to activate and record movement within about fifty to 100 feet. It then sent the first video frames to the internet and recorded the next five minutes. We could get a dump from it by the internet or by triggering it from less than 100 feet."
Gerald, "What was the purpose of this device?"
"It transmitted when Robert or Patricia arrived or departed from the building. A similar one at their home did the same there."
"Why did you care what they were doing?" asked the lawyer.
"Good question. At first, we wanted to know when we could plant our sensors. Later, we knew when to enter their offices and open their file cabinets."
Gerald frowned. "Were the cabinets locked or unlocked?"

She said, "Locked with combination locks. Our video feeds provided the combinations."

"Did you take anything of value from the offices, like the thousands from this condo?"

"No."

"What did you find, and what action did you take?" he asked.

Amelia, "We hit the jackpot with two sets of books and tax records. We took them to our offices and photographed each page."

"And put them back, I presume."

"Yes, back in the exact same order," she confirmed.

Cushing, "So what will the FBI learn when they go through these files?"

Mia, "They'll learn that Southeastern is a holding company for eight insurance LLCs, one in each state, where they also own small office buildings. They will easily see that Patricia calculated the real profit and loss from each building and the insurance and reverse mortgage businesses but filed state and federal taxes using far different numbers. She, Robert, and the CFO, Roscoe Fuller, used every trick in the book to understate revenue and overstate expenses. It's state and federal tax fraud on a grand scale - several million dollars."

"And you have all of this information?"

She said, "We did have it, but now we only could get it if Ratchet squirreled it away somewhere."

"I see. In the files, was there any proof of the murders?" asked Cushing.

"No. Mr. Merriweather kept all the customer data on his laptop computer."

"How many customers were there?" requested Jerry.

"About eleven hundred, just over a hundred in each state."

He whistled. "So, they could execute a small number without it being suspicious?"

"Exactly," Mia affirmed.

"If the customer data was on Robert's computer, how do you know the number?"

"We broke into both of their laptops. He had the customer data, and she had all the financial accounts and bill paying."

"Did you find evidence that proved the murders?"

"Sort of," Amelia said.

"Please explain," asked the lawyer.

"We found regular large payments to Roscoe Fuller, tens of thousands at a time. We think they'd match up with customer deaths but didn't get that far when we were arrested."

"Tell me how you thought this scheme worked."

"Yes sir. First and foremost, we were finally able to clear the Merriweathers of the murders. They were being used as respectable front people by two criminals, Roscoe Fuller and his partner, Johnathon Rivers, who owned all the LLCs. Those two probably arranged the hits and paid the hitmen. They also were siphoning off the illegal profits from the buildings and the murders."

"You said Mr. Fuller is in New York, the state, under surveillance. Where's the other partner?"

Amelia admitted, "We don't know, but he's involved and called the 'Big Boss' by the others."

"By the CFO and the Merriweathers?"

Amelia, "Yes sir. Fuller was scared to death of him. Apparently, Rivers punished poor performance or disloyalty with death. He's ruthless, and no doubt has a long criminal history."

Jerry Cushing put his hands together to his lips. "You two have given me a lot to think about. I suggest we go to the pool and have lunch. You have some action items, and so do I. Miss Talbot, I plan to use private detectives and several professional witnesses for the Prelim. Getting your charges dropped at the Prelim will be expensive but not nearly as much as at a trial."

She asked, "How much are you thinking?"

"Probably as much as two or three hundred thousand."

"Full speed ahead. My parents and I'll cover that."

Gerald Cushing said, "Good. Let's have lunch and take the afternoon off. I have to make several calls."

"Jerry, do you think you can get me off?"

"No promises, but I think there's a chance. It all depends on that damn gun," answered the lawyer.

Gorden announced he was going for a run, but no one else was interested. He changed into his running outfit and checked the map of Paradise Island for a likely route. Once outside, he headed east on Harbour Drive, right on Flamingo Road, and took another right on Paradise Island Drive. It became Ocean Club Drive, and he trotted by all the upscale homes until he reached the dead-end traffic circle. As Gordon passed the Paradise Island Golf Club, he noticed an ATV pull out and begin following him.

He stayed with his planned route and turned right on North Shore Terrace. The four-place ATV stayed about 100 feet behind Gordon, and he counted three riders. As he neared the circle at the end of North Shore Terrace, the ATV pulled abreast of Gordon, and the driver asked if he wanted a ride. Gordon said no thanks, and the three men roared away.

Gordon loped east on Paradise Island Drive, and the same ATV pulled out from Bayview Lane and followed him. He decided to retrace his route and lose them when he entered the Casa Del Sol compound. When Gordon turned left on Flamingo Road, the ATV was right at his heels. Halfway down Flamingo, the driver passed Gordon, put his vehicle at right angles to the road, and the three men got out - two at the front of the ATV and one with a baseball bat at the rear.

Gordon Strong ran off the road into an abandoned industrial area with the three men in pursuit. He had to stand and fight in an open gravel area or run into a wooded area that might be a trap. Gordon picked up a piece of broken cement, jumped up on the hood, and then on top of an abandoned van. The man with the bat was unable to swing it at him. A second assailant climbed on the hood. Gordo took three quick steps and came down on him with the rock bashing in his head and laying open his cheek. The young man screamed in pain, and Strong threw him to the ground. *And then there were two,* he thought.
Gordon jumped back on the roof and said, "Hey guys, I don't have any money – give it up."
The batter replied, "Don' want your money, mon. We want your life."

Gordo then realized this was a hit squad, not a mugging. The man without the bat reached for his ankle, which was a mistake. Gordon stomped on his fingers and grabbed his wrist while he punched him over and over in the face and neck. *Then there is one.*

The bat wielding man came around the van as Gordon moved to the other side of the van's roof.
"Gonna break every bone in your body," threatened the batter.
"Ohh, I'm scared," replied Gordon Strong. "Put down that bat, and I'll fight you man to man."
"No, mon, dis bat is my friend."
Gordon sat in the middle of the roof. "OK, guess we'll wait until the cops come. Someone will complain about your ATV blocking the road."

The young man looked away at the vehicle, giving Gordon an opening to roll off the van. He then put him in a bear hug. Gordo broke the batter's nose with a head butt, punched his Adam's apple, and kicked him in the groin in one fluid motion. The would-be assassin crumpled to the ground, and Gordon used his bat to break a couple of his ribs.

Gordon Strong turned to start batting practice on the other two men but found himself in a punishing choke hold. Realizing he had six to ten seconds before blackout, Gordo shoved the bat tip back into his assailant's face over and over. He could feel warm blood from the beating gush over his neck and back. The man let go, but Gordon felt a searing pain down his right side. He turned and realized the man had cut him with a knife. Gordo smashed the knife wrist with his bat and battered the man's ribs front and back. He wadded up his T-shirt, tried to stem the blood flow, found the keys in the ATV, and drove it to Casa Del Sol.

Alice Cushing applied a bath towel to Gordon's wound while Amelia and Gerald determined that the Doctor's Hospital at Shirley Street and Collins had the best emergency medical care. They flagged a taxi on Harbour Drive, and fifteen minutes later, Gordon was seen by a nurse and then a doctor. The doctor cleaned his wound, sewed it up, and prescribed antibiotics and pain medication.

Gordon returned to the condo and rested except for providing the police with a description of his attackers. The cops later reported that the ATV was stolen.

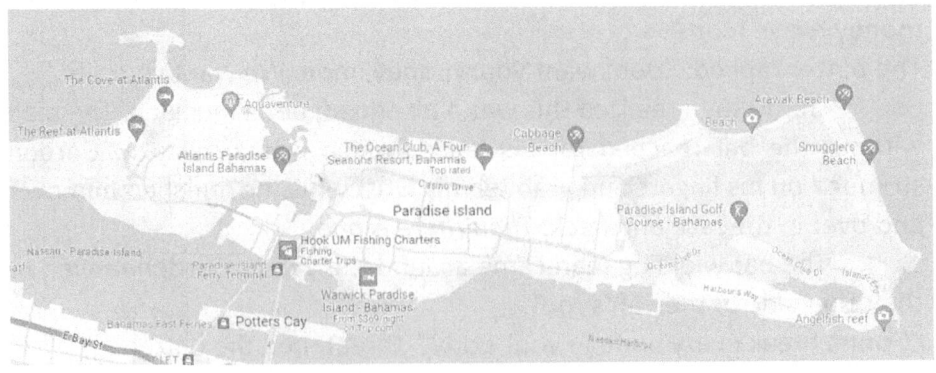

Paradise Island, Nassau, Bahamas (about 3 miles long)
Source: Google Maps

Chapter Thirty-one

PRELIMINARY HEARING – Jacksonville, Fl

Amelia, Gordon, and the Cushings spent five days at Paradise Island. They worked on defense material in the mornings and vacation activities in the afternoon. Before Gordon's incident, the men went fishing and golfing while the women frequented two spas and hit all the shops. Roger Sandstone flew the Talbot G100 to Nassau by midday on their sixth day. Gordon took some pain pills but was still very uncomfortable on the flight back to Gainesville. Gerald Cushing told Amelia and Gordon to take the weekend off while he and his staff prepared testimony and exhibits. Jerry and Alice rented a car and drove to Jacksonville.

While Gordon put their luggage into his car, Sandstone cornered Amelia, "Mia, is there any way I can help with your legal problems?"

"Thanks Roger, but I don't think so."

"Listen, I'm ready to say anything you need said in court. Just give me the word."

"I appreciate your loyalty, but I think we are in good hands with the Cushing team."

"It's not just loyalty, Amelia. Please realize that my offers still stand. Have you given them serious consideration?"

She replied, "Yes, I have, and my answer is the same."

"OK, I understand, but don't go down your present path out of pity for Gordon. He's a good guy but damaged goods."

"Roger, you don't really know him. This conversation is over. Thanks for the flight."

Gordon and Amelia drove to their rental home and answered questions from her parents about their preparation for the Preliminary Hearing. Cushing's staff had already visited them and obtained their affidavits concerning Amelia's whereabouts on the murder day. The two defendants decided to relax and rest for the weekend. They watched a few movies, ordered food delivered, and Amelia helped her parents move out of the Southeast Building.

Amelia and Gordon were back in Cushing's office Monday morning, ready to work night and day if needed.

Gerald Cushing, "Ah, my two favorite clients. Good morning, and thanks for the Bahamas vacation."

Amelia, "You're welcome. Where are we at?"

"First, let's talk about action items. Gordon, were you able to talk with your Ratchet friend?"

"Yes. He told no one about the gun. He has all the Merriweather data available from another hacker friend, and it's locked up on flash drives."

"Both locations?" asked the lawyer.

"Yes."

"Do you have the video from the parking lot sensor?"

"Yes sir, he sent me that day's take, but I haven't looked at it yet. He was also forced to send it to the FBI."

"Hmmm. That could be good or bad. How can we look at it?" asked Cushing.

"It's on my laptop."

"Good. One of my young associates will go over it and make notes. Now, something for both of you. If I put you on the stand and ask why you were armed in Florida, I want you to say the FBI knew you had death threats but provided no protection for months on end."

They both answered, "Yes sir."

"Next, we've some good news. Our blood expert is preparing a report that the detailed color picture Amelia took of the victim shows the murder occurred an hour or more earlier."

Amelia asked, "How can he say that?"

Gerald, "I don't know all the ins and outs, but fresh blood is bright red. As the oxygen in the blood is released, the color fades and is finally nearly black. Also, he told me the wound itself changes with time."

Mia, "That's music to my ears. Anything else?"

"Yes. Our expert mentioned that droplets of blood on a victim's suit coat at first are raised but soak in with time depending on the material."

She smiled. "Maybe more good news. What does my picture show?"

He said, "That Merriweather's sport coat has absorbed them. On another subject, our weapons expert has reported that a hollow nose .38 bullet will probably break into fragments after penetrating the human skull. If so, normal procedures for matching the markings won't work. It may be the prosecution can only talk about the gun and not pin it to the murder."

Gordon raised his hand. "But if the killer used another weapon, the bullet could be intact, right?"

"Yes, it could, but it wouldn't match a test firing from the revolver."

"So, we might argue either way." Strong pointed out.

"You got it, and I will demand forensic proof at the Prelim."
Gordon questioned, "What else do we need to work on?"
"I want one of my associates to walk you through your actions on the day in question and the details of your arrest, booking, detention, and arraignment."
"How will that help?" asked Amelia.
"If we get Mudd again, he will be outraged at how they treated both of you. They could have asked you to come in for questioning, but instead, they treated you like serial criminals. It's a case of prosecutorial intimidation, pure and simple."

They heard a yell from another office, and Cushing's associate came in with Gordon's laptop.
He said, "Hey boss, wait 'til you see this."

The video feed showed Merriweather's car in its parking spot and a white truck arriving and parking next to it. A hooded figure got out of the truck and approached Robert's car. There was a brief conversation, and the person shot Robert in the head. There was no plate on the truck's front, and the camera didn't capture the rear plate, but the type of vehicle was a Toyota Tundra. The single shot time tick on the footage was 5:35 p.m. After some celebration and high-fiving among the team members, Gerald told them to settle down.
He said, "This is a great break, but we are not out of the woods yet."
Amelia challenged him. "Why not? This is cut-and-dried proof of a different killer."
"To us, yes. To the prosecution, not so much."
"Why not?" she demanded.
"For one, they will argue that it is still you, that you slipped away from your house, shot Robert, and returned in ten minutes. Or, Gordon, who said he was going to the bathroom and left the house."
Mia pouted. "They'd do that?"
"They'll do anything to provide evidence that matches their preconceived theories of the crime."
She said, "What can we do?"
"We go over the video time after time and compare it to your arrival at the building. We have a video expert review the evidence. Amelia, I think the person in the tape is taller than you."
"Then that should do it. I should be off the hook."

"Oh no, the prosecution can theorize that you wore elevated shoes or Gordon did it. Also, you both knew you would be recorded, so you disguised yourselves."

"This is a nightmare. Does it ever end?" she agonized.

Cushing, "Yes, it does when we pull all the pieces together and show the government's arguments are far-fetched and biased against common sense and the truth. That's my job and the job of our experts. Our weapons guy has a wild idea, something that is pretty dramatic."

Gordon asked, "What's that?"

"He thinks we can stage the murder using a full-grown hog in the car. Pigs are very close to human beings in several anatomical ways. I have a neighbor with a transplanted pig heart valve."

Amelia, "But we would have to kill the poor animal. I don't think I want to be part of that."

"Yes, that's true, but we would use one the farmer already planned to butcher. We give it a sedative so it feels nothing and dispatch it with less pain and mess than at a slaughterhouse."

She said, "We better shelve that plan for a possible trial. The animal rights groups will be all over us."

Shifting gears, Gerald Cushing asked, "Is your sensor still in the Southeastern parking lot?"

Gordon answered, "It's possible because Rhodes didn't install it. Let me check with my laptop. Yup, it's still there and operating."

"Perfect, tomorrow night at the appropriate times, we will simulate the shooting and Ameilia discovering the body."

"What good will that do?" she asked.

"I'm not entirely sure. Our video interpretation team wants to make a comparison. Mia, is there any chance Robert's blood was on your clothes, your body, or your camera?"

"Hmmm. Maybe after I touched Robert's neck, took my camera out of my jeans, and put it back in my pocket."

"Which pocket?"

"My back right side pocket."

"All good to know. If there's no blood on the gun, the prosecution will have trouble linking it to a close-up shooting," declared the lawyer.

Gordon said, "What else do we need to get done during the next few days?"

"My partner and associates will grill you as if you're testifying with me asking the questions and during cross-examination. We want to prepare you to handle any question or assertion."

Gordon said, "Mr. Cushing, Jerry, we will do what you say. Are our chances getting any better of dismissal?"

"I think they are. I see a logical answer to almost any government evidence. We have the time of death, and the gun blast looks much different than your camera flash an hour later. Mia, could there be any Gun Shot Residue on your clothes?"

"No, I changed clothes when we returned from Gordon's house to Gainesville."

"Gordon, how about you?"

"Nope, I also showered and changed everything."

Amelia asked, "What's our strategy for the rest of the week?"

"We keep working until we have the prosecution blocked at every allegation. We get our arguments and expert witnesses lined up, and then we may move for a Bill of Particulars."

Gordon asked, "What's that?"

"It's a request to the Court for the government to provide us a detailed statement of their charges against both of you."

"Why would we do it?" asked Strong.

"U.S. Attorneys are busy people. They put off developing their cases until the last minute, just like the rest of us. If we ask for this by Friday, it puts more time pressure on them and may reveal what they argued before the federal grand jury. And it makes it difficult for them to waltz into the Prelim with last-minute charges unrelated to the murder. Gordon, all they have on you is guilt by association. For what they know for sure, they might as well have charged the elder Talbots as accessories."

Mia, "My God, could they do that?"

"They can do anything that they want, but doing that would make them look like dicks. Charging you and Gordon as conspirators is much more believable even though you've no criminal records and are decorated veterans."

Amelia added, "And the way we were arrested and detained was over the top, right?"

"How many agents were there?"

"Six."

"All with guns drawn?"

"Yes. Will the judge care about that?" she queried.

"It may show him or her that the FBI was prejudiced against you, but it does not absolve you of any charges at the Prelim or trial. The arrest warrant is a different animal. We have asked for a copy because the original warrant was to arrest you two in Gainesville. Someone whited that out and inserted Jacksonville without informing the original judge."

Gordon, "Jerry, what are the steps in the hearing next week?"

"Good question. Each side will make opening statements. They explain their side of the case, their planned evidence, and any issues for the judge to resolve. Then, we have presentation of the evidence, where the prosecution goes first. You two need to keep your cool. At a Prelim, the government attorney can present hearsay evidence not allowed at a formal trial. Don't get rattled. Write notes to me or my co-counsel. Our objective is to destroy the credibility of the fed's evidence. Next, the judge will rule on matters of law and motions made by either side. After that, we have closing arguments where I go second and the prosecution can rebut my statements."

Amelia, "That doesn't seem fair."

"Maybe not; all's fair in love, war, and trials."

Gordon, "What will the judge do then?"

"A range of things, he can throw out the charges, admonish either side, or even hold them in contempt. He may adjourn to consider all of the material and legal matters presented or bind you over for trial."

Mia, "Again, Jerry, what are our requirements during the coming days?"

"Alice and I want you to work on graphic slides on Saturday. You get Sunday morning off. Sunday afternoon, we will go over all of your possible testimonies again. Also, can you get your friend Herman Rhodes here for his deposition then?"

"We'll try; he says he wants to help us."

"Good. We will file a Motion to Dismiss Gordon's charges with the judge's clerk on Monday morning. We will also ask for most of a full day to present our evidence and witnesses."

Gordon asked, "Do we have a judge and a time?"

"Not yet. It should be Tuesday, and I'm still hoping for Bill Mudd."

"How does this dismiss thing work?" Strong questioned.

"It's a legal motion to dismiss your criminal charges for lack of evidence. We know Amelia did not kill Merriweather, and we can prove it. If so, how can you be an accessory to murder? Only if the prosecutor has your confession or direct evidence that you had foreknowledge of the killing could they charge you."

"Will it work?" asked Gordon.

"Maybe. The government will argue against it, and the judge should see that they don't have specific facts linking you to the murder."

"That would be a great relief to me," sighed Gordon.

Cushing smiled. "Yes Gordon, and also to me. Can you wear your Class A uniform to court on Tuesday?"

"Yes sir, I'll have to go home to get it."

"Excellent. If your charges are dropped, I will be much more inclined to have you testify to Miss Talbot's whereabouts that day. You two will take most of Monday off before the Prelim. Go to a movie, read a book, take a nap, and enjoy a special meal. Charge your batteries to look healthy, rested, relaxed, alert, and innocent the next day.

Alice and I will work on exhibits, testimony, arguments, meetings with our experts, and any additional legal motions. We will leave work at seven and have dinner and fine wine at our favorite restaurant. Our partner and associates will work all night improving our materials and arguments."

Amelia, "Sounds like a plan. Thanks for all of your efforts."

"It's how I make the big bucks. I think I will enjoy crushing the prosecution at your Prelim. They must prove your criminal act beyond a reasonable doubt and your criminal intent to commit the murder. We have to prove that you both are innocent using a preponderance of the evidence, the testimony of our experts, and the truth of the facts, not speculation."

On Thursday, Gordon and Amelia flew to Raleigh, North Carolina, rented a car, and drove to Upchurches Pond. They returned with Gordon's uniform items, service record, and college transcript on Friday. Saturday at the Cushing's offices was a madhouse. Every space had personnel working on some aspect of the case. Gordon and Mia worked on PowerPoint slides showing their findings about Southeastern Assurance and its companies. Jerry Cushing happily reported that they had a ten o'clock court appearance with Judge Mudd on Tuesday.

As promised, Herman Rhodes showed up Sunday morning and was deposed by Gerald and Alice. He also became a client of Cushing so he could discuss his problems with law enforcement. Monday morning, Gerald and his partner trained Amelia, Gordon, and Ratchet to avoid testifying against themselves by invoking the Fifth Amendment. Once complete, they were free to take the day off. Monday afternoon, The U.S. Attorney dismissed Strong's charges. The government only provided a Bill of Particulars for Amelia's charges.

Tuesday morning dawned bright and sunny in Jacksonville. Amelia, Gordon, Ratchet Rhodes, Virginia Wickens, and Mia's parents stayed at the Downtown Marriot. They met for breakfast but didn't talk about the looming Preliminary Hearing. Cushing sent a car for all of them, and Strong stole the show in his Army uniform with combat ribbons, ranger badge, and parachute emblem.

In the courtroom, Gerald Cushing sat closest to the three prosecution attorneys; Alice was next to him, and Amelia was next to Alice. Both Jerry and Alice had laptop computers. Cushing told Mia to give her comments to Alice, who would send them to his laptop in large print. The clerk ordered them all to stand, and in strode Judge William Mudd in his black robe. He was visibly impressed when he saw Gordon standing behind Amelia in his dress uniform.

"Be seated!" boomed Mudd. "The clerk will read the agenda."

"This is the Preliminary Hearing of the United States government against Miss Amelia Rose Talbot. The charges are first-degree murder and second-degree murder."

Mudd, "Is the government ready?"

The tall lawyer across the aisle from Cushing stood and spoke, "If it pleases the court, we request a one-week continuance."

"Why is that?" snapped Mudd.

"Your Honor, the defense dumped a ton of discovery from their experts on us late on Sunday. We need more time to counter all of these arguments."

Mudd, "Let's see, you've had Sunday night, all of Monday, and last night to respond, right?"

"Yes sir."

"Mr. Cushing, does the defense have an opinion on this?"

"Yes sir, we have several people that travelled here ready to testify. I may not be able to produce them after another week."

Judge Mudd, "Mr. Rawlins, your request is denied. This isn't a trial. We are all here to determine the validity of your charges. If you don't have adequate proof, we shouldn't be here in the first place."

Rawlins, "Then the prosecution is ready, Your Honor."

"Good. Mr. Cushing?"

"The defense is ready, Your Honor. Will there be enough time for our presentations?"

"Counselor, you have all day and into the night if need be. Is that enough?"

"Yes sir, thank you sir."

Mudd asked, "Does the defense have any motions before we start?"

Amelia saw Alice rapidly type, "DISMISS!!" on her laptop.

Cushing stood, "Yes, Your Honor. We file a Motion to Dismiss."

"On what grounds?" asked the judge.

"Your Honor, lack of evidence and defects in the Charging Document."

"Denied on the evidence issue. What's wrong with the Charging Document?"

"Sir, the prosecution claims the murder took place at a specific time and place. The time is wrong. We will prove that. They also claim a certain weapon, with the defendant's fingerprints, a .38 caliber revolver, was the murder weapon. We believe that is incorrect."

Judge Mudd, "Good try, Mr. Cushing. It seems to me that you are going to have to prove those assertions to this court. Motion denied. Are you ready to proceed?"

"More than ready, Your Honor. My client is completely innocent."

Mudd frowned, "Stop testifying, counselor. There's no jury here. Stick to the facts."

"Yes sir."

"Mr. Cushing, I'm looking at your witness list and see Major Gordon Strong. Is that correct?"

"Yes sir, he's on the list now that the government dropped his bogus charges."

"Are you going to call him?"

"I haven't decided, Your Honor."

"You won't be able to put him on the stand if he stays in court," said the Judge.

"Yes sir, my mistake. Sorry, Major Strong. Please wait outside."

Strong stood, reached out, held Mia's hand for a moment as coached by Jerry, and left the room. Alice typed, "GOOD ONE!!"

Judge Mudd, "Mr. Rawlins, proceed if you please."

Amelia noticed that Alice and Gerald took notes on their computers as the prosecutor spoke.

Rawlins, "Yes, the prosecution is ready, Your Honor. This case is a slam dunk if there ever was one. For motive, we have a recording of the defendant showing great prejudice against the deceased. She said, quote, 'I will grind him to dust,' unquote. At the time, she had a weak theory that Mr. Merriweather and his companies were trying to kill her. Whether this is true or not, our investigators don't know, but it looks like she struck first. We will provide evidence that Miss Talbot wanted Mr. Merriweather dead and expended a great deal of time and money preparing to carry out her deadly intent.

Regarding opportunity, the defendant and her significant other, Mr. Gordon Strong, traveled from Fayetteville, North Carolina, and rented space in the decedent's office building in Gainesville, Florida. After a few weeks, she shot her landlord in the parking lot of this building. We have the shooting on video file. It's somewhat grainy in quality, but the defendant has testified that she was standing at Merriweather's car at 6:25 p.m. when the murder occurred.

In the video, you can see the flash of her gun when Robert Merriweather was shot once in the left temple. Following the murder, the defendant took several questionable actions that are evidence of her guilt. First, if she was not the shooter, she never called 911. She left fingerprints, even bloody fingerprints, on the dead man's car door. Strangest of all, she's testified that she took a picture of the body, which might be a trophy.

That leads us to means. We will prove the defendant had access to a .38 revolver. It had her fingerprints on both the gun and the shells it contained – every one of them. When tested for gunshot residue the night of the murder, Miss Talbot tested positive – she had recently fired a gun. During her questioning at the Gainesville FBI office, she testified that she fled the murder scene out of fear. Nonsense, Miss Talbot ran to her car and drove away to avoid detection. Realizing that she would probably be charged with this execution style murder, she tried to cover it up by calling an FBI agent, Mr. Jason Finster.

Miss Talbot did voluntarily come to the FBI offices and spun her distorted version of a clear-cut premeditated murder. Of course, her lover, Major Strong, and her parents tried to give her an alibi before she drove to the Merriweather Building on that fateful night. But even they don't know if Amelia took a weapon with her and what her intent was. The prosecution believes she requested a meeting with Robert

Merriweather in his parking lot. When she got there, she walked up to his car and shot him. We have irrefutable evidence of that.

That night, when agents asked her pointed questions about her involvement in the murder, she clammed up and said they could talk to her lawyer. Even more suspicious, this was the third death scene that Miss Talbot fled in just a few months. After speaking to the FBI and the Gainesville Police the night of the murder, she and her lover, Gordon Strong, turned off their phones, left town, and used only cash as they hid here in Jacksonville.

Two days later, they were arrested by FBI agents using standard procedures and found to be heavily armed. Neither has been willing to talk to law enforcement since. And a footnote: Strong and Talbot slipped away to the Caribbean two days after your arraignment hearing. I'm glad they returned, but who knows their intent at the time?"

Judge Mudd, "Mr. Rawlins, are you finished with your opening?"

"Yes, Your Honor."

"We will adjourn for twenty minutes," ordered Judge Mudd.

Chapter Thirty-two

CUSHING'S REBUTTAL – Federal Courthouse

Judge Mudd, "Mr. Cushing, we are ready for your opening."

"Thank you, Judge. My goodness, what a compelling compendium of half-truths and outright lies. I think the late Paul Harvey, a radio personality, said, 'Wait until you hear the rest of the story.' I will respond to the prosecution's misguided assertions and allegations one by one.

First, let's discuss motive. Several months ago, Miss Talbot and Mr. Strong were very upset with Merriweather's companies. Whether right or wrong, they thought Robert Merriweather was part of a conspiracy to have them murdered to collect on their insurance policies and a reverse mortgage. We will expose this evil scheme and identify the main culprits. We will prove that Mr. Merriweather recently discovered this killing scheme and planned to meet with the FBI the day after his murder. He intended to expose the insurance murders and admit to gross tax fraud. Upon learning this, Amelia Talbot and Major Strong transitioned from animosity toward Mr. Merriweather to sympathy for his situation. Ms. Talbot's angry words were spoken many months ago, a fact our opponents left out.

It's essential to pay attention to many evidence points that my learned opponent did not discuss. It is a fact that Amelia suspected Merriweather of homicide and spent much time and money to find out that it was not the case. It is a fact that Talbot had nothing to gain by killing Merriweather. The prosecution has nothing other than stale, out-of-date exclamations to buttress their weak claims of a revenge killing. And it could have only been a revenge killing – they have nothing else.

Once Amelia Talbot realized that Merriweather's Chief Financial Officer, Mr. Roscoe Fuller, and his partner, Mr. Johnathon Rivers, were the actual perpetrators and cold-blooded killers, she felt empathy for Robert and Patricia Merriweather. They were the public face of Southeast Assurance Company and were ill-used by the two criminals. We will not just assert this; we will prove it.

By the way, three other individuals might have done the murder – Fuller and Rivers, and another man who we will identify. To our knowledge, the prosecution has not investigated any of them for this crime. So that's the rest of the story about motive. Let's turn to opportunity.

It certainly is true that Amelia Talbot had plenty of opportunities to kill Robert Merriweather. They had offices in his building for several weeks – even on the same floor. They used the same elevator and parking lot. Strong and Talbot had placed a motion-activated video sensor on the building in front of Robert and Patricia's reserved parking spots. We will explain how that sensor works and what the recordings for the night in question show. They *do* show Miss Talbot walked to Merriweather's car at 6:25 p.m., as claimed by the prosecution.

Her motivation was that of a good Samaritan, not a killer. They show Amelia finding him comatose, and she grabs his car door to keep from fainting. They show Amelia Talbot checking Merriweather's pulse and opening his door to look for a suicide gun. Also, she took a picture of the body. That's the flash that the prosecution has mistaken for a gunshot.

It defies common sense and sound logic that an accomplished and intelligent woman like Miss Talbot would commit a capital crime in front of one of her own video sensors. We will introduce her service and college records to show she's a top performer. Her scores were in the top five percent of tens of thousands of Marine recruits, and her college grades in computer science were straight As.

Why would Miss Talbot kill Mr. Merriweather, knowing there would be a video record of it? It makes no sense. But beyond that, Your Honor, we can pinpoint the murder to an hour before she arrived in that parking lot. We have the proof. We have evidence that Robert Merriweather was murdered when Miss Talbot was still at her rental home having dinner, i.e., the rest of the story.

That takes us to means. The prosecution has pinned their case on a particular .38 caliber revolver because it has my client's fingerprints on the bullets and gun itself. We don't dispute that such a weapon exists, but we believe that it was used to frame Amelia Talbot. Without forensic ballistic confirmation, the prosecution does not have a case. Who would want to frame her and cause her harm? Mr. Fuller and Mr. Rivers are the prime suspects, as her investigation of their murder-for-hire scheme was destroying their unlawful bid for wealth and financial independence.

That particular gun came from the Merriweathers' condo in the Bahamas and was hidden in the Talbot company jet aircraft. Three individuals knew it was there: my client, Major Strong, and Mr. Herman Rhodes. Strong and Talbot have sworn that they did not remove the revolver from the aircraft. That leaves Herman 'Ratchet' Rhodes a man with a criminal past and a penchant for working for the highest bidder. The gun is still a mystery because we haven't received a ballistics report from the prosecution.

Who knows what bullet killed Robert Merriweather? The Gainesville police lab? The FBI? I hate to trade in speculation, but there's one rumor that the Gainesville testing was inconclusive, so the FBI took over and sent the bullet and weapon to Quantico for testing. Hopefully, the government will share its results at this hearing, or the fingerprints on the gun will be moot.

After finding Mr. Merriweather dead, my client panicked and left the scene before calling 911. It was dark, and she was frightened. Amelia partially hid her car in the shadows of the Gainesville Main Library parking lot and called the FBI because she and Major Strong had been working with the FBI for months. The agent she called, Mr. Jake Finster, said he would call the Gainesville police, send FBI agents to the Southeastern Assurance Building, and arrange a protective police escort for my client. Therefore, she didn't need to call 911.

More importantly, before calling the FBI, she called Patricia Merriweather. Why? Because Miss Talbot was afraid that Mrs. Merriweather and her young daughter Amber might be the killer's next targets. She had the guts to break the bad news to Mrs. Merriweather and warn her to flee from her home and not leave a credit card or cell phone trail. This action further diminishes the prosecution's claims of vengeance and motive, as Amelia's first thought was to protect Merriweather's family, not harm them.

Let's get back to means. What you heard, Your Honor, was that my client tested positive for GSR. That is correct. The U.S. Attorney left out that Major Gordon Strong also tested positive. The reason is the two of them fired several magazines of ammo at his home's indoor shooting range only two days before the GSR tests. GSR can remain on one's hands for several days. I have a nephew who was tested by the TSA a week after firing a gun and detained for several hours.

The government has not explained why *both* of these veterans tested positive. The prosecution also left out the results of blood and GSR tests on Talbot's and Strong's clothing confiscated the night of the murder, which I assume were negative for blood and GSR. Also left out were the pictures of each of them, which showed no blood spatter on their skin or clothing. And now, back to *the* gun.

The shooting was close up and personal, from less than two feet. We will prove that beyond a doubt. So, did *the* gun with my client's fingerprints have blood spatter from the deceased? Or not? Only the FBI knows or doesn't know. When will they share that information with the Court and the Defense?

Let's turn to the actions of Strong and Talbot after their FBI interrogation on the night of the murder. Why would they leave town and attempt to leave no trail? Your Honor, they were scared to death. The Southeastern Assurance murders were now in Gainesville. Robert Merriweather was viciously silenced before he could meet with the FBI. Who knew who was next? Gordon and Amelia knew about the murders and that Robert was going to turn himself in, as did Patricia Merriweather. Were they next on the killing list? It's entirely possible.

They were carrying handguns to protect themselves, entirely lawful in Florida. Why would the U.S. Attorney say Miss Talbot and Mr. Strong were arrested using quote 'standard procedures,' unquote? Perhaps it's because six heavily armed agents came into their hotel room in the middle of the night, cuffed them at gunpoint, and manhandled them to the Jacksonville FBI facility like hardened criminals.

Your Honor, I submit that all the FBI had to do was ask them to report in, and they would have done so. Instead, they were booked, fingerprinted, DNA taken, clothes taken, and detained against their will in the facility until your Arraignment Hearing that morning.

I was trying to reach them to protect them from the authorities but was denied access for several hours. This was not standard procedure for two decorated veterans with no criminal records. The FBI regularly lets suspected criminals surrender with counsel. This was a blatant attempt at prosecutorial intimidation. It didn't work. They gave no further information, which was their right. I only mention it because it shows a single-minded prejudice to investigate and charge my clients. Who is examining Roscoe Fuller, Johnathon Rivers, and Herman Rhodes for this crime? No one, to my knowledge. Who in the FBI is working on the recent murder of Mr. Richard Pritchard in Pennsylvania that is tied to this case?

Now let's restate the implausible theory that the two suspects, quote, 'slipped away to the Bahamas,' unquote. My clients asked me if they could take a trip to Nassau that they'd booked and paid for before the murder. I said yes because Your Honor saw their good character and gave them significant leeway on bail. There never was a question that they would not return for this hearing. However, I advised them we had much work to accomplish before this hearing.

They solved that problem by inviting my wife, sitting here beside me, and myself to accompany them. We happily accepted. We worked on the case every morning for five days, had delicious lunches in different locations, and enjoyed the tourist activities in the afternoon. I might add that there was an attempt on Major Strong's life while in Nassau.

Your Honor, you have heard the prosecution whine about the amount of discovery we delivered to them two days ago. I'm holding up a folder of all the discovery the defense received from the government as of two days ago."

Cushing let the empty Manila folder fall open.

Judge Mudd, "Mr. Cushing, are you finished?"

"Yes sir. Thank you, sir."

Mudd banged his gavel. "We will have a fifteen-minute recess and start with the prosecution's witnesses and evidence when we resume."

Chapter Thirty-three
PRELIMINARY HEARING CONTINUED

When the Prelim restarted, the prosecutor called Brenda Smith from the Gainesville Medical Examiner's Office.

After she was sworn in, Rawlins started his questioning. "Ms. Smith, please state your full name and occupation."

"Yes sir, Brenda B. Smith, Assistant Medical Examiner with the Gainesville City Government."

"Ms. Smith, did you examine the body of Robert Merriweather?"

"Yes sir, I had the night duty and performed a full autopsy a few hours after his death."

"How long have you worked in the ME's office?"

"This will be my fifth year."

"Do you have an opinion about the cause of Mr. Merriweather's death?

"Yes sir, it was a single gunshot to the head. There was no other trauma to the body."

"I understand. Did you retrieve the bullet?"

"Yes sir."

"What was the bullet's condition?"

"It was a bit blunt on the nose but a good candidate for comparison. It entered the decedent's left side of his skull and stopped when it hit the right side."

"Was there gunshot residue on the victim's skin?"

"Yes sir."

"In your professional opinion, how far was the murder weapon from the victim when it discharged?"

"Sir, my estimate is twelve to fourteen inches."

"What is your basis for that conclusion?"

She said, "The decedent, Robert Merriweather, had gunpowder residue on the left side of his head and the left shoulder of his suit jacket."

"When did you receive the body for processing?"

"Roughly, about nine p.m. the night of the murder."

"You say murder; could Merriweather have shot himself? Could his death have been a suicide?"

"No sir, not in my opinion," Smith replied.

"Why not?"

"The bullet hole was above his left ear, and there was no GSR on his left hand or a weapon found in his car."

"I understand. Was the body's condition what you expected when you received it with a time of death about two and a half hours earlier?"

"Yes, it was. Rigor mortis had set in on his face muscles and was starting on his limbs."

"What was your estimate of Time Since Death (TSD)?"

"Looking at the eyes and face about 2.5 to 4.5 hours."

"Did you use other means?"

"Yes, algor mortis showed a body cooled to 93 degrees Fahrenheit."

"Please explain algor mortis," asked the lawyer.

"In general, a dead body cools about 1.5 degrees per hour. This can vary with the clothes worn and the outside temperature. We used 98.6 as the starting point, so the decedent had cooled by 5.6 degrees. This is consistent with an estimated TSD of 2.7 to 4.7 hours."

"When did you take the temperature and determine the TSD?"

"At nine-fifteen p.m."

"So, Ms. Smith, a time of death of 6:25 p.m. would exactly match your computations, correct?"

Cushing rose, "Objection, Your Honor. The witness has specified a period of time, not a particular time."

Judge Mudd, "Sustained. Mr. Rawlins, please rephrase."

Rawlins, "Ms. Smith, a time of death of 6:25 p.m. would be consistent with your calculations, correct?"

"Yes sir."

"I have no further questions for this witness."

Judge Mudd, "Your witness, Mr. Cushing."

"Thank you, Your Honor. Ms. Smith, good morning."

"Good morning, sir."

"My understanding of Post-Mortem Intervals (PMI) is Immediate, Early, and Late. Is that correct?"

"Yes, it is."

"At what stage did you receive Merriweather's body for analysis?"

Smith, "All indications were that we received him in Early PMI, which is defined as three to seventy-two hours after death."

"I see. So, his eyes were cloudy, his skin pale, and there were signs of facial rigor mortis?"

"Yes, all of those characteristics were present," she said.

"You have testified that your best guess for TSD was 2.7 to 4.7 hours before 9:15 p.m. Is that correct?"

"Yes sir."

"Why the range of two full hours?"

Ms. Smith was perturbed, "As I said before, there are several variables, and forensic science can provide an accurate period but not a precise time."

Cushing, "I agree and greatly appreciate your efforts. But let's be very specific; if I take your temperature drop of 5.6 degrees Fahrenheit and divide it by a loss of body heat of 1.5 degrees every hour, my answer is 3.73 hours. Do you agree?"

"Yes, that is the mid-point of the period we estimated."

Cushing, "Just to nail this point down, .73 of sixty minutes is 44 minutes, right?"

"It could be, just a minute." Smith did a calculation on her phone. "Yes sir, forty-four if you round up"

Cushing pounced, "Good. And three hours and forty-four minutes before your observation at 9:15 is 5:31 p.m. on the night of the murder."

"That is correct."

"Excellent. Would it surprise you that the defense will present irrefutable proof of the shooting at 5:30 p.m., one minute before your precise calculation?"

Rawlins, "Objection, Your Honor. The witness has provided a two-hour estimate, not a precise time of death."

Mudd, "Sustained. Mr. Cushing, must I warn you about facts not in evidence, testifying again, and your question-wording?"

"No, Your Honor. Sorry."

"Please rephrase your question."

"Yes sir. Ms. Smith, a time of death of 5:30 p.m. would be consistent with your calculations, correct?"

"Yes sir, that is the midpoint of our TSD estimate."

Rawlins, "Objection, Your Honor. Counsel is leading the witness."

Cushing, "Judge, I phrased my question exactly as the prosecutor did before with this witness."

Mudd, "He's got you there, Mr. Rawlins. Overruled."

Cushing continued, "Ms. Smith, did the body show signs of Livor Mortis after 9 p.m.?"

"Yes, there were large patches of purplish discoloration."

"Was the amount of discoloration and persistence of the color consistent with a TSD of 3.7 hours?"

"Not specifically, it was consistent with a TSD of 2.7 to 4.7 hours."

"I see. Let's move on to the fatal bullet. Did you remove the bullet from the body?"

"Yes, I did."

"You said it entered Merriweather's skull above his left ear. Do you know where it impacted the other side of his skull?"

"Yes, there was trauma blow the right ear and one centimeter above the left jaw joint."

"In other words, the bullet traveled downward, indicating a tall shooter, correct?"

"I guess that is possible," she answered.

"If the killer was nearly six foot tall, he or she would have held the gun at an angle to cause a downward trajectory through the brain, right?"

Smith snapped, "That question is outside my area of expertise. An alternate theory could be that the victim leaned to the left, trying to grab the gun. I don't have any scientific opinions on the murderer."

Cushing, "I'm just trying to say that Ms. Talbot is only five foot seven, and if the victim did not move his head, her bullet would have impacted above the right ear."

Rawlins stood. "Asked and answered, Your Honor."

Judge Mudd, "I agree. Move it along, Mr. Cushing."

Cushing smiled. "I'm done with this witness. Thank you, Ms. Smith."

Rawlins, "Redirect Your Honor."

"Go ahead."

"Ms. Smith, can we agree that 6:25 p.m. is three hours and ten minutes before 9:15 p.m.?"

"Yes sir."

"And that specific time is well within the TSD provided by your office?"

"That is correct," she responded.

"Thank you. No further questions."

Mudd, "The witness may step down. Mr. Rawlins, please call your next witness."

"The prosecution calls Officer Chet Wilson to the witness stand."

After Wilson was sworn in, the prosecutor approached. "Please state your full name and your department."

"Yes sir, Officer Charles Newell Wilson from the Gainesville City Police Department."

"Officer Wilson, thank you for your service. How long have you been a policeman?"

"This is my fifth year as a patrolman."

"On the night of Robert Merriweather's murder, where were you patrolling?"

"Me and my partner, a rookie, were driving around the University of Florida campus."

"I understand. You got a call about 6:45 p.m., do you remember that?"

"Yes sir, dispatch needed a unit at the Main Library."

"Did you respond?"

"Yes sir, we took the call and headed east on University Avenue."

"How long did it take you to get there?"

"A little over five minutes, give or take."

"What happened at the library?" asked Rawlins.

"A car in the parking lot blinked its lights at us. By then, we had a text message to protect a lady in the parking lot."

"Do you see that person here in this courthouse?"

Wilson pointed at Amelia. "Yes sir, the defendant, Miss Talbot, is sitting over there."

"She was in the car that blinked at you?"

"Yes sir."

"What were her first words to you?"

"Ummm...something like, 'Thank God, you're here. I just found a man murdered, and I may be next.'"

"What was her demeanor when you found her?"

Cushing stood, "Objection, Your Honor. Calls for a conclusion."

Judge Mudd, "Counselor, could you rephrase and be more specific."

Rawlins, "Officer Wilson, based on your five years of experience, did she seem frightened?"

"Yes sir. Her hands were shaking. She had been crying, and she kept looking around."

"What did she say to you?"

"She said someone was following or tracking her. She found a GPS tracker under a fender and threw it in the trash. And she wanted to use the women's room in the library."

"What did you do?"

"We escorted her into the library. My partner made sure the bathroom was empty, and we waited outside the door."

"This is important; how long was she out of your sight?" asked the prosecutor.

"Not long, less than five minutes, I would say."

"What happened next."

"We escorted her to her car and followed her to a house in the University Park area."

"Did you go inside with her?"

"No sir, we sat on the curb. Uh, we remained in front of the house for about an hour until our next call."

"What was the nature of that call?"

"Dispatch directed us to return to the library parking lot and search the area where her car had been for anything suspicious."

"Who is the her you are referring to?"

"Sorry, Miss Talbot's car."

"What did you and your partner do?"

"We searched around where Miss Talbot' car was parked, the brush behind it, and a trash can nearby."

Rawlins, "What was in the can?"

"Hmmm. Assorted trash, fast food wrappers, cans and bottles, and a gun."

"A gun?" asked the prosecutor.

"Yes sir."

"What type of gun?"

Wilson, "It was a .38 revolver in good condition."

"Did you touch the gun?"

"No sir. I picked it up with my handkerchief and looked it over."

"Was it loaded?"

"Yes, the chambers I could see had rounds in them."

"What did you do next."

"We called it in to central, and they said to bring it to the evidence vault."

"Did you do that?"

"Yes sir."

"Was the revolver ever out of your sight or possession until it was logged into the vault?"

"No sir."

Rawlins, "Thank you very much, officer. Your witness."

Gerald Cushing rose, buttoned his suit jacket, and said, "Officer Wilson, I also thank you for your service."

"Yes sir."

"When you first found Miss Talbot in her car, did you shine your flashlight on her and around her car?"

"Yes sir, we wanted to clear the area."

"Did you see anything suspicious at that time?"

"No sir."

"You said you saw her hands shaking."

"Yes sir."

"Did you see any blood on her hands or face?"

"Ummm. There might have been a spot of blood on her right hand."

"Might have been? Are you sure one way or the other?"

"No sir."

"I've been in the library, and it is well-lighted. When you went in with Miss Talbot, did you see any blood on her skin or clothing?"

"Sir, I wasn't looking for blood."

Gerald pressed his point, "Yes, but you are an experienced and well-trained policeman. If she had blood specks on her white blouse, head, neck, bare arms, or tan pants, you would have alerted, would you not?"

"Yes sir."

"Think back, to when your partner entered the women's bathroom. Did you see any blood spots on Amelia Talbot?"

"No sir"

"You're sure?"

"Yes sir."

Cushing, "Excellent. Let's talk about the revolver you found."

"Yes sir."

"When you searched the trash can, did you find the GPS tracking unit that Miss Talbot mentioned to you?"

Wilson scratched his head. "No, we didn't?"

"You're sure?"

"Yes sir, I would have realized that right away. There were no electronic devices in the can."

"Did that surprise you?"

Wilson, "Honestly, no, I was pretty fixated on the gun. It had all my attention. I knew I had to collect it and not screw up."

"Not touch it?" stated Cushing.

"Yes."

"Did you think it was odd that if the gun was associated with Miss Talbot, would she tell you about throwing something in the trashcan?"

Rawlins stood. "Objection, Your Honor, calls for a conclusion based on events not known by the Officer."

Judge Mudd, "Sustained."

Cushing, "Officer Wilson, you shined your bright flashlight on the revolver, right?"

"Yes sir."

"You carefully picked it up and examined it in a bright light."

"Yes sir, both of our flashlights."

"Did you or your partner see any blood specks on the gun?"

Rawlins, "Objection, Your Honor."

Mudd, "Overruled. The witness may answer."

"I don't know about Billy, but I saw no blood."

"Thank you, Officer Wilson. You have been very helpful. One more question, well, maybe two."

"Have you ever seen hollow point bullets?"

"Yes sir, they have a hole in the center."

"Correct. Now, think back. When you shined your bright flashlight on the gun and saw some bullets, were they hollow points?"

"Well, yes sir, now that I think about it, they were."

"I apologize, Officer Wilson; I have one more."

"Did you smell the gun?"

"Did I what?" asked the cop.

Cushing, "You are experienced in handling firearms; it's only natural that you might have sniffed the barrel to see if it was recently fired. Did you sniff it?"

"I guess I did," replied the Officer.

"You guess, or are you sure?" probed Cushing.

"No, I mean, yes, I smelled it."

"What did it smell like?" asked the lawyer.

"An oiled weapon," answered the officer.

Cushing pounced. "Not fired an hour before?"

"No."

"Thank you for your testimony."

Rawlins stood. "Your Honor, redirect."

Judge Mudd, "Go ahead."

"Officer Wilson, when you saw some of the bullets in the revolver were hollow point, you could not see any of the other bullets, correct?"
"No sir."
"So, they could have been regular rounds? You didn't spin the cylinder, right?"
"No sir."
"Thank you. You are dismissed. Your Honor, the prosecution would like to submit Exhibit One, the .38 revolver recovered from the library parking lot."
Judge Mudd, "Mr. Cushing, any objections?"
"No, Your Honor. Our weapons expert has examined the revolver, and we will prove it isn't the murder weapon."
Mudd snapped, "Counselor, stop testifying."
"Yes sir."
Judge Mudd, "We will have a ten-minute recess."

Chapter Thirty-four
GAINESVILLE DETECTIVE – U.S. District Court

Judge William Mudd, "Mr. Rawlins, call your next witness."

"The prosecution calls Detective Brian L. Granger from the Gainesville homicide squad."

Granger was sworn in, and Rawlins commenced establishing his expertise.

Cushing stood, "Your Honor, the Defense will stipulate as to Mr. Granger's experience and training."

"Very well, Mr. Rawlins, please proceed."

"Detective Granger, where were you at 6:55 the night of Robert Merriweather's murder?"

"I was having dinner with my family."

"And what happened at that time?"

"I received a call about a homicide at the Arnholdt Building and instruction to proceed there as soon as possible."

"When did you arrive?"

"7:15"

"What did you find?"

"There were several Gainesville police cars with flashing lights at the scene, and their headlights illuminated a four-door late-model Mercedes. That car had police tape around it that stretched to the building."

"What did you find in the car?"

"There was a gentleman, probably in his forties, shot in the head and apparently dead."

"Did you touch or disturb the body in any way?"

"No sir. I made sure the scene was secure and waited for forensics."

"When did they arrive?"

"7:25. They confirmed that the man was dead, that it was probably a homicide, made their tests, and took pictures."

"Your Honor, the Prosecution now enters into evidence our Exhibit Two, the Gainesville Forensic Report of the murder scene, and Exhibit Three, the pictures that were taken."

Cushing called out, "Without objection."

"Detective Granger, when forensics was done, what did you do?"

"I wore gloves and went through the man's wallet."

"What did you determine?"

"The ID matched the victim, a Mr. Robert Merriweather, living at 4589 North East 16th Terrace."

"How was that important?"

"I called in the name and address to Central so someone could notify his family before the press splashed it all over radio and TV."

"What did you do next?"

"I looked in the car for a gun, considering it might have been a suicide."

"Did you think it was a suicide?"

"No sir."

"Why not?"

"Merriweather had his watch on his left arm, and the wound was on his left side of the head."

Rawlins, "Please explain."

"Usually, only a left-handed person would shoot himself in the left side of his head. If left-handed, his watch would be on the other arm."

Rawlins asked, "Did you find a gun?"

"No. I directed several of the officers to start a search of the parking lot and all of the nearby dumpsters and trashcans."

"Did that include the one at the Main Library more than a mile away?"

"No sir. At that time, I was unaware of Miss Talbot's involvement with the murder."

Cushing, "Objection!"

Rawlins, "I will rephrase, you were not aware that Miss Talbot was first to find the body, correct?"

Granger glared at Cushing, "Yes sir, that's correct."

"When did you find out about Miss Talbot's involvement?"

"Officer Wilson and his partner came to the crime scene and told me about securing her at the library and escorting her home. They said she found the body and was scared for her life and called the police from the library parking lot."

"What did you do?"

"I told them to return to the library and search the area with a fine-tooth comb, the parking lot, nearby trash cans, and inside the library, including the restroom, etc."

"Did that complete your activity regarding the murder that night?"

Granger smiled. "No sir. Officer Wilson called me on my cell and said they'd found a gun near where Talbot was parked."

"What did you respond?"

"I told them to take it to the Evidence Vault."
"When you were at the crime scene, was the FBI also there?"
"Yes sir, two agents took pictures with their phones."
"Did you tell them about the gun that Officer Wilson found?"
"Yes sir."
"What did you do next?"
"I went to my office to research who the deceased was. It turned out Robert Merriweather was a notable person in the community, and this was a high-profile murder."
"Understood. Did you call the Medical Examiner's office?"
"No. I called my boss, the head of the Homicide Division, and the District Attorney's office. Then I checked if his family had been notified."
"His, meaning Robert Merriweather?"
"Sorry. Yes, the squad car went to his house, and no one was there."
"What next?"
"I called my partner, Doug Schmidt, informed him of the killing, and asked him to report in because it looked like an all-nighter."
"Did you receive a call from the FBI?"
"Yes, an agent, Jason Finster, called me and said they were taking the lead on the murder case."
"What else did he say?"
"He explained that they were aware of possible criminal activity by Merriweather's company and had been monitoring Miss Talbot and Mr. Strong for several months."
"What else did he say?"
"He invited me to sit in on their interrogation of Talbot and Strong and requested I bring the .38 revolver to their building in Gainesville."
"Did you do that?"
"Yes sir."
"What was your impression of Miss Amelia Talbot?"
"She seemed very intelligent and somewhat arrogant."
Cushing rose, "Objection, Your Honor."
Mudd, "Overruled. I'm interested in this seasoned investigator's evaluations."
Rawlins, "Did you think she was capable of the murder?"
Cushing, "Objection, Your Honor. Calls for a conclusion not based on evidence."
"Sustained. Move on, Mr. Rawlins."

"Detective Granger, what did you think of Mr. Gordon Strong?"
"I never met him. He went to another interrogation room. I heard he refused to cooperate."
"But Miss Talbot did answer Finster's questions briefly?"
"Yes, she gave us her version of finding Merriweather and her actions."
Cushing, "Objection, Your Honor. What other version would she be able to provide?"
"Sustained."
"Detective Granger, in your professional opinion, was Talbot a person of interest for the crime?"
"Yes sir, definitely. The FBI seemed to have plenty of damaging information on her."
Cushing, "Really, Your Honor?"
Judge Mudd, "I'll allow it. It's his opinion. Remember, this is a Preliminary Hearing where even hearsay is allowed."
Rawlins, "I'm done with this witness for now."
Judge Mudd, "We'll take a ten-minute recess before the defense's cross."
Clerk, "All rise."
During the recess, Cushing asked Mia, "Did Granger speak during your initial testimony to the FBI?"
She said, "No. It was just Finster and me who talked. It seemed conversational until Jake mentioned suspicious things I had said."
"What about the night of your arrest in Jacksonville? Granger was there for that also, right?"
"Yes. Again, it was mainly Finster's party. Granger did wave the revolver at me and asserted they had my murder weapon with my fingerprints on it. He called me Missy."
"Whoa, did he point the gun at you?"
"No, he thumped it and picked it up."
Judge Mudd returned. "Mr. Cushing, please proceed."
"Yes sir. Detective Granger, good morning."
"Good morning to you, counselor."
"Detective, the defendant informed me that you didn't talk during the interrogation at the Gainesville FBI Office. Is that correct?"
"Yes. That's correct."
"Why is that? Didn't you have some questions of your own?"
"Well, the Feds had taken the lead and seemed to know much more about Miss Talbot than me."

"I see. Several days later, at the second interrogation of my client at the Jacksonville FBI Office, you were also present. Why is that?"

"Agent Finster called me and asked if I would like to be present after they arrested Talbot and Strong. He requested I arrive with all current knowledge from the Gainesville M-E's Office and our forensic staff."

"Did you obtain that information?"

"Yes, I did."

"What were you told?"

"The M-E ruled the death as a homicide from a gunshot to the head. They had the bullet; it was a .38 caliber."

"Did it match the gun?"

"We didn't know yet because the FBI had the gun."

"What did you do?"

"I called Agent Finster and asked if they'd test-fired the revolver."

"What did he say?"

"He said the gun was at their Jacksonville office, and he thought they'd fired it. He requested I bring the bullet to Jacksonville, which I did."

"You were pretty quiet during the interview after Miss Talbot's arrest, right?"

"Again, the FBI had the lead."

"But you brought what you thought was the murder gun and bullet to the table, correct?"

"Yes, I did."

"Why did you do that?"

"By that time, counselor, we all knew that Miss Talbot's fingerprints were on the revolver found in the library trash can. I brought the gun and bullet that killed Merriweather to confront her. Many criminals break down and confess when you challenge them with damning evidence."

"Did she break down?"

"No. She wanted a closer view of the weapon and the bullet."

"Did you do that?"

"Sure, why not? I thought it still might work."

"Detective Granger, did you know when you showed the defendant that evidence that it would help her defense?"

Granger's eyes narrowed, "Huh? What are you talking about?"

Cushing turned to the Judge, "Your Honor, I need to bring up some facts not yet in evidence that I will introduce later to speed along the testimony of this witness."

Judge Mudd, "I'll allow it."

"Detective Granger, when Miss Talbot first found this gun at the Merriweather's condo in Nassau, it had hollow point bullets in every chamber. Did you know that?"

"No. I did not."

"She took all of those shells out of the gun and put them in a plastic bag. When she returned from the Bahamas to Gainesville, she left the gun and the shells in her private aircraft. Did you know the revolver you showed her still had hollow point bullets in the chambers that she could see?"

"No. I didn't know that. So what?"

Cushing said, "She knew it was the gun from the Merriweather's condo. She also knew that her fingerprints were on the firearm and on the shells."

"All very convincing evidence of guilt in my opinion," said the lawman.

"Yes, mine too, except you were showing her an intact bullet that killed Merriweather. Her Marine Corps training and years of handling weapons taught her that a hollow-point bullet would have splintered into many pieces when it hit Robert Merriweather's skull. Therefore, if this was the murder gun, someone must have replaced one or more of the hollow points with a regular round."

"So what? She could have been the one to do that," Granger argued.

Cushing, "You're right, except why would a person knowledgeable about guns and ammunition replace a round that was not traceable with one that was? It is not logical and defies common sense."

"Maybe she's not that smart after all," smirked the detective.

Gerald, "You might say so, but when you showed her that intact bullet, she knew the shell wouldn't have her prints on it."

"She could have worn gloves.

"I suppose so, but why go to all that trouble? Why not wipe the gun and the shells? Was her print on the trigger?"

Granger shrugged. "I don't know, and I don't think it matters."

"Detective, does the FBI still have that expended shell?"

"I believe they do."

"I bet you a thousand dollars it has different manufacturing markings, and Amelia's prints are not on that substituted round."

"Nonsense. Save it for a jury," challenged Granger.

Cushing retorted, "I don't think we will have a trial. When you showed Miss Talbot the weapon, did you call her Missy?"

"I don't know. I might have, so what?"
"Don't you know that is a pejorative, sexist term and shows prejudice against my client?"
"That's not what I intended," claimed the detective.
"I see. Let's turn to another subject. On the night of the murder, did you receive a copy of the photograph Miss Talbot took of the deceased?"
"I did. Agent Finster received it from her after the interrogation, and he emailed me a copy."
"Good. Did you notice anything important in that photo?"
"No. I looked at it on my phone."
"Did you later see a high-definition, full-color version on your computer display or a printout?"
"No, I had a secretary in our office add it to our case file."
"As a hard copy or in digital form?"
"Digital."
Cushing, "Can we receive a copy here from your office?"
Granger, "No, case file computers aren't connected to the internet."
"Your Honor, to speed the completion of this testimony, I request the prosecution to enter Talbot's photo into the record."
"Mr. Rawlins?"
"Without objection, we enter Exhibit 4, the photograph in question."
Cushing, "Thank you, counselor, whoa. I object. This printout is black and white. My client sent a color picture; that's the one we need."
Rawlins, "Your Honor, I think the FBI had some problems with their color printer when they sent us this."
Gerald Cushing was angry. "Your Honor, I can't tell you how bogus that sounds. That color picture is critical to our defense."
"Figure out how to get it, Mr. Cushing, without wasting too much of the court's time."
"Yes sir."
Amelia whispered to Alice, "It's on my email. We can pull it up on a computer and print it."
Alice typed on the two laptops, "ON HER EMAIL, HAVE CLERK ACCESS AND PRINT."
Cushing rose and said, "Your Honor, we can go back in Miss Talbot's emails and send it to your Clerk."
"How long will that take?"

"About ten minutes, Your Honor. Hold it; maybe there's a better way. Detective Granger, do you still have that file on your phone?"

"I suppose so; I didn't delete it."

Cushing, "Even better. Judge, Mr. Granger, will send it to the Clerk."

Rawlins, "Objection, Your Honor. This is very nonstandard procedure."

Mudd, "Yes, it is. Objection denied. Ten-minute recess."

Ten minutes later, Cushing handed the photograph to the Detective, "Mr. Granger, what do you see?"

"I see the deceased, Mr. Merriweather, sitting in his car. The driver's door is open. He is slumped forward and has blood seeping out of a bullet hole above his left ear."

"Is the blood seeping or somewhat coagulated?" asked the lawyer.

"Hmmm. It could be partially clotted."

"Detective, look at the color. Is that fresh blood from a man shot one minute before?"

Rawlins shot to his feet, "Objection, Detective Granger isn't a forensic scientist."

Cushing snapped back, "Judge, he's had six years as a homicide detective. Surely, he must know what fresh blood looks like."

Mudd, "Overruled. The witness may answer."

Granger, "Now that you call attention to it, Mr. Cushing, this is not fresh blood. It is too dark, and the droplets on the victim's shoulder aren't standing up."

"I agree. When you arrived at the scene, did forensics give you an estimated time of death?"

"Yes sir, from an hour to two hours before."

"Looking at the deceased blood in this printout, would it surprise you to learn time of death was an hour before Miss Talbot took this picture?"

Rawlins, "Objection!"

Judge Mudd, "The witness may answer. He's your witness, Mr. Rawlins."

Granger said, "No, it would not surprise me. The blood is pretty dark."

"Please look closely at the bullet hole. Do you see a slight darkening around it?"

"Yes, yes I do," responded Granger.

Cushing, "Does that happen immediately after someone has been shot?"

"No, it takes a significant amount of time, many minutes at a minimum."

"Thank you, Detective Granger. Your Honor, I'm done with this witness."

Mudd, "We will have a twenty-minute recess. Mr. Rawlins, plan on questioning one or two witnesses before lunch."
"Yes sir."
Clerk, "All rise."

Chapter Thirty-five
PROSECUTION'S CASE – U.S. District Courthouse

During recess, Gerald Cushing asked Amelia and Gordon if they'd ever received their clothes back from the FBI. Their answer was negative. Cushing used the bathroom, splashed water on his face, and drank coffee.

The hearing resumed, and Judge Mudd said, "Will the prosecution call its next witness."

Rawlins rose. "We call FBI technician Roy Iverson."

Iverson took the oath and sat on the witness stand.

Rawlins approached and said, "Agent Iverson, please state your full name and organization."

"Yes sir, Roger L. Iverson, Federal Bureau of Investigation, Jacksonville crime lab."

"What is your primary area of expertise?"

"Matching fingerprints, DNA, and now face prints."

"Did you find fingerprints on our Exhibit One?"

"Yes, I did."

"More than one set?"

"Yes, several sets from one individual."

"And who is that person?"

"Amelia Talbot, the defendant."

"Did you also find her prints on the cartridges in the revolver?"

"Yes, I did."

"All of them?"

"No, all but two."

"I understand. Were there different types of ammunition in the gun?"

"Yes sir, two shells were standard .38 rounds, and the rest were hollow point rounds."

"Have you compared a bullet fired from this revolver to the one removed from Robert Merriweather's skull?"

"That is happening as we speak by an expert from Quatico and defense representative. It should be completed during lunch."

"Thank you. No further questions."

Judge Mudd, "Cross-examine Mr. Cushing?"

"Yes Judge. Thank you. Mr. Iverson, were the fingerprints on the gun consistent with it having been recently fired?"

Iverson, "I'm not sure what you mean."

"Well, were they on the grip, the cylinder, and the trigger?"

"The grip is knurled, so only some partial prints were on there. There were no prints on the trigger, and Miss Talbot's prints were on the cylinder, the barrel, and hollow point shells."

"I see. I'm most interested in whether there was a clear right-hand index fingerprint below the cylinder?"

"No, I don't believe so."

"Agent Iverson, you are aware that most military shooters keep their index finger straight forward and off the trigger until they're ready to fire, right?"

Iverson was reluctant. "Yes, I guess so."

Cushing, "Could you say Miss Talbot's prints are more consistent with holding the gun and unloading the rounds rather than firing the weapon?"

"No, I can't say that one way or the other," answered the technician.

"Did you check the barrel before test-firing the weapon?" asked Gerald.

"Check it for what?"

"Well, to see if it was dirty or clean and whether it had been recently fired."

Iverson was irritated, "No, I did not."

"Did you sniff it for the smell of gunpowder?"

"Negative."

"Agent Iverson, you took a pretty close look at this weapon, right?"

"Yes sir."

"Did you see any blood spots or blood splatter on it?"

"Negative."

"Thank you, that is all."

Judge Mudd, "One more witness before lunch, Mr. Rawlins.

"Yes sir, the prosecution calls Jason Higgons."

Higgons was sworn in, and Rawlins approached. "Please state your full name and where you work."

"Jason Odum Higgons and I work in the Gainesville FBI Building."

"Thank you, Jason. What is your specialty?"

"Yes sir. I do a lot of varied computer and information technology work and specialize in computer graphics."

"Were you tasked to prepare some slides for this hearing?"

"Yes sir. I was provided several frames of a video file that showed the murder of Robert Merriweather. I've turned them into hard copies, and PowerPoint slides for your demonstration."

"Good. Your Honor, we submit Exhibit 5, which is a series of photos showing the defendant approaching Merriweather's car, talking to him, shooting him, and running back to her car."

Mudd, "Mr. Cushing?"

"No objections until I see them and cross the witness, Judge."

The judge queried, "You haven't seen them?"

"No, sir. I have not seen Mr. Higgons's product. I've seen the original video file."

Judge Mudd, "Continue, Mr. Rawlins."

"Jason, which of these photos shows the defendant shooting a gun?"

"Number 8, sir. It's a bit grainy. I cleaned it up the best I could and put a contrast filter on it. You can see the time of 6:25 and Miss Talbot standing at the car window with a gun in her hand and a gunfire explosion that lights the left side of the victim's face."

Rawlins rubbed his hands together. "Thank you, a picture is worth a thousand words. I'm done with this witness."

Cushing approached the witness, "Good morning, Mr. Higgons."

"Good morning."

"Could you put Number 8 up on the screen so everyone can see it?"

"Yes, just a moment. The projector is ready to go. There it is."

"Good. Would you be surprised if I told you that isn't a gun firing but Miss Talbot taking a picture of the body?"

"Yes, I would. I was told it was the time of the murder."

"Mr. Higgons, who told you that?"

"My boss."

"What else did he tell you?"

"He said to make it look as good as possible."

"So, what did you do?" asked the lawyer.

"I used a bunch of video tools to enhance the image, especially the gunshot."

Cushing pounced, "I see. What was wrong with the gunshot?"

"On the original file, it was a bright ball of light, and not clearly coming from Miss Talbot's hand."

Gerald persisted, "So you made it look more like a gun firing, right?"

"I guess you could say that. I screened out some of the light so you can see the origin."

"Mr. Higgons, why is your product not in color?"

"Oh, the color was hopeless. It didn't have enough pixels or shades to be meaningful at that time of night."

"So, you made a lot of alterations to the original frames of video, is that correct?"

Higgons, "Yes, I used a trial-and-error method until I had a set of tools to apply to all frames. I sharpened the objects so you can see it's a woman walking to the car, not a man."

Cushing, "Was your boss pleased?"

"Oh, very pleased. He may put me in for an award."

"Your Honor, now I object to this so-called evidence. It has been doctored to show the prosecution's version of the murder."

Judge Mudd, "Mr. Rawlins?"

"Judge, I disagree with the counselor's choice of words. The video has been enhanced, not doctored."

"The objection is sustained. Mr. Cushing, will we see these pictures again?"

"Yes sir, we will see the time of the murder as 5:30 p.m. and compare it to the 6:25 video. I'm done with this witness but reserve the right to call him back."

Judge Mudd, "Noted. We will break for lunch and reconvene at one o'clock."

Chapter Thirty-six

THE DEFENSE ATTACKS – Federal Courthouse

Alice Cushing had two cars waiting outside the courthouse to take the Talbots, Gordon Strong, Ratchet Rhodes, the Cushings, and two associates to the BB&T Building. The lawyer's conference room table was covered with lunch items and multiple chilled nonalcoholic drinks.

Amelia took a cobb salad and queried, "Jerry, what comes next?"

He replied, "Let's go to my office and consider our options."

Jerry Cushing sipped his iced tea as the others dug into their lunches. "Amelia, we've about an hour to prepare for the prosecution's next moves and decide on our strategies."

She took a drink from her Perrier bottle and said, "What do you think they'll do?"

"I think they'll wrap it up with an FBI agent and try and do as much damage as possible with him or her summarizing the case."

Gordon broke in. "Jerry, how are we doing so far?"

Cushing smiled. "It couldn't be better. Judge Mudd is sharp. He's seen how they're twisting the evidence, and I expect he's seething from how they treated you the night of your arrest. Do you know who they might put on the stand from the FBI?"

Mia answered, "It has to be Jake Finster. He has stayed involved since we met him five months ago."

Gerald nodded. "Next question, how did you know Merriweather was not involved in the murders? Was it your illegal sensors in his home, or did you have any other means?"

Amelia said, "We first learned from their conversation in the kitchen. Then we backtracked on his telephone file and listened to his calls to Richard Pritchard. Pritchard was an insurance actuary and analyzed the deaths of Southeast's customers. He called Robert and declared that they were statistically impossible."

"In what way?" asked the lawyer.

"They were too soon for the age of the customers. Too many accidents paid double indemnity, and the geographical spread and distribution over several different insurance companies was highly suspect."

"How did you hack Merriweather's phone?"

"Ratchet did it. He has dark web software to compromise most cell phones from the major carriers."

Cushing reacted. "Ouch. I'll be more careful in the future."
Amelia, "Too right; Gordon and I use burner phones briefly and then chuck them in the trash."
"Hmmm. I think it's better to say Ratchet monitored Robert's phone than you had bugs in their house."
"I suppose so," answered Mia.
"I was thinking of using Rhodes as a witness, but now it seems it could be a can of worms."
She responded, "He knows all of our sins. I would keep him off the stand if possible."
"Do you know how much he has revealed to the FBI?"
"No, we don't. He says he's on our side and will take the fifth if the Feds ask him about our questionable activities."
Cushing, "I'm going to talk to him next. Gordon, I want you to testify to the history of your involvement with the murderers. You must explain the viewgraphs on the Southeastern companies and office locations. We will reveal the hacking of the CFO's phone and Robert Merriweather's. On cross-examination, you'll take the fifth for any other possible crimes except the murder, understood?"
"Understood. Exactly what do I say when I take the fifth?" asked Strong.
"I will give you a statement to read in court."
"Outstanding. Gerald, aren't you going to have something to eat?"
"No, no food until we get these charges dropped. Being hungry keeps my energy focused on the case and super alert in court."
"You're doing a terrific job, and we both appreciate it," said Gordon.
"Thanks. Now get out of here and send Rhodes to talk to me."
"Yes sir."

An hour later, Amelia and the Cushings were back in the courtroom. Gordon, Rhodes, and four expert defense witnesses waited outside.
Judge Mudd, "Mr. Rawlins, is the prosecution ready to continue?"
"Yes, Your Honor. We call FBI Special Agent Jason Finster to the stand."

Finster entered the room wearing a pin-striped suit, white shirt, and an expensive silk tie.
Rawlins, "Agent Finster, please state your full name and organization."
"Jason Lester Finster, Special Agent from the Fayetteville, North Carolina FBI office."
"Agent Finster, what brought you here to Florida?"

"I was the first to interview Major Strong and Miss Amelia Talbot. My home is near Gordon Strong's, and he set up a meeting. They claimed there was a conspiracy to murder them. I thought it questionable."

"Questionable, how?" asked Rawlins.

"Miss Talbot had brought two folders to Gordon, or so they said. The folders had pictures and personal information about each of them, their daily routines, and activities."

"What were your first thoughts?" asked Rawlins.

"It seemed very far-fetched, and anyone could have created the material, even them."

"Why would they do that?"

"At the time, I didn't know, and they couldn't explain why anyone would murder Amelia Talbot in Virginia and Gordon Strong in North Carolina."

"Did they manufacture a theory?"

Cushing on his feet, "Objection to the innuendo of manufacture, Your Honor."

Mudd, "Sustained. Please rephrase Mr. Rawlins."

"Agent Finster, did they come to your office in Fayetteville within forty-eight hours with a new theoretical conclusion?"

"Yes sir, they did."

"Please briefly describe their assertions."

Finster, "They believed that two different insurance companies wanted them dead to collect on their insurance policies and Strong's reverse mortgage. They asserted that both companies and perhaps others were subsidiaries of Mr. Robert Merriweather's Florida Corporation, Southeast Assurance Company."

"Did you believe them?"

"I wanted to. I had known Gordon Strong for several years and thought he was an honorable man and exemplary soldier. I was unsure about Miss Talbot as a quick check of her record showed payments from the CIA, DIA, and even the FBI for classified consulting."

"What else did you discover about her?"

"Through her testimony that she had left the scene of two deaths in Bumpass, Virginia."

Rawlins, "What was the nature of these deaths?"

"She said they were accidental."

"What did you do?"

"I opened a case file and asked our Richmond, Virginia office to investigate the circumstances."

"What were they?" asked the prosecutor.

"One was a nighttime car accident where the driver exited a narrow two-lane, black-topped road at high speed and hit a tree."

"That sounds accidental, doesn't it?"

"Yes sir, it did until our Virginia agents did some canvasing, and two neighbors reported Miss Talbot's powerful motorcycle was chasing the dead man in a screaming low gear."

Rawlins, "Is that suspicious?"

"Yes and no. Talbot knew the hairpin turn was coming up, and the victim didn't. In a way, she was herding him to his death."

Cushing, "Objection, Your Honor. This is all conjecture, and no charges have been filed against Miss Talbot."

Mudd, "But it did happen, did it not?"

"Yes sir, but not in the sinister way that's been portrayed."

"Objection denied. You will have your chance to rebut the testimony, counselor," said the judge.

"Yes sir, I will."

Judge Mudd, "Mr. Rawlins, please continue."

"Yes sir. Agent Finster, what about the other death scene you mentioned."

"Sir, it was even more suspicious. Miss Talbot said a woman assassin broke into her home armed with a knife and fell down the stairs from the second floor to the ground floor."

"How did she die?"

Finster, "Talbot argued that she cracked her skull open on a bottom stair baseboard."

"Why was that suspicious?"

"Sir, there was no evidence whether she fell or was pushed. Miss Talbot had a very elaborate security system, and someone erased the sensor outputs during the woman's fall. Amelia Talbot's location and actions during that time are not in evidence."

Rawlins, "Theoretically, what could she have done?"

Cushing, "Objection. For all we know, she went to her kitchen and baked a cake."

Judge Mudd, "Overruled. The witness may answer."

Finster, "In theory, she could have attacked her intruder at the bottom of the stairs with a blunt instrument and then placed her against the baseboard."

"I understand. Was there any evidence that the intruder fell down the stairs?"

"No, none. No blood, no scrape marks, or damage to the oak stairs," replied the agent.

"What happened after Strong and Talbot came to your home?"

"They conducted their own research and decided that Robert Merriweather and his companies in eight states were out to get them. Oh, and also, the parent company CFO, one Roscoe Fuller, was probably involved."

"Please list the states," requested Rawlins.

"Yes, uh, Florida, Georgia, South Carolina, North Carolina, Virginia, Pennsylvania, New York, and Connecticut. They claimed without any substantiation that insurance companies in those states were killing their customers to collect on insurance policies and reverse mortgages."

"What did you do?"

"I entered the information into their file and asked our Gainesville office to investigate Merriweather's Southeast Assurance Company."

"During those ensuing weeks, what did Strong and Talbot do?"

Finster, "I was not sure as I lost track of them and decided they went into hiding."

"Did you get a report back from Gainesville?"

"Yes sir, they replied that Robert and Patricia Merriweathers were respected community members. They donated to many charities, were regular churchgoers, and filed their yearly taxes on time. Our agents saw no illegal abuse of their Florida customers."

Rawlins, "They more or less gave them a clean bill of health?"

"Yes sir, but the report had one very disturbing tidbit."

"What was that?"

"Amelia Talbot was listed as one of the tenants in Merriweather's building."

"What did you do?" questioned Rawlins.

"I reported this to my boss and asked permission to go to Gainesville to see if they were both there and what they were up to."

"Both meaning Gordon Strong and Amelia Talbot?"

"Yes sir."

"Agent Finster, did you take that trip to Gainesville, Florida?"

"Yes sir, I did. I spent the better part of a week surveilling the Talbot activities."

"What did you find out?"

"Miss Talbot's parents had flown in from Seattle and were working with her, and a known computer hacker, one Herman 'Ratchet' Rhodes, was also in their offices. Her company had purchased a private jet, and they'd flown to Albany, New York, and the Bahamas."

Rawlins, "The Bahamas, why there?"

"I'm not sure, perhaps to establish offshore accounts," answered the FBI Agent.

Cushing stood, "Objection, Your Honor, there's no evidence of that. Talbot and Strong took a vacation like any of us might have."

Mudd, "Sustained."

Rawlins continued, "Agent Finster, what were your concerns and actions at this point?"

"I was concerned that they were illegally spying on the Merriweathers and some of their other offices, especially the CFO, Mr. Fuller, in the Saratoga Springs office. I found out that our New York City office was using Ratchet Rhodes as a Confidential Informant (CI) and collecting evidence on the Talbot gang."

Cushing standing, "Object to the word 'gang.' Your Honor."

"Sustained. Mr. Rawlins, please restate."

Rawlins, "They were collecting evidence on the Talbot group or team, right?"

Finster, "Yes sir."

"Did you start receiving that evidence from New York?"

"Yes, sir."

"Was any of it concerning to you?" asked Rawlins.

"Yes, it was. On one transcript, Miss Talbot said she would grind the Merriweathers to dust, and when she got done with them, the family, including a ten-year-old daughter, would be sleeping in their car and begging for food."

Rawlins, "Did you construe this as the Talbot group taking the law into their own hands?"

"Yes, I did."

"What else concerned you?"

Finster said, "Rhodes provided a recording of Roscoe Fuller and another man in a restaurant bar that sounded like the CFO plotting a murder or murders."

"Did you listen to the recording?"

"No, I received a transcript," answered the agent.

"What were your actions after that?" asked Rawlins.

"I went to my boss and said there may be proof of what Strong and Talbot claimed. I requested a temporary assignment to the Gainesville office for a month to sort things out."

Rawlins, "What do you mean...to sort what out?"

"First, to determine what the Talbots were up to, and second, to take a closer look at the Southeastern Assurance companies."

"What did you find out when you went to Gainesville?"

"I found the Talbots, Strong, and Mr. Rhodes were all staying in a rented home near the Southeastern Assurance Building. They worked out of offices on the third floor and kept odd hours."

"Odd in what way?"

"Well, mostly Rhodes might come at night and work several hours."

"What was he doing?"

Jake Finster, "I don't know. The Talbot offices had high-speed internet, so he could be working on just about anything."

Rawlins, "Did he report his activities with the Talbots to your New York office?"

"No, he stopped. And the New York office was pressuring him that he was violating his plea agreement."

"Did you learn anything significant about Southeastern?" questioned Rawlins.

"I looked at their federal taxes and suspected they were cooking the books."

"How so?"

"They paid a small amount of income tax, but their income seemed low, and expenses were excessive. I have an accountant in my home office reviewing all their state and federal taxes, including personal filings by the Merriweathers and the CFO."

Rawlins, "Thank you, Agent Finster. Your witness, Mr. Cushing."

Judge Mudd, "Ten-minute recess."

Clerk, "All rise."

Chapter Thirty-seven

PRELIMINARY COMPLETION – U.S. District Court

When the hearing reconvened, Cushing approached Finster, "Agent Finster, have you ever provided any protection for Gordon Strong or Amelia Talbot in the past few months?"

"No, I have not."

"Nothing?"

"No."

"Did you ever attempt to help them carry weapons from state to state so they could protect themselves?"

"No, I did not."

Cushing, "So, you basically left them defenseless, even as sitting targets for the Southeastern murder squads?"

"I wouldn't say that," replied Finster.

"I suppose not, but it almost looks like you were using them for bait and then were surprised when Merriweather was murdered."

Finster, "Nonsense. I've worked nonstop to charge Miss Talbot with the murder."

"Yes, we can all see that. What have you done to stop the Southeastern Assurance murders?"

"We lack evidence that there were several premeditated murders for financial gain. It seems more like a story made up by Strong and Talbot to cover their questionable activities."

"Are you familiar with a Mr. Richard Pritchard from Philadelphia, Pennsylvania?"

"No, I am not."

"Did you know that he was an insurance actuary who convinced Robert Merriweather that his clients were being killed?"

"I do not."

"Do you know Robert was going to meet with the Gainesville FBI the morning after his murder?"

"Yes, I was going to be part of the team questioning him."

"Do you know that Pritchard was murdered in Philadelphia by a hit-and-run car the night before Robert Merriweather was shot?"

"No, I don't."

"For the FBI lead on this case, it seems there's a lot you don't know."

Rawlins, "Objection, Your Honor. Does counsel have a question?"

"Objection sustained, Mr. Cushing, are you done?"
"Yes sir."
"Mr. Rawlins, please call your next witness."
"Your Honor, the prosecution rests."
"Very well. Mr. Cushing, please proceed."
"Yes, Your Honor. We call Major Gordon Strong, United States Army."
Gordon took the oath, and Cushing approached, "Major Strong, until last Friday, were you concerned that you would be appearing here today as a co-defendant?"
"Yes, I was. The U.S. Attorney planned to charge me as an accessory to Robert Merriweather's murder."
"I see. Did you have anything to do with Merriweather's murder?"
"No, I did not."
"What is your relationship with the defendant, Miss Amelia Talbot?"
Gordon, "We started out as friends and teammates against the Southeast Assurance criminals."
"And now?"
"We've become very close and are lovers. We spend most of our time together and sleep in the same bed."
"In your opinion, do you believe she would kill someone without consulting you?" asked Cushing.
"Never."
"Have the two of you discussed the possibility of killing the officers of Southeast Assurance."
"Yes. But we decided we would only hurt the officers and their hitmen in defense of our lives."
"You believed the threat to you two and other Southeast customers was real and imminent?"
"Yes sir."
"Please tell the court why you had this tangible belief."
"Yes sir. We flew from Gainesville to Albany, New York, to locate the CFO, Mr. Roscoe Fuller."
"Who is the we? How many of you?"
"Myself, Miss Talbot, her parents, and Herman Rhodes."
"Did you find Fuller?"
"Yes sir, he was in Saratoga Springs, living in a small office building."
"Did you or Miss Talbot ever meet him or accuse him of his crimes."
"No, we never had that kind of meeting with him."

"Your team did rent some office space in his building, right?"
"Yes, we did. Mr. and Mrs. Talbot talked to Roscoe Fuller about doing that. Amelia and I were afraid he might recognize us."
Cushing, "Why is that?"
"There had been an attempt on Miss Talbot's life by a man and a woman. They had background material on Mia and myself."
"What kind of material?"
"Our pictures, location, occupations, activities, and daily routines."
"And you thought this might be tied to Fuller? That he might have sent them?"
"We didn't know. It was highly likely, so we decided to surveil Roscoe for a few days."
"Did you become convinced he was part of a murder-for-hire conspiracy?"
"Yes sir, one hundred percent."
"Why is that?"
Strong, "We overheard him on his cell phone arranging for a new hit team to kill Miss Talbot and me."
"How much was he going to pay them?"
"Twenty thousand up front and thirty thousand when the job was done."
Cushing, "Was the hit man directed to make it look like an accident?"
"No sir. He had the flexibility to kill us in any way possible."
"Did Fuller provide your location either in Saratoga Springs or Gainesville?"
"No sir, that was the only good news. He said we were tracked to North Florida, and our trail went cold."
"Can you tell us why that happened?" asked Cushing.
"We started at my house at Upchurches Pond, North Carolina, and drove to Jacksonville. Then we disabled our phones and rented a car using cash."
"Where were you headed?"
"To Gainesville to monitor the head of the Southeastern Assurance Companies, Mr. Robert Merriweather."
"That was before you went to Saratoga Springs?"
"Yes sir."
"Why did you go to Gainesville and rent space in Merriweather's building?"

"Amelia's research showed Robert Merriweather, his wife Patricia, and Roscoe Fuller were corporate officers in multiple state insurance companies. She also surmised that they probably had office buildings in each state."

"How could she do that?" asked the lawyer.

"Gerald, she's smart as a whip and provided forensic financial accounting for the CIA, DIA, and FBI."

"Can you explain forensic accounting to the court?"

Strong shrugged. "As best that I understand it, she can find bad guys, their organizations, and their monetary accounts."

Cushing, "Let's return to your surveillance of Fuller in Saratoga. What did you know at that time?"

"We knew Southeastern had a building in Gainesville where the Merriweathers worked and in Saratoga Springs where Roscoe lived and worked. Also, we knew they had insurance companies in both those states and Virginia and North Carolina."

"Why did Miss Talbot deduce that they had modest office buildings in each state?"

Gordon, "Like I said, she's super bright and figured out their whole criminal scheme the second day I met her."

"Please explain," directed the lawyer.

"First, we both had sold our whole life insurance policies to Southeastern companies. I also took out a reverse mortgage with them. By arranging our untimely deaths, Southeast would rake in nearly $800K if they looked like accidents."

Cushing, "Why have the buildings?"

"Amelia explained to me that they could use the buildings to cheat on the depreciation, rent, and expenses to launder the criminal receipts from their killings. Otherwise, state and federal taxes would cut their cash flow in half."

"Pretty slick, huh?" said Cushing.

"Diabolical and evil were the words she used," replied Gordon.

"When you left Saratoga and returned to Gainesville, what were your objectives?"

Gordon Strong, "First, not to get killed. Second, to find all of the Southeast companies and buildings. Third, to surveil the Merriweathers and determine if they knew about the murders."

"Did you locate all the companies and office buildings?"

"Yes sir, we did. I have the list of the states, company names, and cities in this folder."

"Good. Your Honor, this list will be the defense's Exhibit 1."

Judge Mudd, "Mr. Rawlins?"

Rawlins, "Without objection, Your Honor."

Cushing, "Please read the list, Major."

"Yes sir, state of Florida, Southeast Assurance Company, building in Gainesville, Florida; New York, New York Mutual Assurance Company, Saratoga Springs; Georgia, Assurance Trust of Georgia, Macon, Georgia; South Carolina, Southeast Assurance Association, Sumpter; North Carolina, Northeast Assurance Association, Charlotte; Virginia, Mutual Assurance of Virginia, Richmond; Pennsylvania, Northeast Mutual Assurance Company, Harrisburg; Connecticut, Northeastern Assurance Association, Hartford."

Were the officers the same in each state?"

"Yes, sir. Robert Merriweather was CEO, his wife Patricia was Secretary and Treasurer, and Roscoe Fuller was the CFO."

What did you learn about the managers of these buildings?"

"Sir, except for the Merriweathers in Gainesville and Roscoe Fuller in Saratoga Springs, none of the managers knew about the insurance companies or participated in insurance activity. They also were unaware of taxes paid on their buildings. They don't file the forms or pay any tax bills."

"How do you know this?"

"Our team members located each building and interviewed the managers."

"Thank you. Could you give the court an overview of the Southeastern business relationships?"

"Yes sir, I have it here on this diagram. Each office building is owned by an LLC, the J and R LLC, in their respective state. Roscoe Fuller and his partner, Johnathon Rivers, own all the LLCs. They also own all the stock in each insurance company in every state except in Florida, where the Merriweathers own twenty percent of the stock.

"Your Honor, this diagram is defense Exhibit 2."

"Rawlins, "Without objection."

"Major Strong, on the day of Mr. Merriweather's murder, did you or Miss Talbot have any grudge against him?"

"No sir, we felt sorry for him."

"Why is that?" asked the lawyer.

"He had just learned about the murders and planned to turn himself in to the FBI the next morning for tax fraud. The other two partners owned all the company's assets, and he was being exploited as the public representative of their criminal endeavors."

"So, neither you nor Miss Talbot had any reason to kill Robert Merriweather?"

"No sir, we were celebrating."

Cushing, "Why is that?"

"We knew when he met with the FBI, they'd have proof of what we had told them."

"As you learned the information you have shared with us today, you passed it to the FBI."

"Yes sir, to Agent Finster in Fayetteville, North Carolina."

"The day of Robert's murder, you were in your rental home all afternoon and evening, correct?"

"Yes, sir."

"Was Miss Talbot with you?"

"Affirmative until she left to go to our offices."

"Offices at Merriweather's Building?

"Yes, sir."

"What time did she leave?"

"I'm sure it was after six o'clock."

"Why are you sure?" asked Cushing.

"Because we all watched the five-thirty news together while eating dinner."

"What did you have for dinner?" asked the lawyer.

"Mia, eh...Miss Talbot ordered a large Kentucky Fried Chicken Family Bucket."

"When did it arrive? Who paid the delivery person?"

Gordon, "A guy from Uber Eats arrived just as the news started. Amelia paid him in cash and gave him a large tip. I have the receipt right here."

"Your Honor, defense's Exhibit 3."

Rawlins, "Without objection except it could have been paid by anyone there."

Cushing, "Major, would it surprise you to learn the man who delivered your dinner remembers Amelia paying him and the $20 tip."

Gordon winked at Amelia. "No sir, she's a very memorable woman."

Cushing, "Your Honor, we have that delivery person here today ready to testify."

Rawlins stood. "Your Honor, in the interest of expediting this hearing, prosecution stipulates Miss Talbot was in her rental home until after six o'clock."

Cushing, "Thank you, counselor, Your Honor, our Exhibits 4 and 5 are affidavits from the Major and her parents that she ordered and paid for dinner at about five thirty, ate dinner with them during the news program, and left their rental home after six o'clock."

Rawlins, "Without objection. We know she killed Merriweather after that."

Cushing threw up his hands. "Your Honor?"

Judge Mudd, "Stop testifying, Mr. Rawlins. The recorder will delete everything after 'without objection.'"

Cushing, "Major, how did you know Mr. Merriweather learned about the murder plots of his companies?"

"We had hacked his phone and heard him talking to a Mr. Richard Pritchard in Philadelphia."

"What was the nature of that conversation?" asked the lawyer.

"Pritchard was an insurance actuary warning Robert that the deaths of his customers in various states were statistically impossible."

"How so?"

Strong, "As I understood it, they were too soon for the customers' ages. The numbers were the same in each state, and the geographical spread in different counties looked contrived, as did the distribution of insurance companies."

"Could you expand on your comments?"

"Yes sir. Pritchard claimed that the death rates were five times what his tables predicted, and the accidental death rate was ten times a normal expectation for customers of those ages."

"Did you share that data with the FBI?"

"No sir."

"Why not?"

"Well, we thought Merriweather was going to the FBI anyway, and hacking his phone might be an issue."

Cushing, "Do you have any other comments for the court?"

"Yes sir, Miss Talbot is the most intelligent person I've ever met. It makes no sense she would murder Robert Merriweather in front of one of our video sensors – none at all. It makes sense that she acted as a good Samaritan and went to help him. She knew he had a loving wife and a young daughter. No way would she have taken him away from them."

"Thank you, Major. Your Honor, defense Exhibits 6 and 7, are service records, and university grades for Miss Talbot. Both of these veterans have served their country with distinction and deserve our fullest appreciation."

Mudd, "Are you done with the witness?"

"Yes sir, I am."

"Mr. Rawlins, your turn."

"Thank you, Judge. I have a few questions. Major Strong, thank you for your service. What is your current status with the U.S. Army?"

"I'm not sure what you mean."

"Well, it doesn't seem you go to work each day from your testimony. Have you been on leave during these surveillance efforts?"

"Yes sir. I took thirty days' leave after returning from Afghanistan and was placed on convalescent leave to recover from head wounds and PTSD."

"Major, please describe your surveillance activities in Gainesville, Florida."

"Yes sir. We rented some offices in the Southeastern Building and placed outside sensors to determine the daily routine of Robert and Patricia Merriweather. Amelia's parents convinced Robert that we could provide security for the building, so we could install additional sensors in the common areas."

Rawlins, "Please define common areas."

"The first-floor mezzanine, the elevator and hallways."

"You admitted your team broke into Robert Merriweather's phone. Do you think that was illegal?"

"Sir, I'm not a lawyer. I don't know."

Rawlins, "Well, it is. Who in your team hacked his phone?"

Gordon, "I can't answer that question without committing self-incrimination."

"Really? Did you or anyone on your team place sensors in the Merriweather's offices?"

"Sir, I'll have to invoke my Fifth Amendment privilege against self-incrimination and respectfully decline to answer your question."

"You said your team hacked the CFO's phone, right?"

"Yes sir."

"Who did that? Name the person."

Strong, "On advice of counsel, I invoke my fifth amendment rights again."

"Did you place sensors in Roscoe Fuller's office and living spaces?"

"Sorry, sir, fifth amendment."

Rawlins, "Let's try a new subject. When the FBI arrested you, you and Miss Talbot were armed, right?"

"Yes, we had handguns under our pillows to protect ourselves from the Southeastern hitmen."

"Did you have carry permits in Florida?"

"Not necessarily, but it seems a gray area when you consider Florida's 'stand your ground laws.'"

"About what time did Amelia Talbot return to the rental home?"

"About 7 p.m.."

"How do you know that?"

Gordon smiled. "Jeopardy was coming on the TV, and we had to turn it off to listen to her dreadful experience."

"What was her demeanor at the house?"

"She was terrified and shaking. She got her piece and held it in her lap."

"Her piece?"

"Her nine-millimeter Glock."

Rawlins, "Did she have any blood splatter on her hands, arms, legs, shoes, or face?"

"None, sir."

"How about her clothes?"

"Also, none, sir."

"How about gunpowder? Did you see any black specks on her skin and clothes?"

"No sir, none, and she wore a white silk blouse."

"You're sure you saw no blood or black powder?

Cushing rose. "Asked and answered, Your Honor."

Mudd, "Yes, move along, counselor."

Rawlins, "Major, if not Miss Talbot, who do you think killed Robert Merriweather?"

"Sir, I don't have evidence, but I think it probably was Roscoe Fuller or Johnny Rivers who was called 'The Big Boss' by Fuller and the Merriweathers."

"Where can we find this Rivers character?" questioned Rawlins.

"Sir, we don't know. We suspect he is offshore somewhere and orders the murders."

Rawlins, "On the night of the murder, why did you and Miss Talbot turn off your phones and flee to the Jacksonville seaside, where you paid cash for all your expenses?"

Gordon, "There's a simple answer: we were afraid we were next on the hit list. Ratchet found a call from Robert to the actuary's home that really fed our paranoia."

"Why is that?"

"Richard Pritchard, the man who proved that the Southeastern deaths were not random, had been killed by a deliberate hit-and-run truck in front of a Walmart."

"When did that happen?"

"The night before Merriweather's murder."

"This Ratchet fellow, he's a notorious computer hacker, correct?"

"I believe so."

"What illegal acts did he perform as a member of your surveillance team?"

"Sir, on the advice of counsel, I invoke my Fifth Amendment privilege against self-incrimination."

Rawlins, in disgust, "I'm done with this witness. Major, one more question: who is your counsel?"

"Why, sir, it's Mr. Cushing sitting right over there."

Rawlins, "I might have known!"

Cushing, "Is there a question there, Your Honor?"

Judge Mudd, "The recorder will strike the prosecution's last remark. Mr. Cushing, could you provide the court with an estimate of your remaining witnesses?"

"Yes, sir. We have a weapons expert next, then a video expert, then a murder scene staging expert, and my closing will be about thirty minutes."

"Thank you. Twenty-minute recess." 'Bang' went the gavel.

Chapter Thirty-eight

THE DECISION – U.S. District Court, Jacksonville

Judge Mudd, "Mr. Cushing, please call your next witness."

"Yes sir. The defense calls Mr. Roy Jenkins."

Jenkins was sworn in and sat in the witness box.

Cushing, "Mr. Jenkins, you have testified at many trials during the past twenty years, right?"

"Yes, I'm an expert on all types of guns and fingerprints."

Rawlins, "The prosecution agrees that Mr. Jenkins is a weapons expert."

Cushing, "Did you examine the prosecution's Exhibit 1 for Miss Talbot's prints?"

"I did."

"Were her prints consistent with firing that revolver?"

"No, they were not. They were consistent with someone unloading the weapon. Her prints weren't on the hammer, the trigger, or the body of the gun on the right side."

"Why would they be on the right side of the frame?"

"Miss Talbot is right-handed and a former Marine who was awarded a pistol Marksman Badge. She was trained to carry a handgun with her right forefinger forward on the frame, not on the trigger.

"Maybe she wiped that print off the gun?"

"That doesn't make any sense. If someone wipes a weapon, they do the whole thing, including the ammo."

"In your expert opinion, was that .38 revolver the gun that killed Robert Merriweather?"

"No, it was not."

"Why not?" asked Cushing.

"Merriweather was shot up close and personal. The weapon that did this from less than two feet away would have some blood spatter and GSR on it. Neither is on this weapon."

"I see. Could Miss Talbot have wiped those off?"

"No, not completely, and if she tried, most of her prints would be gone."

"Were you observing today the government's comparison of the bullet from Merriweather's head to one shot from this same .38 revolver?"

"I was."

"What were the results of the comparison?"

"The two bullets were similar but not a match."

"Similar in what way?" asked the lawyer.

"It's possible the murderer bought the same Smith & Wesson model and mistakenly thought the lands and grooves markings would be identical to the other revolver. The FBI had one of their most experienced ballistics experts do the second evaluation, which I observed."

Cushing was surprised. "Why a second evaluation?"

"I don't know the whole story, but it seems either the Gainesville or Jacksonville lab initially thought there was a match."

"Based on your decades of experience, what do you think happened to the gun that Miss Talbot left on her aircraft?"

"I think someone retrieved the revolver and the sack of bullets. They realized the hollow points wouldn't provide good ballistic testing, so they took the spent shell from the other gun and put it in the one that was found near the library."

"How can you say that?"

"The hammer strike mark on the substituted shell is slightly different than the mark on the shell shot by the FBI technician into a tub of water."

"Allow me to review your testimony. The gun found in the Gainesville Library trashcan isn't the one that killed Robert Merriweather."

"No, it is not," asserted Jenkins.

"Someone tried to make it look like it was that weapon and blame the murder on Amelia Talbot."

"That's my conclusion."

"Thank you. Mr. Rawlins, your turn.

Rawlins, "Thank you, counselor. Mr. Jenkins, do you know the defendant?"

"No, I don't."

"Even though you don't know her, you have accepted her story as the truth."

"Yes sir, it fits the evidence. She took the rounds out of the revolver, and someone else put four of them with her prints back into it. She handled the gun but did not fire it."

"Could she have killed Merriweather with a similar gun and sent us all in the wrong direction with Exhibit 1?"

"I suppose that's possible, but she would have had blood splatter on her and some powder residue.

Rawlins pounced. "So, is it possible that Miss Talbot is the killer?"

"Anything is possible. The important part of my testimony is that the gun with her fingerprints on it and the hollow point shells isn't the one that killed the deceased. Someone tried to make it look like Talbot used the revolver on Merriweather, but she did not."

Rawlins persisted, "Isn't it possible that she staged this entire ruse to confuse the investigation?"

"Again, when you get into a theoretical, anything can be claimed," said Jenkins.

"I'm done with this witness."

Cushing leaped to his feet. "Your Honor, redirect."

Judge Mudd, "Go ahead."

Cushing, "Mr. Jenkins, the government does not have the murder weapon, correct?"

"Correct."

"The bullet from the dead man's head isn't a match to one fired from prosecution's Exhibit 1."

"It is not."

"You don't know who killed Robert Merriweather, do you?"

"No. I do not."

"The prosecutor was asking you theoretical questions, so I have one. Do you think Amelia Talbot killed Robert Merriweather?"

"No, I don't."

"Based on your decades of experience, why not?"

"It doesn't make sense. Miss Talbot knows guns, so she would have known better than to shoot someone at close range."

"Thank you. You may step down. The defense calls Rudolf Jankowski."

Judge Mudd, "We will have a fifteen-minute recess before this witness."

Amelia had tears in her eyes. "Jerry, that went very well indeed."

"Yes," he replied. "We have them on the run, and it's time to destroy the rest of their case."

Mudd returned from his bathroom break, and Cushing started with his witness, "Mr. Jankowski, please tell us about your expertise."

"Yes, I am a graphic artist and work with all types of video files. I have developed some of the now standard video formats. I helped write some of the founding software for the Adobe Company."

Rawlins stood. "The prosecution stipulates that Mr. Jankowski is a computer expert for video processing."

Cushing, "Rudolf, I sent you a large video file two weeks ago. Have you been able to process all of it and show us the most important events?"
"Yes, the files consist of multiple transmissions from a motion-activated sensor on the Southeastern Building that monitored Mr. and Mrs. Merriweather's parking spots. The data are sent to the internet with a time stamp."
Once activated, is the video continuous?"
"No sir. A moving person or car causes transmission of still frames of video every five seconds until two minutes after the movement ceases."
"I see. What is the quality of the frames? They're low-quality color pictures, right?"
"Yes, they are." Said the witness.
"What is the first event you will show us?"
"It is Robert Merriweather arriving at 1615 in his Mercedes. Here it is on the projector. He pulls in, exits his car, and walks toward the entrance."
"Your Honor, these series of pictures of the Merriweathers are defense Exhibit 8."
Mudd, "Mr. Rawlins?"
"No objection, Your Honor."
Cushing, Mr. Jankowski, what's next?"
"Mrs. Merriweather is leaving at 1630. I'm told that this is her normal departure time."
"That's correct. Go on."
"At 1715, Mr. Merriweather walks to his car and makes a phone call. You can see from further frames that he stays in his car."
"Your Honor, the next series of photographs are defense Exhibit 9."
Mudd, "Mr. Rawlins?"
"Without objection until I see them."
Jankowski, "At 1721, a white truck pulls in next to Merriweather's Mercedes. A man or very tall woman gets out and talks to Robert, still in his driver's seat. The video doesn't identify the person from the white truck. Also, he or she is wearing a hoodie which hides their facial detail."
Cushing, "What do the next frames show?"
"I'll put them up one by one. You can see the person's arms gesturing like they're arguing."
"What happens at 1729?"

Witness, "The person from the truck pulls out a gun and shoots Robert Merriweather. First, you see the gun coming up in this frame, then it is pointing at Robert, and here's the gunshot."

Cushing, "Mr. Jankowski, is there any doubt that this is a gun firing?"

"None, sir."

"What happens during the next hour?"

"The shooter goes back to the truck, a late model Toyota Tacoma, and drives away."

"Does the sensor show the license plate?"

"No, there was none on the front, and the rear plate was at a right angle to the camera."

"What's next?"

"A few cars left the parking lot, but no one went toward the Merriweather car until 1823.

"Your Honor, let the record show that defense's Exhibit 10 provides images of Miss Talbot's arrival at the building and her actions at Robert Merriweather's car."

Judge Mudd, "Mr. Rawlins?"

"No objection, Your Honor."

Cushing, "Mr. Jankowski, please continue.

"Yes sir. Here is Miss Talbot arriving, parking, and starting toward the building. She goes out of range but must have stopped and decided to check on Mr. Merriweather. See her walking to his car, here, here, and here. She gets to the car and grabs his windowsill to keep from fainting. Here, Miss Talbot opens his door to look for a gun, and you can see the light on her phone here and here. It's getting dark, but you can see that she is holding up her phone and taking a flash picture here. The timestamp is 1833."

Cushing, "Let me stop you. Could that be a gunshot?"

Jenkins, "No way. The video is mainly white light."

"Could you make it look more like a gunshot?" asked the lawyer.

"I suppose you could, but why do that? This is the raw video that tells an accurate story."

Cushing, "You said in your email that you have a comparison of the 1729 gunshot and the 1826 camera flash."

"Yes sir."

"Your Honor, defense's Exhibit 11 a comparison of the gunshot at 1729 and Miss Talbot taking a picture of the deceased at 1833.

Rawlins, "Without objection."
Jankowski, "Here's a slide with the gun explosion at the top and Talbot's picture flash at the bottom. Note the difference in colors."
"Mr. Jenkins, thank you for your expertise and testimony. Mr. Rawlins, your witness."
Rawlins, "Your Honor, I need a few minutes to confer with my staff."
Judge Mudd, "I imagine you do - ten-minute recess."
After the recess, Rawlins questioned the witness, "Mr. Jenkins, you said the person who fired a gun at 1725 could have been a man or a woman, right?"
"Yes, a man nearly six feet in height or an unusually tall and burly woman."
"So, in your opinion, it could have been the defendant, Miss Talbot."
"No sir. She is neither tall nor heavy set."
"What if she wore elevated shoes and extra clothing simulating a man."
Cushing rose, "Objection, Your Honor. The prosecution has already stipulated that Miss Talbot was at her rental home until after 6 p.m.."
Mudd, "Noted, and overruled. The witness may answer."
Jenkins, "What was the question again?"
Rawlins, "The defendant knew the video sensor was at the scene. Might she have worn a disguise to confuse the police?"
"I guess it's possible but not likely. I've been on hundreds of cases and never seen a defendant wear shoes to make them five inches taller."
Rawlins persisted. "But it could be possible, correct?"
Jenkins, "Again, possible, but not probable. We tried to connect Amelia Talbot to the white truck but found no such vehicle readily available."
"I understand, but she could have stolen one in her neighborhood, right?" stated Rawlins.
"Yes sir, but there are none registered in her area," said Jenkins.
Rawlins, "How can you say that?"
"We identified the white truck as a late model Toyota Tacoma TRD off-road model. There are only five in Gainesville and none in her neighborhood."
Rawlins, "Gainesville is a college town. Maybe there's a student there with such a vehicle?"
Cushing, "Your Honor, I object."
"Overruled."
Rawlins, "I'm done with this witness."

Judge Mudd, "Mr. Cushing, call your next witness. Is he or she your last?"

"Yes sir. The testimony will be short and sweet. The defense calls Hildebrand Hessman."

Cushing, "Ms. Hessman, what type of services do you offer for criminal trials?"

"Yes, Mr. Cushing. My company provides re-enactment of crimes, virtual modeling of figures involved, and photography evidence when needed."

"Did my firm engage you to re-enact the Robert Merriweather murder?"

"Yes, you did."

"Please tell the court what you did and how you did it."

"We obtained a Mercedes like Mr. Merriweather's and placed it at the crime scene. We then had a series of men exit a truck and walk to the car until we found one of the same height and weight as the 1725 video."

"How can you do that?"

"We take dimensions off the car, like the height of the roof and the width of the grille, and compare them with our model and the video of the murderer."

"What was the killer's height?"

"Five foot, eleven inches – his hat made it six feet."

"And what weight seemed about right?"

"One hundred and ninety pounds."

"So, the murderer was probably a man, right?"

Rawlins, "Objection. We have already postulated it could be a burly tall woman or Miss Talbot in disguise."

Mudd, "Overruled. You will have your chance to make your case, counselor."

Cushing, "Ms. Hessman, based on your many years of providing these services, what is the probability that the figure in the 1729 shooting was a man?"

Hessman, "Ninety percent or more. Men commit far more murders than women, especially violent murders."

"Thank you. Can you show us that simulated video?"

"Yes sir, here it is on the projector."

"Your Honor, this video is defense Exhibit 19."

Mudd, "Very well."

"Ms. Hildebrand, what else did you do?"

"We had the defendant, Miss Talbot, re-enact the scene to show she was much shorter and smaller in girth."

"Can you show that, please?"

"Yes sir, here it is."

"Can you show the male model and the defendant standing next to each other by the Mercedes?"

"Yes, here is a photograph of that.

"Defense Exhibit 20, Your Honor."

"Ms. Hessman, Hildebrand, thank you for your expertise and testimony. I'm done, Your Honor."

Mudd, "Your witness, Mr. Rawlins."

Rawlins, "Ms. Hessman, could Miss Talbot have worn a disguise to look like a man?"

Hessman frowned. "Your question is silly and stupid. Why would she do that?"

Rawlins, "To confuse the prosecution. She knew there was a camera there."

"Ridiculous! No woman is going to do that."

"Why is that? Please explain."

"We had her stand there with a revolver eighteen inches from the dead man's head. She's a smart cookie and wouldn't have wanted his blood and brains to explode onto her face and arms – no way."

Rawlins, "I'm done with this witness.

Mudd, "Mr. Cushing, do you have any additional witnesses or cross-examination requests?"

"No, Your Honor. We've proved our case. The defendant is innocent."

Judge Mudd, "Mr. Rawlins, do you have more witnesses, evidence, or a need to cross-examine?"

Rawlins sighed. "No sir. The prosecution rests."

Mudd, "Mr. Cushing, you made a motion at the beginning of these proceedings. Do you still believe that motion is relevant?"

Alice typed on the laptops, "DISMISS."

Cushing stood. Your Honor, I renew my Motion to Dismiss these charges. The hearing showed a woeful lack of evidence from the government. Our defense has shown their murder theories to be weak and without substance. This is a hearing of fact, not speculation. In addition, the Charging Document was defective and full of surplusage not proven in this hearing. It claimed the defendant murdered Merriweather at 1825 with a .38 revolver that had her prints on it – another example of their unreliable evidence.

There are even questions of Due Process. The defendant testified freely about her actions on the night of the murder. There was no reason other than intimidation for the FBI to arrest her a week later at gunpoint and handcuff her."

Judge Mudd, "Mr. Rawlins, what is the prosecution's response?"

"Your Honor, we vehemently disagree with the defense's motion. We believe we have presented clear and convincing evidence to the court of probable cause for first and second-degree murder on the part of the defendant. Mr. Cushing brings several paid so-called experts here and has attempted to muddy the water. Ooops, no pun intended, Judge."

Judge Mudd, "None was taken. Mr. Rawlins, when you lost the gun, your case collapsed. I see no reason to spend another hour with each side rehashing their theories and assertions. The government's evidence was not clear or convincing. Defense's motion is granted." 'Bang!' went the gavel. "Miss Talbot, you are free to go. I apologize for how the FBI treated you and Major Strong."

Mia hugged Gerald and Alice and gave Gordon an enthusiastic kiss. Her parents came forward, and they had a Talbot family hug. Alice had two cars waiting to take them to the Cushings' offices. Champagne corks were popped, and the entire staff enjoyed drinks and canapes. Gerald was especially hungry as this was his first food since the night before.

The Talbots and Gordon returned to their rental home in Gainesville, and Herman Rhodes caught a flight from Jacksonville to New York.

Agent Jake Finster called that night and apologized to Strong, "Gordo, I apologize to you and Amelia. As soon as we found her prints on that gun, I got tunnel vision."

"Apology accepted, Jake. Does this mean we are still golfing buddies?"

"Yes. I'm game if you are."

Gordon, "Count me in."

"Oh, by the way, we had agents go to arrest Rosco Fuller in his building," reported Finster.

"Good move."

"He was found with a shot to his head that apparently is a suicide."

"I see, I'll let Mia know."

Gordon put the phone down. "What are you going to tell me?" asked Amelia.

"Roscoe is dead from a gunshot. It was probably a suicide."
"I doubt that," she said.
"Mia, what are we going to do now?"
"I have some ideas. The first one is to take a week off in Nassau. Maybe my parents will join us."

Chapter Thirty-nine

BAHAMAS FLIGHT – Bermuda - Nassau

Roger Sandstone pushed the throttles forward, and the sleek G100 Gulfstream took off and started climbing to cruising altitude. He headed for Saint Augustine on Florida's east coast and set a heading of 080 degrees on the plane's autopilot.

The day before, he had convinced Amelia to accompany him to Bermuda to evaluate a flying service for sale. He argued the trip would provide more flying time for Gordon, and he, Sandstone, would pay for all the fuel to Bermuda and then to Nassau. Also, he said when he picked them up for the return flight to Gainesville, Strong would fly in the left seat for his G100 certification.

Over St. Augustine, Gordon got a phone call. "Hello? Yeah. Are you sure? Good to know; thanks for the call."

Sandstone, "Who was that?"

"Our lawyer. The FBI wants to return our clothes, and there's more paperwork to sign."

"Can they wait a week?" asked Roger.

"They're gonna have to," replied Gordon.

Over the Florida coast, Roger Sandstone continued climbing through fifteen thousand feet as he thought about his conversation with Amelia the previous day. She had agreed to consider a partnership in the new flying service if her company provided security systems for all of Sandstone's facilities. Once again, he requested she dump Strong and make their proposed partnership an intimate affair.

Amelia declined, and he said, "Mia, when you had your trouble with the FBI, I made plans to fly you anywhere in the world. Could Gordon do that? I think not."

She replied, "Dear Roger, I know you meant well, but my parents would have lost their house if I had run."

He shrugged. "No problem. I would have bought them another one. I learned Albania is the place to go if you have plenty of money. If you spread enough cash around, you can fend off extradition for years."

"Luckily, we don't have that problem," she responded.

"You're turning me down again?"

"Sorry, Roger, yes I am. Gordon and I will probably return from Paradise Island engaged."

Passing 25,000 feet, Sandstone glanced over at Gordon. Strong sat to his right in the Co-pilot seat, sipping his Starbucks cappuccino coffee. Amelia was in the passenger seat behind Gordon, also drinking coffee Roger had provided. He turned and gave her the thumbs-up signal, which she returned.

Roger leveled the jet off at 31,500 feet and checked the altimeter set at 29.92. Then he made a slight course change for Bermuda's L.F. Wade International Airport. Gordon Strong was the first to nod off, as he often did if not at the controls. Amelia reviewed her action items for dismantling the Southeast Assurance Company organization. Instead of bankrupting Patricia Merriweather, Amelia had a new plan. She had reached a tentative agreement with the FBI, IRS, and tax authorities in eight states that Talbot Security would act as a legal receiver and liquidate all of Southeast's assets. The various jurisdictions offered Patricia Merriweather criminal immunity if she cooperated with Amelia and paid all taxes, interest, and penalties.

Amelia would be free to sell all insurance and building assets once she signed the final contracts. She had proposed a ten percent fee on the total asset value for her new company, Talbot Receivers. Mia could legally recover cash, sell assets, and recommend a final settlement to each state and the federal government.

Talbot's original team shelved its plans on maxing the Merriweathers' credit cards, emptying their bank accounts, and stopping payment on their bills. Instead, Gordon and Gerald Cushing were authorized to dissolve all the J&R LLCs and combine their assets. Virginia Wickens, Merriweather's secretary, now paid the mortgage fees, credit card bills, utilities, car leases, and employee checks.

After flying eastward over the Atlantic for thirty minutes, Sandstone changed course to the south into the Bermuda Triangle. He checked Amelia Talbot and saw her slumped over. *Stupid amateurs*, he thought. *Hmmm, sleeping powder in your coffee will do that every time. Now, we start my plan. I never filed for Bermuda.*

They were at 30,000 feet when he began bleeding off the cabin pressure while descending using the autopilot. He pulled the pressurization circuit breakers until the cabin altitude increased to 19,000 feet. Roger kept the breakers out until he felt short of breath and let the loud warning horn sound.

Gordon roused from his chemical-induced slumber and said, "What's going on? Why the alarm?"

Sandstone feigned fear and disarray. "Cabin pressure has dumped. Get an oxygen mask on Amelia and put yours on. Select 100%!"

Strong did as he was told and scanned the instruments. Their cabin pressure was approaching 20,000 feet.

Gordon warned, "Roger, we need an emergency descent."

Sandstone replied, "Naw, I'll get it working, and we all have our masks on. Give it a couple of minutes."

In a few minutes, Gordon felt punchy and nauseous. "Roger, I don't feel good. We need to go down."

Sandstone popped the breakers in and showed his co-pilot that the cabin altitude was decreasing. "Look, you pussy, we'll have these masks off soon. Check you selected 100%, you dumb shit."

He then saw Gordon's hands shake and his eyes close as the lack of oxygen rendered him unconscious. Roger reversed the breakers, commanded a descent to fifteen thousand feet on autopilot, and switched to the walk-around oxygen bottle.

He checked Amelia and confirmed she was comatose. Gordon and his lover had selected 100% oxygen, but it did no good. Before the flight, Sandstone had replaced their oxygen bottles with two that had compressed air, not pure oxygen.

He stood beside Amelia and yelled through his mask, "Not so high and mighty now, are you? You stuck-up bitch. Why don't you ask Mr. Muscles to come back here and save you? I gave you plenty of chances to see my business talent - seven years of nonstop work to create a high-income-paying platform. You and Gordo Biceps are trying to disrupt my life. You could have been my partner in business and in bed. But no, you pick a PTSD vet who plays your lap dog. Screw you, your parents, and the hacker. I'll take care of them when I get back."

Sandstone stood before Amelia, unfastened her seatbelt, and tore off her useless oxygen mask.

He yelled, "Get ready to fly, you teasing whore bitch! You think you're smarter than me, huh? I'm Mensa, 150 IQ+; you and your boyfriend are dumb-ass meatheads. I'm going to enjoy your womanhood before it turns cold."

He started removing her jeans and said, "Got panties on, Mia? I hope so. I'll keep them as a reminder of my conquest."

Her eyes flicked open, and she kicked him hard in the groin with a leather boot. Roger Sandstone screamed in pain as she then stuck her forked fingers into his eyes. A strong arm wrapped his throat in a death grip.

Sandstone exclaimed, "What the hell? What the hell is happening here?"

Gordon spoke into his right ear, "We knew either you or Ratchet were disrupting our plans. When our security cameras showed you changing out the bottles, we knew it was you. I put new oxygen-filled bottles in while you talked to Amelia in your office. Admit it; you're Johnny Rivers."

"Why do you think that?" spat Roger.

Strong explained, "That was Ratchet who called over St Augustine. He said there's no record of a Roger Sandstone before six years ago. Your history started in Orlando, but you have no ex-wife or child there. You came to Gainesville to monitor the Merriweathers, and you had access to the pistol in this plane. You're the Big Boss."

Roger gasped for air and nodded his head up and down. "Join forces with me, and I'll make you rich."

Gordon snorted, "Too late, asshole. A judge and jury of your peers have found you guilty of murder and a host of other crimes. Your sentence is death. Mia, put your mask back on and put Roger's on me."

"You can't do that! I'll get hypoxia and die!" complained Sandstone.

Strong said, "No, Rivers, that's not our plan."

"Your plan is flawed," said Sandstone. "I only filed a flight plan with one soul onboard. How are you going to explain yourself and Amelia to customs?"

"Not to worry, Johnny. I added myself to your Nassau flight plan. You're the one going for a free fall flight."

Rivers pleaded, "No. You can't do this. I'll turn over all my properties to you. They're worth many millions more than what the Merriweathers have."

"We don't want your blood money property," retorted Amelia.

Johnny Rivers cried, "What about Roscoe? He's the one that set up all the hits."

Amelia responded, "Roscoe's apartment was raided by the FBI yesterday. He took his own life. Or, that's what they think. Gordon and I know you were involved."

"You can't do this!" Rivers cried. "I've worked so hard for so long. I deserve the money."

Gordon replied, "Yes, we can. Soon, you'll be woozy. That's when you leave the plane. As you get below 10,000 feet, you'll revive and experience the sheer panic you wanted to force on Amelia and me. There's only one approach to buy your way out of this."
"What is it? Tell me. Tell me," begged the frantic pilot.
Gordon, "All right. Did the Merriweathers know what you and Roscoe were doing?"
Rivers sneered. "Of course, they knew. They paid all the bills."
Gordon grimaced. "But did they know you murdered their customers? Did they have foreknowledge of the hits?"
"What's it to you, Mr. Biceps? They had to be idiots not to know what was going on. Why would Fuller pay people thousands of dollars in cash? I'm getting weak; give me some oxygen!" complained Rivers.
Gordon, "Mia, take the mask off me and hold it on his face. Then, move the small tank from his back to mine."
She nodded and said, "Sandstone or Rivers, whoever you are, I almost fell for you. Shame on you, killing innocent customers for money."
Rivers jeered, "Kiss my ass, Amelia. It's a dog-eat-dog world. If you don't realize that, you're a putz. The rule to getting the gold is to 'do onto others before they do onto you.'"
Mia said, "You're wrong, Rivers. You must have had an awful upbringing."
Johnathon Rivers replied, "No, I got smart at an early age. I cheated, and I stole at every opportunity."
She gave Rivers a glaring look. "Gordon, don't kill him in our plane, but do get rid of this scum."
Gordon, "OK, put the mask back on my face, return to your seat, and get your mask back on."
"Hold it, I told you about the Merriweathers. You have to let me live!" sobbed Johnny Rivers.
Gordon smiled. "No, I don't. I was lying. Sorry about that."
Amelia said, "Gordo, wait. Let's talk about this. If we kill him, aren't we just as immoral as Roscoe and Rivers?"
"Mia, that may be, but we know he's a killer with tons of money. His case could drag through the justice system for years. God forbid, he might even get out on bail."

Rivers gasped for breath and doubled up as Gordon dragged him to the couch and tied his hands and ankles with zip ties.
Amelia, "What do you want me to do?" asked Gordon.

She looked deep in thought. "I think we need more information. We need to make sure we're not making a mistake."
Gordon, "All right, I have some of my joy juice in my backpack. I'll give him a shot, and he'll sing like a canary."
"Do it," she directed.
Rivers wailed, "I need more oxygen. I'm dying!"
"Give it a rest," warned Gordon. "Our pressurization is back on, and we're descending to ten thousand feet."
Amelia asked, "Is the aircraft OK? Don't you need to be in the cockpit?"
Gordon said, "It's fine; the autopilot is dependable, and we're heading in the general direction of Nassau. Rivers will be unconscious for a few minutes after this shot. When he wakes, act like his best friend. Compliment him on everything you can think of. Be on his side, and he will blab like a baby."

Amelia moved to the couch and started stroking Johnny's arm.
As he awoke, his first words were, "Are you going to kill me?"
She smiled and held his left hand. "You silly boy. I sent Mr. Biceps back to the cockpit so we can talk heart to heart."
"Will you consider my offers?" he pleaded.
She said, "I will. I want to know you better. The businesses you built are amazing, Johnny. Where were you born?"
"Kansas City, Kansas."
She queried, "Did you have a family there?"
"Yes, my older sister, mom and dad. When I was ten, my parents were killed in a car crash."
She squeezed his hand. "Oh my, that's terrible. What happened to you and your sister?"
"We had to go live with my aunt and uncle on a dairy farm."
"I bet that was a lot of work."
He said, "It was brutal and awful. They treated us like slaves. We had to work in the morning, go to school all day, and do more work at night."
She hugged his shoulders. "I feel for you, but that experience made you the tough businessman you are today. Please tell me your birth date. I want to know how old you are."
"May 8th, 1981."
"I knew it; you are three years older than me. I like to date mature men. Did your mama name you Johnathon Rivers?"
"Naw. I was John or Johnny Reardon until I changed it."

"Good for you," she gushed. "I like Johnny Rivers even more – sounds a little like a riverboat gambler."

Rivers smiled as she kissed him on the cheek.

"How many people did Roscoe Fuller kill?" she questioned.

"Eighteen."

"You couldn't stop him?"

"No, I was afraid for my own life. He was a bad dude."

"But Johnny, you were the one who shot Merriweather, right?"

"Roscoe ordered me to do it – kill Robert or die myself."

"Why did you try and implicate me?"

He hung his head. "I'm sorry, so sorry. I was angry and hurt that you were choosing Gordon instead of me. I wanted to damage you."

"How did you know we hid the revolver in this airplane?"

"After we shut down the engines, I heard that guy, Rhodes, say something to you about the seat. I returned later, took the weapon and the cash."

She patted his hands. "You naughty boy. I want that money back. Where is it?"

"In a floor safe under my desk at the main hanger," he volunteered.

"You were very clever following me the night Robert was killed. What gun did you use?"

"I bought a .38 exactly like yours and put regular bullets in it. After shooting Merriweather, I put the spent shell in your gun. When you went into the library with the cops, I put the piece in the trash can and took my GPS tracker."

"You're a very smart man. I admire that. Your scheme almost worked, except you needed to hold my pistol in your other hand during the shooting and fire a bullet through it that day."

"Why is that?" he demanded.

Mia replied, "One, there was no blood on my gun, and two, it did not smell like it was recently fired."

"I should not have framed you. My mistake," apologized Rivers.

"Johnny, you were the one leaking information to the FBI, correct?"

"I gave them some info, yeah. You aren't the only ones who can place listening devices."

"Where do you send your offshore money?"

He frowned. "That's a trick question. I'm not falling for it."

She took his hand. "Dear Jonathon, I need to hide some money. Where do you recommend?"

"Oh, you can't go wrong with Bali."

"Bali?"

He replied, "Yeah, the island and National Bank of Bali. I have a question. Where's Patricia Merriweather?"

Amelia, "She's in hiding. When I found Robert, I called her and told her to leave town."

"Why did you do that?"

"I figured she and her daughter might be the next people killed. Johnny, why do you care where she is?"

"She's a loose end in this mess that you and Mr. Biceps have created."

"You had Richard Pritchard murdered in Philly, didn't you?"

"Who's he? I don't know what you're talking about."

"Yes, you do. Roscoe told you that Pritchard figured out your murderous business plan, and Merriweather was turning himself over to the police. So, you decided to kill both of them."

He sneered. "Prove it."

"I think we will once we review Roscoe Fuller's phone calls and conversations in his living quarters."

He was surprised. "You recorded him?"

"Yes."

"Shit."

"One last thing," she said.

"What?"

"It was you that had the men attack Gordon on Paradise Island, right?"

"Again, prove it."

"Dear Johnny, you are so smart. How much did you pay them?"

"I didn't have to pay them. Mr. Biceps beat the shit out of them."

Gordon returned from the cockpit and reported they were level at 9,500 feet.

He said, "Mia, we can go to Miami, back to Gainesville, the Bahamas, or Fayetteville. How was your little chat with this imposter?"

"It was good. Johnny's real name is Jonathon Reardon, and he was born in Kansas City in 1981. We'll no doubt find a criminal record in the Midwest."

Gordon asked, "What's your recommendation? What do we do with him?"

"Gordo, his crimes are beyond comprehension. He admitted to eighteen murders and blamed them on Roscoe. But we know Roscoe Fuller was not the boss and was deathly afraid of Rivers."
Strong asked, "So, he's the one we've been after all along?"
"Yes, and he as much as confirmed he killed Robert Merriweather, Roscoe, and Pritchard. He's an evil, evil man with no conscience."
Rivers complained, "Hold it, you drugged me, and that was a private conversation."
Mia said, "He's half right, Gordon. I have it on my phone, but it won't be admissible in court."
"Amelia, what's your decision?" asked Gordon.
"We take him back and turn him over to the FBI."
Strong responded, "No."
"No? Why"
"Amelia, as long as this piece of shit is living, we'll have to look over our shoulders and fear his revenge."
Johnny said, "I give you my word. It's over. Let me go, and I'll pay you five million dollars."
Gordon smiled. "See, there's the problem. Your word is not worth a plugged nickel. You have no honor, none. Mia and I have only one way to live normal lives. That's to end yours."
Amelia, "Gordon, are you sure?"
"More than sure. We are the judge and jury. For God's sake, Rivers killed at least twenty innocent people. He doesn't love you. He tried to put you in prison for life."
She said, "I know, but it makes us just as bad as him."
Gordon, "Wrong. Rivers is the ultimate evil, a psychopath. If he could kill us right now, he would do so."
Rivers pleaded, "No, I wouldn't. Be my partners. We can make millions together."
Gordon pushed back, "No thanks. We saw what happened to your last two partners. Mia, he was going to dump us out of this aircraft. It's poetic justice if we do the same to him. Remember, he has millions to fight the courts and prosecutors."
"Gordon, I've caused people to die before; it's a bad feeling," she said.
"I know, but whether we have a family together or with someone else, we'll have to worry about this pile of crap kidnapping them or killing them."

Johnny protested, "I would never do something like that!"
Gordo retorted, "Give it a rest, Rivers or Reardon. We know who and what you are. You can't stand to lose and will always threaten us and those we love. Therefore, you are a dead man."

Gordon went into the cockpit and pulled the pressurization breakers. Then he went aft and opened a luggage access hatch. Loose papers and a blanket were sucked out of the howling opening.

Gordon approached Rivers, and the jet pilot used his last burst of energy to smash Gordon's foot with his boot. Gordon lost his grip on the man's neck; Rivers twisted around and hopped to the cockpit. He deselected the autopilot and put the plane in a hard port turn, pinning his two companions to the deck with high g-forces. Johnny's movements were hindered by the tight zip ties on his wrists and ankles, but he managed to don his seatbelt. He pushed both throttles full forward and pulled the wheel back, putting the agile craft into a loop. Gordon tried to crawl forward, but Rivers rolled the G100 at the loop's top and slammed his passengers against the overhead.

Gordon sprained his left wrist and passed out. Johnny turned hard to starboard, and Amelia dropped from the ceiling and bounced off the couch. She found herself on the deck, close to Strong's backpack. Mia extracted the syringe, held it in her mouth, and used all of her strength to crawl and inch forward. Once near Rivers, she jammed the needle into his hip and pushed the remaining sedative into him before he knocked her hand away.

Johnny felt woozy, and his self-preservation instinct caused him to engage the autopilot before he lost consciousness. Mia pulled herself into the co-pilot's seat and scanned the instrument panel. They were in level flight at 11,000 feet and heading east. She had two problems. They needed to head south to Nassau and neutralize Rivers before he revived.

Amelia went back into the main cabin and found Strong with a nasty gash on his forehead and disoriented.
She yelled, "Gordon, wake up. I need you. We're flying in the wrong direction, and Johnny might come to at any time."
Gordon, "My head hurts. What's Rivers doing?"
"He's passed out in the left seat. I injected the rest of the joy juice into his hip."
"Good girl. Help me up."

Gordon went to the cockpit, punched Rivers in the head with his good arm, and undid the seatbelt. He and Amelia dragged the criminal aft, cut off the zip ties, and pushed and kicked the limp body out into the howling slipstream.

Gordon told Mia how to replace the door. Then he went to the pilot's seat, pushed in the pressurization breakers, and turned the plane south using the autopilot. Amelia took the co-pilot's seat and plugged in the microphone.

"Gordon, what's next?"

"We continue south and head for Lynden Pindling Airport at Nassau."

"That was close. Rivers almost got us," she sighed.

"Yeah, he had a good plan," Gordon replied.

"How did you know about the tanks?"

"Ratchet called me yesterday and said to check the hanger camera at minute 0712. I saw the tank switch. That's why I decided we should pretend to drink the coffee and pretend to black out."

"Gordon, will Roger or Johnny really revive below 10,000 feet?"

"Possibly. I like to think he would and know our sentence of death."

She sighed. "He was right, you know. I think I'm a real smart ass, but I need someone like you to protect me."

"Woof, woof. You mean your Mr. Biceps, the lap dog?"

"Stop that; I've grown very fond of your biceps – more than fond. I'll show my appreciation when we get to the Merriweather condo."

He looked over at her profile. "Mia, I like all your hills and valleys also. I was incensed that Rivers wanted to kill you – the woman I love."

"You just used the L-word, big guy."

"I know. It slipped out, but I meant it."

"Well, the same for me, Gordon Strong. I love you."

He said, "I want to have kids. Is that going to be a problem?"

"No, two or three should do nicely." she answered.

He reached to his right and took her hand. "It's been quite a journey, Mia."

"Gordo, it's just beginning."

EPILOGUE

Amelia Talbot and Gordon Strong landed at Nassau and took a taxi to the Merriweather condo. They decided not to involve the Bahama authorities in their deadly flight details. The next day, Amelia sent a text message to Jake Finster. "Dear Jake, we are in Nassau and will return in a few days. We need to meet with you to review a problem with Johnny Rivers yesterday. Please text us your location, and we will fly to meet with you. Best regards, Amelia & Gordon."

She called Ratchet Rhodes in New York and directed him to enter Roger Sandstone's hanger, recover as much cash as possible, hack his computer for financial accounts, and look for connections with Bali. She and Gordon opened the condo safes and took control of $100K of cash.

Amelia's parents, Doris and Henry, returned to Bellevue, WA, and continued their employment with Microsoft.

Gordon bought an engagement ring in Nassau City, and Mia proudly wore it. She met with a real estate agent to discuss selling Merriweather's condo.

Mia and Gordo returned to Jacksonville to meet with Jerry and Alice Cushing. Cushing sent the following message to Jake Finster, "Dear Agent Finster, five days ago, Amelia Talbot and Gordon Strong boarded a private jet in Gainesville for a flight to Bermuda and then the Bahamas. Their pilot was Roger Sandstone from the Sandstone Flying Service at Gainesville's Regional Airport. Sandstone attempted to drug them and planned to hurl them from the aircraft. They foiled his plan and determined that he was actually Johnathon Rivers, a partner of Roscoe Fuller in Saratoga Springs, NY. Born in Kansas City, Kansas (May 8th 1981), his birth name was Johnathon Reardon.

Rivers admitted to 18 homicides, not including Fuller and Robert Merriweather. He was the one who attempted to frame Ms. Talbot. Sandstone AKA Rivers, became very agitated during the flight and stated that he would rather die than return to prison. Without warning, Rivers opened an access door in the baggage compartment and jumped from the aircraft. The location was roughly 110 miles east of Cape Canaveral, and the plane was heading south at 11,000 feet. This is Talbot and Strong's last and final statement concerning this distressing matter. Please address all questions and inquiries to my office. Respectfully, Gerald Cushing, attorney at law."

Amelia signed all the necessary contracts for Talbot receivers to dissolve the J&R assets and close the various insurance companies. She turned over $100K to Patricia Merriweather when the bookkeeper returned to her home in Gainesville. Pat and Virginia managed the Arnholdt Building until it sold for $4.5 million. Martha, the hairdresser, managed the Brown Building in the 'Springs' until it sold for $3.7 million.

Through the efforts of Gerald Cushing, Ratchet Rhodes was rid of his agreement with the FBI. Herman moved to Gainesville and became engaged to Ginny Wickens.

Amelia Talbot sold her Virginia home and moved in with Gordon at Upchurches Pond, NC. She earned over two million dollars from the dissolution of the Fuller/Rivers/Merriweather companies. Mia sent $50K to the Pritchard family along with an apology from Patricia.

Alice and Gerald Cushing provided legal support to Talbot Receivers and submitted the winning bid for the Paradise Island condominium.

Amelia flew to Atlanta and met with Graham Rabinski to transfer Roscoe's stock and trust accounts. As near as she could tell, Graham was Roscoe's only upstanding friend and the only one who attended Fuller's burial.

Over time, Gordon and Amelia Strong grew tired of rural Upchurches Pond and moved to Wilmington, NC. They and their two children settled in a waterfront home on South Harbor Island. The Gulfstream G100 and its monstrous yearly upkeep fees were long gone. Instead, they had a fishing boat, a ski boat, and a small sailboat on their dock. They also docked a cabin cruiser nearby at the Seapath Yacht Club.

Lawyer "Bull" Ralston, in the Saratoga Springs 'Brown Building,' sued Talbot Receivers for one million dollars of dubious Roscoe Fuller legal fees. The claim was settled out of court for $250K.

Rolo Three Fingers didn't receive any additional payments. It was just as well since he died during a poker game when an inmate stabbed him in the heart with a sharpened toothbrush.

ACKNOWLEDGEMENTS

The author thanks his friends and family, who urged him to write this book. The first reader was Clare S. Law, Jim's lovely wife of fifty-four years. She provided a sanity check on the characters and plot and identified many typos.

Bill Fenton, a local friend in Las Cruces, once again gave cogent recommendations and essential corrections. His inputs were responsible for a significant improvement in the book's quality.

Dozens of upgrades were forthcoming from professional editor Jim Oliveri (yeeditor27@yahoo.com).

Several excellent comments and a positive review were received from Candy Richards in San Diego, who has read the other Lawman books. Fellow RV Club members John and Loretta Sutton, former police professionals, provided some insights on bullet wounds and bleeding.

The cover material was designed by Robert Reno from weareIT, Las Cruces, NM.

My niece, Karen A. Overstreet, a retired federal judge, corrected several errors in the final draft. Her input on legal matters was priceless.

We have all done our best to make "Deader Than a Doornail" accurate and consistent. As always, errors, mistakes, and confusing material are the author's sole responsibility.

James W. Law

MORE BOOKS BY THIS AUTHOR

VOLUME ONE introduces Captain Harry "Rats" Mueller, USMC, and his transport aircraft crew. It traces his pilot training at NAS Pensacola, carrier landing qualifications, and rating as a C-46 Plane Commander.

Harry is a hero but no saint. He and his "Ratpack" crew modify and fly the first "Commando" aircraft to Hawaii before the attack on Pearl Harbor.

VOLUME TWO provides the training experience of a destroyer captain before FDR declares war on Japan. After 7 December 1941, LCDR Pelham received orders to a heavy Destroyer and flew to Hawaii with Captain Mueller and his crew.

As Captain of USS Selfridge, David A. Pelham employs unusual methods and objectives to pay the Japanese back for the sneak attack on Pearl Harbor. He's aided in some of his schemes by Mueller's aircrew and their plane nicknamed "Ginger Snap."

VOLUME THREE provides the adventures of a Patrol Torpedo Boat officer and the competition for building the American boat. New boats and squadrons are deployed before the attack on Pearl Harbor. The story features the battle for Midway Island and continues the saga of "Rats" Mueller and CDR David Pelham. Ensign Wilbur Wright trains in PT Boats and visits the Higgins Boatworks in New Orleans before the war begins for America.

VOLUME FOUR explains how submarines work and follows a reserve Ensign through his training and first war patrols. The book also introduces the initial defensive battles in New Guinea (MacArthur) and Guadalcanal (Nimitz). Ltjg Lyle Littleton is thrust into the command of an attack sub and hot water when a boarding party overachieves. "Rats" Mueller and CDR Pelham also are fighting "down under."

Made in the USA
Coppell, TX
13 May 2024

32341944R00164